H.P. LOVECRAFT'S
FAVORITE
WEIRD TALES

Discover the roots of modern horror by reading the master's favorite stories, those which inspired, awed, and scared him! This is the only collection in print of stories selected by Lovecraft himself.

ALSO BY DOUGLAS A. ANDERSON

The Annotated Hobbit

Tales Before Tolkien

Seekers of Dreams: Masterpieces of Fantasy

H.P. LOVECRAFT'S FAVORITE WEIRD TALES

Edited by Douglas A. Anderson

𝕮old 𝕾pring 𝕻ress

P.O. Box 284, Cold Spring Harbor, NY 11724
E-mail: Jopenroad@aol.com

Acknowledgments

For assistance with various aspects of this anthology, I am grateful to Ned Brooks, Kevin Cook, Stefan Dziemianowicz, Kenneth W. Faig, Jr., Morgan Holmes, Jim Rockhill, and Robert Weinberg.

Contents

To my friend
Kenneth W. Faig, Jr.,
who should have done this book years ago

H. P. LOVECRAFT (1890-1937) was the premiere writer of weird fiction in the first half of twentieth century, and his influence has been wide-reaching—not only from his fiction, but also his nonfiction, and in particular his seminal essay "Supernatural Horror in Literature," which was one of the earliest historical studies of the weird tradition from its beginnings. First published in 1927, and revised in 1933-34, it has long been a used as a reading list by devotees of the genre, and it was the basis for one previous anthology, *H. P. Lovecraft's Book of Horror* (1993), edited by Stephen Jones and Dave Carson, which gives a selection of stories—chosen by the editors—from the works and authors praised by Lovecraft in his essay.

This anthology represents Lovecraft's own choices for what he viewed as the best weird tales, based upon his published lists and letters, and thus comprises a compilation of the particular stories that Lovecraft himself would have selected for the anthology of weird tales that he at one time hoped to compile. This volume overlaps with the book edited by Jones and Carson in only three stories.

Lovecraft's first list of what he considered the best came about through his correspondence with the literary editor B[ertrand] K[elton] Hart (1892-1941) of the *Providence Journal*, the newspaper in Lovecraft's hometown of Providence, Rhode Island. In 1929, Hart began a column of literary chat entitled "The Sideshow," and when Lovecraft was interested by the various topics covered, he sent letters and postcards to Hart, who in turn printed some of Lovecraft's comments.

In mid-November 1929, Hart brought up the topic of what might be the most eerie story ever told, and this brought forth a letter from Lovecraft, which Hart duly quoted in his column of 23 November 1929:

> It was while talking of the lost railroad train that we discussed also the question of the most eery [sic] story ever written. You may possibly remember that we spoke of Kipling's "Morrowbie Jukes," of "Halpin Frayser," of "The

Rue Morgue" and many more. I have since had an extremely interesting correspondence with Mr. H. P. Lovecraft of Providence, who has made a lifelong study of the macabre in literature, and who has written with high authority on the subject. . . .

Mr. Lovecraft, and I think rightly, suggests that our casual list leaned toward the mechanically clever in eery stories, whereas the best examples of the mood are to be found (often in less well known authors) among those whose work "is actually profound and disturbing in its intimations of morbid violations of the order of the universe." A good definition of the field we are hunting! He cites Poe's delicately artistic "House of Usher" as against his "Rue Morgue" and some other merely ingenious works. "The difference is one between the workings of the deeper subconscious emotions and the conscious but superficial processes of a brilliant objective intellect. 'Usher' represents art; 'The Rue Morgue,' scientific image-carpentry."

The intimations of an exhaustive research embodied in Mr. Lovecraft's letters sent me on a somewhat gruesome but vastly stimulating lurk through the libraries. He provided me with several tables of selections of "the best" in the field from which I endeavored to reach an independent opinion; and I am convinced that his own list is a little masterpiece of comparative criticism.

Here is it—and by no means must you consider reading these stories by midnight lamplight in a lonely house:

THE WILLOWS by Algernon Blackwood
THE WHITE POWDER by Arthur Machen
THE WHITE PEOPLE by Arthur Machen
THE BLACK LAKE [i.e., SEAL] by Arthur Machen
THE FALL OF THE HOUSE OF USHER by E. A. Poe
THE HOUSE OF SOUNDS by M. P. Shiel
THE YELLOW SIGN by Robert W. Chambers

The superiority of Machen in his métier is undoubted. It is not at all out of proportion to allot him three places in a list of seven, and I am glad Mr. Lovecraft offers an opportunity to print Machen's important but steadily forgotten name here. . . .

"As a group of second choices," writes Mr. Lovecraft, "I would suggest these:"

COUNT MAGNUS by M. R. James
HALPIN FRAYSER by Ambrose Bierce
THE SUITABLE SURROUNDINGS by Ambrose Bierce
SEATON'S AUNT by Walter de la Mare

... "I fight shy of tales dependent on a trick ending," notes Mr. Lovecraft. "Real horror dwells in atmosphere—even in language itself—not in obviously stage-managed dénouements and literary cap-pistol cracks."

Nearly five years later, a list of ten selections labeled as "The Favourite Weird Stories of H. P. Lovecraft" appeared in the fanzine *The Fantasy Fan* (October 1934). This list is believed to have come from a letter by Lovecraft sent to H. C. Koenig. The list is given as follows:

Algernon Blackwood: "The Willows"
Arthur Machen: "The Novel of the White Powder"
Arthur Machen: "The Novel of the Black Seal"
Arthur Machen: "The White People"
Edgar Allan Poe: "The Fall of the House of Usher"
M. P. Shiel: "The House of Sounds"
Robert W. Chambers: "The Yellow Sign"
M. R. James: "Count Magnus"
Ambrose Bierce: "The Death of Halpin Frayser"
A. Merritt: "The Moon Pool"

For the Merritt story, Lovecraft specified the original novelette version (from *All-Story Weekly*, 22 June 1918), not the later version as incorporated into the novel *The Moon Pool* (1919), which Lovecraft regarded as inferior.

It is interesting to compare the two lists, both of which begin with "The Willows" (which Lovecraft considered the best weird tale in all of literature) and contain the same first nine selections. The 1929 lists gives in total eleven stories, and in making the 1934 list Lovecraft dropped the final two choices ("The Suitable Surroundings" and "Seaton's Aunt") and replaced them with one new one ("The Moon Pool"). Combining both lists, the resultant twelve stories are presented in this volume, and constitute Lovecraft's selections of his favorite literary weird tales.

There remains the area of the popular weird tale, particularly as exemplified in *Weird Tales* magazine (to which Lovecraft and many of his friends contributed), considering it as a sub-genre complementary with that of the literary weird tale. We are fortunate to have evidence of Lovecraft's favorites in this area too, dating from the same time period as the lists of his favorite literary weird tales. In the July 1930 issue of *Weird Tales*, editor Farnsworth Wright wrote:

H. P. Lovecraft writes that he has gone through his file of *Weird Tales* from the beginning [i.e., 1923] and has picked out the following stories as having the greatest amount of truly cosmic horror and macabre convincingness: "Beyond the Door" by Paul Suter; "The Floor Above" by M. L. Humphreys; "The Night Wire" by H. F. Arnold; "The Canal" by Everil Worrell; "Bells of Oceana" by Arthur J. Burks; and "In Amundsen's Tent" by John Martin Leahy. All or most of these will be used later as Weird Story Reprints.

In letters from the early 1930s (e.g., to J. Vernon Shea, and to Richard Ely Morse), Lovecraft repeated this list of popular favorites. Thus in combining Lovecraft's lists of favorite literary and popular weird tales, we end up with the eighteen selections that are included in this volume, which can be safely said to contain Lovecraft's preferences as dating to the early 1930s. And it makes for a fine collection indeed.

–Douglas A. Anderson

Works Consulted

Faig, Kenneth W. "Lovecraft's Own Book of Weird Fiction," *The HPL Supplement*, no. 2 (July 1973): 4-15.

Hart, B. K. "The Sideshow," *The Providence Journal*, 23 November 1929.

Jones, Stephen, and Dave Carson, eds. *H. P. Lovecraft's Book of Horror* (New York: Barnes & Noble, 1993).

Joshi, S. T. *H. P. Lovecraft: A Life* (West Warwick, RI: Necronomicon Press, 1996)

Joshi, S. T., and David E. Schultz. *An H. P. Lovecraft Encyclopedia* (Westport, CT: Greenwood Press, 2001).

Lovecraft, H. P. *The Annotated Supernatural Horror in Literature*. Edited by S. T. Joshi (New York: Hippocampus Press, 2000).

I. THE LITERARY WEIRD TALE

EDGAR ALLAN POE (1809-1849) has been called the father of the modern horror story, as well as the father of the detective story. His pioneering influence pervades both fields. In the history of the weird tale, Poe was the first to bring psychological depth to the field, and to cast aside literary and popular conventions that otherwise limited the effectiveness and the scope of the horror story.

Lovecraft first read Poe at the age of eight, and by February 1916, in a letter to his friend Rheinhart Kleiner, he referred to Poe as "my God of fiction." Lovecraft devoted a chapter to Poe in "Supernatural Horror in Literature," and wrote a travelogue of "Homes and Shrines of Poe," after visiting most of the sites. The Poe-scholar T. O. Mabbott credited Lovecraft with solving one of the problems of interpretation of "The Fall of the House of Usher." Mabbott wrote that Lovecraft's "recognition of the central theme of the House of Usher as the possession of but one soul by brother, sister, and the house itself seems to have been as novel as it is obviously correct."

"The Fall of the House of Usher" was first published in *Burton's Gentleman's Magazine* for September 1839, and collected in *Tales of the Grotesque and Arabesque* (1839) and *Tales by Edgar A. Poe* (1845).

THE FALL OF THE HOUSE OF USHER
by Edgar Allan Poe

Son coeur est un luth suspendu;
Sitôt qu'on le touche il résonne.
De Béranger

During the whole of a dull, dark, and soundless day in the autumn of the year, when the clouds hung oppressively low in the heavens, I had been passing alone, on horseback, through a singularly dreary tract of country; and at length found myself, as the shades of the evening drew on, within view of the melancholy House of Usher. I know not how it was—but, with the first glimpse of the building, a sense of insufferable gloom pervaded my spirit. I say insufferable; for the feeling was unrelieved by any of that half-pleasureable, because poetic, sentiment, with which the mind usually receives even the sternest natural images of the desolate or terrible. I looked upon the scene before me—upon the mere house, and the simple landscape features of the domain—upon the bleak walls—upon the vacant eye-like windows—upon a few rank sedges—and upon a few white trunks of decayed trees—with an utter depression of soul which I can compare to no earthly sensation more properly than to the after-dream of the reveller upon opium—the bitter lapse into everyday life—the hideous dropping off of the veil. There was an iciness, a sinking, a sickening of the heart—an unredeemed dreariness of thought which no goading of the imagination could torture into aught of the sublime. What was it—I paused to think— what was it that so unnerved me in the contemplation of the House of Usher? It was a mystery all insoluble; nor could I grapple with the shadowy fancies that crowded upon me as I pondered. I was forced to fall back upon the unsatisfactory conclusion, that while, beyond doubt, there *are* combinations of very simple natural objects which have the power of thus affecting us, still the analysis of this power lies among considerations beyond our depth. It was possible, I reflected, that a mere different arrangement of the particulars of the scene, of the details of the picture, would be sufficient to modify, or perhaps to annihilate its capacity for sorrowful impression; and, acting upon this idea, I reined my horse to the precipitous brink of a black and lurid tarn that lay in unruffled lustre by the dwelling, and gazed down—but with a shudder even more thrilling than before—upon the remodelled and inverted images of the gray sedge, and the ghastly tree-stems, and the vacant and eye-like windows.

Nevertheless, in this mansion of gloom I now proposed to myself a sojourn of some weeks. Its proprietor, Roderick Usher, had been one of my boon companions in boyhood; but many years had elapsed since our last meeting. A letter, however, had lately reached me in a distant part of the country—a letter from him—which, in its wildly importunate nature, had admitted of no other than a personal reply. The MS. gave evidence of nervous agitation. The writer spoke of acute bodily illness—of a mental disorder which oppressed him—and of an earnest desire to see me, as his best, and indeed his only personal friend, with a view of attempting, by the cheerfulness of my society, some alleviation of his malady. It was the manner in which all this, and much more, was said—it was the apparent *heart* that went with his request—which allowed me no room for hesitation; and I accordingly obeyed forthwith what I still considered a very singular summons.

Although, as boys, we had been even intimate associates, yet I really knew little of my friend. His reserve had been always excessive and habitual. I was aware, however, that his very ancient family had been noted, time out of mind, for a peculiar sensibility of temperament, displaying itself, through long ages, in many works of exalted art, and manifested, of late, in repeated deeds of munificent yet unobtrusive charity, as well as in a passionate devotion to the intricacies, perhaps even more than to the orthodox and easily recognisable beauties, of musical science. I had learned, too, the very remarkable fact, that the stem of the Usher race, all time-honored as it was, had put forth, at no period, any enduring branch; in other words, that the entire family lay in the direct line of descent, and had always, with very trifling and very temporary variation, so lain. It was this deficiency, I considered, while running over in thought the perfect keeping of the character of the premises with the accredited character of the people, and while speculating upon the possible influence which the one, in the long lapse of centuries, might have exercised upon the other—it was this deficiency, perhaps, of collateral issue, and the consequent undeviating transmission, from sire to son, of the patrimony with the name, which had, at length, so identified the two as to merge the original title of the estate in the quaint and equivocal appellation of the "House of Usher"—an appellation which seemed to include, in the minds of the peasantry who used it, both the family and the family mansion.

I have said that the sole effect of my somewhat childish experiment—that of looking down within the tarn—had been to deepen the first singular impression. There can be no doubt that the consciousness of the rapid increase of my superstition—for why should I not so term it?—served mainly to accelerate the increase itself. Such, I have long known, is the paradoxical law of all sentiments having terror as a basis. And it might have been for this reason only, that, when I again uplifted my eyes to the house itself, from its image in the pool, there grew in my mind a strange fancy—a fancy so ridiculous, indeed, that I but mention it to show the vivid force of the sensations which oppressed me. I had so worked upon my imagination as really to believe that about the whole mansion and domain there hung an atmosphere peculiar to themselves and their immediate vicinity—an atmosphere which had no affinity with the air of heaven, but which had reeked up from the decayed trees, and the gray wall, and the silent tarn— a pestilent and mystic vapor, dull, sluggish, faintly discernible, and leaden-hued.

Shaking off from my spirit what *must* have been a dream, I scanned more narrowly the real aspect of the building. Its principal feature seemed to be that of an excessive antiquity. The discoloration of ages had been great. Minute fungi overspread the whole exterior, hanging in a fine tangled web-work from the eaves. Yet all this was apart from any extraordinary dilapidation. No portion of the masonry had fallen; and there appeared to be a wild inconsistency between its still perfect adaptation of parts, and the crumbling condition of the individual stones. In this there was much that reminded me of the specious totality of old wood-work which has rotted for long years in some neglected vault, with no disturbance from the breath of the external air. Beyond this indication of extensive decay, however, the fabric gave little token of instability. Perhaps the eye of a scrutinizing observer might have discovered a barely perceptible fissure, which, extending from the roof of the building in front, made its way down the wall in a zigzag direction, until it became lost in the sullen waters of the tarn.

Noticing these things, I rode over a short causeway to the house. A servant in waiting took my horse, and I entered the Gothic archway of the hall. A valet, of stealthy step, thence conducted me, in silence, through many dark and intricate passages in my progress to the *studio* of his master. Much that I encountered on the way contributed, I know not how, to heighten the vague sentiments of which I have already spoken. While the objects around me—while the carvings of the ceilings, the sombre tapestries of the walls, the ebon blackness of the floors, and the phantasmagoric armorial trophies which rattled as I strode, were but matters to which, or to such as which, I had been accustomed from my infancy—while I hesitated not to acknowledge how familiar was all this—I still wondered to find how unfamiliar were the fancies which ordinary images were stirring up. On one of the staircases, I met the physician of the family. His countenance, I thought, wore a mingled expression of low cunning and perplexity. He accosted me with trepidation and passed on. The valet now threw open a door and ushered me into the presence of his master.

The room in which I found myself was very large and lofty. The windows were long, narrow, and pointed, and at so vast a distance from the black oaken floor as to be altogether inaccessible from within. Feeble gleams of encrimsoned light made their way through the trellissed panes, and served to render sufficiently distinct the more prominent objects around; the eye, however, struggled in vain to reach the remoter angles of the chamber, or the recesses of the vaulted and fretted ceiling. Dark draperies hung upon the walls. The general furniture was profuse, comfortless, antique, and tattered. Many books and musical instruments lay scattered about, but failed to give any vitality to the scene. I felt that I breathed an atmosphere of sorrow. An air of stern, deep, and irredeemable gloom hung over and pervaded all.

Upon my entrance, Usher arose from a sofa on which he had been lying at full length, and greeted me with a vivacious warmth which had much in it, I at first thought, of an overdone cordiality—of the constrained effort of the *ennuyé* man of the world. A glance, however, at his countenance, convinced me of his perfect sincerity. We sat down; and for some moments, while he spoke not, I gazed upon him with a feeling half of pity, half of awe. Surely, man had never before so terribly altered, in so brief a period, as had Roderick Usher! It was with difficulty that I could bring myself to admit the identity of the wan being before me with the companion of my early boyhood. Yet the character of his face had been at all times remarkable. A cadaverousness of complexion; an eye large, liquid, and luminous beyond comparison; lips somewhat thin and very pallid, but of a surpassingly beautiful curve; a nose of a delicate Hebrew model, but with a breadth of nostril unusual in similar formations; a finely moulded chin, speaking, in its want of prominence, of a want of moral energy; hair of a more than web-like softness and tenuity; these features, with an inordinate expansion above the regions of the temple, made up altogether a countenance not easily to be forgotten. And now in the mere exaggeration of the prevailing character of these features, and of the expression they were wont to convey, lay so much of change that I doubted to whom I spoke. The now ghastly pallor of the skin, and the now miraculous lustre of the eye, above all things startled and even awed me. The silken hair, too, had been suffered to grow all unheeded, and as, in its wild gossamer texture, it floated rather than fell about the face, I could not, even with effort, connect its Arabesque expression with any idea of simple humanity.

In the manner of my friend I was at once struck with an incoherence—an inconsistency; and I soon found this to arise from a series of feeble and futile struggles to overcome an habitual trepidancy—an excessive nervous agitation. For something of this nature I had indeed been prepared, no less by his letter, than by reminiscences of certain boyish traits, and by conclusions deduced from his peculiar physical conformation and temperament. His action was alternately vivacious and sullen. His voice varied rapidly from a tremulous indecision (when the animal spirits seemed utterly in abeyance) to that species of energetic concision—that abrupt, weighty, unhurried, and hollow-sounding enunciation—that leaden, self-balanced and perfectly modulated guttural utterance, which may be observed in the lost drunkard, or the irreclaimable eater of opium, during the periods of his most intense excitement.

It was thus that he spoke of the object of my visit, of his earnest desire to see me, and of the solace he expected me to afford him. He entered, at some length, into what he conceived to be the nature of his malady. It was, he said, a constitutional and a family evil, and one for which he despaired to find a remedy—a mere nervous affection, he immediately added, which would undoubtedly soon pass off. It displayed itself in a host of unnatural sensations. Some of these, as he detailed them, interested and bewildered me; although, perhaps, the terms, and the general manner of the narration had their weight. He suffered much from a morbid acuteness of the senses; the most insipid food was alone endurable; he could wear only garments of certain texture; the odors of all flowers were oppressive; his eyes were tortured by even a faint light; and there were but peculiar sounds, and these from stringed instruments, which did not inspire him with horror.

To an anomalous species of terror I found him a bounden slave. "I shall perish," said he, "I *must* perish in this deplorable folly. Thus, thus, and not otherwise, shall I be lost. I dread the events of the future, not in themselves, but in their results. I shudder at the thought of any, even the most trivial, incident, which may operate upon this intolerable agitation of soul. I have, indeed, no abhorrence of danger, except in its absolute effect—in terror. In this unnerved—in this pitiable condition—I feel that the period will sooner or later arrive when I must abandon life and reason together, in some struggle with the grim phantasm, FEAR."

I learned, moreover, at intervals, and through broken and equivocal hints, another singular feature of his mental condition. He was enchained by certain superstitious impressions in regard to the dwelling which he tenanted, and whence, for many years, he had never ventured forth—in regard to an influence whose supposititious force was conveyed in terms too shadowy here to be re-stated—an influence which some peculiarities in the mere form and substance of his family mansion, had, by dint of long sufferance, he said, obtained over his spirit—an effect which the *physique* of the gray walls and turrets, and of the dim tarn into which they all looked down, had, at length, brought about upon the *morale* of his existence.

He admitted, however, although with hesitation, that much of the peculiar gloom which thus afflicted him could be traced to a more natural and far more palpable origin—to the severe and long-continued illness—indeed to the evidently approaching dissolution—of a tenderly beloved sister—his sole companion for long years—his last and only relative on earth. "Her decease," he said, with a bitterness which I can never forget, "would leave him (him the hopeless and the frail) the last of the ancient race of the Ushers." While he spoke, the lady Madeline (for so was she called) passed slowly through a remote portion of the apartment, and, without having noticed my presence, disappeared. I regarded her with an utter astonishment not unmingled with dread—and yet I found it impossible to account for such feelings. A sensation of stupor oppressed me, as my eyes followed her retreating steps. When a door, at length, closed upon her, my glance sought instinctively and eagerly the countenance of the brother—but he had buried his face in his hands, and I could only perceive that a far more than ordinary wanness had overspread the emaciated fingers through which trickled many passionate tears.

The disease of the lady Madeline had long baffled the skill of her physicians. A settled apathy, a gradual wasting away of the person, and frequent although transient affections of a partially cataleptical character, were the unusual diagnosis. Hitherto she had steadily borne up against the pressure of her malady, and had not betaken herself finally to bed; but, on the closing in of the evening of my arrival at the house, she succumbed (as her brother told me at night with inexpressible agitation) to the prostrating power of the destroyer; and I learned that the glimpse I had obtained of her person would thus probably be the last I should obtain—that the lady, at least while living, would be seen by me no more.

For several days ensuing, her name was unmentioned by either Usher or myself: and during this period I was busied in earnest endeavors to alleviate the melancholy of my friend. We painted and read together; or I listened, as if in a dream, to the wild improvisations of his speaking guitar. And thus, as a closer and still closer intimacy admitted me more unreservedly into the recesses of his spirit, the more bitterly did I perceive the futility of all attempt at cheering a mind from which darkness, as if an inherent positive quality, poured forth upon all objects of the moral and physical universe, in one unceasing radiation of gloom.

I shall ever bear about me a memory of the many solemn hours I thus spent alone with the master of the House of Usher. Yet I should fail in any attempt to convey an idea of the exact character of the studies, or of the occupations, in which he involved me, or led me the way. An excited and highly distempered ideality threw a sulphurous lustre over all. His long improvised dirges will ring for ever in my ears. Among other things, I hold painfully in mind a certain singular perversion and amplification of the wild air of the last waltz of Von Weber. From the paintings over which his elaborate fancy brooded, and which grew, touch by touch, into vaguenesses at which I shuddered the more thrillingly, because I shuddered knowing not why; —from these paintings (vivid as their images now are before me) I would in vain endeavor to educe more than a small portion which should lie within the compass of merely written words. By the utter simplicity, by the nakedness of his designs, he arrested and overawed attention. If ever mortal painted an idea, that mortal was Roderick Usher. For me at least— in the circumstances then surrounding me—there arose out of the pure abstractions which the hypochondriac contrived to throw upon his canvas, an intensity of intolerable awe, no shadow of which felt I ever yet in the contemplation of the certainly glowing yet too concrete reveries of Fuseli.

One of the phantasmagoric conceptions of my friend, partaking not so rigidly of the spirit of abstraction, may be shadowed forth, although feebly, in words. A small picture presented the interior of an immensely long and rectangular vault or tunnel, with low walls, smooth, white, and without interruption or device. Certain accessory points of the design served well to convey the idea that this excavation lay at an exceeding depth below the surface of the earth. No outlet was observed in any portion of its vast extent, and no torch, or other artificial source of light was discernible; yet a flood of intense rays rolled throughout, and bathed the whole in a ghastly and inappropriate splendor.

I have just spoken of that morbid condition of the auditory nerve which rendered all music intolerable to the sufferer, with the exception of certain effects of stringed instruments. It was, perhaps, the narrow limits to which he thus confined himself upon the guitar, which gave birth, in great measure, to the fantastic character of the performances. But the fervid *facility* of his *impromptus* could not be so accounted for. They must have been, and were, in the notes, as well as in the words of his wild fantasias (for he not unfrequently accompanied himself with rhymed verbal improvisations), the result of that intense mental collectedness and concentration to which I have previously alluded as observable only in particular moments of the highest artificial excitement. The words of one of these rhapsodies I have easily remembered. I was, perhaps, the more forcibly impressed with it, as he gave it, because, in the under or mystic current of its meaning, I fancied that I perceived, and for the first time, a full consciousness on the part of Usher, of the tottering of his lofty reason upon her throne. The verses, which were entitled "The Haunted Palace," ran very nearly, if not accurately, thus:

I

In the greenest of our valleys,
  By good angels tenanted,
Once a fair and stately palace—
  Radiant palace—reared its head.
In the monarch Thought's dominion—
  It stood there!
Never seraph spread a pinion
  Over fabric half so fair.

II

Banners yellow, glorious, golden,
  On its roof did float and flow;
(This—all this—was in the olden
  Time long ago)
And every gentle air that dallied,
  In that sweet day,
Along the ramparts plumed and pallid,
  A winged odor went away.

III

Wanderers in that happy valley
  Through two luminous windows saw
Spirits moving musically
  To a lute's well tunéd law,
Round about a throne, where sitting
  (Porphyrogene!)
In state his glory well befitting,
  The ruler of the realm was seen.

IV

And all with pearl and ruby glowing
  Was the fair palace door,
Through which came flowing, flowing, flowing,
  And sparkling evermore,
A troop of Echoes whose sweet duty
  Was but to sing,
In voices of surpassing beauty,
  The wit and wisdom of their king.

V

But evil things, in robes of sorrow,
  Assailed the monarch's high estate;
(Ah, let us mourn, for never morrow
  Shall dawn upon him, desolate!)
And, round about his home, the glory
  That blushed and bloomed
Is but a dim-remembered story,
  Of the old time entombed.

VI.

And travellers now within that valley,
  Through the red-litten windows, see
Vast forms that move fantastically
  To a discordant melody;
While, like a rapid ghastly river,
  Through the pale door,
A hideous throng rush out forever,
  And laugh—but smile no more.

I well remember that suggestions arising from this ballad, led us into a train of thought wherein there became manifest an opinion of Usher's which I mention not so much on account of its novelty, (for other men[†] have thought thus,) as on account of the pertinacity with which he maintained it. This opinion, in its general form, was that of the sentience of all vegetable things. But, in his disordered fancy, the idea had assumed

[†]Watson, Dr. Percival, Spallanzani, and especially the Bishop of Landaff.—See "Chemical Essays," vol. v.

a more daring character, and trespassed, under certain conditions, upon the kingdom of inorganization. I lack words to express the full extent, or the earnest *abandon* of his persuasion. The belief, however, was connected (as I have previously hinted) with the gray stones of the home of his forefathers. The conditions of the sentience had been here, he imagined, fulfilled in the method of collocation of these stones—in the order of their arrangement, as well as in that of the many *fungi* which overspread them, and of the decayed trees which stood around—above all, in the long undisturbed endurance of this arrangement, and in its reduplication in the still waters of the tarn. Its evidence—the evidence of the sentience—was to be seen, he said, (and I here started as he spoke,) in the gradual yet certain condensation of an atmosphere of their own about the waters and the walls. The result was discoverable, he added, in that silent, yet importunate and terrible influence which for centuries had moulded the destinies of his family, and which made *him* what I now saw him—what he was. Such opinions need no comment, and I will make none.

Our books—the books which, for years, had formed no small portion of the mental existence of the invalid—were, as might be supposed, in strict keeping with this character of phantasm. We pored together over such works as the Ververt et Chartreuse of Gresset; the Belphegor of Machiavelli; the Heaven and Hell of Swedenborg; the Subterranean Voyage of Nicholas Klimm by Holberg; the Chiromancy of Robert Flud, of Jean d'Indaginé, and of De la Chambre; the Journey into the Blue Distance of Tieck; and the City of the Sun by Campanella. One favourite volume was a small octavo edition of the *Directorium Inquisitorum*, by the Dominican Eymeric de Gironne; and there were passages in Pomponius Mela, about the old African Satyrs and Œgipans, over which Usher would sit dreaming for hours. His chief delight, however, was found in the perusal of an exceedingly rare and curious book in quarto Gothic—the manual of a forgotten church—the *Vigiliae Mortuorum secundum Chorum Ecclesiae Maguntinae.*

I could not help thinking of the wild ritual of this work, and of its probable influence upon the hypochondriac, when, one evening, having informed me abruptly that the lady Madeline was no more, he stated his intention of preserving her corpse for a fortnight, (previously to its final interment,) in one of the numerous vaults within the main walls of the building. The worldly reason, however, assigned for this singular proceeding, was one which I did not feel at liberty to dispute. The brother had been led to his resolution (so he told me) by consideration of the unusual character of the malady of the deceased, of certain obtrusive and eager inquiries on the part of her medical men, and of the remote and exposed situation of the burial-ground of the family. I will not deny that when I called to mind the sinister countenance of the person whom I met upon the staircase, on the day of my arrival at the house, I had no desire to oppose what I regarded as at best but a harmless, and by no means an unnatural, precaution.

At the request of Usher, I personally aided him in the arrangements for the temporary entombment. The body having been encoffined, we two alone bore it to its rest. The vault in which we placed it (and which had been so long unopened that our torches, half smothered in its oppressive atmosphere, gave us little opportunity for investigation) was small, damp, and entirely without means of admission for light; lying, at great depth, immediately beneath that portion of the building in which was my own sleeping apartment. It had been used, apparently, in remote feudal times, for the worst purposes of a donjon-keep, and, in later days, as a place of deposit for powder, or some other highly combustible substance, as a portion of its floor, and the whole interior of a long archway through which we reached it, were carefully sheathed with copper. The door, of massive iron, had been, also, similarly protected. Its immense weight caused an unusually sharp grating sound, as it moved upon its hinges.

Having deposited our mournful burden upon tressels within this region of horror, we partially turned aside the yet unscrewed lid of the coffin, and looked upon the face of the tenant. A striking similitude between the brother and sister now first arrested my attention; and Usher, divining, perhaps, my thoughts, murmured out some few words from which I learned that the deceased and himself had been twins, and that sympathies of a scarcely intelligible nature had always existed between them. Our glances, however, rested not long upon the dead—for we could not regard her unawed. The disease which had thus entombed the lady in the maturity of youth, had left, as usual in all maladies of a strictly cataleptical character, the mockery of a faint blush upon the bosom and the face, and that suspiciously lingering smile upon the lip which is so terrible in death. We replaced and screwed down the lid, and, having secured the door of iron, made our way, with toil, into the scarcely less gloomy apartments of the upper portion of the house.

And now, some days of bitter grief having elapsed, an observable change came over the features of the mental disorder of my friend. His ordinary manner had vanished. His ordinary occupations were neglected or forgotten. He roamed from chamber to chamber with hurried, unequal, and objectless step. The pallor of his countenance had assumed, if possible, a more ghastly hue—but the luminousness of his eye had utterly gone out. The once occasional huskiness of his tone was heard no more; and a tremulous quaver, as if of extreme terror, habitually characterized his utterance. There were times, indeed, when I thought his unceasingly agitated mind was laboring with some oppressive secret, to divulge which he struggled for the necessary courage. At times, again, I was obliged to resolve all into the mere inexplicable vagaries of madness, for I beheld him gazing upon vacancy for long hours, in an attitude of the profoundest attention, as if listening to some imaginary sound. It was no wonder that his condition terrified—that it infected me. I felt creeping upon me, by slow yet certain degrees, the wild influences of his own fantastic yet impressive superstitions.

It was, especially, upon retiring to bed late in the night of the seventh or eighth day after the placing of the lady Madeline within the donjon, that I experienced the full power of such feelings. Sleep came not near my couch—while the hours waned and waned away. I struggled to reason off the nervousness which had dominion over me. I endeavored to believe that much, if not all of what I felt, was due to the bewildering influence of the gloomy furniture of the room—of the dark and tattered draperies, which, tortured into motion by the breath of a rising tempest, swayed fitfully to and fro upon the walls, and rustled uneasily about the decorations of the bed. But my efforts were fruitless. An irrepressible tremor gradually pervaded my frame; and, at length, there sat upon my very heart an incubus of utterly causeless alarm. Shaking this off with a gasp and a struggle, I uplifted myself upon the pillows, and, peering earnestly within the intense darkness of the chamber, hearkened—I know not why, except that an instinctive spirit prompted me—to certain low and indefinite sounds which came, through the pauses of the storm, at long intervals, I knew not whence. Overpowered by an intense sentiment of horror, unaccountable yet unendurable, I threw on my clothes with haste (for I felt that I should sleep no more during the night), and endeavored to arouse myself from the pitiable condition into which I had fallen, by pacing rapidly to and fro through the apartment.

I had taken but few turns in this manner, when a light step on an adjoining staircase arrested my attention. I presently recognized it as that of Usher. In an instant afterwards he rapped, with a gentle touch, at my door, and entered, bearing a lamp. His countenance was, as usual, cadaverously wan—but, moreover, there was a species of mad hilarity in his eyes—an evidently restrained *hysteria* in his whole demeanor. His air appalled me—but anything was preferable to the solitude which I had so long endured, and I even welcomed his presence as a relief.

"And you have not seen it?" he said abruptly, after having stared about him for some moments in silence—"you have not then seen it?—but, stay! you shall." Thus speaking, and having carefully shaded his lamp, he hurried to one of the casements, and threw it freely open to the storm.

The impetuous fury of the entering gust nearly lifted us from our feet. It was, indeed, a tempestuous yet sternly beautiful night, and one wildly singular in its terror and its beauty. A whirlwind had apparently collected its force in our vicinity; for there were frequent and violent alterations in the direction of the wind; and the exceeding density of the clouds (which hung so low as to press upon the turrets of the house) did not prevent our perceiving the life-like velocity with which they flew careering from all points against each other, without passing away into the distance. I say that even their exceeding density did not prevent our perceiving this—yet we had no glimpse of the moon or stars—nor was there any flashing forth of the lightning. But the under surfaces of the huge masses of agitated vapor, as well as all terrestrial objects immediately around us, were glowing in the unnatural light of a faintly luminous and distinctly visible gaseous exhalation which hung about and enshrouded the mansion.

"You must not—you shall not behold this!" said I, shudderingly, to Usher, as I led him, with a gentle violence, from the window to a seat. "These appearances, which bewilder you, are merely electrical phenomena not uncommon—or it may be that they have their ghastly origin in the rank miasma of the tarn. Let us close this casement; —the air is chilling and dangerous to your frame. Here is one of your favorite romances. I will read, and you shall listen; —and so we will pass away this terrible night together."

The antique volume which I had taken up was the "Mad Trist" of Sir Launcelot Canning; but I had called it a favorite of Usher's more in sad jest than in earnest; for, in truth, there is little in its uncouth and unimaginative prolixity which could have had interest for the lofty and spiritual ideality of my friend. It was, however, the only book immediately at hand; and I indulged a vague hope that the excitement which now agitated the hypochondriac, might find relief (for the history of mental disorder is full of similar anomalies) even in the extremeness of the folly which I should read. Could I have judged, indeed, by the wild overstrained air of vivacity with which he hearkened, or apparently hearkened, to the words of the tale, I might well have congratulated myself upon the success of my design.

I had arrived at that well-known portion of the story where Ethelred, the hero of the Trist, having sought in vain for peaceable admission into the dwelling of the hermit, proceeds to make good an entrance by force. Here, it will be remembered, the words of the narrative run thus:

"And Ethelred, who was by nature of a doughty heart, and who was now mighty withal, on account of the powerfulness of the wine which he had drunken, waited no longer to hold parley with the hermit, who, in sooth, was of an obstinate and maliceful turn, but, feeling the rain upon his shoulders, and fearing the rising of the tempest, uplifted his mace outright, and, with blows, made quickly room in the plankings of the door for his gauntleted hand; and now pulling therewith sturdily, he so cracked, and ripped, and tore all asunder, that the noise of the dry and hollow-sounding wood alarmed and reverberated throughout the forest."

At the termination of this sentence I started, and for a moment, paused; for it appeared to me (although I at once concluded that my excited fancy had deceived me)—it appeared to me that, from some very remote portion of the mansion, there came, indistinctly, to my ears, what might have been, in its exact similarity of character, the echo (but a stifled and dull one certainly) of the very cracking and ripping sound which Sir Launcelot had so particularly described. It was, beyond doubt, the coincidence alone which had arrested my attention; for, amid the rattling of the sashes of the casements, and the ordinary commingled noises of the still increasing storm, the sound, in itself, had nothing, surely, which should have interested or disturbed me. I continued the story:

"But the good champion Ethelred, now entering within the door, was sore enraged and amazed to perceive no signal of the maliceful hermit; but, in the stead thereof, a dragon of a scaly and prodigious demeanor, and of a fiery tongue, which sate in guard before a palace of gold, with a floor of silver; and upon the wall there hung a shield of shining brass with this legend enwritten—

Who entereth herein, a conquerer hath bin;
Who slayeth the dragon, the shield he shall win.

And Ethelred uplifted his mace, and struck upon the head of the dragon, which fell before him, and gave up his pesty breath, with a shriek so horrid and harsh, and withal so piercing, that Ethelred had fain to close his ears with his hands against the dreadful noise of it, the like whereof was never before heard."

Here again I paused abruptly, and now with a feeling of wild amazement—for there could be no doubt whatever that, in this instance, I did actually hear (although from what direction it proceeded I found it impossible to say) a low and apparently distant, but harsh, protracted, and most unusual screaming or grating sound—the exact counterpart of what my fancy had already conjured up for the dragon's unnatural shriek as described by the romancer.

Oppressed, as I certainly was, upon the occurrence of the second and most extraordinary coincidence, by a thousand conflicting sensations, in which wonder and extreme terror were predominant, I still retained sufficient presence of mind to avoid exciting, by any observation, the sensitive nervousness of my companion. I was by no means certain that he had noticed the sounds in question; although, assuredly, a strange alteration had, during the last few minutes, taken place in his demeanor. From a position fronting my own, he had gradually brought round his chair, so as to sit with his face to the door of the chamber; and thus I could but partially perceive his features, although I saw that his lips trembled as if he were murmuring inaudibly. His head had dropped upon his breast— yet I knew that he was not asleep, from the wide and rigid opening of the eye as I caught a glance of it in profile. The motion of his body, too, was at variance with this idea—for he rocked from side to side with a gentle yet constant and uniform sway. Having rapidly taken notice of all this, I resumed the narrative of Sir Launcelot, which thus proceeded:

"And now, the champion, having escaped from the terrible fury of the dragon, bethinking himself of the brazen shield, and of the breaking up of the enchantment which was upon it, removed the carcass from out of the way before him, and approached valorously over the silver pavement of the castle to where the shield was upon the wall; which in sooth tarried not for his full coming, but fell down at his feet upon the silver floor, with a mighty great and terrible ringing sound."

No sooner had these syllables passed my lips, than—as if a shield of brass had indeed, at the moment, fallen heavily upon a floor of silver—I became aware of a distinct, hollow, metallic, and clangorous, yet apparently muffled reverberation. Completely unnerved, I leaped to my feet; but the measured rocking movement of Usher was undisturbed. I rushed to the chair in which he sat. His eyes were bent fixedly before him, and throughout his whole countenance there reigned a stony rigidity. But, as

I placed my hand upon his shoulder, there came a strong shudder over his whole person; a sickly smile quivered about his lips; and I saw that he spoke in a low, hurried, and gibbering murmur, as if unconscious of my presence. Bending closely over him, I at length drank in the hideous import of his words.

"Not hear it?—yes, I hear it, and *have* heard it. Long—long—long—many minutes, many hours, many days, have I heard it—yet I dared not—oh, pity me, miserable wretch that I am!—I dared not—I *dared* not speak! *We have put her living in the tomb!* Said I not that my senses were acute? I *now* tell you that I heard her first feeble movements in the hollow coffin. I heard them—many, many days ago—yet I dared not—*I dared not speak!* And now—to-night—Ethelred—ha! ha!—the breaking of the hermit's door, and the death-cry of the dragon, and the clangor of the shield!—say, rather, the rending of her coffin, and the grating of the iron hinges of her prison, and her struggles within the coppered archway of the vault! Oh whither shall I fly? Will she not be here anon? Is she not hurrying to upbraid me for my haste? Have I not heard her footsteps on the stair? Do I not distinguish that heavy and horrible beating of her heart? Madman!"—here he sprang furiously to his feet, and shrieked out his syllables, as if in the effort he were giving up his soul—"*Madman! I tell you that she now stands without the door!*"

As if in the superhuman energy of his utterance there had been found the potency of a spell—the huge antique pannels to which the speaker pointed, threw slowly back, upon the instant, their ponderous and ebony jaws. It was the work of the rushing gust—but then without those doors there *did* stand the lofty and enshrouded figure of the lady Madeline of Usher. There was blood upon her white robes, and the evidence of some bitter struggle upon every portion of her emaciated frame. For a moment she remained trembling and reeling to and fro upon the threshold, —then, with a low moaning cry, fell heavily inward upon the person of her brother, and in her violent and now final death-agonies, bore him to the floor a corpse, and a victim to the terrors he had anticipated.

From that chamber, and from that mansion, I fled aghast. The storm was still abroad in all its wrath as I found myself crossing the old causeway. Suddenly there shot along the path a wild light, and I turned to see whence a gleam so unusual could have issued; for the vast house and its shadows were alone behind me. The radiance was that of the full, setting, and blood-red moon which now shone vividly through that once barely-discernible fissure of which I have before spoken as extending from the roof of the building, in a zigzag direction, to the base. While I gazed, this fissure rapidly widened—there came a fierce breath of the whirlwind—the entire orb of the satellite burst at once upon my sight—my brain reeled as I saw the mighty walls rushing asunder—there was a long tumultuous shouting sound like the voice of a thousand waters—and the deep and dank tarn at my feet closed sullenly and silently over the fragments of the *"House of Usher."*

AMBROSE BIERCE (1842-1913?) was a journalist and short story writer. He is remembered today for his acidic wit, best represented in *The Devil's Dictionary* (1911), though some of his short stories, collected in *Tales of Soldiers and Civilians* (1891) and *Can Such Things Be?* (1893), are probably his best literary work.

Lovecraft discovered Bierce in 1919, through his friend Samuel Loveman, who had corresponded with Bierce. In "Supernatural Horror in Literature," Lovecraft notes that "The Suitable Surroundings" "evokes with singular subtlety yet apparent simplicity a piercing sense of the terror which may reside in the written word."

"The Suitable Surroundings" was first published in the *San Francisco Examiner*, 14 July 1889, with the subtitle "Instruction by Example in the Art of Reading a Ghost Story." It was collected in *Tales of Soldiers and Civilians*.

THE SUITABLE SURROUNDINGS
by Ambrose Bierce

The Night

One midsummer night a farmer's boy living about ten miles from the city of Cincinnati was following a bridle path through a dense and dark forest. He had lost himself while searching for some missing cows, and near midnight was a long way from home, in a part of the country with which he was unfamiliar. But he was a stout-hearted lad, and knowing his general direction from his home, he plunged into the forest without hesitation, guided by the stars. Coming into the bridle path, and observing that it ran in the right direction, he followed it.

The night was clear, but in the woods it was exceedingly dark. It was more by the sense of touch than by that of sight that the lad kept the path.

He could not, indeed, very easily go astray; the, undergrowth on both sides was so thick as to be almost impenetrable. He had gone into the forest a mile or more when he was surprised to see a feeble gleam of light shining through the foliage skirting the path on his left. The sight of it startled him and set his heart beating audibly.

"The old Breede house is somewhere about here," he said to himself. "This must be the other end of the path which we reach it by from our side. Ugh! what should a light be doing there?"

Nevertheless, he pushed on. A moment later he had emerged from the forest into a small, open space, mostly upgrown to brambles. There were remnants of a rotting fence. A few yards from the trail, in the middle of the "clearing," was the house from which the light came, through an unglazed window. The window had once contained glass, but that and its supporting frame had long ago yielded to missiles flung by hands of venturesome boys to attest alike their courage and their hostility to the supernatural; for the Breede house bore the evil reputation of being haunted. Possibly it was not, but even the hardiest sceptic could not deny that it was deserted—which in rural regions is much the same thing.

Looking at the mysterious dim light shining from the ruined window the boy remembered with apprehension that his own hand had assisted at the destruction. His penitence was of course poignant in proportion to its tardiness and inefficacy. He half expected to be set upon by all the unworldly and bodiless malevolences whom he had outraged by assisting to break alike their windows and their peace. Yet this stubborn lad, shaking in every limb, would not retreat. The blood in his veins was strong and rich with the iron of the frontiersman. He was but two removes from the generation that had subdued the Indian. He started to pass the house.

As he was going by he looked in at the blank window space and saw a strange and terrifying sight,—the figure of a man seated in the centre of the room, at a table upon which lay some loose sheets of paper. The elbows rested on the table, the hands supporting the head, which was uncovered. On each side the fingers were pushed into the hair. The face showed dead-yellow in the light of a single candle a little to one side. The flame illuminated that side of the face, the other was in deep shadow. The man's eyes were fixed upon the blank window space with a stare in which an older and cooler observer might have discerned something of apprehension, but which seemed to the lad altogether soulless. He believed the man to be dead.

The situation was horrible, but not without its fascination. The boy stopped to note it all. He was weak, faint and trembling; he could feel the blood forsaking his face. Nevertheless, he set his teeth and resolutely advanced to the house. He had no conscious intention—it was the mere courage of terror. He thrust his white face forward into the illuminated opening. At that instant a strange, harsh cry, a shriek, broke upon the silence of the night—the note of a screech-owl. The man sprang to his feet, overturning the table and extinguishing the candle. The boy took to his heels.

The Day Before

"Good-morning, Colston. I am in luck, it seems. You have often said that my commendation of your literary work was mere civility, and here you find me absorbed—actually merged—in your latest story in the *Messenger*. Nothing less shocking than your touch upon my shoulder would have roused me to consciousness."

"The proof is stronger than you seem to know," replied the man addressed: "so keen is your eagerness to read my story that you are willing to renounce selfish considerations and forego all the pleasure that you could get from it."

"I don't understand you," said the other, folding the newspaper that he held and putting it into his pocket. "You writers are a queer lot, anyhow. Come, tell me what I have done or omitted in this matter. In what way does the pleasure that I get, or might get, from your work depend on me?"

"In many ways. Let me ask you how you would enjoy your breakfast if you took it in this street car. Suppose the phonograph so perfected as to be able to give you an entire opera,—singing, orchestration, and all; do you think you would get much pleasure out of it if you turned it on at your office during business hours? Do you really care for a serenade by Schubert when you hear it fiddled by an untimely Italian on a morning ferryboat? Are you always cocked and primed for enjoyment? Do you keep every mood on tap, ready to any demand? Let me remind you, sir, that the story which you have done me the honor to begin as a means of becoming oblivious to the discomfort of this car is a ghost story!"

"Well?"

"Well! Has the reader no duties corresponding to his privileges? You have paid five cents for that newspaper. It is yours. You have the right to read it when and where you will. Much of what is in it is neither helped nor harmed by time and place and mood; some of it actually requires to be read at once—while it is fizzing. But my story is not of that character. It is not 'the very latest advices' from Ghostland. You are not expected to keep yourself *au courant* with what is going on in the realm of spooks. The stuff will keep until you have leisure to put yourself into the frame of mind appropriate to the sentiment of the piece—which I respectfully submit that you cannot do in a street car, even if you are the only passenger. The solitude is not of the right sort. An author has rights which the reader is bound to respect."

"For specific example?"

"The right to the reader's undivided attention. To deny him this is immoral. To make him share your attention with the rattle of a street car, the moving panorama of the crowds on the sidewalks, and the buildings beyond—with any of the thousands of distractions which make our customary environment—is to treat him with gross injustice. By God, it is infamous!"

The speaker had risen to his feet and was steadying himself by one of the straps hanging from the roof of the car. The other man looked up at him in sudden astonishment, wondering how so trivial a grievance could seem to justify so strong language. He saw that his friend's face was uncommonly pale and that his eyes glowed like living coals.

"You know what I mean," continued the writer, impetuously crowding his words—"you know what I mean, Marsh. My stuff in this morning's *Messenger* is plainly sub-headed 'A Ghost Story.' That is ample notice to all. Every honorable reader will understand it as prescribing by implication the conditions under which the work is to be read."

The man addressed as Marsh winced a trifle, then asked with a smile: "What conditions? You know that I am only a plain business man who cannot be supposed to understand such things. How, when, where should I read your ghost story?"

"In solitude—at night—by the light of a candle. There are certain emotions which a writer can easily enough excite—such as compassion or merriment. I can move you to tears or laughter under almost any circumstances. But for my ghost story to be effective you must be made to feel fear—at least a strong sense of the supernatural—and that is a difficult matter. I have a right to expect that if you read me at all you will give me a chance; that you will make yourself accessible to the emotion that I try to inspire."

The car had now arrived at its terminus and stopped. The trip just completed was its first for the day and the conversation of the two early passengers had not been interrupted. The streets were yet silent and desolate; the house tops were just touched by the rising sun. As they stepped from the car and walked away together Marsh narrowly eyed his companion, who was reported, like most men of uncommon literary ability, to be addicted to various destructive vices. That is the revenge which dull minds take upon bright ones in resentment of their superiority. Mr. Colston was known as a man of genius. There are honest souls who believe that genius is a mode of excess. It was known that Colston did not drink liquor, but many said that he ate opium. Something in his appearance that morning—a certain wildness at the eyes, an unusual pallor, a thickness and rapidity of speech—were taken by Mr. Marsh to confirm the report. Nevertheless, he had not the self-denial to abandon a subject which he found interesting, however it might excite his friend.

"Do you mean to say," he began, "that if I take the trouble to observe your directions—place myself in the conditions that you demand: solitude, night and a tallow candle—you can with your ghostly work give me an uncomfortable sense of the supernatural, as you call it? Can you accelerate my pulse, make me start at sudden noises, send a nervous chill along my spine and cause my hair to rise?"

Colston turned suddenly and looked him squarely in the eyes as they walked. "You would not dare—you have not the courage," he said, He emphasized the words with a contemptuous gesture. "You are brave enough to read me in a street car, but—in a deserted house—alone—in the forest—at night! Bah! I have a manuscript in my pocket that would kill you."

Marsh was angry. He knew himself courageous, and the words stung him. "If you know such a place," he said, "take me there to-night and leave me your story and a candle. Call for me when I've had time enough to read it and I'll tell you the entire plot and—kick you out of the place."

"That is how it occurred that the farmer's boy, looking in at an unglazed window of the Breede house, saw a man sitting in the light of a candle.

The Day After

Late in the afternoon of the next day three men and a boy approached the Breede house from that point of the compass toward which the boy had fled the preceding night. The men were in high spirits; they talked very loudly and laughed. They made facetious and good-humored ironical remarks to the boy about his adventure, which evidently they did not believe in. The boy accepted their raillery with seriousness, making no reply. He had a sense of the fitness of things and knew that one who professes to have seen a dead man rise from his seat and blow out a candle is not a credible witness.

Arriving at the house and finding the door unlocked, the party of investigators entered without ceremony. Leading out of the passage into which this door opened was another on the right and one on the left. They entered the room on the left—the one which had the blank front window. Here was the dead body of a man.

It lay partly on one side, with the forearm beneath it, the cheek on the floor. The eyes were wide open; the stare was not an agreeable thing to encounter. The lower jaw had fallen; a little pool of saliva had collected beneath the mouth. An overthrown table, a partly burned candle, a chair and some paper with writing on it were all else that the room contained. The men looked at the body, touching the face in turn. The boy gravely stood at the head, assuming a look of ownership. It was the proudest moment of his life. One of the men said to him, "You're a good 'un"—a remark which was received by the two others with nods of acquiescence. It was Scepticism apologizing to Truth. Then one of the men took from the floor the sheet of manuscript and stepped to the window, for already the evening shadows were glooming the forest. The song of the whip-poor-will was heard in the distance and a monstrous beetle sped by the window on roaring wings and thundered away out of hearing. The man read:

The Manuscript

"Before committing the act which, rightly or wrongly, I have resolved on and appearing before my Maker for judgment, I, James R. Colston, deem it my duty as a journalist to make a statement to the public. My name is, I believe, tolerably well known to the people as a writer of tragic tales, but the somberest imagination never conceived anything so tragic as my own life and history. Not in incident: my life has been destitute of adventure and action. But my mental career has been lurid with experiences such as kill and damn. I shall not recount them here—some of them are written and ready for publication elsewhere. The object of these lines is to explain to whomsoever may be interested that my death is voluntary—my own act.

I shall die at twelve o'clock on the night of the 15th of July—a significant anniversary to me, for it was on that day, and at that hour, that my friend in time and eternity, Charles Breede, performed his vow to me by the same act which his fidelity to our pledge now entails upon me. He took his life in his little house in the Copeton woods. There was the customary verdict of 'temporary insanity.' Had I testified at that inquest—had I told all I knew, they would have called *me* mad!"

Here followed an evidently long passage which the man reading read to himself only. The rest he read aloud.

"I have still a week of life in which to arrange my worldly affairs and prepare for the great change. It is enough, for I have but few affairs and it is now four years since death became an imperative obligation.

"I shall bear this writing on my body; the finder will please hand it to the coroner.

"JAMES R. COLSTON.

"P. S.—Willard Marsh, on this the fatal fifteenth day of July I hand you this manuscript, to be opened and read under the conditions agreed upon, and at the place which I designated. I forego my intention to keep it on my body to explain the manner of my death, which is not important. It will serve to explain the manner of yours. I am to call for you during the night to receive assurance that you have read the manuscript. You know me well enough to expect me. But, my friend, *it will be after twelve o'clock*. May God have mercy on our souls!

"J. R. C."

Before the man who was reading this manuscript had finished, the candle had been picked up and lighted. When the reader had done, he quietly thrust the paper against the flame and despite the protestations of the others held it until it was burnt to ashes. The man who did this, and who afterward placidly endured a severe reprimand from the coroner, was a son-in-law of the late Charles Breede. At the inquest nothing could elicit an intellig-ent account of what the paper had contained.

From *"The Times"*

"Yesterday the Commissioners of Lunacy committed to the asylum Mr. James R. Colston, a writer of some local reputation, connected with the *Messenger*. It will be remembered that on the evening of the 15th inst. Mr. Colston was given into custody by one of his fellow-lodgers in the

Baine House, who had observed him acting yery suspiciously, baring his throat and whetting a razor—occasionally trying its edge by actually cutting through the skin of his arm, etc. On being handed over to the police, the unfortunate man made a desperate resistance, and has ever since been so violent that it has been necessary to keep him in a strait-jacket. Most of our esteemed contemporary's other writers are still at large."

IN "SUPERNATURAL HORROR IN LITERATURE," Lovecraft refers to "The Death of Halpin Frayser" as one of the "permanent mountain-peaks of American weird writing," noting that critic Frederic Taber Cooper called it "the most fiendishly ghastly tale in the literature of the Anglo-Saxon race." It first appeared in *The Wave*, 19 December 1891, and was collected in *Can Such Things Be?* (1893).

THE DEATH OF HALPIN FRAYSER
by Ambrose Bierce

I

For by death is wrought greater change than hath been shown. Whereas in general the spirit that removed cometh back upon occasion, and is sometimes seen of those in flesh (appearing in the form of the body it bore) yet it hath happened that the veritable body without the spirit hath walked. And it is attested of those encounter-ing who have lived to speak thereon that a lich so raised up hath no natural affection, nor remembrance thereof, but only hate. Also, it is known that some spirits which in life were benign become by death evil altogether.—*Hali.*

One dark night in midsummer a man waking from a dreamless sleep in a forest lifted his head from the earth, and staring a few moments into the blackness, said: "Catherine Larue." He said nothing more; no reason was known to him why he should have said so much.

The man was Halpin Frayser. He lived in St. Helena, but where he lives now is uncertain, for he is dead. One who practices sleeping in the woods with nothing under him but the dry leaves and the damp earth, and nothing over him but the branches from which the leaves have fallen and the sky from which the earth has fallen, cannot hope for great longevity, and Frayser had already attained the age of thirty-two. There are persons in this world, millions of persons, and far and away the best persons, who regard that as a very advanced age. They are the children. To those who view the voyage of life from the port of departure the bark that has accomplished any considerable distance appears already in close approach to the far-ther shore. However, it is not certain that Halpin Frayser came to his death by exposure.

He had been all day in the hills west of the Napa Valley, looking for doves and such small game as was in season. Late in the aft-ernoon it had come on to be cloudy, and he had lost his bearings; and although he had only to go always downhill—everywhere the way to safety when one is lost— the absence of trails had so impeded him that he was overtaken by night while still in the forest. Unable in the darkness to penetrate the thickets of manzanita and other undergrowth, utterly bewildered and overcome with fatigue, he had lain down near the root of a large madroño and fallen into a dreamless sleep. It was hours later, in the very middle of the night, that one of God's mysterious messengers, gliding ahead of the incalculable host of his companions sweeping westward with the dawn line, pronounced the awakening word in the ear of the sleeper, who sat upright and spoke, he knew not why, a name, he knew not whose.

Halpin Frayser was not much of a philosopher, nor a scientist. The circumstance that, waking from a deep sleep at night in the midst of a forest, he had spoken aloud a name that he had not in memory and hardly had in mind did not arouse an enlightened curiosity to investigate the phenomenon. He thought it odd, and with a little perfunctory shiver, as if in deference to a seasonal presumption that the night was chill, he lay down again and went to sleep. But his sleep was no longer dreamless.

He thought he was walking along a dusty road that showed white in the gathering darkness of a summer night. Whence and whither it led, and why he traveled it, he did not know, though all seemed simple and natural, as is the way in dreams; for in the Land Beyond the Bed surprises cease from troubling and the judgment is at rest. Soon he came to a parting of the ways; leading from the highway was a road less traveled, having the appearance, indeed, of having been long abandoned, because, he thought, it led to something evil; yet he turned into it without hesitation, impelled by some imperious necessity.

As he pressed forward he became conscious that his way was haunted by invisible existences whom he could not definitely figure to his mind. From among the trees on either side he caught broken and incoherent whispers in a strange tongue which yet he partly understood. They seemed to him fragmentary utterances of a monstrous conspiracy against his body and soul.

It was now long after nightfall, yet the interminable forest through which he journeyed was lit with a wan glimmer having no point of diffusion, for in its mysterious lumination nothing cast a shadow. A shallow pool in the guttered depression of an old wheel rut, as from a recent rain, met his eye with a crimson gleam. He stooped and plunged his hand into it. It stained his fingers; it was blood! Blood, he then observed, was about him everywhere. The weeds growing rankly by the roadside showed it in blots and splashes on their big, broad leaves. Patches of dry dust between the wheelways were pitted and spattered as with a red rain. Defiling the trunks of the trees were broad maculations of crimson, and blood dripped like dew from their foliage.

All this he observed with a terror which seemed not incompatible with the fulfillment of a natural expectation. It seemed to him that it was all in expiation of some crime which, though conscious of his guilt, he could not rightly remember. To the menaces and mysteries of his surroundings the consciousness was an added horror. Vainly he sought by tracing life backward in memory, to reproduce the moment of his sin; scenes and incidents came crowding tumultuously into his mind, one picture effacing another, or commingling with it in confusion and obscurity, but nowhere could he catch a glimpse of what he sought. The failure augmented his terror; he felt as one who has murdered in the dark, not knowing whom nor why. So frightful was the situation—the mysterious light burned with so silent and awful a menace; the noxious plants, the trees that by common consent are invested with a melancholy or baleful character, so openly in his sight conspired against his peace; from overhead and all about came so audible and startling whispers and the sighs of creatures so obviously not of earth—that he could endure it no longer, and with a great effort to break some malign spell that bound his faculties to silence and inaction, he shouted with the full strength of his lungs! His voice broken, it seemed, into an infinite multitude of unfamiliar sounds, went babbling and stammering away into the distant reaches of the forest, died into silence, and all was as before. But he had made a beginning at resistance and was encouraged. He said:

"I will not submit unheard. There may be powers that are not malignant traveling this accursed road. I shall leave them a record and an appeal. I shall relate my wrongs, the persecutions that I endure—I, a helpless mortal, a penitent, an unoffending poet!" Halpin Frayser was a poet only as he was a penitent: in his dream.

Taking from his clothing a small red-leather pocketbook, one-half of which was leaved for memoranda, he discovered that he was without a pencil. He broke a twig from a bush, dipped it into a pool of blood and wrote rapidly. He had hardly touched the paper with the point of his twig when a low, wild peal of laughter broke out at a measureless distance away, and growing ever louder, seemed approaching ever nearer; a soulless, heartless, and unjoyous laugh, like that of the loon, solitary by the lakeside at midnight; a laugh which culminated in an unearthly shout close at hand, then died away by slow gradations, as if the accursed being that uttered it had withdrawn over the verge of the world whence it had come. But the man felt that this was not so—that it was near by and had not moved.

A strange sensation began slowly to take possession of his body and his mind. He could not have said which, if any, of his senses was affected; he felt it rather as a consciousness—a mysterious mental assurance of some overpowering presence—some supernatural malevolence different in kind from the invisible existences that swarmed about him, and superior to them in power. He knew that it had uttered that hideous laugh. And now it seemed to be approaching him; from what direction he did not know— dared not conjecture. All his former fears were forgotten or merged in the gigantic terror that now held him in thrall. Apart from that, he had but one thought: to complete his written appeal to the benign powers who, traversing the haunted wood, might some time rescue him if he should be denied the blessing of annihilation. He wrote with terrible rapidity, the twig in his fingers rilling blood without renewal; but in the middle of a sentence his hands denied their service to his will, his arms fell to his sides, the book to the earth; and powerless to move or cry out, he found himself staring into the sharply drawn face and blank, dead eyes of his own mother, standing white and silent in the garments of the grave!

II

In his youth Halpin Frayser had lived with his parents in Nashville, Tennessee. The Fraysers were well-to-do, having a good position in such society as had survived the wreck wrought by civil war. Their children had the social and educational opportunities of their time and place, and had responded to good associations and instruction with agreeable manners and cultivated minds. Halpin being the youngest and not over robust was perhaps a trifle "spoiled." He had the double disadvantage of a mother's assiduity and a father's neglect. Frayser *père* was what no Southern man of means is not—a politician. His country, or rather his section and State, made demands upon his time and attention so exacting that to those of his family he was compelled to turn an ear partly deafened by the thunder of the political captains and the shouting, his own included.

Young Halpin was of a dreamy, indolent and rather romantic turn, somewhat more addicted to literature than law, the profession to which he was bred. Among those of his relations who professed the modern faith of heredity it was well understood that in him the character of the late Myron Bayne, a maternal great-grandfather, had revisited the glimpses of the moon—by which orb Bayne had in his lifetime been sufficiently affected to be a poet of no small Colonial distinction. If not specially observed, it was observable that while a Frayser who was not the proud possessor of a sumptuous copy of the ancestral "poetical works" (printed at the family expense, and long ago withdrawn from an inhospitable market) was a rare Frayser indeed, there was an illogical indisposition to honor the great deceased in the person of his spiritual successor. Halpin was pretty generally deprecated as an intellectual black sheep who was likely at any moment to disgrace the flock by bleating in meter. The Tennessee Fraysers were a practical folk—not practical in the popular sense of devotion to sordid pursuits, but having a robust contempt for any qualities unfitting a man for the wholesome vocation of politics.

In justice to young Halpin it should be said that while in him were pretty faithfully reproduced most of the mental and moral characteristics ascribed by history and family tradition to the famous Colonial bard, his succession to the gift and faculty divine was purely inferential. Not only had he never been known to court the muse, but in truth he could not have written correctly a line of verse to save himself from the Killer of the Wise. Still, there was no knowing when the dormant faculty might wake and smite the lyre.

In the meantime the young man was rather a loose fish, anyhow. Between him and his mother was the most perfect sympathy, for secretly the lady was herself a devout disciple of the late and great Myron Bayne, though with the tact so generally and justly admired in her sex (despite the hardy calumniators who insist that it is essentially the same thing as cunning) she had always taken care to conceal her weakness from all eyes but those of him who shared it. Their common guilt in respect of that was an added tie between them. If in Halpin's youth his mother had "spoiled" him, he had assuredly done his part toward being spoiled. As he grew to such manhood as is attainable by a Southerner who does not care which way elections go the attachment between him and his beautiful mother—whom from early childhood he had called Katy—became yearly stronger and more tender. In these two romantic natures was manifest in a signal way that neglected phenomenon, the dominance of the sexual element in all the relations of life, strengthening, softening, and beautifying even those of consanguinity. The two were nearly inseparable, and by strangers observing their manner were not infrequently mistaken for lovers.

Entering his mother's boudoir one day Halpin Frayser kissed her upon the forehead, toyed for a moment with a lock of her dark hair which had escaped from its confining pins, and said, with an obvious effort at calmness:

"Would you greatly mind, Katy, if I were called away to California for a few weeks?"

It was hardly needful for Katy to answer with her lips a question to which her telltale cheeks had made instant reply. Evidently she would greatly mind; and the tears, too, sprang into her large brown eyes as corroborative testimony.

"Ah, my son," she said, looking up into his face with infinite tenderness, "I should have known that this was coming. Did I not lie awake a half of the night weeping because, during the other half, Grandfather Bayne had come to me in a dream, and standing by his portrait—young, too, and handsome as that—pointed to yours on the same wall? And when I looked it seemed that I could not see the features; you had been painted with a face cloth, such as we put upon the dead. Your father has laughed at me, but you and I, dear, know that such things are not for nothing. And I saw below the edge of the cloth the marks of hands on your throat—forgive me, but we have not been used to keep such things from each other. Perhaps you have another interpretation. Perhaps it does not mean that you will go to California. Or maybe you will take me with you?"

It must be confessed that this ingenious interpretation of the dream in the light of newly discovered evidence did not wholly commend itself to the son's more logical mind; he had, for the moment at least, a conviction that it foreshadowed a more simple and immediate, if less tragic, disaster than a visit to the Pacific Coast. It was Halpin Frayser's impression that he was to be garroted on his native heath.

"Are there not medicinal springs in California?" Mrs. Frayser resumed before he had time to give her the true reading of the dream—"places where one recovers from rheumatism and neuralgia? Look—my fin-gers feel so stiff; and I am almost sure they have been giving me great pain while I slept."

She held out her hands for his inspection. What diagnosis of her case the young man may have thought it best to conceal with a smile the historian is unable to state, but for himself he feels bound to say that fingers looking less stiff, and showing fewer evidences of even insensible pain, have seldom been submitted for medical inspection by even the fairest patient desiring a prescription of unfamiliar scenes.

The outcome of it was that of these two odd persons having equally odd notions of duty, the one went to California, as the interest of his client required, and the other remained at home in compliance with a wish that her husband was scarcely conscious of entertaining.

While in San Francisco Halpin Frayser was walking one dark night along the water front of the city, when, with a suddenness that surprised and disconcerted him, he became a sailor. He was in fact "shanghaied" aboard a gallant, gallant ship, and sailed for a far countree. Nor did his misfortunes end with the voyage; for the ship was cast ashore on an island of the South Pacific, and it was six years afterward when the survivors were taken off by a venturesome trading schooner and brought back to San Francisco.

Though poor in purse, Frayser was no less proud in spirit than he had been in the years that seemed ages and ages ago. He would accept no assistance from strangers, and it was while living with a fellow survivor near the town of St. Helena, awaiting news and remittances from home, that he had gone gunning and dreaming.

III

The apparition confronting the dreamer in the haunted wood —the thing so like, yet so unlike his mother—was horrible! It stirred no love nor longing in his heart; it came unattended with pleasant memories of a golden past—inspired no sentiment of any kind; all the finer emotions were swallowed up in fear. He tried to turn and run from before it, but his legs were as lead; he was unable to lift his feet from the ground. His arms hung helpless at his sides; of his eyes only he retained control, and these he dared not remove from the lusterless orbs of the apparition, which he knew was not a soul without a body, but that most dreadful of all existences infesting that haunted wood—a body without a soul! In its blank stare was neither love, nor pity, nor intelligence—nothing to which to address an appeal for mercy. "An appeal will not lie," he thought, with an absurd reversion to professional slang, making the situation more horrible, as the fire of a cigar might light up a tomb.

For a time, which seemed so long that the world grew gray with age and sin, and the haunted forest, having fulfilled its purpose in this monstrous culmination of its terrors, vanished out of his consciousness with all its sights and sounds, the apparition stood within a pace, regarding him with the mindless malevolence of a wild brute; then thrust its hands forward and sprang upon him with appalling ferocity! The act released his physical energies without unfettering his will; his mind was still spellbound, but his powerful body and agile limbs, endowed with a blind, insensate life of their own, resisted stoutly and well. For an instant he seemed to see this unnatural contest between a dead intelligence and a breathing mechanism only as a spectator—such fancies are in dreams; then he regained his identity almost as if by a leap forward into his body, and the straining automaton had a directing will as alert and fierce as that of its hideous antagonist.

But what mortal can cope with a creature of his dream? The imagination creating the enemy is already vanquished; the combat's result is the combat's cause. Despite his struggles—despite his strength and activity, which seemed wasted in a void, he felt the cold fingers close upon his throat. Borne backward to the earth, he saw above him the dead and drawn face within a hand's breadth of his own, and then all was black. A sound as of the beating of distant drums—a murmur of swarming voices, a sharp, far cry signing all to silence, and Halpin Frayser dreamed that he was dead.

IV

A warm, clear night had been fol-lowed by a morning of drenching fog. At about the middle of the afternoon of the preceding day a little whiff of light vapor—a mere thickening of the atmosphere, the ghost of a cloud— had been observed clinging to the western side of Mount St. Helena, away up along the barren altitudes near the summit. It was so thin, so diaphanous, so like a fancy made visible, that one would have said: "Look quickly! in a moment it will be gone."

In a moment it was visibly larger and denser. While with one edge it clung to the mountain, with the other it reached farther and farther out into the air above the lower slopes. At the same time it extended itself to north and south, joining small patches of mist that appeared to come out of the mountainside on exactly the same level, with an intelligent design to be absorbed. And so it grew and grew until the summit was shut out of view from the valley, and over the valley itself was an ever-extending canopy, opaque and gray. At Calistoga, which lies near the head of the valley and the foot of the mountain, there were a starless night and a sunless morning. The fog, sinking into the valley, had reached southward, swallowing up ranch after ranch, until it had blotted out the town of St. Helena, nine miles away. The dust in the road was laid; trees were adrip with moisture; birds sat silent in their coverts; the morning light was wan and ghastly, with neither color nor fire.

Two men left the town of St. Helena at the first glimmer of dawn, and walked along the road northward up the valley toward Calistoga. They carried guns on their shoulders, yet no one having knowledge of such matters could have mistaken them for hunters of bird or beast. They were a deputy sheriff from Napa and a detective from San Francisco—Holker and Jaralson, respectively. Their business was man-hunting.

"How far is it?" inquired Holker, as they strode along, their feet stirring white the dust beneath the damp surface of the road.

"The White Church? Only a half mile farther," the other answered. "By the way," he added, "it is neither white nor a church; it is an abandoned schoolhouse, gray with age and neglect. Religious services were once held in it—when it was white, and there is a graveyard that would delight a poet. Can you guess why I sent for you, and told you to come heeled?"

"Oh, I never have bothered you about things of that kind. I've always found you communicative when the time came. But if I may hazard a guess, you want me to help you arrest one of the corpses in the graveyard."

"You remember Branscom?" said Jaralson, treating his companion's wit with the inattention that it deserved.

"The chap who cut his wife's throat? I ought; I wasted a week's work on him and had my expenses for my trouble. There is a reward of five hundred dollars, but none of us ever got a sight of him. You don't mean to say—"

"Yes, I do. He has been under the noses of you fellows all the time. He comes by night to the old graveyard at the White Church."

"The devil! That's where they buried his wife."

"Well, you fellows might have had sense enough to suspect that he would return to her grave some time."

"The very last place that anyone would have expected him to return to."

"But you had exhausted all the other places. Learning your failure at them, I 'laid for him' there."

"And you found him?"

"Damn it! he found *me*. The rascal got the drop on me—regularly held me up and made me travel. It's God's mercy that he didn't go through me. Oh, he's a good one, and I fancy the half of that reward is enough for me if you're needy."

Holker laughed good humoredly, and explained that his creditors were never more importunate.

"I wanted merely to show you the ground, and arrange a plan with you," the detective explained. "I thought it as well for us to be heeled, even in daylight."

"The man must be insane," said the deputy sheriff. "The reward is for his capture and conviction. If he's mad he won't be convicted."

Mr. Holker was so profoundly affected by that possible failure of justice that he involuntarily stopped in the middle of the road, then resumed his walk with abated zeal.

"Well, he looks it," assented Jaralson. "I'm bound to admit that a more unshaven, unshorn, unkempt, and uneverything wretch I never saw outside the ancient and honorable order of tramps. But I've gone in for him, and can't make up my mind to let go. There's glory in it for us, anyhow. Not another soul knows that he is this side of the Mountains of the Moon."

"All right," Holker said; "we will go and view the ground," and he added, in the words of a once favorite inscription for tombstones: "'where you must shortly lie'—I mean, if old Branscom ever gets tired of you and your impertinent intrusion. By the way, I heard the other day that 'Branscom' was not his real name."

"What is?"

"I can't recall it. I had lost all interest in the wretch, and it did not fix itself in my memory—something like Pardee. The woman whose throat he had the bad taste to cut was a widow when he met her. She had come to California to look up some relatives—there are persons who will do that sometimes. But you know all that."

"Naturally."

"But not knowing the right name, by what happy inspiration did you find the right grave? The man who told me what the name was said it had been cut on the headboard."

"I don't know the right grave." Jaralson was apparently a trifle reluctant to admit his ignorance of so important a point of his plan. "I have been watching about the place generally. A part of our work this morning will be to identify that grave. Here is the White Church."

For a long distance the road had been bordered by fields on both sides, but now on the left there was a forest of oaks, madroños, and gigantic spruces whose lower parts only could be seen, dim and ghostly in the fog. The undergrowth was, in places, thick, but nowhere impenetrable. For some moments Holker saw nothing of the building, but as they turned into the woods it revealed itself in faint gray outline through the fog, looking huge and far away. A few steps more, and it was within an arm's length, distinct, dark with moisture, and insignificant in size. It had the usual country-schoolhouse form—belonged to the packing-box order of architecture; had an underpinning of stones, a moss-grown roof, and blank window spaces, whence both glass and sash had long departed. It was ruined, but not a ruin—a typical Californian substitute for what are known to guide-bookers abroad as "monu-ments of the past." With scarcely a glance at this uninteresting structure Jaralson moved on into the dripping undergrowth beyond.

"I will show you where he held me up," he said. "This is the graveyard."

Here and there among the bushes were small inclosures containing graves, sometimes no more than one. They were recognized as graves by the discolored stones or rotting boards at head and foot, leaning at all angles, some prostrate; by the ruined picket fences surrounding them; or, infrequently, by the mound itself showing its gravel through the fallen leaves. In many instances nothing marked the spot where lay the vestiges of some poor mortal—who, leaving "a large circle of sorrowing friends," had been left by them in turn—except a depression in the earth, more lasting than that in the spirits of the mourners. The paths, if any paths had been, were long obliterated; trees of a considerable size had been permitted to grow up from the graves and thrust aside with root or branch the inclosing fences. Over all was that air of abandonment and decay which seems nowhere so fit and significant as in a village of the forgotten dead.

As the two men, Jaralson leading, pushed their way through the growth of young trees, that enterprising man suddenly stopped and brought up his shotgun to the height of his breast, uttered a low note of warning, and stood motionless, his eyes fixed upon something ahead. As well as he could, obstructed by brush, his companion, though seeing nothing, imitated the posture and so stood, prepared for what might ensue. A moment later Jaralson moved cautiously forward, the other following.

Under the branches of an enormous spruce lay the dead body of a man. Standing silent above it they noted such particulars as first strike the attention—the face, the attitude, the clothing; whatever most promptly and plainly answers the unspoken question of a sympathetic curiosity.

The body lay upon its back, the legs wide apart. One arm was thrust upward, the other outward; but the latter was bent acutely, and the hand was near the throat. Both hands were tightly clenched. The whole attitude was that of desperate but ineffectual resistance to—what?

Near by lay a shotgun and a game bag through the meshes of which was seen the plumage of shot birds. All about were evid-ences of a furious struggle; small sprouts of poison-oak were bent and denuded of leaf and bark; dead and rotting leaves had been pushed into heaps and ridges on both sides of the legs by the action of other feet than theirs; alongside the hips were unmistakable impressions of human knees.

The nature of the struggle was made clear by a glance at the dead man's throat and face. While breast and hands were white, those were purple—almost black. The shoulders lay upon a low mound, and the head was turned back at an angle otherwise impossible, the expanded eyes staring blankly backward in a direction opposite to that of the feet. From the froth filling the open mouth the tongue protruded, black and swollen. The throat showed horrible contusions; not mere finger-marks, but bruises and lacerations wrought by two strong hands that must have buried themselves in the yielding flesh, maintaining their terrible grasp until long after death. Breast, throat, face, were wet; the clothing was saturated; drops of water, condensed from the fog, studded the hair and mustache.

All this the two men observed without speaking—almost at a glance. Then Holker said:

"Poor devil! he had a rough deal."

Jaralson was making a vigilant circumspection of the forest, his shotgun held in both hands and at full cock, his finger upon the trigger.

"The work of a maniac," he said, without withdrawing his eyes from the inclosing wood. "It was done by Branscom—Pardee."

Something half hidden by the disturbed leaves on the earth caught Holker's attention. It was a red-leather pocketbook. He picked it up and opened it. It contained leaves of white paper for memoranda, and upon the first leaf was the name "Halpin Frayser." Written in red on several succeeding leaves—scrawled as if in haste and barely legible—were the following lines, which Holker read aloud, while his companion continued scann-ing the dim gray confines of their narrow world and hearing matter of apprehension in the drip of water from every burdened branch:

> "Enthralled by some mysterious spell, I stood
> In the lit gloom of an enchanted wood.
>   The cypress there and myrtle twined their boughs,
> Significant, in baleful brotherhood.
>
> "The brooding willow whispered to the yew;
> Beneath, the deadly nightshade and the rue,
>   With immortelles self-woven into strange
> Funereal shapes, and horrid nettles grew.
>
> "No song of bird nor any drone of bees,
> Nor light leaf lifted by the wholesome breeze:
>   The air was stagnant all, and Silence was
> A living thing that breathed among the trees.
>
> "Conspiring spirits whispered in the gloom,
> Half-heard, the stilly secrets of the tomb.
>   With blood the trees were all adrip; the leaves
> Shone in the witch-light with a ruddy bloom.
>
> "I cried aloud!—the spell, unbroken still,
> Rested upon my spirit and my will.
>   Unsouled, unhearted, hopeless and forlorn,
> I strove with monstrous presages of ill!
>
> "At last the viewless——"

Holker ceased reading; there was no more to read. The manuscript broke off in the middle of a line.

"That sounds like Bayne," said Jaralson, who was something of a scholar in his way.

He had abated his vigilance and stood looking down at the body.

"Who's Bayne?" Holker asked rather incuriously.

"Myron Bayne, a chap who flourished in the early years of the nation—more than a century ago. Wrote mighty dismal stuff; I have his collected works. That poem is not among them, but it must have been omitted by mistake."

"It is cold," said Holker; "let us leave here; we must have up the coroner from Napa."

Jaralson said nothing, but made a movement in compliance. Passing the end of the slight elevation of earth upon which the dead man's head and shoulders lay, his foot struck some hard substance under the rotting forest leaves, and he took the trouble to kick it into view. It was a fallen headboard, and painted on it were the hardly decipherable words, "Catharine Larue."

"Larue, Larue!" exclaimed Holker, with sudden animation. "Why, that is the real name of Branscom—not Pardee. And—bless my soul! how it all comes to me—the murdered woman's name had been Frayser!"

"There is some rascally mystery here," said Detective Jaralson. "I hate anything of that kind."

There came to them out of the fog—seemingly from a great distance—the sound of a laugh, a low, deliberate, soulless laugh, which had no more of joy than that of a hyena night-prowling in the desert; a laugh that rose by slow gradation, louder and louder, clearer, more distinct and terrible, until it seemed barely outside the narrow circle of their vision; a laugh so unnatural, so unhuman, so devilish, that it filled those hardy man-hunters with a sense of dread unspeakable! They did not move their weapons nor think of them; the menace of that horrible sound was not of the kind to be met with arms. As it had grown out of silence, so now it died away; from a culminating shout which had seemed almost in their ears, it drew itself away into the distance, until its failing notes, joyless and mechanical to the last, sank to silence at a measureless remove.

LOVECRAFT DESCRIBED THE Welsh writer Arthur Machen (1863-1947) as "a general man of letters and a master of an exquisitely lyrical and expressive prose style" who wrote "some dozen tales long and short, in which the elements of hidden horror and brooding fright attain an almost incomparable substance and realistic acuteness." One of Machen's favorite themes, according to Lovecraft, was "the notion that beneath the mounds and rocks of the wild Welsh hills dwell subterraneously that squat primitive race whose vestiges gave rise to our common folk legends of fairies, elves, and the 'little people'." And Lovecraft felt that "this theme receives its finest treatment in the episode entitled 'The Novel of the Black Seal'," a part of Machen's episodic novel *The Three Impostors* (1895). Lovecraft discovered Machen's writings in the late spring of 1923, and in a letter to Frank Belknap Long from June 1923 Lovecraft referred to Machen as "perhaps the greatest living author."

NOVEL OF THE BLACK SEAL
by Arthur Machen

"I see you are a determined rationalist," she said. "Did you not hear me say that I have had experiences even more terrible? I too was once a sceptic, but after what I have known I can no longer doubt."

"Madam," replied Mr. Phillipps, "no one shall make me deny my faith. I will never believe, nor will pretend to believe that two and two make five, nor will I on any pretences admit the existence of two-sided triangles."

"You are a little hasty," rejoined the lady. "But may I ask you if you ever heard the name of Professor Gregg, the authority on ethnology and kindred subjects?"

"I have done much more than merely hear of Professor Gregg," said Phillipps. "I always regarded him as one of our most acute and clear-headed observers; and his last publication, the 'Textbook of Ethnology,' struck me as being admirable in its kind. Indeed, the book had but come into my hands when I heard of the terrible accident which cut short Gregg's career. He had, I think, taken a country house in the West of England for the summer, and is supposed to have fallen into a river. So far as I remember, his body was never recovered."

"Sir, I am sure that you are discreet. Your conversation seems to declare as much, and the very title of that little work of yours which you mentioned assures me that you are no empty trifler. In a word, I feel that I may depend on you. You appear to be under the impression that Professor Gregg is dead; I have no reason to believe that that is the case."

"What?" cried Phillipps, astonished and perturbed. "You do not hint that there was anything disgraceful? I cannot believe it. Gregg was a man of the clearest character; his private life was one of great benevolence; and though I myself am free from delusions, I believe him to have been a sincere and devout Christian. Surely you cannot mean to insinuate that some disreputable history forced him to flee the country?"

"Again you are in a hurry," replied the lady. "I said nothing of all this. Briefly, then, I must tell you that Professor Gregg left his house one morning in full health both of mind and body. He never returned, but his watch and chain, a purse containing three sovereigns in gold, and some loose silver, with a ring that he wore habitually, were found three days later on a wild and savage hillside, many miles from the river. These articles were placed beside a limestone rock of fantastic form; they had been wrapped into a parcel with a kind of rough parchment which was secured with gut. The parcel was opened, and the inner side of the parchment bore an inscription done with some red substance; the characters were undecipherable, but seemed to be a corrupt cuneiform."

"You interest me intensely," said Phillipps. "Would you mind continuing your story? The circumstance you have mentioned seems to me of the most inexplicable character, and I thirst for elucidation."

The young lady seemed to meditate for a moment, and she then proceeded to relate the

NOVEL OF THE BLACK SEAL

I must now give you some fuller particulars of my history. I am the daughter of a civil engineer, Steven Lally by name, who was so unfortunate as to die suddenly at the outset of his career, and before he had accumulated sufficient means to support his wife and her two children.

My mother contrived to keep the small household going on resources which must have been incredibly small; we lived in a remote country village, because most of the necessaries of life were cheaper than in a town, but even so we were brought up with the severest economy. My father was a clever and well-read man, and left behind him a small but select collection of books, containing the best Greek, Latin, and English classics, and these books were the only amusement we possessed. My brother, I remember, learnt Latin out of Descartes' "Meditationes," and I, in place of the little tales which children are usually told to read, had nothing more charming than a translation of the "Gesta Romanorum." We grew up thus, quiet, and studious children, and in course of time my brother provided for himself in the manner I have mentioned. I continued to live at home; my poor mother had become an invalid, and demanded my continual care, and about two years ago she died after many months of painful illness. My situation was a terrible one; the shabby furniture barely sufficed to pay the debts I had been forced to contract, and the books I dispatched to my brother, knowing how he would value them. I was absolutely alone; I was aware how poorly my brother was paid; and though I came up to London in the hope of finding employment, with the understanding that he would defray my expenses, I swore it should only be for a month, and that if I could not in that time find some work, I would starve rather than deprive him of the few miserable pounds he had laid by for his day of trouble. I took a little room in a distant suburb, the cheapest that I could find; I lived on bread and tea, and I spent my time in vain answering of advertisements, and vainer walks to addresses I had noted. Day followed on day, and week on week, and still I was unsuccessful, till at last the term I had appointed drew to a close, and I saw before me the grim prospect of slowly dying of starvation. My landlady was good-natured in her way; she knew the slenderness of my means, and I am sure that she would not have turned me out of doors; it remained for me then to go away, and to try to die in some quiet place. It was winter then and a thick white fog gathered in the early part of the afternoon, becoming more dense as the day wore on; it was a Sunday, I remember, and the people of the house were at chapel. At about three o'clock I crept out and walked away as quickly as I could, for I was weak from abstinence. The white mist wrapped all the streets in silence, a hard frost had gathered thick upon the bare branches of the trees, and frost crystals glittered on the wooden fences, and on the cold, cruel ground beneath my feet. I walked on, turning to right and left in utter haphazard, without caring to look up at the names of the streets, and all that I remember of my walk on that Sunday afternoon seems but the broken fragments of an evil dream. In a confused vision I stumbled on, through roads half town and half country, grey fields melting into the cloudy world of mist on one side of me, and on the other comfortable villas with a glow of firelight flickering on the walls, but all unreal; red brick walls and lighted windows, vague trees, and glimmering country, gas-lamps beginning to star the white shadows, the vanishing perspectives of the railway line beneath high embankments, the green and red of the signal lamps,—all these were but momentary pictures flashed on my tired brain and senses numbed by hunger. Now and then I would hear a quick step ringing on the iron road, and men would pass me well wrapped up, walking fast for the sake of warmth, and no doubt eagerly foretasting the pleasures of a glowing hearth, with curtains tightly drawn about the frosted panes, and the welcomes of their friends; but as the early evening darkened and night approached, foot-passengers got fewer and fewer, and I passed through street after street alone. In the white silence I stumbled on, as desolate as if I trod the streets of a buried city; and as I grew more weak and exhausted, something of the horror of death was folding thickly round my heart. Suddenly, as I turned a corner, some one accosted me courteously beneath the lamp-post, and I heard a voice asking if I could kindly point the way to Avon Road. At the sudden shock of human accents I was prostrated, and my strength gave way; I fell all huddled on the sidewalk, and wept and sobbed and laughed in violent hysteria. I had gone out prepared to die, and as I stepped across the threshold that had sheltered me, I consciously bade adieu to all hopes and all remembrances; the door clanged behind me with the noise of thunder, and I felt that an iron curtain had fallen on the brief passages of my life, that henceforth I was to walk a little way in a world of gloom and shadow; I entered on the stage of the first act of death. Then came my wandering in the mist, the whiteness wrapping all things, the void streets, and muffled silence, till when that voice spoke to me it was as if I had died and life returned to me. In a few minutes I was able to compose my feelings, and as I rose I saw that I was confronted by a middle-aged gentleman of pleasing appearance, neatly and correctly dressed. He looked at me with an expression of great pity, but before I could stammer out my ignorance of the neighbourhood, for indeed I had not the slightest notion of where I had wandered, he spoke.

"My dear madam," he said, "you seem in some terrible distress. You cannot think how you alarmed me. But may I inquire the nature of your trouble? I assure you that you can safely confide in me."

"You are very kind," I replied, "but I fear there is nothing to be done. My condition seems a hopeless one."

"Oh, nonsense, nonsense! You are too young to talk like that. Come, let us walk down here, and you must tell me your difficulty. Perhaps I may be able to help you."

There was something very soothing and persuasive in his manner, and as we walked together I gave him an outline of my story, and told of the despair that had oppressed me almost to death.

"You were wrong to give in so completely," he said, when I was silent. "A month is too short a time in which to feel one's way in London. London, let me tell you, Miss Lally, does not lie open and undefended; it is a fortified place, fossed and double-moated with curious intricacies. As must always happen in large towns, the conditions of life have become hugely artificial; no mere simple palisade is run up to oppose the man or woman who would take the place by storm, but serried lines of subtle contrivances, mines, and pitfalls which it needs a strange skill to overcome. You, in your simplicity, fancied you had only to shout for these walls to sink into nothingness, but the time is gone for such startling victories as these. Take courage; you will learn the secret of success before long."

"Alas I sir," I replied, "I have no doubt your conclusions are correct, but at the present moment I seem to be in a fair way to die of starvation. You spoke of a secret; for heaven's sake tell it me, if you have any pity for my distress."

He laughed genially. "There lies the strangeness of it all. Those who know the secret cannot tell it if they would; it is positively as ineffable as the central doctrine of Freemasonry. But I may say this, that you yourself have penetrated at least the outer husk of the mystery," and he laughed again.

"Pray do not jest with me," I said. "What have I done, *que sçais-je?* I am so far ignorant that I have not the slightest idea of how my next meal is to be provided."

"Excuse me. You ask what you have done. You have met me. Come, we will fence no longer. I see you have self-education, the only education which is not infinitely pernicious, and I am in want of a governess for my two children. I have been a widower for some years; my name is Gregg. I offer you the post I have named, and shall we say a salary of a hundred a year?"

I could only stutter out my thanks, and slipping a card with his address, and a banknote by way of earnest into my hand, Mr. Gregg bade me good-bye, asking me to call in a day or two.

Such was my introduction to Professor Gregg, and can you wonder that the remembrance of despair and the cold blast that had blown from the gates of death upon me made me regard him as a second father? Before the close of the week I was installed in my new duties. The professor had leased an old brick manor-house in a western suburb of London, and here, surrounded by pleasant lawns and orchards, and soothed with the murmur of ancient elms that rocked their boughs above the roof, the new chapter of my life began. Knowing as you do the nature of the professor's occupations, you will not be surprised to hear that the house teemed with books, and cabinets full of strange, and even hideous, objects filled every available nook in the vast low rooms. Gregg was a man whose one thought was for knowledge, and I too before long caught something of his enthusiasm, and strove to enter into his passion for research. In a few months I was perhaps more his secretary than the governess of the two children, and many a night I have sat at the desk in the glow of the shaded lamp while he, pacing up and down in the rich gloom of the firelight, dictated to me the substance of his "Textbook of Ethnology." But amidst these more sober and accurate studies I always detected a something hidden, a longing and desire for some object to which he did not allude; and now and then he would break short in what he was saying and lapse into reverie, entranced, as it seemed to me, by some distant prospect of adventurous discovery. The text-book was at last finished, and we began to receive proofs from the printers, which were entrusted to me for a first reading, and then underwent the final revision of the professor. All the while his weariness of the actual business he was engaged on increased, and it was with the joyous laugh of a schoolboy when term is over that he one day handed me a copy of the book. "There," he said, "I have kept my word; I promised to write it, and it is done with. Now I shall be free to live for stranger things; I confess it, Miss Lally, I covet the renown of Columbus; you will, I hope, see me play the part of an explorer."

"Surely," I said, "there is little left to explore. You have been born a few hundred years too late for that."

"I think you are wrong," he replied; "there are still, depend upon it, quaint, undiscovered countries and continents of strange extent. Ah, Miss Lally! believe me, we stand amidst sacraments and mysteries full of awe, and it doth not yet appear what we shall be. Life, believe me, is no simple thing, no mass of grey matter and congeries of veins and muscles to be laid naked by the surgeon's knife; man is the secret which I am about to explore, and before I can discover him I must cross over weltering seas indeed, and oceans and the mists of many thousand years. You know the myth of the lost Atlantis; what if it be true, and I am destined to be called the discoverer of that wonderful land?"

I could see the excitement boiling beneath his words, and in his face was the heat of the hunter; before me stood a man who believed himself summoned to tourney with the unknown. A pang of joy possessed me when I reflected that I was to be in a way associated with him in the adventure, and I too burned with the lust of the chase, not pausing to consider that I knew not what we were to unshadow.

The next morning Professor Gregg took me into his inner study, where, ranged against the wall, stood a nest of pigeon-holes, every drawer neatly labelled, and the results of years of toil classified in a few feet of space.

"Here," he said, "is my life; here are all the facts which I have gathered together with so much pains, and yet it is all nothing. No, nothing to what I am about to attempt. Look at this"; and he took me to an old bureau, a piece fantastic and faded, which stood in a corner of the room. He unlocked the front and opened one of the drawers.

"A few scraps of paper," he went on, pointing to the drawer, "and a lump of black stone, rudely annotated with queer marks and scratches—that is all that drawer holds. Here you see is an old envelope with the dark red stamp of twenty years ago, but I have pencilled a few lines at the back; here is a sheet of manuscript, and here some cuttings from obscure local journals. And if you ask me the subject-matter of the collection, it will not seem extraordinary—a servant-girl at a farm-house, who disappeared from her place and has never been heard of, a child supposed to have slipped down some old working on the mountains, some queer scribbling on a limestone rock, a man murdered with a blow from a strange weapon; such is the scent I have to go upon. Yes, as you say, there is a ready explanation for all this; the girl may have run away to London, or Liverpool, or New York; the child may be at the bottom of the disused shaft; and the letters on the rock may be the idle whims of some vagrant. Yes, yes, I admit all that; but I know I hold the true key. Look!" and he held out a slip of yellow paper.

Characters found inscribed on a limestone rock on the Grey Hills, I read, and then there was a word erased, presumably the name of a county, and a date some fifteen years back. Beneath was traced a number of uncouth characters, shaped somewhat like wedges or daggers, as strange and outlandish as the Hebrew alphabet.

"Now the seal," said Professor Gregg, and he handed me the black stone, a thing about two inches long, and something like an old-fashioned tobacco-stopper, much enlarged.

I held it up to the light, and saw to my surprise the characters on the paper repeated on the seal.

"Yes," said the professor, "they are the same. And the marks on the limestone rock were made fifteen years ago, with some red substance. And the characters on the seal are four thousand years old at least. Perhaps much more."

"Is it a hoax?" I said.

"No, I anticipated that. I was not to be led to give my life to a practical joke. I have tested the matter very carefully. Only one person besides myself knows of the mere existence of that black seal. Besides, there are other reasons which I cannot enter into now."

"But what does it all mean?" I said. "I cannot understand to what conclusion all this leads."

"My dear Miss Lally, that is a question I would rather leave unanswered for some little time. Perhaps I shall never be able to say what secrets are held here in solution; a few vague hints, the outlines of village tragedies, a few marks done with red earth upon a rock, and an ancient seal. A queer set of data to go upon? Half a dozen pieces of evidence, and twenty years before even so much could be got together; and who knows what mirage or *terra incognita* may be beyond all this? I look across deep waters, Miss Lally, and the land beyond may be but a haze after all. But still I believe it is not so, and a few months will show whether I am right or wrong."

He left me, and alone I endeavoured to fathom the mystery, wondering to what goal such eccentric odds and ends of evidence could lead. I myself am not wholly devoid of imagination, and I had reason to respect the professor's solidity of intellect; yet I saw in the contents of the drawer but the materials of fantasy, and vainly tried to conceive what theory could be founded on the fragments that had been placed before me. Indeed, I could discover in what I had heard and seen but the first chapter of an extravagant romance; and yet deep in my heart I burned with curiosity, and day after day I looked eagerly in Professor Gregg's face for some hint of what was to happen.

It was one evening after dinner that the word came.

"I hope you can make your preparations without much trouble," he said suddenly to me. "We shall be leaving here in a week's time."

"Really!" I said in astonishment. "Where are we going?"

"I have taken a country house in the west of England, not far from Caermaen, a quiet little town, once a city, and the headquarters of a Roman legion. It is very dull there, but the country is pretty, and the air is wholesome."

I detected a glint in his eyes, and guessed that this sudden move had some relation to our conversation of a few days before.

"I shall just take a few books with me," said Professor Gregg, "that is all. Everything else will remain here for our return. I have got a holiday," he went on, smiling at me, "and I shan't be sorry to be quit for a time of my old bones and stones and rubbish. Do you know," he went on, "I have been grinding away at facts for thirty years; it is time for fancies."

The days passed quickly; I could see that the professor was all quivering with suppressed excitement, and I could scarce credit the eager appetence of his glance as we left the old manor-house behind us and began our journey. We set out at midday, and it was in the dusk of the evening that we arrived at a little county station. I was tired and excited, and the drive through the lanes seems all a dream. First the deserted streets of a forgotten village, while I heard Professor Gregg's voice talking of the Augustan Legion and the clash of arms, and all the tremendous pomp that followed the eagles; then the broad river swimming to full tide with the last afterglow glimmering duskily in the yellow water, the wide meadows, the cornfields whitening, and the deep lane winding on the slope between the hills and the water. At last we began to ascend, and the air grew rarer. I looked down and saw the pure white mist tracking the outline of the river like a shroud, and a vague and shadowy country; imaginations and fantasy of swelling hills and hanging woods, and half-shaped outlines of hills beyond, and in the distance the glare of the furnace fire on the mountain, growing by turns a pillar of shining flame and fading to a dull point of red. We were slowly mounting a carriage drive, and then there came to me the cool breath and the secret of the great wood that was above us; I seemed to wander in its deepest depths, and there was the sound of trickling water, the scent of the green leaves, and the breath of the summer night. The carriage stopped at last, and I could scarcely distinguish the form of the house as I waited a moment at the pillared porch. The rest of the evening seemed a dream of strange things bounded by the great silence of the wood and the valley and the river.

The next morning, when I awoke and looked out of the bow window of the big, old-fashioned bedroom, I saw under a grey sky a country that was still all mystery. The long, lovely valley, with the river winding in and out below, crossed in mid-vision by a mediæval bridge of vaulted and buttressed stone, the clear presence of the rising ground beyond, and the woods that I had only seen in shadow the night before, seemed tinged with enchantment, and the soft breath of air that sighed in at the opened pane was like no other wind. I looked across the valley, and beyond, hill followed on hill as wave on wave, and here a faint blue pillar of smoke rose still in the morning air from the chimney of an ancient grey farm-house, there was a rugged height crowned with dark firs, and in the distance I saw the white streak of a road that climbed and vanished into some unimagined country. But the boundary of all was a great wall of mountain, vast in the west, and ending like a fortress with a steep ascent and a domed tumulus clear against the sky.

I saw Professor Gregg walking up and down the terrace path below the windows, and it was evident that he was revelling in the sense of liberty, and the thought that he had for a while bidden good-bye to task-work. When I joined him there was exultation in his voice as he pointed out the sweep of valley and the river that wound beneath the lovely hills.

"Yes," he said, "it is a strangely beautiful country; and to me, at least, it seems full of mystery. You have not forgotten the drawer I showed you, Miss Lally? No; and you guessed that I have come here not merely for the sake of the children and the fresh air?"

"I think I have guessed as much as that," I replied; "but you must remember I do not know the mere nature of your investigations; and as for the connection between the search and this wonderful valley, it is past my guessing."

He smiled queerly at me. "You must not think I am making a mystery for the sake of a mystery," he said. "I do not speak out because, so far, there is nothing to be spoken, nothing definite, I mean, nothing that can be set down in hard black and white, as dull and sure and irreproachable as any blue-book. And then I have another reason: Many years ago a chance paragraph in a news-paper caught my attention, and focussed in an instant the vagrant thoughts and half-formed fancies of many idle and speculative hours into a certain hypothesis. I saw at once that I was treading on a thin crust; my theory was wild and fantastic in the extreme, and I would not for any consideration have written a hint of it for publication. But I thought that in the company of scientific men like myself, men who knew the course of discovery, and were aware that the gas that blazes and flares in the gin-palace was once a wild hypothesis—I thought that with such men as these I might hazard my dream—let us say Atlantis, or the philosopher's stone, or what you like—without danger of ridicule. I found I was grossly mistaken; my friends looked blankly at me and at one another, and I could see something of pity, and something also of insolent contempt, in the glances they exchanged. One of them called on me next day, and hinted that I must be suffering from overwork and brain exhaustion. 'In plain terms,' I said, 'you think I am going mad. I think not'; and I showed him out with some little appearance of heat. Since that day I vowed that I would never whisper the nature of my theory to any living soul; to no one but yourself have I ever shown the contents of that drawer. After all, I may be following a rainbow; I may have been misled by the play of coincidence; but as I stand here in this mystic hush and silence amidst the woods and the wild hills, I am more than ever sure that I am hot on the scent. Come, it is time we went in."

To me in all this there was something both of wonder and excitement; I knew how in his ordinary work Professor Gregg moved step by step, testing every inch of the way, and never venturing on assertion without proof that was impregnable. Yet I divined more from his glance and the vehemence of his tone than from the spoken word, that he had in his every thought the vision of the almost incredible continually with him; and I, who was with some share of imagination no little of a sceptic, offended at a hint of the marvellous, could not help asking myself whether he were cherishing a monomania, and barring out from this one subject all the scientific method of his other life.

Yet, with this image of mystery haunting my thoughts, I surrendered wholly to the charm of the country. Above the faded house on the hillside began the great forest—a long, dark line seen from the opposing hills, stretching above the river for many a mile from north to south, and yielding in the north to even wilder country, barren and savage hills, and ragged common-land, a territory all strange and unvisited, and more unknown to Englishmen than the very heart of Africa. The space of a couple of steep fields alone sepa-rated the house from the wood, and the children were delighted to follow me up the long alleys of undergrowth, between smooth pleached walls of shining beech, to the highest point in the wood, whence one looked on one side across the river and the rise and fall of the country to the great western mountain wall, and on the other over the surge and dip of the myriad trees of the forest, over level meadows and the shining yellow sea to the faint coast beyond. I used to sit at this point on the warm sunlit turf which marked the track of the Roman Road, while the two children raced about hunting for the whinberries that grew here and there on the banks. Here beneath the deep blue sky and the great clouds rolling, like olden galleons with sails full-bellied, from the sea to the hills, as I listened to the whispered charm of the great and ancient wood, I lived solely for delight, and only remembered strange things when we would return to the house and find Professor Gregg either shut up in the little room he had made his study, or else pacing the terrace with the look, patient and enthusiastic, of the determined seeker.

One morning, some eight or nine days after our arrival, I looked out of my window and saw the whole landscape transmuted before me. The clouds had dipped low and hidden the mountain in the west; a southern wind was driving the rain in shifting pillars up the valley, and the little brooklet that burst the hill below the house now raged, a red torrent, down the river. We were perforce obliged to keep snug within-doors; and when I had attended to my pupils, I sat down in the morning-room where the ruins of a library still encumbered an old-fashioned bookcase. I had inspected the shelves once or twice, but their contents had failed to attract me; volumes of eighteenth-century sermons, an old book on farriery, a collection of *Poems* by "persons of quality," Prideaux's *Connection*, and an odd volume of Pope, were the boundaries of the library, and there seemed little doubt that everything of interest or value had been removed. Now however, in desperation, I began to re-examine the musty sheepskin and calf bindings, and found, much to my delight, a fine old quarto printed by the Stephani, containing the three books of Pomponius Mela, *De Situ Orbis*, and other of the ancient geographers. I knew enough of Latin to steer my way through an ordinary sentence, and I soon became absorbed in the odd mixture of fact and fancy—light shining on a little space of the world, and beyond, mist and shadow and awful forms. Glancing over the clear-printed pages, my attention was caught by the heading of a chapter in Solinus, and I read the words:—

> "MIRA DE INTIMIS GENTIBUS LIBYAE, DE LAPIDE HEXECONTALITHO,"

—"The wonders of the people that inhabit the inner parts of Libya, and of the stone called Sixtystone."

The odd title attracted me, and I read on:—"Gens ista avia et secreta habitat, in montibus horrendis frœda mysteria celebrat. De hominibus nihil aliud illi praeferunt quam figuram, ab humano ritu prorsus exulant, oderunt deum lucis. Stridunt potius quam loquuntur; vox absona nec sine horrore auditur. Lapide quodam gloriantur, quem Hexecontalithon vocant; dicunt enim hunc lapidem sexaginta notas ostendere. Cujus lapidis nomen secretum ineffabile colunt: quod Ixaxar."

"This folk," I translated to myself, "dwells in remote and secret places, and celebrates foul mysteries on savage hills. Nothing have they in common with men save the face, and the customs of humanity are wholly strange to them; and they hate the sun. They hiss rather than speak; their voices are harsh, and not to be heard without fear. They boast of a certain stone, which they call Sixtystone; for they say that it displays sixty characters. And this stone has a secret unspeakable name; which is Ixaxar."

I laughed at the queer inconsequence of all this, and thought it fit for "Sinbad the Sailor," or other of the supplementary Nights. When I saw Professor Gregg in the course of the day, I told him of my find in the bookcase, and the fantastic rubbish I had been reading. To my surprise he looked up at me with an expression of great interest.

"That is really very curious," he said. "I have never thought it worth while to look into the old geographers, and I dare say I have missed a good deal. Ah, that is the passage, is it? It seems a shame to rob you of your entertainment, but I really think I must carry off the book."

The next day the professor called me to come to the study. I found him sitting at a table in the full light of the window, scrutinizing something very attentively with a magnifying glass.

"Ah, Miss Lally," he began, "I want to use your eyes. This glass is pretty good, but not like my old one that I left in town. Would you mind examining the thing yourself, and telling me how many characters are cut on it?"

He handed me the object in his hand. I saw that it was the black seal he had shown me in London, and my heart began to beat with the thought that I was presently to know something. I took the seal, and, holding it up to the light, checked off the grotesque dagger-shaped characters one by one.

"I make sixty-two," I said at last.

"Sixty-two? Nonsense; it's impossible. Ah, I see what you have done, you have counted that and that," and he pointed to two marks which I had certainly taken as letters with the rest.

"Yes, yes," Professor Gregg went on, "but those are obvious scratches, done accidentally; I saw that at once. Yes, then that's quite right. Thank you very much, Miss Lally."

I was going away, rather disappointed at my having been called in merely to count the number of marks on the black seal, when suddenly there flashed into my mind what I had read in the morning.

"But, Professor Gregg," I cried, breathless, "the seal, the seal. Why, it is the stone Hexecontalithos that Solinus writes of; it is Ixaxar."

"Yes," he said, "I suppose it is. Or it may be a mere coincidence. It never does to be too sure, you know, in these matters. Coincidence killed the professor."

I went away puzzled at what I had heard, and as much as ever at a loss to find the ruling clue in this maze of strange evidence. For three days the bad weather lasted, changing from driving rain to a dense mist, fine and dripping, and we seemed to be shut up in a white cloud that veiled all the world away from us. All the while Professor Gregg was darkling in his room, unwilling, it appeared, to dispense confidences or talk of any kind, and I heard him walking to and fro with a quick, impatient step, as if he were in some way wearied of inaction. The fourth morning was fine, and at breakfast the professor said briskly—

"We want some extra help around the house; a boy of fifteen or sixteen, you know. There are a lot of little odd jobs that take up the maids' time which a boy could do much better."

"The girls have not complained to me in any way," I replied. "Indeed, Anne said there was much less work than in London, owing to there being so little dust."

"Ah, yes, they are very good girls. But I think we shall do much better with a boy. In fact, that is what has been bothering me for the last two days."

"Bothering you?" I said in astonishment, for as a matter of fact the professor never took the slightest interest in the affairs of the house.

"Yes," he said, "the weather, you know. I really couldn't go out in that Scotch mist; I don't know the country very well, and I should have lost my way. But I am going to get the boy this morning."

"But how do you know there is such a boy as you want anywhere about?"

"Oh, I have no doubt as to that. I may have to walk a mile or two at the most, but I am sure to find just the boy I require."

I thought the professor was joking, but though his tone was airy enough there was something grim and set about his features that puzzled me. He got his stick, and stood at the door looking meditatively before him, and as I passed through the hall he called to me.

"By the way, Miss Lally, there was one thing I wanted to say to you. I dare say you may have heard that some of these country lads are not over bright; idiotic would be a harsh word to use, and they are usually called 'naturals,' or something of the kind. I hope you won't mind if the boy I am after should turn out not too keen-witted; he will be perfectly harmless, of course, and blacking boots doesn't need much mental effort."

With that he was gone, striding up the road that led to the wood, and I remained stupified; and then for the first time my astonishment was mingled with a sudden note of terror, arising I knew not whence, and all unexplained even to myself, and yet I felt about my heart for an instant something of the chill of death, and that shapeless, formless dread of the unknown that is worse than death itself. I tried to find courage in the sweet air that blew up from the sea, and in the sunlight after rain, but the mystic woods seemed to darken around me; and the vision of the river coiling between the reeds, and the silver grey of the ancient bridge, fashioned in my mind symbols of vague dread, as the mind of a child fashions terror from things harmless and familiar.

Two hours later Professor Gregg returned. I met him as he came down the road, and asked quietly if he had been able to find a boy.

"Oh, yes," he answered; "I found one easily enough. His name is Jervase Cradock, and I expect he will make himself very useful. His father has been dead for many years, and the mother, whom I saw, seemed very glad at the prospect of a few shillings extra coming in on Saturday nights. As I expected, he is not too sharp, has fits at times, the mother said; but as he will not be trusted with the china, that doesn't much matter, does it? And he is not in any way dangerous, you know, merely a little weak."

"When is he coming?"

"To-morrow morning at eight o'clock. Anne will show him what he has to do, and how to do it. At first he will go home every night, but per-haps it may ultimately turn out more convenient for him to sleep here, and only go home for Sundays."

I found nothing to say to all this; Professor Gregg spoke in a quiet tone of matter-of-fact, as indeed was warranted by the circumstance; and yet I could not quell my sensation of astonishment at the whole affair. I know that in reality no assistance was wanted in the housework, and the professor's prediction that the boy he was to engage might prove a little "simple," followed by so exact a fulfilment, struck me as bizarre in the extreme. The next morning I heard from the house-maid that the boy Cradock had come at eight, and that she had been trying to make him useful. "He doesn't seem quite all there, I don't think, miss," was her comment, and later in the day I saw him helping the old man who worked in the garden. He was a youth of about fourteen, with black hair and black eyes and an olive skin, and I saw at once from the curious vacancy of his expression that he was mentally weak. He touched his forehead awkwardly as I went by, and I heard him answering the gardener in a queer, harsh voice that caught my attention; it gave me the impression of some one speaking deep below under the earth, and there was a strange sibilance, like the hissing of the phonograph as the pointer travels over the cylinder. I heard that he seemed anxious to do what he could, and was quite docile and obedient, and Morgan the gardener, who knew his mother, assured me he was perfectly harmless. "He's always been a bit queer," he said, "and no wonder, after what his mother went through before he was born. I did know his father, Thomas Cradock, well, and a very fine workman he was too, indeed. He got something wrong with his lungs owing to working in the wet woods, and never got over it, and went off quite sudden like. And they do say as how Mrs. Cradock was quite off her head; anyhow, she was found by Mr. Hillyer, Ty Coch, all crouched up on the Grey Hills, over there, crying and weeping like a lost soul. And Jervase, he was born about eight months afterwards, and as I was saying, he was a bit queer always; and they do say when he could scarcely walk he would frighten the other children into fits with the noises he would make."

A word in the story had stirred up some remembrance within me, and, vaguely curious, I asked the old man where the Grey Hills were.

"Up there," he said, with the same gesture he had used before; "you go past the 'Fox and Hounds,' and through the forest, by the old ruins. It's a good five mile from here, and a strange sort of a place. The poorest soil between this and Monmouth, they do say, though it's good feed for sheep. Yes, it was a sad thing for poor Mrs. Cradock."

The old man turned to his work, and I strolled on down the path between the espaliers, gnarled and gouty with age, thinking of the story I had heard, and groping for the point in it that had some key to my memory. In an instant it came before me; I had seen the phrase "Grey Hills" on the slip of yellowed paper that Professor Gregg had taken from the drawer in his cabinet. Again I was seized with pangs of mingled curiosity and fear; I remembered the strange characters copied from the limestone rock, and then again their identity with the inscription on the age-old seal, and the fantastic fables of the Latin geographer. I saw beyond doubt that, unless coincidence had set all the scene and disposed all these bizarre events with curious art, I was to be a spectator of things far removed from the usual and customary traffic and jostle of life. Professor Gregg I noted day by day; he was hot on his trail, growing lean with eagerness; and in the evenings, when the sun was swimming on the verge of the mountain, he would pace the terrace to and fro with his eyes on the ground, while the mist grew white in the valley, and the stillness of the evening brought far voices near, and the blue smoke rose a straight column from the diamond-shaped chimney of the grey farm-house, just as I had seen it on the first morning. I have told you I was of sceptical habit; but though I understood little or nothing, I began to dread, vainly proposing to myself the iterated dogmas of science that all life is material, and that in the system of things there is no undiscovered land, even beyond the remotest stars, where the supernatural can find a footing. Yet there struck in on this the thought that matter is as really awful and unknown as spirit, that science itself but dallies on the threshold, scarcely gaining more than a glimpse of the wonders of the inner place.

There is one day that stands up from amidst the others as a grim red beacon, betokening evil to come. I was sitting on a bench in the garden, watching the boy Cradock weeding, when I was suddenly alarmed by a harsh and choking sound, like the cry of a wild beast in anguish, and I was unspeakably shocked to see the unfortunate lad standing in full view before me, his whole body quivering and shaking at short intervals as though shocks of electricity were passing through him, his teeth grinding, foam gathering on his lips, and his face all swollen and blackened to a hideous mask of humanity. I shrieked with terror, and Professor Gregg came running; and as I pointed to Cradock, the boy with one convulsive shudder fell face forward, and lay on the wet earth, his body writhing like a wounded blind worm, and an inconceivable babble of sounds bursting and rattling and hissing from his lips. He seemed to pour forth an infamous jargon, with words, or what seemed words, that might have belonged to a tongue dead since untold ages, and buried deep beneath Nilotic mud, or in the inmost recesses of the Mexican forest. For a moment the thought passed through my mind, as my ears were still revolted with that infernal clamour, "Surely this is the very speech of hell," and then I cried out again and again, and ran away shuddering to my inmost soul. I had seen Professor Gregg's face as he stooped over the wretched boy and raised him, and I was appalled by the glow of exultation that shone on every lineament and feature. As I sat in my room with drawn blinds, and my eyes hidden in my hands, I heard heavy steps beneath, and I was told afterwards that Professor Gregg had carried Cradock to his study, and had locked the door. I heard voices murmur indistinctly, and I trembled to think of what might be passing within a few feet of where I sat; I longed to escape to the woods and sunshine, and yet I dreaded the sights that might confront me on the way; and at last, as I held the handle of the door nervously, I heard Professor Gregg's voice calling to me with a cheerful ring. "It's all right now, Miss Lally," he said. "The poor fellow has got over it, and I have been arranging for him to sleep here after to-morrow. Perhaps I may be able to do something for him."

"Yes," he said later, "it was a very painful sight, and I don't wonder you were alarmed. We may hope that good food will build him up a little, but I am afraid he will never be really cured," and he affected the dismal and conventional air with which one speaks of hopeless illness; and yet beneath it I detected the delight that leapt up rampant within him, and fought and struggled to find utterance. It was as if one glanced down on the even surface of the sea, clear and immobile, and saw beneath raging depths and a storm of con-tending billows. It was indeed to me a torturing and offensive problem that this man, who had so bounteously rescued me from the sharpness of death, and showed himself in all the relations of life full of benevolence, and pity, and kindly forethought, should so manifestly be for once on the side of the demons, and take a ghastly pleasure in the torments of an afflicted fellow-creature. Apart, I struggled with the horned difficulty, and strove to find the solution; but without the hint of a clue, beset by mystery and contradiction. I saw nothing that might help me, and began to wonder whether, after all, I had not escaped from the white mist of the suburb at too dear a rate. I hinted something of my thought to the professor; I said enough to let him know that I was in the most acute perplexity, but the moment after regretted that I had done when I saw his face contort with a spasm of pain.

"My dear Miss Lally," he said, "you surely do not wish to leave us? No, no, you would not do it. You do not know how I rely on you; how confidently I go forward, assured that you are here to watch over my children. You, Miss Lally, are my rearguard; for let me tell you the business in which I am engaged is not wholly devoid of peril. You have not forgotten what I said the first morning here; my lips are shut by an old and firm resolve till they can open to utter no ingenious hypothesis or vague surmise but irrefragable fact, as certain as a demonstration in mathematics. Think over it, Miss Lally: not for a moment would I endeavour to keep you here against your own instincts, and yet I tell you frankly that I am persuaded it is here, here amidst the woods, that your duty lies."

I was touched by the eloquence of his tone, and by the remembrance that the man, after all, had been my salvation, and I gave him my hand on a promise to serve him loyally and without question. A few days later the rector of our church—a little church, grey and severe and quaint, that hovered on the very banks of the river and watched the tides swim and return—came to see us, and Professor Gregg easily persuaded him to stay and share our dinner. Mr. Meyrick was a member of an antique family of squires, whose old manor-house stood amongst the hills some seven miles away, and thus rooted in the soil, the rector was a living store of all the old fading customs and lore of the country. His manner, genial, with a deal of retired oddity, won on Professor Gregg; and towards the cheese, when a curious Burgundy had begun its incantations, the two men glowed like the wine, and talked of philology with the enthusiasm of a burgess over the peerage. The parson was expounding the pronunciation of the Welsh *ll*, and producing sounds like the gurgle of his native brooks, when Professor Gregg struck in.

"By the way," he said, "that was a very odd word I met the other day. You know my boy, poor Jervase Cradock? Well, he has got the bad habit of talking to himself, and the day before yesterday I was walking in the garden here and heard him; he was evidently quite unconscious of my presence. A lot of what he said I couldn't make out, but one word struck me distinctly. It was such an odd sound, half sibilant, half guttural, and as quaint as those double *ls* you have been demonstrating. I do not know whether I can give you an idea of the sound; 'Ishakshar' is perhaps as near as I can get. But the *k* ought to be a Greek *chi* or a Spanish *j*. Now what does it mean in Welsh?"

"In Welsh?" said the parson. "There is no such word in Welsh, nor any word remotely re-sembling it. I know the book-Welsh, as they call it, and the colloquial dialects as well as any man, but there's no word like that from Anglesea to Usk. Besides, none of the Cradocks speaks a word of Welsh; it's dying out about here."

"Really. You interest me extremely, Mr. Meyrick. I confess the word didn't strike me as having the Welsh ring. But I thought it might be some local corruption."

"No, I never heard such a word, or anything like it. Indeed," he added, smiling whimsically, "if it belongs to any language, I should say it must be that of the fairies—the Tylwydd Têg, as we call them."

The talk went on to the discovery of a Roman villa in the neighbourhood; and soon after I left the room, and sat down apart to wonder at the drawing together of such strange clues of evidence. As the professor had spoken of the curious word, I had caught the glint of his eye upon me; and though the pronunciation he gave was grotesque in the extreme, I recognized the name of the stone of sixty characters mentioned by Solinus, the black seal shut up in some secret drawer of the study, stamped for ever by a vanished race with signs that no man could read, signs that might, for all I knew, be the veils of awful things done long ago, and forgotten before the hills were moulded into form.

When the next morning I came down, I found Professor Gregg pacing the terrace in his eternal walk.

"Look at that bridge," he said, when he saw me; "observe the quaint and Gothic design, the angles between the arches, and the silvery grey of the stone in the awe of the morning light. I confess it seems to me symbolic; it should illustrate a mystical allegory of the passage from one world to another."

"Professor Gregg," I said quietly, "it is time that I knew something of what has happened, and of what is to happen."

For the moment he put me off, but I returned again with the same question in the evening, and then Professor Gregg flamed with excitement. "Don't you understand yet?" he cried. "But I have told you a good deal; yes, and shown you a good deal; you have heard pretty nearly all that I have heard, and seen what I have seen; or at least," and his voice chilled as he spoke, "enough to make a good deal clear as noonday. The servants told you, I have no doubt, that the wretched boy Cradock had another seizure the night before last; he awoke me with cries in that voice you heard in the garden, and I went to him, and God forbid you should see what I saw that night. But all this is useless; my time here is drawing to a close; I must be back in town in three weeks, as I have a course of lectures to prepare, and need all my books about me. In a very few days it will all be over, and I shall no longer hint, and no longer be liable to ridicule as a madman and a quack. No, I shall speak plainly, and I shall be heard with such emotions as perhaps no other man has ever drawn from the breasts of his fellows."

He paused, and seemed to grow radiant with the joy of great and wonderful discovery.

"But all that is for the future, the near future certainly, but still the future," he went on at length. "There is something to be done yet; you will remember my telling you that my researches were not altogether devoid of peril? Yes, there is a certain amount of danger to be faced; I did not know how much when I spoke on the subject before, and to a certain extent I am still in the dark. But it will be a strange adventure, the last of all, the last demonstration in the chain."

He was walking up and down the room as he spoke, and I could hear in his voice the contending tones of exultation and despondence, or perhaps I should say awe, the awe of a man who goes forth on unknown waters, and I thought of his allusion to Columbus on the night he had laid his book before me. The evening was a little chilly, and a fire of logs had been lighted in the study where we were; the remittent flame and the glow on the walls reminded me of the old days. I was sitting silent in an armchair by the fire, wondering over all I had heard, and still vainly speculating as to the secret springs concealed from me under all the phantasmagoria I had witnessed, when I became suddenly aware of a sensation that change of some sort had been at work in the room, and that there was something unfamiliar in its aspect. For some time I looked about me, trying in vain to localize the alteration that I knew had been made; the table by the window, the chairs, the faded settee were all as I had known them. Suddenly, as a sought-for recollection flashes into mind, I knew what was amiss. I was facing the professor's desk, which stood on the other side of the fire, and above the desk was a grimy-looking bust of Pitt, that I had never seen there before. And then I remembered the true position of this work of art; in the furthest corner by the door was an old cupboard, projecting into the room, and on the top of the cupboard, fifteen feet from the floor, the bust had been, and there, no doubt, it had delayed, accumulating dirt, since the early years of the century.

I was utterly amazed, and sat silent still, in a confusion of thought. There was, so far as I knew, no such thing as a step-ladder in the house, for I had asked for one to make some alterations in the curtains of my room, and a tall man standing on a chair would have found it impossible to take down the bust. It had been placed, not on the edge of the cupboard, but far back against the wall; and Professor Gregg was, if anything, under the average height.

"How on earth did you manage to get down Pitt?" I said at last.

The professor looked curiously at me, and seemed to hesitate a little.

"They must have found you a step-ladder, or perhaps the gardener brought in a short ladder from outside?"

"No, I have had no ladder of any kind. Now, Miss Lally," he went on with an awkward simulation of jest, "there is a little puzzle for you; a problem in the manner of the inimitable Holmes; there are the facts, plain and patent; summon your acuteness to the solution of the puzzle. For Heaven's sake," he cried with a breaking voice, "say no more about it! I tell you, I never touched the thing," and he went out of the room with horror manifest on his face, and his hand shook and jarred the door behind him.

I looked round the room in vague surprise, not at all realizing what had happened, making vain and idle surmises by way of explanation, and wondering at the stirring of black waters by an idle word and the trivial change of an ornament. "This is some petty business, some whim on which I have jarred," I reflected; "the professor is perhaps scrupulous and superstitious over trifles, and my question may have outraged unacknowledged fears, as though one killed a spider or spilled the salt before the very eyes of a practical Scotchwoman." I was immersed in these fond suspicions, and began to plume myself a little on my immunity from such empty fears, when the truth fell heavily as lead upon my heart, and I recognized with cold terror that some awful influence had been at work. The bust was simply inaccessible; without a ladder no one could have touched it.

I went out to the kitchen and spoke as quietly as I could to the housemaid.

"Who moved that bust from the top of the cupboard, Anne?" I said to her. "Professor Gregg says he has not touched it. Did you find an old step-ladder in one of the outhouses?"

The girl looked at me blankly.

"I never touched it," she said. "I found it where it is now the other morning when I dusted the room. I remember now, it was Wednesday morning, because it was the morning after Cradock was taken bad in the night. My room is next to his, you know, miss," the girl went on piteously, "and it was awful to hear how he cried and called out names that I couldn't understand. It made me feel all afraid; and then master came, and I heard him speak, and he took down Cradock to the study and gave him something."

"And you found that bust moved the next morning?"

"Yes, miss. There was a queer sort of smell in the study when I came down and opened the windows; a bad smell it was, and I wondered what it could be. Do you know, miss, I went a long time ago to the Zoo in London with my cousin Thomas Barker, one afternoon that I had off, when I was at Mrs. Prince's in Stanhope Gate, and we went into the snake-house to see the snakes, and it was just the same sort of smell; very sick it made me feel, I remember, and I got Barker to take me out. And it was just the same kind of a smell in the study, as I was saying, and I was wondering what it could be from, when I see that bust with Pitt cut in it, standing on the master's desk, and I thought to myself, Now who has done that, and how have they done it? And when I came to dust the things, I looked at the bust, and I saw a great mark on it where the dust was gone, for I don't think it can have been touched with a duster for years and years, and it wasn't like finger-marks, but a large patch like, broad and spread out. So I passed my hand over it, without thinking what I was doing, and where that patch was it was all sticky and slimy, as if a snail had crawled over it. Very strange, isn't it, miss? and I wonder who can have done it, and how that mess was made."

The well-meant gabble of the servant touched me to the quick; I lay down upon my bed, and bit my lip that I should not cry out loud in the sharp anguish of my terror and bewilderment. Indeed, I was almost mad with dread; I believe that if it had been daylight I should have fled hot foot, forgetting all courage and all the debt of gratitude that was due to Professor Gregg, not caring whether my fate were that I must starve slowly, so long as I might escape from the net of blind and panic fear that every day seemed to draw a little closer round me. If I knew, I thought, if I knew what there were to dread, I could guard against it; but here, in this lonely house, shut in on all sides by the olden woods and the vaulted hills, terror seems to spring inconsequent from every covert, and the flesh is aghast at the half--heard murmurs of horrible things. All in vain I strove to summon scepticism to my aid, and endeavoured by cool common sense to buttress my belief in a world of natural order, for the air that blew in at the open window was a mystic breath, and in the darkness I felt the silence go heavy and sorrowful as a mass of requiem, and I conjured images of strange shapes gathering fast amidst the reeds, beside the wash of the river.

In the morning from the moment that I set foot in the breakfast-room, I felt that the unknown plot was drawing to a crisis; the professor's face was firm and set, and he seemed hardly to hear our voices when we spoke.

"I am going out for a rather long walk," he said when the meal was over. "You mustn't be expecting me, now, or thinking anything has happened if I don't turn up to dinner. I have been getting stupid lately, and I dare say a miniature walking tour will do me good. Perhaps I may even spend the night in some little inn, if I find any place that looks clean and comfortable."

I heard this and knew by my experience of Professor Gregg's manner that it was no ordinary business or pleasure that impelled him. I knew not, nor even remotely guessed, where he was bound, nor had I the vaguest notion of his errand, but all the fear of the night before returned; and as he stood, smiling, on the terrace ready to set out, I implored him to stay, and to forget all his dreams of the undiscovered continent.

"No, no, Miss Lally," he replied still smiling, "it's too late now. *Vestigia nulla retrorsum*, you know, is the device of all true explorers, though I hope it won't be literally true in my case. But, indeed, you are wrong to alarm yourself so; I look upon my little expedition as quite commonplace; no more exciting than a day with the geological hammers. There is a risk, of course, but so there is on the commonest excursion. I can afford to be jaunty; I am doing nothing so hazardous as 'Arry does a hundred times over in the course of every Bank Holiday. Well, then, you must look more cheerfully; and so good-bye till tomorrow at latest."

He walked briskly up the road, and I saw him open the gate that marks the entrance of the wood, and then he vanished in the gloom of the trees.

All the day passed heavily with a strange dark-ness in the air, and again I felt as if imprisoned amidst the ancient woods, shut in an olden land of mystery and dread, and as if all was long ago and forgotten by the living outside. I hoped and dreaded; and when the dinner-hour came I waited, expecting to hear the professor's step in the hall, and his voice exulting at I knew not what triumph. I composed my face to welcome him gladly, but the night descended dark, and he did not come.

In the morning, when the maid knocked at my door, I called out to her, and asked if her master had returned; and when she replied that his bed-room stood open and empty, I felt the cold clasp of despair. Still, I fancied he might have discovered genial company, and would return for luncheon, or perhaps in the afternoon, and I took the children for a walk in the forest, and tried my best to play and laugh with them, and to shut out the thoughts of mystery and veiled terror. Hour after hour I waited, and my thoughts grew darker; again the night came and found me watching, and at last, as I was making much ado to finish my dinner, I heard steps outside and the sound of a man's voice.

The maid came in and looked oddly at me. "Please, miss," she began, "Mr. Morgan the gardener wants to speak to you for a minute, if you didn't mind."

"Show him in, please," I answered, and set my lips tight.

The old man came slowly into the room, and the servant shut the door behind him.

"Sit down, Mr. Morgan," I said; "what is it that you want to say to me?"

"Well, miss, Mr. Gregg he gave me something for you yesterday morning, just before he went off; and he told me particular not to hand it up before eight o'clock this evening exactly, if so be as he wasn't back home again before, and if he should come home before I was just to return it to him in his own hands. So, you see, as Mr. Gregg isn't here yet, I suppose I'd better give you the parcel directly."

He pulled out something from his pocket, and gave it to me, half rising. I took it silently, and seeing that Morgan seemed doubtful as to what he was to do next, I thanked him and bade him good-night, and he went out. I was left alone in the room with the parcel in my hand—a paper parcel neatly sealed and directed to me, with the instructions Morgan had quoted, all written in the professor's large loose hand. I broke the seals with a choking at my heart, and found an envelope inside, addressed also, but open, and I took the letter out.

"My Dear Miss Lally," it began, —"To quote the old logic manual, the case of your reading this note is a case of my having made a blunder of some sort, and, I am afraid, a blunder that turns these lines into a farewell. It is practically certain that neither you nor anyone else will ever see me again. I have made my will with provision for this eventuality, and I hope you will consent to accept the small remembrance addressed to you, and my sincere thanks for the way in which you joined your fortunes to mine. The fate which has come upon me is desperate and terrible beyond the remotest dreams of man; but this fate you have a right to know—if you please. If you look in the left-hand drawer of my dressing-table, you will find the key of the escritoire, properly labelled. In the well of the escritoire is a large envelope sealed and addressed to your name. I advise you to throw it forthwith into the fire; you will sleep better of nights if you do so. But if you must know the history of what has happened, it is all written down for you to read."

The signature was firmly written below, and again I turned the page and read out the words one by one, aghast and white to the lips, my hands cold as ice, and sickness choking me. The dead silence of the room, and the thought of the dark woods and hills closing me in on every side, oppressed me, helpless and without capacity, and not knowing where to turn for counsel. At last I resolved that though knowledge should haunt my whole life and all the days to come, I must know the meaning of the strange terrors that had so long tormented me, rising grey, dim, and awful, like the shadows in the wood at dusk. I carefully carried out Professor Gregg's directions, and not without reluctance broke the seal of the envelope, and spread out his manuscript before me. That manuscript I always carry with me, and I see that I cannot deny your unspoken request to read it. This, then, was what I read that night, sitting at the desk, with a shaded lamp beside me.

The young lady who called herself Miss Lally then proceeded to recite

The Statement of William Gregg, F. R. S., etc.

It is many years since the first glimmer of the theory which is now almost, if not quite, reduced to fact dawned on my mind. A somewhat extensive course of miscellaneous and obsolete reading had done a good deal to prepare the way, and, later, when I became somewhat of a specialist, and immersed myself in the studies known as ethnological, I was now and then startled by facts that would not square with orthodox scientific opinion, and by discoveries that seemed to hint at something still hidden for all our research. More particularly I became convinced that much of the folk-lore of the world is but an exaggerated account of events that really happened, and I was especially drawn to consider the stories of the fairies, the good folk of the Celtic races. Here I thought I could detect the fringe of embroidery and exaggeration, the fantastic guise, the little people dressed in green and gold sporting in the flowers, and I thought I saw a distinct analogy between the name given to this race (supposed to be imaginary) and the description of their appearance and manners. Just as our remote ancestors called the dreadful beings "fair" and "good" precisely because they dreaded them, so they had dressed them up in charming forms, knowing the truth to be the very reverse. Literature, too, had gone early to work, and had lent a powerful hand in the transformation, so that the playful elves of Shakespeare are already far removed from the true original, and the real horror is disguised in a form of prankish mischief. But in the older tales, the stories that used to make men cross themselves as they sat round the burning logs, we tread a different stage; I saw a widely opposed spirit in certain histories of children and of men and women who vanished strangely from the earth. They would be seen by a peasant in the fields walking towards some green and rounded hillock, and seen no more on earth; and there are stories of mothers who have left a child quietly sleeping, with the cottage door rudely barred with a piece of wood, and have returned, not to find the plump and rosy little Saxon, but a thin and wizened creature, with sallow skin and black, piercing eyes, the child of another race. Then, again, there were myths darker still; the dread of witch and wizard, the lurid evil of the Sabbath, and the hint of demons who mingled with the daughters of men. And just as we have turned the terrible "fair folk" into a company of benignant, if freakish, elves, so we have hidden from us the black foulness of the witch and her companions under a popular *diablerie* of old women and broomsticks and a comic cat with tail on end. So the Greeks called the hideous furies benevolent ladies, and thus the northern nations have followed their example. I pursued my investigations, stealing odd hours from other and more imperative labours, and I asked myself the question: Supposing these traditions to be true, who were the demons who are reported to have attended the Sabbaths? I need not say that I laid aside what I may call the supernatural hypothesis of the Middle Ages, and came to the conclusion that fairies and devils were of one and the same race and origin; invention, no doubt, and the Gothic fancy of old days, had done much in the way of exaggeration and distortion; yet I firmly believe that beneath all this imagery there was a black background of truth. As for some of the alleged wonders, I hesitated. While I should be very loath to receive any one specific instance of modern spiritualism as containing even a grain of the genuine, yet I was not wholly pre-pared to deny that human flesh may now and then, once perhaps in ten million cases, be the veil of powers which seem magical to us—powers which, so far from proceeding from the heights and leading men thither, are in reality survivals from the depth of being. The amœba and the snail have powers which we do not possess; and I thought it possible that the theory of reversion might explain many things which seem wholly inexplicable. Thus stood my position; I saw good reason to believe that much of the tradition, a vast deal of the earliest and uncorrupted tradition of the so-called fairies, represented solid fact, and I thought that the purely supernatural element in these traditions was to be accounted for on the hypothesis that a race which had fallen out of the grand march of evolution might have retained, as a survival, certain powers which would be to us wholly miraculous. Such was my theory as it stood conceived in my mind; and working with this in view, I seemed to gather confirmation from every side, from the spoils of a tumulus or a barrow, from a local paper reporting an antiquar-ian meeting in the country, and from general literature of all kinds. Amongst other instances, I remember being struck by the phrase "articulate-speaking men" in Homer, as if the writer knew or had heard of men whose speech was so rude that it could hardly be termed articulate; and on my hypothesis of a race who had lagged far behind the rest, I could easily conceive that such a folk would speak a jargon but little removed from the inarticulate noises of brute beasts.

Thus I stood, satisfied that my conjecture was at all events not far removed from fact, when a chance paragraph in a small country print one day arrested my attention. It was a short account of what was to all appearance the usual sordid tragedy of the village—a young girl un-accountably missing, and evil rumour blatant and busy with her reputa-tion. Yet, I could read between the lines that all this scandal was purely hypocritical, and in all probability invented to account for what was in any other manner unaccountable. A flight to London or Liverpool, or an undiscovered body lying with a weight about its neck in the foul depths of a woodland pool, or perhaps murder—such were the theories of the wretched girl's neighbours. But as I idly scanned the paragraph, a flash of thought passed through me with the violence of an electric shock: what if the obscure and horrible race of the hills still survived, still remained haunting the wild places and barren hills, and now and then repeating the evil of Gothic legend, unchanged and unchangeable as the Turanian Shelta, or the Basques of Spain? I have said that the thought came with violence; and indeed I drew in my breath sharply, and clung with both hands to my elbow-chair, in a strange confusion of horror and elation. It was as if one of my *confrères* of physical science, roaming in a quiet English wood, had been sud-denly stricken aghast by the presence of the slimy and loathsome terror of the ichthyosaurus, the original of the stories of the awful worms killed by valorous knights, or had seen the sun darkened by the pterodactyl, the dragon of tradition. Yet as a resolute explorer of knowledge, the thought of such a discovery threw me into a passion of joy, and I cut out the slip from the paper and put it in a drawer in my old bureau, resolved that it should be but the first piece in a collection of the strangest significance. I sat long that evening dreaming of the conclusions I should establish, nor did cooler reflection at first dash my confidence. Yet as I began to put the case fairly, I saw that I might be building on an unstable foundation; the facts might possibly be in accordance with local opinion, and I regarded the affair with a mood of some reserve. Yet I resolved to remain perched on the look-out, and I hugged to myself the thought that I alone was watching and wakeful, while the great crowd of thinkers and searchers stood heedless and indifferent, perhaps letting the most prerogative facts pass by unnoticed.

Several years elapsed before I was enabled to add to the contents of the drawer; and the second find was in reality not a valuable one, for it was a mere repetition of the first, with only the variation of another and distant locality. Yet I gained something; for in the second case, as in the first, the tragedy took place in a desolate and lonely country, and so far my theory seemed justified. But the third piece was to me far more decisive. Again, amongst outland hills, far even from a main road of traffic, an old man was found done to death, and the instrument of execution was left beside him. Here, indeed, there were rumour and conjecture, for the deadly tool was a primitive stone axe, bound by gut to the wooden handle, and surmises the most extravagant and improbable were indulged in. Yet, as I thought with a kind of glee, the wildest conjectures went far astray; and I took the pains to enter into correspondence with the local doctor, who was called at the inquest. He, a man of some acuteness, was dumb-foundered. "It will not do to speak of these things in country places," he wrote to me; "but frankly, there is some hideous mystery here. I have obtained possession of the stone axe, and have been so curious as to test its powers. I took it into the back-garden of my house one Sunday afternoon when my family and the servants were all out, and there, sheltered by the poplar hedges, I made my experiments. I found the thing utterly unmanageable; whether there is some peculiar balance, some nice adjustment of weights, which require incessant practice, or whether an effectual blow can be struck only by a certain trick of the muscles, I do not know; but I can assure you that I went into the house with but a sorry opinion of my athletic capacities. It was like an inexperienced man trying 'putting the hammer'; the force exerted seemed to return on oneself, and I found myself hurled backwards with violence, while the axe fell harmless to the ground. On another occasion I tried the experiment with a clever woodman of the place; but this man, who had handled his axe for forty years, could do nothing with the stone implement, and missed every stroke most ludicrously. In short, if it were not so supremely absurd, I should say that for four thousand years no one on earth could have struck an effective blow with the tool that undoubtedly was used to murder the old man." This, as may be imagined, was to me rare news; and afterwards, when I heard the whole story, and learned that the unfortunate old man had babbled tales of what might be seen at night on a certain wild hillside, hinting at unheard-of wonders, and that he had been found cold one morning on the very hill in question, my exultation was extreme, for I felt I was leaving conjecture far behind me. But the next step was of still greater importance. I had possessed for many years an extraordinary stone seal—a piece of dull black stone, two inches long from the handle to the stamp, and the stamping end a rough hexagon an inch and a quarter in diameter. Altogether, it presented the appearance of an enlarged tobacco stopper of an old-fashioned make. It had been sent to me by an agent in the East, who informed me that it had been found near the site of the ancient Babylon. But the characters engraved on the seal were to me an intolerable puzzle. Somewhat of the cuneiform pattern, there were yet striking differences, which I detected at the first glance, and all efforts to read the inscription on the hypothesis that the rules for deciphering the arrow-headed writing would apply proved futile. A riddle such as this stung my pride, and at odd moments I would take the Black Seal out of the cabinet, and scrutinize it with so much idle perseverance that every letter was familiar to my mind, and I could have drawn the inscription from memory without the slightest error. Judge, then, of my surprise when I one day received from a correspondent in the west of England a letter and an enclosure that positively left me thunderstruck. I saw carefully traced on a large piece of paper the very characters of the Black Seal, without alteration of any kind, and above the inscription my friend had written: *Inscription found on a limestone rock on the Grey Hills, Monmouthshire. Done in some red earth, and quite recent.* I turned to the letter. My friend wrote: "I sent you the enclosed inscription with all due reserve. A shepherd who passed by the stone a week ago swears that there was then no mark of any kind. The characters, as I have noted, are formed by drawing some red earth over the stone, and are of an average height of one inch. They look to me like a kind of cuneiform character, a good deal altered, but this, of course, is impossible. It may be either a hoax, or more probably some scribble of the gipsies, who are plentiful enough in this wild country. They have, as you are aware, many hieroglyphics which they use in communicating with one another. I happened to visit the stone in question two days ago in connection with a rather painful incident which has occurred here."

As may be supposed, I wrote immediately to my friend, thanking him for the copy of the inscription, and asking him in a casual manner the history of the incident he mentioned. To be brief, I heard that a woman named Cradock, who had lost her husband a day before, had set out to communicate the sad news to a cousin who lived some five miles away. She took a short cut which led by the Grey Hills. Mrs. Cradock, who was then quite a young woman, never arrived at her relative's house. Late that night a farmer who had lost a couple of sheep, supposed to have wandered from the flock, was walking over the Grey Hills, with a lantern and his dog. His attention was attracted by a noise, which he described as a kind of wailing, mournful and pitiable to hear; and, guided by the sound, he found the unfortunate Mrs. Cradock crouched on the ground by the limestone rock, swaying her body to and fro, and lamenting and crying in so heart-rending a manner that the farmer was, as he says, at first obliged to stop his ears, or he would have run away. The woman allowed herself to be taken home, and a neighbour came to see to her necessities. All the night she never ceased her crying, mixing her lament with words of some unintelligible jargon, and when the doctor arrived he pronounced her insane. She lay on her bed for a week, now wailing, as people said, like one lost and damned for eternity, and now sunk in a heavy coma; it was thought that grief at the loss of her husband had unsettled her mind, and the medical man did not at one time expect her to live. I need not say that I was deeply interested in this story, and I made my friend write to me at intervals with all the particulars of the case. I heard then that in the course of six weeks the woman gradually recovered the use of her faculties, and some months later she gave birth to a son, christened Jervase, who unhappily proved to be of weak intellect. Such were the facts known to the village; but to me, while I whitened at the suggested thought of the hideous enormities that had doubtless been committed, all this was nothing short of conviction, and I incautiously hazarded a hint of something like the truth to some scientific friends. The moment the words had left my lips I bitterly regretted having spoken, and thus given way the great secret of my life, but with a good deal of relief mixed with indignation I found my fears altogether misplaced, for my friends ridiculed me to my face, and I was regarded as a madman; and beneath a natural anger I chuckled to myself, feeling as secure amidst these blockheads as if I had confided what I knew to the desert sands.

But now, knowing so much, I resolved I would know all, and I concentrated my efforts on the task of deciphering the inscription on the Black Seal. For many years I made this puzzle the sole object of my leisure moments; for the greater portion of my time was, of course, devoted to other duties, and it was only now and then that I could snatch a week of clear research. If I were to tell the full history of this curious investigation, this statement would be wearisome in the extreme, for it would contain simply the account of long and tedious failure. By what I knew already of ancient scripts I was well equipped for the chase, as I always termed it to myself. I had correspondents amongst all the scientific men in Europe, and indeed, in the world, and I could not believe that in these days any character, however ancient and however perplexed, could long resist the search-light I should bring to bear upon it. Yet, in point of fact, it was fully fourteen years before I succeeded. With every year my professional duties increased, and my leisure became smaller. This no doubt retarded me a good deal; and yet, when I look back on those years, I am astonished at the vast scope of my investigation of the Black Seal. I made my bureau a centre, and from all the world and from all the ages I gathered transcripts of ancient writing. Nothing, I resolved, should pass me unawares, and the faintest hint should be welcomed and followed up. But as one covert after another was tried and proved empty of result, I began in the course of years to despair, and to wonder whether the Black Seal were the sole relic of some race that had vanished from the world and left no other trace of its existence—had perished, in fine, as Atlantis is said to have done, in some great cataclysm, its secrets perhaps drowned beneath the ocean or moulded into the heart of the hills. The thought chilled my warmth a little, and though I still persevered, it was no longer with the same certainty of faith. A chance came to the rescue. I was staying in a considerable town in the north of England, and took the opportunity of going over the very creditable museum that had for some time been established in the place. The curator was one of my correspondents; and, as we were looking through one of the mineral cases, my attention was struck by a specimen, a piece of black stone some four inches square, the appearance of which reminded me in a measure of the Black Seal. I took it up carelessly, and was turning it over in my hand, when I saw, to my astonishment, that the under side was inscribed. I said, quietly enough, to my friend the curator that the specimen interested me, and that I should be much obliged if he would allow me to take it with me to my hotel for a couple of days. He, of course, made no objection, and I hurried to my rooms and found that my first glance had not deceived me. There were two inscriptions; one in the regular cuneiform character, another in the character of the Black Seal, and I realized that my task was accomplished. I made an exact copy of the two inscriptions; and when I got to my London study, and had the Seal before me, I was able seriously to grapple with the great problem. The interpreting inscription on the museum specimen, though in itself curious enough, did not bear on my quest, but the transliteration made me master of the secret of the Black Seal. Conjecture, of course, had to enter into my calculations; there was here and there uncertainty about a particular ideograph, and one sign recurring again and again on the seal baffled me for many successive nights. But at last the secret stood open before me in plain English, and I read the key of the awful transmutation of the hills. The last word was hardly written, when with fingers all trembling and unsteady I tore the scrap of paper into the minutest fragments, and saw them flame and blacken in the red hollow of the fire, and then I crushed the grey films that remained into finest powder. Never since then have I written those words; never will I write the phrases which tell how man can be reduced to the slime from which he came, and be forced to put on the flesh of the reptile and the snake. There was now but one thing remaining. I knew, but I desired to see, and I was after some time able to take a house in the neighbourhood of the Grey Hills, and not far from the cottage where Mrs. Craddock and her son Jervase resided. I need not go into a full and detailed account of the apparently inexplicable events which have occurred here, where I am writing this. I knew that I should find in Jervase Craddock some-thing of the blood of the "Little People," and I found later that he had more than once encountered his kinsmen in lonely places in that lonely land. When I was summoned one day to the garden, and found him in a seizure speaking or hissing the ghastly jargon of the Black Seal, I am afraid that exultation prevailed over pity. I heard bursting from his lips the secrets of the underworld, and the word of dread, "Ishakshar," signification of which I must be excused from giving.

But there is one incident I cannot pass over unnoticed. In the waste hollow of the night I awoke at the sound of those hissing syllables I knew so well; and on going to the wretched boy's room, I found him convulsed and foaming at the mouth, struggling on the bed as if he strove to escape the grasp of writhing demons. I took him down to my room and lit the lamp, while he lay twisting on the floor, calling on the power within his flesh to leave him. I saw his body swell and become distended as a bladder, while the face blackened before my eyes; and then at the crisis I did what was necessary according to the directions on the Seal, and putting all scruple on one side, I became a man of science, observant of what was passing. Yet the sight I had to witness was horrible, almost beyond the power of human conception and the most fearful fantasy. Something pushed out from the body there on the floor, and stretched forth, a slimy, wavering tentacle, across the room, grasped the bust upon the cupboard, and laid it down on my desk.

When it was over, and I was left to walk up and down all the rest of the night, white and shuddering, with sweat pouring from my flesh, I vainly tried to reason with myself: I said, truly enough, that I had seen nothing really supernatural, that a snail pushing out his horns and drawing them in was but an instance on a smaller scale of what I had witnessed; and yet horror broke through all such reasonings and left me, shattered and loathing myself for the share I had taken in the night's work.

There is little more to be said. I am going now to the final trial and encounter; for I have determined that there shall be nothing wanting, and I shall meet the "Little People" face to face. I shall have the Black Seal and the knowledge of its secrets to help me, and if I unhappily do not return from my journey, there is no need to con-jure up here a picture of the awfulness of my fate.

Pausing a little at the end of Professor Gregg's statement, Miss Lally continued her tale in the following words:—

Such was the almost incredible story that the professor had left behind him. When I had finished reading it, it was late at night, but the next morning I took Morgan with me, and we proceeded to search the Grey Hills for some trace of the lost professor. I will not weary you with a description of the savage desolation of that tract of country, a tract of utterest loneliness, of bare green hills dotted over with grey limestone boulders, worn by the ravages of time into fantastic semblances of men and beasts. Finally, after many hours of weary searching, we found what I told you—the watch and chain, the purse, and the ring—wrapped in a piece of coarse parchment. When Morgan cut the gut that bound the parcel together, and I saw the professor's property, I burst into tears, but the sight of the dreaded characters of the Black Seal repeated on the parchment froze me to silent horror, and I think I understood for the first time the awful fate that had come upon my late employer.

I have only to add that Professor Gregg's lawyer treated my account of what had happened as a fairy tale, and refused even to glance at the documents I laid before him. It was he who was responsible for the statement that appeared in the public press, to the effect that Professor Gregg had been drowned, and that his body must have been swept into the open sea.

Miss Lally stopped speaking, and looked at Mr. Phillipps, with a glance of some inquiry. He, for his part, was sunken in a deep reverie of thought; and when he looked up and saw the bustle of the evening gathering in the square, men and women hurrying to partake of dinner, and crowds already besetting the music-halls, all the hum and press of actual life seemed unreal and visionary, a dream in the morning after an awakening.

"I thank you," he said at last, "for your most interesting story; interesting to me, because I feel fully convinced of its exact truth."

"Sir," said the lady, with some energy of indignation, "you grieve and offend me. Do you think I should waste my time and yours by concocting fictions on a bench in Leicester Square?"

"Pardon me, Miss Lally, you have a little misunderstood me. Before you began I knew that whatever you told would be told in good faith, but your experiences have a far higher value than that of *bona fides*. The most extraordinary circumstances in your account are in perfect harmony with the very latest scientific theories. Professor Lodge would, I am sure, value a communication from you extremely; I was charmed from the first by his daring hypothesis in explanation of the wonders of spiritualism (so called), but your narrative puts the whole matter out of the range of mere hypothesis."

"Alas! sir, all this will not help me. You forget, I have lost my brother under the most startling and dreadful circumstances. Again, I ask you, did you not see him as you came here? His black whiskers, his spectacles, his timid glance to right and left; think, do not these particulars recall his face to your memory?"

"I am sorry to say I have never seen anyone of the kind," said Phillipps, who had forgotten all about the missing brother. "But let me ask you a few questions. Did you notice whether Professor Gregg—"

"Pardon me, sir, I have stayed too long. My employers will be expecting me. I thank you for your sympathy. Good-bye."

Before Mr. Phillipps had recovered from his amazement at this abrupt departure Miss Lally had disappeared from his gaze, passing into the crowd that now thronged the approaches to the Empire. He walked home in a pensive frame of mind, and drank too much tea. At ten o'clock he had made his third brew, and had sketched out the outlines of a little work to be called "Protoplasmic Reversion."

"NOVEL OF THE WHITE POWDER," which Lovecraft described as approaching "the absolute culmination of loathsome fright," also comes from Machen's episodic novel *The Three Impostors* (1895).

NOVEL OF THE WHITE POWDER
by Arthur Machen

My name is Leicester; my father, Major-General Wyn Leicester, a distinguished officer of artillery, succumbed five years ago to a complicated liver complaint acquired in the deadly climate of India. A year later my only brother, Francis, came home after an exceptionally brilliant career at the University, and settled down with the resolution of a hermit to master what has been well called the great legend of the law. He was a man who seemed to live in utter indifference to everything that is called pleasure; and though he was handsomer than most men, and could talk as merrily and wittily as if he were a mere vagabond, he avoided society, and shut himself up in a large room at the top of the house to make himself a lawyer. Ten hours a day of hard reading was at first his allotted portion; from the first light in the east to the late afternoon he remained shut up with his books, taking a hasty half-hour's lunch with me as if he grudged the wasting of the moments, and going out for a short walk when it began to grow dusk. I thought that such relentless application must be injurious, and tried to cajole him from the crabbed text-books, but his ardour seemed to grow rather than diminish, and his daily tale of hours increased. I spoke to him seriously, suggesting some occasional relaxation, if it were but an idle afternoon with a harmless novel; but he laughed, and said that he read about feudal tenures when he felt in need of amusement, and scoffed at the notions of theatres, or a month's fresh air. I confessed that he looked well, and seemed not to suffer from his labours, but I knew that such unnatural toil would take revenge at last, and I was not mistaken. A look of anxiety began to lurk about his eyes, and he seemed languid, and at last he avowed that he was no longer in perfect health; he was troubled, he said, with a sensation of dizziness, and awoke now and then of nights from fearful dreams, terrified and cold with icy sweats. "I am taking care of myself," he said, "so you must not trouble; I passed the whole of yesterday afternoon in idleness, leaning back in that comfortable chair you gave me, and scribbling nonsense on a sheet of paper. No, no; I will not overdo my work; I shall be well enough in a week or two, depend upon it."

Yet in spite of his assurances I could see that he grew no better, but rather worse; he would enter the drawing-room with a face all miserably wrinkled and despondent, and endeavour to look gaily when my eyes fell on him, and I thought such symptoms of evil omen, and was frightened sometimes at the nervous irritation of his movements, and at glances which I could not decipher. Much against his will, I prevailed on him to have medical advice, and with an ill grace he called in our old doctor.

Dr. Haberden cheered me after examination of his patient.

"There is nothing really much amiss," he said to me. "No doubt he reads too hard and eats hastily, and then goes back again to his books in too great a hurry, and the natural sequence is some digestive trouble and a little mischief in the nervous system. But I think—I do indeed, Miss Leicester—that we shall be able to set this all right. I have written him a prescription which ought to do great things. So you have no cause for anxiety."

My brother insisted on having the prescription made up by a chemist in the neighbourhood. It was an odd, old-fashioned shop, devoid of the studied coquetry and calculated glitter that make so gay a show on the counters and shelves of the modern apothecary; but Francis liked the old chemist, and believed in the scrupulous purity of his drugs. The medicine was sent in due course, and I saw that my brother took it regularly after lunch and dinner. It was an innocent-looking white powder, of which a little was dissolved in a glass of cold water; I stirred it in, and it seemed to disappear, leaving the water clear and colorless. At first Francis seemed to benefit greatly; the weariness vanished from his face, and he became more cheerful than he had ever been since the time when he left school; he talked gaily of reforming himself, and avowed to me that he had wasted his time.

"I have given too many hours to law," he said, laughing; "I think you have saved me in the nick of time. Come, I shall be Lord Chancellor yet, but I must not forget life. You and I will have a holiday together before long; we will go to Paris and enjoy ourselves, and keep away from the Bibliothèque Nationale."

I confessed myself delighted with the prospect.

"When shall we go?" I said. "I can start the day after to-morrow if you like."

"Ah! that is perhaps a little too soon; after all, I do not know London yet, and I suppose a man ought to give the pleasures of his own country the first choice. But we will go off together in a week or two, so try and furbish up your French. I only know law French myself, and I am afraid that wouldn't do."

We were just finishing dinner, and he quaffed off his medicine with a parade of carousal as if it had been wine from some choicest bin.

"Has it any particular taste?" I said.

"No; I should not know I was not drinking water," and he got up from his chair and began to pace up and down the room as if he were un-decided as to what he should do next.

"Shall we have coffee in the drawing-room?" I said; "or would you like to smoke?"

"No, I think I will take a turn; it seems a pleasant evening. Look at the afterglow; why, it is as if a great city were burning in flames, and down there between the dark houses it is raining blood fast. Yes, I will go out; I may be in soon, but I shall take my key; so good-night, dear, if I don't see you again."

The door slammed behind him, and I saw him walk lightly down the street, swinging his malacca cane, and I felt grateful to Dr. Haberden for such an improvement.

I believe my brother came home very late that night, but he was in a merry mood the next morning.

"I walked on without thinking where I was going," he said, "enjoying the freshness of the air, and livened by the crowds as I reached more fre-quented quarters. And then I met an old college friend, Orford, in the press of the pavement, and then—well, we enjoyed ourselves. I have felt what it is to be young and a man; I find I have blood in my veins, as other men have. I made an appointment with Orford for to-night; there will be a little party of us at the restaurant. Yes; I shall enjoy myself for a week or two, and hear the chimes at midnight, and then we will go for our little trip together."

Such was the transmutation of my brother's character that in a few days he became a lover of pleasure, a careless and merry idler of western pavements, a hunter out of snug restaurants, and a fine critic of fantastic dancing; he grew fat before my eyes, and said no more of Paris, for he had clearly found his paradise in London. I rejoiced, and yet wondered a little; for there was, I thought, something in his gaiety that indefinitely displeased me, though I could not have defined my feeling. But by degrees there came a change; he returned still in the cold hours of the morning, but I heard no more about his pleasures, and one morning as we sat at breakfast together I looked suddenly into his eyes and saw a stranger before me.

"Oh, Francis!" I cried. "Oh, Francis, Francis, what have you done?" and rending sobs cut the words short. I went weeping out of the room; for though I knew nothing, yet I knew all, and by some odd play of thought I remembered the evening when he first went abroad, and the picture of the sunset sky glowed before me; the clouds like a city in burning flames, and the rain of blood. Yet I did battle with such thoughts, resolving that perhaps, after all, no great harm had been done, and in the evening at dinner I resolved to press him to fix a day for our holiday in Paris. We had talked easily enough, and my brother had just taken his medicine, which he continued all the while. I was about to begin my topic when the words forming in my mind vanished, and I wondered for a second what icy and intolerable weight oppressed my heart and suffocated me as with the unutterable horror of the coffin-lid nailed down on the living.

We had dined without candles; the room had slowly grown from twilight to gloom, and the walls and corners were indistinct in the shadow. But from where I sat I looked out into the street; and as I thought of what I would say to Francis, the sky began to flush and shine, as it had done on a well-remembered evening, and in the gap between two dark masses that were houses an awful pageantry of flame appeared—lurid whorls of writhed cloud, and utter depths burning, grey masses like the fume blown from a smoking city, and an evil glory blazing far above shot with tongues of more ardent fire, and below as if there were a deep pool of blood. I looked down to where my brother sat facing me, and the words were shaped on my lips, when I saw his hand resting on the table. Between the thumb and forefinger of the closed hand there was a mark, a small patch about the size of a sixpence, and somewhat of the colour of a bad bruise. Yet, by some sense I cannot define, I knew that what I saw was no bruise at all; oh! if human flesh could burn with flame, and if flame could be black as pitch, such was that before me. Without thought or fashioning of words grey horror shaped within me at the sight, and in an inner cell it was known to be a brand. For the moment the stained sky became dark as midnight, and when the light returned to me I was alone in the silent room, and soon after I heard my brother go out.

Late as it was, I put on my hat and went to Dr. Haberden, and in his great consulting room, ill lighted by a candle which the doctor brought in with him, with stammering lips, and a voice that would break in spite of my resolve, I told him all, from the day on which my brother began to take the medicine down to the dreadful thing I had seen scarcely half an hour before.

When I had done, the doctor looked at me for a minute with an expression of great pity on his face.

"My dear Miss Leicester," he said, "you have evidently been anxious about your brother; you have been worrying over him, I am sure. Come, now, is it not so?"

"I have certainly been anxious," I said. "For the last week or two I have not felt at ease."

"Quite so; you know, of course, what a queer thing the brain is?"

"I understand what you mean; but I was not deceived. I saw what I have told you with my own eyes."

"Yes, yes, of course. But your eyes had been staring at that very curious sunset we had tonight. That is the only explanation. You will see it in the proper light tomorrow, I am sure. But, remember, I am always ready to give any help that is in my power; do not scruple to come to me, or to send for me if you are in any distress."

I went away but little comforted, all confusion and terror and sorrow, not knowing where to turn. When my brother and I met the next day, I looked quickly at him, and noticed, with a sicken-ing at heart, that the right hand, the hand on which I had clearly seen the patch as of a black fire, was wrapped up with a handkerchief.

"What is the matter with your hand, Francis?" I said in a steady voice.

"Nothing of consequence. I cut a finger last night, and it bled rather awkwardly. So I did it up roughly to the best of my ability."

"I will do it neatly for you, if you like."

"No, thank you, dear; this will answer very well. Suppose we have breakfast; I am quite hungry."

We sat down and I watched him. He scarcely ate or drank at all, but tossed his meat to the dog when he thought my eyes were turned away; there was a look in his eyes that I had never yet seen, and the thought flashed across my mind that it was a look that was scarcely human. I was firmly convinced that awful and incredible as was the thing I had seen the night before, yet it was no illusion, no glamour of bewildered sense, and in the course of the evening I went again to the doctor's house.

He shook his head with an air puzzled and incredulous, and seemed to reflect for a few minutes.

"And you say he still keeps up the medicine? But why? As I understand, all the symptoms he complained of have disappeared long ago; why should he go on taking the stuff when he is quite well? And by the by, where did he get it made up? At Sayce's? I never send anyone there; the old man is getting careless. Suppose you come with me to the chemist's; I should like to have some talk with him."

We walked together to the shop; old Sayce knew Dr. Haberden, and was quite ready to give any information.

"You have been sending that in to Mr. Leicester for some weeks, I think, on my prescription," said the doctor, giving the old man a pencilled scrap of paper.

The chemist put on his great spectacles with trembling uncertainty, and held up the paper with a shaking hand.

"Oh, yes," he said, "I have very little of it left; it is rather an uncommon drug, and I have had it in stock some time. I must get in some more if Mr. Leicester goes on with it."

"Kindly let me have a look at the stuff," said Haberden, and the chemist gave him a glass bottle. He took out the stopper and smelt the contents, and looked strangely at the old man.

"Where did you get this?" he said, "and what is it? For one thing, Mr. Sayce, it is not what I prescribed. Yes, yes, I see the label is right enough, but I tell you this is not the drug."

"I have had it a long time," said the old man in feeble terror; "I got it from Burbage's in the usual way. It is not prescribed often, and I have had it on the shelf for some years. You see there is very little left."

"You had better give it to me," said Haberden. "I am afraid something wrong has happened."

We went out of the shop in silence, the doctor carrying the bottle neatly wrapped in paper under his arm.

"Dr. Haberden," I said, when we had walked a little way—"Dr. Haberden."

"Yes," he said, looking at me gloomily enough.

"I should like you to tell me what my brother has been taking twice a day for the last month or so."

"Frankly, Miss Leicester, I don't know. We will speak of this when we get to my house."

We walked on quickly without another word till we reached Dr. Haberden's. He asked me to sit down, and began pacing up and down the room, his face clouded over, as I could see, with no common fears.

"Well," he said at length, "this is all very strange; it is only natural that you should feel alarmed, and I must confess that my mind is far from easy. We will put aside, if you please, what you told me last night and this morning, but the fact remains that for the last few weeks Mr. Leicester has been impregnating his system with a drug which is completely unknown to me. I tell you, it is not what I ordered; and what the stuff in the bottle really is remains to be seen."

He undid the wrapper, and cautiously tilted a few grains of the white powder on to a piece of paper, and peered curiously at it.

"Yes," he said, "it is like the sulphate of quinine, as you say; it is flaky. But smell it."

He held the bottle to me, and I bent over it. It was a strange, sickly smell, vaporous and overpowering, like some strong anæsthetic.

"I shall have it analysed," said Haberden; "I have a friend who has devoted his whole life to chemistry as a science. Then we shall have something to go upon. No, no; say no more about that other matter; I cannot listen to that; and take my advice and think no more about it yourself."

That evening my brother did not go out as usual after dinner.

"I have had my fling," he said with a queer laugh, "and I must go back to my old ways. A little law will be quite a relaxation after so sharp a dose of pleasure," and he grinned to himself, and soon after went up to his room. His hand was still all bandaged.

Dr. Haberden called a, few days later.

"I have no special news to give you," he said. "Chambers is out of town, so I know no more about that stuff than you do. But I should like to see Mr. Leicester, if he is in."

"He is in his room," I said; "I will tell him you are here."

"No, no, I will go up to him; we will have a little quiet talk together. I dare say that we have made a good deal of fuss about a very little; for, after all, whatever the powder may be, it seems to have done him good."

The doctor went upstairs, and standing in the hall I heard his knock, and the opening and shutting of the door; and then I waited in the silent house for an hour, and the stillness grew more and more intense as the hands of the clock crept round. Then there sounded from above the noise of a door shut sharply, and the doctor was coming down the stairs. His footsteps crossed the hall, and there was a pause at the door; I drew a long, sick breath with difficulty, and saw my face white in a little mirror, and he came in and stood at the door. There was an unutterable horror shining in his eyes; he steadied himself by holding the back of a chair with one hand, his lower lip trembled like a horse's, and he gulped and stammered unintelligible sounds before he spoke.

"I have seen that man," he began in a dry whisper. "I have been sitting in his presence for the last hour. My God! And I am alive and in my senses! I, who have dealt with death all my life, and have dabbled with the melting ruins of the earthly tabernacle. But not this, oh! not this," and he covered his face with his hands as if to shut out the sight of something before him.

"Do not send for me again, Miss Leicester," he said with more composure. "I can do nothing in this house. Good-bye."

As I watched him totter down the steps, and along the pavement towards his house, it seemed to me that he had aged by ten years since the morning.

My brother remained in his room. He called out to me in a voice I hardly recognized that he was very busy, and would like his meals brought to his door and left there, and I gave the order to the servants. From that day it seemed as if the arbitrary conception we call time had been annihilated for me; I lived in an ever-present sense of horror, going through the routine of the house mechanically, and only speaking a few necessary words to the servants. Now and then I went out and paced the streets for an hour or two and came home again; but whether I were without or within, my spirit delayed before the closed door of the upper room, and, shuddering, waited for it to open. I have said that I scarcely reckoned time; but I suppose it must have been a fortnight after Dr. Haberden's visit that I came home from my stroll a little refreshed and lightened. The air was sweet and pleasant, and the hazy form of green leaves, floating cloud-like in the square, and the smell of blossoms, had charmed my senses, and I felt happier and walked more briskly. As I delayed a moment at the verge of the pavement, waiting for a van to pass by before crossing over to the house, I happened to look up at the windows, and instantly there was the rush and swirl of deep cold waters in my ears, my heart leapt up and fell down, down as into a deep hollow, and I was amazed with a dread and terror without form or shape. I stretched out a hand blindly through the folds of thick darkness, from the black and shadowy valley, and held myself from falling, while the stones beneath my feet rocked and swayed and tilted, and the sense of solid things seemed to sink away from under me. I had glanced up at the window of my brother's study, and at that moment the blind was drawn aside, and something that had life stared out into the world. Nay, I cannot say I saw a face or any human likeness; a living thing, two eyes of burning flame glared at me, and they were in the midst of something as formless as my fear, the symbol and presence of all evil and all hideous corruption. I stood shuddering and quaking as with the grip of ague, sick with unspeakable agonies of fear and loathing, and for five minutes I could not summon force or motion to my limbs. When I was within the door, I ran up the stairs to my brother's room and knocked.

"Francis, Francis," I cried, "for Heaven's sake, answer me. What is the horrible thing in your room? Cast it out, Francis; cast it from you."

I heard a noise as of feet shuffling slowly and awkwardly, and a choking, gurgling sound, as if some one was struggling to find utterance, and then the noise of a voice, broken and stifled, and words that I could scarcely understand.

"There is nothing here," the voice said. "Pray do not disturb me. I am not very well to-day."

I turned away, horrified, and yet helpless. I could do nothing, and I wondered why Francis had lied to me, for I had seen the appearance beyond the glass too plainly to be deceived, though it was but the sight of a moment. And I sat still, conscious that there had been something else, something I had seen in the first flash of terror, before those burning eyes had looked at me. Suddenly I remembered; as I lifted my face the blind was being drawn back, and I had had an instant's glance of the thing that was moving it, and in my recollection I knew that a hideous image was engraved forever on my brain. It was not a hand; there were no fingers that held the blind, but a black stump pushed it aside, the mouldering outline and the clumsy movement as of a beast's paw had glowed into my senses before the darkling waves of terror had overwhelmed me as I went down quick into the pit. My mind was aghast at the thought of this, and of the awful presence that dwelt with my brother in his room; I went to his door and cried to him again, but no answer came. That night one of the servants came up to me and told me in a whisper that for three days food had been regularly placed at the door and left untouched; the maid had knocked but had received no answer; she had heard the noise of shuffling feet that I had noticed. Day after day went by, and still my brother's meals were brought to his door and left untouched; and though I knocked and called again and again, I could get no answer. The servants began to talk to me; it appeared they were as alarmed as I; the cook said that when my brother first shut himself up in his room she used to hear him come out at night and go about the house; and once, she said, the hall door had opened and closed again, but for several nights she had heard no sound. The climax came at last; it was in the dusk of the evening, and I was sitting in the darkening dreary room when a terrible shriek jarred and rang harshly out of the silence, and I heard a frightened scurry of feet dashing down the stairs. I waited, and the servant-maid staggered into the room and faced me, white and trembling.

"Oh, Miss Helen!" she whispered; "oh! for the Lord's sake, Miss Helen, what has happened? Look at my hand, miss; look at that hand!"

I drew her to the window, and saw there was a black wet stain upon her hand.

"I do not understand you," I said. "Will you explain to me?"

"I was doing your room just now," she began. "I was turning down the bed-clothes, and all of a sudden there was something fell upon my hand, wet, and I looked up, and the ceiling was black and dripping on me."

I looked hard at her and bit my lip.

"Come with me," I said. "Bring your candle with you."

The room I slept in was beneath my brother's, and as I went in I felt I was trembling. I looked up at the ceiling, and saw a patch, all black and wet, and a dew of black drops upon it, and a pool of horrible liquor soaking into the white bed-clothes.

I ran upstairs and knocked loudly.

"Oh, Francis, Francis, my dear brother," I cried, "what has happened to you."

And I listened. There was a sound of choking, and a noise like water bubbling and regurgitating, but nothing else, and I called louder, but no answer came.

In spite of what Dr. Haberden had said, I went to him; with tears streaming down my cheeks I told him all that had happened, and he listened to me with a face set hard and grim.

"For your father's sake," he said at last, "I will go with you, though I can do nothing."

We went out together; the streets were dark and silent, and heavy with heat and a drought of many weeks. I saw the doctor's face white under the gas-lamps, and when we reached the house his hand was shaking.

We did not hesitate, but went upstairs directly. I held the lamp, and he called out in a loud, determined voice—

"Mr. Leicester, do you hear me? I insist on seeing you. Answer me at once."

There was no answer, but we both heard that choking noise I have mentioned.

"Mr. Leicester, I am waiting for you. Open the door this instant, or I shall break it down." And he called a third time in a voice that rang and echoed from the walls—

"Mr. Leicester! For the last time I order you to open the door."

"Ah!" he said, after a pause of heavy silence, "we are wasting time here. Will you be so kind as to get me a poker, or something of the kind?"

I ran into a little room at the back where odd articles were kept, and found a heavy adze-like tool that I thought might serve the doctor's purpose.

"Very good," he said, "that will do, I dare say. I give you notice, Mr. Leicester," he cried loudly at the keyhole, "that I am now about to break into your room."

Then I heard the wrench of the adze, and the wood-work split and cracked under it; with a loud crash the door suddenly burst open, and for a moment we started back aghast at a fearful screaming cry, no human voice, but as the roar of a monster, that burst forth inarticulate and struck at us out of the darkness.

"Hold the lamp," said the doctor, and we went in and glanced quickly round the room.

"There it is," said Dr. Haberden, drawing a quick breath; "look, in that corner."

I looked, and a pang of horror seized my heart as with a white-hot iron. There upon the floor was a dark and putrid mass, seething with corruption and hideous rottenness, neither liquid nor solid, but melting and changing before our eyes, and bubbling with unctuous oily bubbles like boiling pitch. And out of the midst of it shone two burning points like eyes, and I saw a writhing and stirring as of limbs, and something moved and lifted up what might have been an arm. The doctor took a step forward, raised the iron bar and struck at the burning points; he drove in the weapon, and struck again and again in the fury of loathing.

*　　　*　　　*　　　*　　　*

A week or two later, when I had recovered to some extent from the terrible shock, Dr. Haberden came to see me.

"I have sold my practice," he began, "and to-morrow I am sailing on a long voyage. I do not know whether I shall ever return to England; in all probability I shall buy a little land in California, and settle there for the remainder of my life. I have brought you this packet, which you may open and read when you feel able to do so. It contains the report of Dr. Chambers on what I submitted to him. Good-bye, Miss Leicester, good-bye."

When he was gone I opened the envelope; I could not wait, and proceeded to read the papers within. Here is the manuscript, and if you will allow me, I will read you the astounding story it contains.

"My dear Haberden," the letter began, "I have delayed inexcusably in answering your questions as to the white substance you sent me. To tell you the truth, I have hesitated for some time as to what course I should adopt, for there is a bigotry and orthodox standard in physical science as in theology, and I knew that if I told you the truth I should offend rooted prejudices which I once held dear myself. However, I have determined to be plain with you, and first I must enter into a short personal explanation.

"You have known me, Haberden, for many years as a scientific man; you and I have often talked of our profession together, and discussed the hopeless gulf that opens before the feet of those who think to attain to truth by any means whatsoever except the beaten way of experiment and observation in the sphere of material things. I remember the scorn with which you have spoken to me of men of science who have dabbled a little in the unseen, and have timidly hinted that perhaps the senses are not, after all, the eternal, impenetrable bounds of all knowledge, the everlasting walls beyond which no human being has ever passed. We have laughed together heartily, and I think justly, at the 'occult' follies of the day, disguised under various names—the mesmerisms, spiritualisms, materializations, theosophies, all the rabble rout of imposture, with their machinery of poor tricks and feeble conjuring, the true back-parlour of shabby London streets. Yet, in spite of what I have said, I must confess to you that I am no materialist, taking the word of course in its usual signification. It is now many years since I have convinced myself—convinced myself, a sceptic, remember—that the old ironbound theory is utterly and entirely false. Perhaps this confession will not wound you so sharply as it would have done twenty years ago; for I think you cannot have failed to notice that for some time hypotheses have been advanced by men of pure science which are nothing less than transcendental, and I suspect that most modern chemists and biologists of repute would not hesitate to subscribe the *dic-*

tum of the old Schoolman, *Omnia exeunt in mysterium,* which means, I take it, that every branch of human knowledge if traced up to its source and final principles vanishes into mystery. I need not trouble you now with a detailed account of the painful steps which led me to my conclusions; a few simple experiments suggested a doubt as to my then standpoint, and a train of thought that rose from circumstances comparatively trifling brought me far; my old conception of the universe has been swept away, and I stand in a world that seems as strange and awful to me as the endless waves of the ocean seen for the first time, shining, from a peak in Darien. Now I know that the walls of sense that seemed so impenetrable, that seemed to loom up above the heavens and to be founded below the depths, and to shut us in for evermore, are no such everlasting impassable barriers as we fancied, but thinnest and most airy veils that melt away before the seeker, and dissolve as the early mist of the morning about the brooks. I know that you never adopted the extreme materialistic position; you did not go about trying to prove a universal negative, for your logical sense withheld you from that crowning absurdity; but I am sure that you will find all that I am saying strange and repellent to your habits of thought. Yet, Haberden, what I tell you is the truth, nay, to adopt our common language, the sole and scientific truth, verified by experience; and the universe is verily more splendid and more awful than we used to dream. The whole universe, my friend, is a tremendous sacrament; a mystic, ineffable force and energy, veiled by an outward form of matter; and man, and the sun and the other stars, and the flower of the grass, and the crystal in the test-tube, are each and everyone as spiritual, as material, and subject to an inner working.

"You will perhaps wonder, Haberden, whence all this tends; but I think a little thought will make it clear. You will understand that from such a standpoint the whole view of things is changed, and what we thought incredible and absurd may be possible enough. In short, we must look at legend and belief with other eyes, and be prepared to accept tales that had become mere fables. Indeed this is no such great demand. After all, modern science will concede as much, in a hypocritical manner; you must not, it is true, believe in witchcraft, but you may credit hypnotism; ghosts are out of date, but there is a good deal to be said for the theory of telepathy. Give superstition a Greek name, and believe in it, should almost be a proverb.

"So much for my personal explanation. You sent me, Haberden, a phial, stoppered and sealed, containing a small quantity of flaky white powder, obtained from a chemist who has been dispensing it to one of your patients. I am not surprised to hear that this powder refused to yield any results to your analysis. It is a substance which was known to a few many hundred years ago, but which I never expected to have submitted to me from the shop of a modern apothecary. There seems no reason to doubt the truth of the man's tale; he no doubt got, as he says, the rather uncommon salt you prescribed from the wholesale chemist's; and it has probably remained on his shelf for twenty years, or perhaps longer. Here what we call chance and coincidence begin to work; during all these years the salt in the bottle was exposed to certain recurring variations of temperature, variations probably ranging from 40° to 80°, And, as it happens, such changes, recurring year after year at irregular intervals, and with varying degrees of intensity and duration, have constituted a process, and a process so complicated and so delicate, that I question whether modern scientific apparatus directed with the utmost precision could produce the same result. The white powder you sent me is something very different from the drug you prescribed; it is the powder from which the wine of the Sabbath, the *Vinum Sabbati*, was prepared. No doubt you have read of the Witches' Sabbath, and have laughed at the tales which terrified our ancestors; the black cats, and the broomsticks, and dooms pronounced against some old woman's cow. Since I have known the truth I have often reflected that it is on the whole a happy thing that such burlesque as this is believed, for it serves to conceal much that it is better should not be known generally. However, if you care to read the appendix to Payne Knight's monograph, you will find that the true Sabbath was something very different, though the writer has very nicely refrained from printing all he knew. The secrets of the true Sabbath were the secrets of remote times surviving into the Middle Ages, secrets of an evil science which existed long before Aryan man entered Europe. Men and women, seduced from their homes on specious pretences, were met by beings well qualified to assume, as they did assume, the part of devils, and taken by their guides to some desolate and lonely place, known to the initiate by long tradition, and unknown to all else. Perhaps it was a cave in some bare and windswept hill, perhaps some inmost recess of a great forest, and there the Sabbath was held. There, in the blackest hour of night, the *Vinum Sabbati* was prepared, and this evil graal was poured forth and offered to the neophytes, and they partook of an infernal sacrament; *sumentes calicem principis inferorum*, as an old author well expresses it. And suddenly, each one that had drunk found himself attended by a companion, a shape of glamour and unearthly allurement, beckoning him apart, to share in joys more exquisite, more piercing than the thrill of any dream, to the consummation of the marriage of the Sabbath. It is hard to write of such things as these, and chiefly because that shape that allured with loveliness was no hallucination, but, awful as it is to express, the man himself. By the power of that Sabbath wine, a few grains of white powder thrown into a glass of water, the house of life was riven asunder and the human trinity dissolved, and the worm which never dies, that which lies sleeping within us all, was made tangible and an external thing, and clothed with a garment of flesh. And then, in the hour of midnight, the primal fall was repeated and represented, and the awful thing veiled in the mythos of the Tree in the Garden was done anew. Such was the *nuptiæ Sabbati*.

"I prefer to say no more; you, Haberden, know as well as I do that the most trivial laws of life are not to be broken with impunity; and for so terrible an act as this, in which the very inmost place of the temple was broken open and defiled, a terrible vengeance followed. What began with corruption ended also with corruption."

Underneath is the following in Dr. Haberden's writing:—

"The whole of the above is unfortunately strictly and entirely true. Your brother confessed all to me on that morning when I saw him in his room. My attention was first attracted to the bandaged hand, and I forced him to show it me. What I saw made me, a medical man of many years' standing, grow sick with loathing, and the story I was forced to listen to was infinitely more frightful than I could have believed possible. It has tempted me to doubt the Eternal Goodness which can permit nature to offer such hideous possibilities; and if you had not with your own eyes seen the end, I should have said to you—disbelieve it all. I have not, I think, many more weeks to live, but you are young, and may forget all this.

"JOSEPH HABERDEN, M. D."

In the course of two or three months I heard that Dr. Haberden had died at sea shortly after the ship left England.

ROBERT W. CHAMBERS (1865-1933) was a very prolific author of popular novels, most of which are justly forgotten, but early in his career, he wrote some notable horror stories that today form the entire basis upon which he is remembered. His second book, *The King in Yellow* (1895), is a collection of ten stories that Lovecraft read in early 1927 and described to his friend Donald Wandrei as "a series of vaguely connected short tales having as a background a horrible book—abhorred & suppressed—whose perusal brings fright, madness, & spectral tragedy. There is a bit of *fin de siècle* affectation about the thing, but it's great for all that. The best tale is 'The Yellow Sign'." Chambers derived some of the allusions in his tale (e.g., Hastur, Carcosa, etc.) from Ambrose Bierce. In "Supernatural Horror in Literature," Lovecraft noted that "other early works of Mr. Chambers displaying the outré and macabre element are *The Makers of Moons* and *In Search of the Unknown*. One cannot help regretting that he did not further develop a vein in which he could so easily have become a recognised master."

THE YELLOW SIGN
By Robert W. Chambers

"Let the red dawn surmise
What we shall do,
When this blue starlight dies
And all is through."

There are so many things which are impossible to explain! Why should certain chords in music make me think of the brown and golden tints of autumn foliage? Why should the Mass of Sainte Cécile send my thoughts wandering among the caverns whose walls blaze with ragged masses of virgin silver? What was it in the roar and turmoil of Broadway at six o'clock that flashed before my eyes the picture of a still Breton forest where sunlight filtered through spring foliage and Sylvia bent, half curiously, half tenderly, over a small green lizard, murmuring: "To think that this also is a little ward of God!"

When I first saw the watchman his back was toward me. I looked at him indifferently until he went into the church. I paid no more attention to him than I had to any other man who lounged through Washington Square that morning, and when I shut my window and turned back into the my studio I had forgotten him. Late in the afternoon, the day being warm, I raised the window again and leaned out to get a sniff of air. A man was standing in the courtyard of the church, and I noticed him again with as little interest as I had that morning. I looked across the square to where the fountain was playing and then, with my mind filled with vague impressions of trees, asphalt drives, and the moving groups of nursemaids and holiday-makers, I started to walk back to my easel. As I turned, my listless glance included the man below in the churchyard. His face was toward me now, and with a perfectly involuntary movement I bent to see it. At the same moment he raised his head and looked at me. Instantly I thought of a coffin-worm. Whatever it was about the man that repelled me I did not know, but the impression of a plump white grave-worm was so intense and nauseating that I must have shown it in my expression, for he turned his puffy face away with a movement which made me think of a disturbed grub in a chestnut.

I went back to my easel and motioned the model to resume her pose. After working awhile I was satisfied that I was spoiling what I had done as rapidly as possible, and I took up a palette knife and scraped the color out again. The flesh tones were sallow and unhealthy, and I did not understand how I could have painted such sickly color into a study which before that had glowed with healthy tones.

I looked at Tessie. She had not changed, and the clear flush of health dyed her neck and cheeks as I frowned.

"Is it something I've done?" she said.

"No—I've made a mess of this arm, and for the life of me I can't see how I came to paint such mud as that into the canvas," I replied.

"Don't I pose well?" she insisted.

"Of course, perfectly."

"Then isn't not my fault?"

"No. It's my own."

"I'm very sorry," she said.

I told her she could rest while I applied rag and turpentine to the plague spot on my canvas, and she went off to smoke a cigarette and look over the illustrations in the *Courier Français*.

I did not know whether it was something in the turpentine or a defect of the canvas, but the more I scrubbed the more that gangrene defect seemed to spread. I worked like a beaver to get it out, and yet the disease appeared to creep from limb to limb of the study before me. Alarmed I strove to arrest it, but now the color on the breast changed and the whole figure seemed to absorb the infection as a sponge soaks up water. Vigorously I plied palette knife, turpentine, and scraper, thinking all the time what a séance I should hold with Duval who had sold me the canvas; but soon I noticed that it was not the canvas which was defective nor yet the colors of Edward. "It must be the turpentine," I thought angrily, "or else my eyes have become so blurred and confused by the afternoon light that I can't see straight." I called Tessie, the model. She came and leaned over my chair blowing rings of smoke into the air.

"What *have* you been doing to it?" she exclaimed.

"Nothing," I growled, "it must be this turpentine!"

"What a horrible color it is now," she continued. "Do you think my flesh resembles green cheese?"

"No, I don't," I said angrily, "did you ever know me to paint like that before?"

"No, indeed!"

"Well, then!"

"It must be the turpentine, or something," she admitted.

She slipped on a Japanese robe and walked to the window. I scraped and rubbed until I was tired and finally picked up my brushes and hurled them through the canvas with a forcible expression, the tone alone of which reached Tessie's ears.

Nevertheless she promptly began: "That's it! Swear and act silly and ruin your brushes! You have been three weeks on that study, and now look! What's the good of ripping the canvas? What creatures artists are!"

I felt about as much ashamed as I usually did after such an outbreak, and I turned the ruined canvas to the wall. Tessie helped me clean my brushes, and then danced away to dress. From the screen she regaled me with bits of advice concerning whole or partial loss of temper, until, thinking, perhaps, I had been tormented sufficiently, she came out to implore me to button her waist where she could not reach it on the shoulder.

"Everything went wrong from the time you came back from the window and talked about that horrid-looking man you saw in the church-yard," she announced.

"Yes, he probably bewitched the picture," I said, yawning. I looked at my watch.

"It's after six, I know," said Tessie, adjusting her hat before the mirror.

"Yes," I replied, "I didn't mean to keep you so long." I leaned out of the window but recoiled with disgust, for the young man with the pasty face stood below in the churchyard. Tessie saw my gesture of disapproval and leaned from the window.

"Is that the man you don't like?" she whispered.

I nodded.

"I can't see his face, but he does look fat and soft. Someway or other," she continued, turning to look at me, "he reminds me of a dream—an awful dream I once had. Or," she mused, looking down at her shapely shoes, "was it a dream after all?"

"How should I know?" I smiled.

Tessie smiled in reply.

"You were in it," she said, "so perhaps you might know something about it."

"Tessie! Tessie!" I protested, "don't you dare flatter by saying you dream about me!"

"But I did," she insisted; "shall I tell you about it?"

"Go ahead," I replied, lighting a cigarette. Tessie leaned back on the open window-sill and began very seriously.

"One night last winter I was lying in bed thinking about nothing at all in particular. I had been posing for you and I was tired out, yet it seemed impossible for me to sleep. I heard the bells in the city ring ten, eleven, and midnight. I must have fallen asleep about midnight because I don't remember hearing the bells after that. It seemed to me that I had scarcely closed my eyes when I dreamed that something impelled me to go to the window. I rose, and raising the sash, leaned out. Twenty-fifth Street was deserted as far as I could see. I began to be afraid; everything outside seemed so—so black and uncomfortable. Then the sound of wheels in the distance came to my ears, and it seemed to me as though that was what I must wait for. Very slowly the wheels approached, and, finally, I could make out a vehicle moving along the street. It came nearer and nearer, and when it passed beneath my window I saw it was a hearse. Then, as I trembled with fear, the driver turned and looked straight at me. When I awoke I was standing by the open window shivering with cold, but the black-plumed hearse and the driver were gone. I dreamed this dream again in March last, and again awoke beside the open window. Last night the dream came again. You remember how it was raining; when I awoke, standing at the open window, my night-dress was soaked."

"But where did I come into the dream?" I asked.

"You—you were in the coffin; but you were not dead."

"In the coffin?"

"Yes."

"How did you know? Could you see me?"

"No; I only knew you were there."

"Had you been eating Welsh rarebits, or lobster salad?" I began laughing, but the girl interrupted me with a frightened cry.

"Hello! What's up?" I said, as she shrank into the embrasure by the window.

"The—the man below in the churchyard—he drove the hearse."

"Nonsense," I said, but Tessie's eyes were wide with terror. I went to the window and looked out. The man was gone. "Come, Tessie," I urged, "don't be foolish. You have posed too long; you are nervous."

"Do you think I could forget that face?" she murmured. "Three times I saw the hearse pass below my window, and every time the driver turned and looked up at me. Oh, his face was so white and—and soft? It looked dead—it looked as if it had been dead a long time."

I induced the girl to sit down and swallow a glass of Marsala. Then I sat down beside her, and tried to give her some advice.

"Look here, Tessie," I said, "you go to the country for a week or two, and you'll have no more dreams about hearses. You pose all day, and when night comes your nerves are upset. You can't keep this up. Then again, instead of going to bed when your day's work is done, you run off to picnics at Sulzer's Park, or go to the Eldorado or Coney Island, and when you come down here next morning you are fagged out. There was no real hearse. That was a soft-shelled crab dream."

She smiled faintly.

What about the man in the churchyard?"

"Oh, he's only an ordinary unhealthy, everyday creature."

"As true as my name is Tessie Reardon, I swear to you, Mr. Scott, that the face of the man below in the churchyard is the face of the man who drove the hearse."

"What of it?" I said. "It's an honest trade."

"Then you think I *did* see the hearse?"

"Oh," I said, diplomatically, "if you really did, it might not be unlikely that the man below drove it. There is nothing in it."

Tessie rose, unrolled her scented handkerchief, and taking a bit of gum from a knot in the hem, placed it in her mouth. Then drawing on her gloves she offered me her hand, with a frank, "Good-night, Mr. Scott," and walked out.

II

The next morning, Thomas, the bellboy, brought me the *Herald* and a bit of news. The church next door had been sold. I thanked Heaven for it, not that it being a Catholic I had any repugnance for the congregation next door, but because my nerves were shattered by a blatant exhorter, whose every word echoed though the aisle of the church as if it had been my own rooms, and who insisted on his r's with a nasal persistence which revolted my every instinct. Then, too, there was a fiend in human shape, an organist, who reeled off some of the grand old hymns with an interpretation of his own, and I longed for the blood of a creature who could play the doxology with an amendment of minor chords which one hears only in a quartet of very young undergraduates. I believe the minister was a good man, but when he bellowed: "And the Lorrrrd said unto Moses, the Lorrrd is a man of war; the Lorrrd is his name. My wrath shall wax hot and I will kill you with the sworrrd!" I wondered how many centuries of purgatory it would take to atone for such a sin.

"Who bought the property?" I asked Thomas.

"Nobody that I knows, sir. They do say the gent wot owns this 'ere 'Amilton flats was lookin' at it. 'E might be a bildin' more studios."

I walked to the window. The young man with the unhealthy face stood by the churchyard gate, and at the mere sight of him the same overwhelming repugnance took possession of me.

"By the way, Thomas," I said, "who is that fellow down there?"

Thomas sniffed. "That there worm, sir? 'E's night-watchman of the church, sir. 'E makes me tired a-sittin' out all night on them steps and lookin' at you insultin' like. I'd punched 'is 'ed, sir—beg pardon, sir "

"Go on, Thomas."

"One night a comin' 'ome with 'Arry, the other English boy, I sees 'im sittin' there on them steps. We 'ad Molly and Jen with us, sir, the two girls on the tray service, an' 'e looks so insultin' at us that I up and sez: 'Wat you looking hat, you fat slug?'—beg pardon, sir, but that's 'ow I sez, sir. Then 'e don't say nothin' and I sez: 'Come out and I'll punch that puddin' 'ed.' Then I hopens the gate an' goes in, but 'e don't say nothin', only looks insultin' like. Then I 'its 'im one, but, ugh! 'is 'ed was that cold and mushy it ud sicken you to touch 'im."

"What did he do then?" I asked, curiously.

"'Im? Nawthin'."

"And you, Thomas?"

The young fellow flushed with embarrassment and smiled uneasily.

"Mr. Scott, sir, I ain't no coward an' I can't make it out at all why I run. I was in the 5th Lawncers, sir, bugler at Tel-el-Kebir, an' was shot by the wells."

"You don't mean to say you ran away?"

"Yes, sir; I run."

"Why?"

"That's just what I want to know, sir. I grabbed Molly an' run, an' the rest was as frightened as I."

"But what were they frightened at?"

Thomas refused to answer for a while, but now my curiosity was aroused about the repulsive young man below and I pressed him. Three years' sojourn in America had not only modified Thomas' cockney dialect but had given him the American's fear of ridicule.

"You won't believe me, Mr. Scott, sir?"

"Yes, I will."

"You will lawf at me, sir?"

"Nonsense!"

He hesitated. "Well, sir, it's God's truth that when I 'it 'im 'e grabbed me wrists, sir, and when I twisted 'is soft, mushy fist one of 'is fingers come off in me 'and."

The utter loathing and horror of Thomas' face must have been reflected in my own for he added:

"It's orful, an' now when I see 'im I just go away. 'E maikes me hill."

When Thomas had gone I went to the window. The man stood beside the church-railing with both hands on the gate, but I hastily retreated to my easel again, sickened and horrified, for I saw that the middle finger of his right hand was missing.

At nine o'clock Tessie appeared and vanished behind the screen with a merry "good-morning, Mr. Scott." When she had reappeared and taken her pose upon the model-stand I started a new canvas much to her delight.

She remained silent as long as I was on the drawing, but as soon as the scrape of the charcoal ceased and I took up my fixative she began to chatter.

"Oh, I had such a lovely time last night. We went to Tony Pastor's."

"Who are 'we'?" I demanded.

"Oh, Maggie, you know, Mr. Whyte's model, and Pinkie McCormick—we call her Pinkie because she's got that beautiful red hair you artists like so much—and Lizzie Burke."

I sent a shower of spray from the fixative over the canvas, and said: "Well, go on."

"We saw Kelly and Baby Barnes the skirt-dancer and—and all the rest. I made a mash."

"Then you have gone back on me, Tessie?"

She laughed and shook her head.

"He's Lizzie Burke's brother, Ed. He's a perfect gen'l'man."

I felt constrained to give her some parental advice concerning mashing, which she took with a bright smile.

"Oh, I can take care of a strange mash," she said, examining her chewing gum, "but Ed is different. Lizzie is my best friend."

Then she related how Ed had come back from the stocking mill in Lowell, Massachusetts, to find her and Lizzie grown up, and what an accomplished young man he was, and how he thought nothing of squandering half a dollar for ice-cream and oysters to celebrate his entry as clerk into the woollen department of Macy's. Before she finished I began to paint and she resumed the pose, smiling and chattering like a sparrow. By noon I had the study fairly well rubbed in and Tessie came to look at it.

"That's better," she said.

I thought so too, and ate my lunch with a satisfied feeling that all was going well. Tessie spread her lunch on a drawing table opposite me and we drank our claret from the same bottle and lighted out cigarettes from the same match. I was very much attached to Tessie. I had watched her shoot up into a slender but exquisitely formed woman from a frail, awkward child. She had posed for me during the last three years, and among all my models she was my favorite. It would have troubled me very much indeed had she become "tough" or "fly," as the phrase goes, but I never noticed any deterioration of her manner, and felt at heart that she was all right. She and I never discussed morals at all, and I had no intention of doing so, partly because I had none myself, and partly because I knew she would do what she like in spite of me. Still I did hope she would steer clear of complications, because I wished her well, and then also I had a selfish desire to retain the best model I had. I knew that mashing, as she termed it, had no significance with girls like Tessie, and that such things in America did not resemble in the least the same things in Paris. Yet, having lived with my eyes open, I also knew that somebody would take Tessie away some day, in one manner or another, and though I professed to myself that marriage was nonsense, I sincerely hoped that, in this case, there would be a priest at the end of the vista. I am a Catholic. When I listen to high mass, when I sign myself, I feel that everything, including myself, is more cheerful, and when I confess, it does me good. A man who lives as much alone as I do must confess to somebody. Then, again, Sylvia was Catholic, and it was reason enough for me. But I was speaking of Tessie, which is very different. Tessie also was Catholic and much more devout than I, so taking it all in all, I had little fear for my pretty model until she should fall in love. But *then* I knew that fate alone would decide her future for her, and I prayed inwardly that fate would keep her away from men like me and throw into her path nothing but Ed Burkes and Jimmy McCormicks, bless her sweet face!

Tessie sat blowing rings of smoke up to the ceiling and tinkling the ice in her tumbler.

"Do you know that I also had a dream last night?" I observed.

"Not about that man," she laughed.

"Exactly. A dream similar to yours, only much worse."

It was foolish and thoughtless of me to say this, but you know how little tact the average painter has.

"I must have fallen asleep about 10 o'clock," I continued, "and after a while I dreamt that I awoke. So plainly did I hear the midnight bells, the wind in the tree-branches, and the whistle of steamers from the bay, that even now I can scarcely believe I was not awake. I seemed to be lying in a box which had a glass cover. Dimly I saw the street lamps as I passed, for I must tell you, Tessie, the box in which I reclined appeared to lie in a cushioned wagon which jolted me over the stony pavement. After a while I became impatient and tried to move but the box was too narrow. My hands were crossed on my breast so I could not raise them to help myself. I listened and then tried to call. My voice was gone. I could hear the trample of the horses attached to the wagon and even the breathing of the driver. Then another sound broke upon my ears like the raising of a window sash. I managed to turn my head a little, and found I could look, not only through the glass cover of my box. but also through the glass panes in the sides of the covered vehicle. I saw houses, empty and silent, with neither light nor life about any of them excepting one. In that house a window was open on the first floor and a figure all in white stood looking down into the street. It was you."

Tessie has turned her face away from me and leaned on the table with her elbow.

"I could see your face," I resumed, "and it seemed to me to be very sorrowful. Then we passed on and turned into a narrow black lane. Presently the horses stopped. I waited and waited, closing my eyes with fear and impatience, but all was silent as the grave. After what seemed to me hours, I began to feel uncomfortable. A sense that somebody was close to me made me unclose my eyes. Then I saw the white face of the hearse-driver looking at me through the coffin-lid—"

A sob from Tessie interrupted me. She was trembling like a leaf. I saw I had made an ass of myself and attempted to repair the damage.

"Why, Tess," I said, "I only told you this to show you what influence your story might have on another person's dreams. You don't suppose I really lay in a coffin, do you? What are you trembling for? Don't you see that your dream and my unreasonable dislike for that inoffensive watchman of the church simply set my brain working as soon as I fell asleep?"

She laid her head between her arms and sobbed as if her heart would break. What a precious triple donkey I had made of myself! But I was about to break my record. I went over and put my arm about her.

"Tessie dear, forgive me," I said; "I had no business to frighten you with such nonsense. You are too sensible a girl, too good a Catholic to believe in dreams."

Her hand tightened on mine and her head fell back upon my shoulder, but she still trembled and I petted her and comforted her.

"Come, Tess, open your eyes and smile."

Her eyes opened with a slow languid movement and met mine, but their expression was so queer that I hastened to reassure her again.

"It's all humbug, Tessie, you surely are not afraid that any harm will come to you because of that."

"No," she said, but her scarlet lips quivered.

"Then what's the matter? Are you afraid?"

"Yes. Not for myself."

"For me, then?" I demanded gayly.

"For you," she murmured in a voice almost inaudible, "I—I care for you."

At first I started to laugh, but when I understood her, a shock passed through me and I sat like one turned to stone. This was the crowning bit of idiocy I had committed. During the moment which elapsed between her reply and my answer I thought of a thousand responses to that innocent confession. I could pass it by with a laugh, I could misunderstand her and reassure her as to my health, I could simply point out that it was impossible she could love me. But my reply was quicker than my thoughts, and I might think and think now when it was too late, for I had kissed her on the mouth.

That evening I took my usual walk in Washington Park, pondering over the occurrences of the day. I was thoroughly committed. There was no back out now, and I stared the future straight in the face. I was not good, not even scrupulous, but I had no idea of deceiving either myself or Tessie. The one passion of my life lay buried in the sunlit forests of Brittany. Was it buried forever? Hope cried "No!" For three years I had been listening to the voice of Hope, and for three years I had waited for a footstep on my threshold. Had Sylvia forgotten? "No!" cried Hope.

I said that I was not good. That is true, but still I was not exactly a comic opera villain. I had led an easy-going reckless life, taking what invited me of pleasure, deploring and sometimes bitterly regretting consequences. In one thing alone, except my painting, was I serious, and that was something which lay hidden if not lost in the Breton forests.

It was too late now for me to regret what had occurred during the day. Whatever it had been, pity, a sudden tenderness for sorrow, or the more brutal instinct of gratified vanity, it was all the same now, and unless I wished to bruise an innocent heart my path lay marked before me. The fire and strength, the depth of passion of a love which I had never even suspected, with all my imagined experience in the world, left me no alternative but to respond or send her away. Whether because I am so cowardly about giving pain to others, or whether it was that I have little of the gloomy Puritan in me, I do not know, but I shrank from disclaiming responsibility for that thoughtless kiss, and in fact had no time to do so before the gate of her heart opened and the flood poured forth. Others who habitually do their duty and find a sullen satisfaction in making themselves and everybody else unhappy, might have withstood it. I did not. I dared not. After the storm had abated I did tell her that she might better have loved Ed Burke and worn a plain gold ring, but she would not hear of it, and I thought perhaps that as long as she had decided to love somebody she could not marry, it had better be me. I, at least, could treat her with an intelligent affection, and whenever she became tired of her infatuation she could go none the worse for it. For I was decided on that point although I knew how hard it would be. I remembered the usual termination of Platonic liaisons and thought how disgusted I had been whenever I heard of one. I knew I was undertaking a great deal for so unscrupulous a man as I was, and I dreaded the future, but never for one moment did I doubt that she was safe with me. Had it been anybody but Tessie I should not have bothered my head about scruples. For it did not occur to me to sacrifice Tessie as I would have sacrificed a woman of the world. I looked the future squarely in the face and saw the several probable endings to the affair. She would either tire of the whole thing, or become so unhappy that I should have either to marry her or go away. If I married her we would be unhappy. I with a wife unsuited to me, and she with a husband unsuitable for any woman. For my past life could scarcely entitle me to marry. If I went away she might either fall ill, recover, and marry some Eddie Burke, or she might recklessly or deliberately go and do something foolish. On the other hand if she tired of me, then her whole life would be before her with beautiful vistas of Eddie Burkes and marriage rings and twins and Harlem flats and Heaven knows what. As I strolled along through the trees by the Washington Arch, I decided that she should find a substantial friend in me anyway and the future could take care of itself. Then I went into the house and put on my evening dress for the little faintly perfumed note on my dresser said, "Have a cab at the stage door at eleven," and the note was signed "Edith Carmichel, Metropolitan Theatre."

I took supper that night, or rather we took supper, Miss Carmichel and I, at Solari's and the dawn was just beginning to gild the cross on the Memorial Church as I entered Washington Square after leaving Edith at the Brunswick. There was not a soul in the park as I passed among the trees and took the walk which leads from the Garibaldi statue to the Hamilton Apartment House, but as I passed the churchyard I saw a figure sitting on the stone steps. In spite of myself a chill crept over me at the sight of the white puffy face, and I hastened to pass. Then he said something which might have been addressed to me or might merely have been a mutter to himself, but a sudden furious anger flamed up within me that such a creature should address me. For an instant I felt like wheeling about and smashing my stick over his head, but I walked on, and entering the Hamilton went to my apartment. For some time I tossed about the bed trying to get the sound of his voice out of my ears, but could not. It filled my head, that muttering sound, like thick oily smoke from a fat-rending vat or an odor of noisome decay. And as I lay and tossed about, the voice in my ears seemed more distinct, and I began to understand the words he had muttered. They came to me slowly as if I had forgotten them, and at last I could make some sense out of the sounds. It was this:

"Have you found the Yellow Sign?"

"Have you found the Yellow Sign?"

"Have you found the Yellow Sign?"

I was furious. What did he mean by that? Then with a curse upon him and his I rolled over and went to sleep, but when I awoke later I looked pale and haggard, for I had dreamed the dream of the night before and it troubled me more than I cared to think.

I dressed and went down into my studio. Tessie sat by the window, but as I came in she rose and put both arms around my neck for an innocent kiss. She looked so sweet and dainty that I kissed her again and then sat down before my easel.

"Hello! Where's the study I began yesterday?" I asked.

Tessie looked conscious, but did no answer. I began to hunt among the pile of canvases, saying, "Hurry up, Tess, and get ready; we must take advantage of the morning light."

When at last I gave up the search among the other canvases and turned to look around the room for the missing study I noticed Tessie standing by the screen with her clothes on.

"What's the matter," I asked, "don't you feel well?"

"Yes."

"Then hurry."

"Do you want me to pose as—as I have always posed?"

Then I understood. Here was a new complication. I had lost, of course, the best nude model I had ever seen. I looked at Tessie. Her face was scarlet. Alas! Alas! We had eaten of the tree of knowledge, and Eden and native innocence were dreams of the past—I mean for her.

I suppose she noticed the disappointment on my face, for she said: "I will pose if you wish. The study is behind the screen here where I put it."

"No," I said, "we will begin something new;" and I went into my wardrobe and picked out a Moorish costume which fairly blazed with tinsel. It was a genuine costume, and Tessie retired to the screen with it enchanted. When she came forth again I was astonished. Her long black hair was bound above her forehead with a circlet of turquoises, and the ends curled about her glittering girdle. Her feet were encased in the embroidered pointed slippers and the skirt of her costume, curiously wrought with arabesques in silver, fell to her ankles. The deep metallic blue vest embroidered with silver and the short Mauresque jacket spangled and sewn with turquoises became her wonderfully. She came up to me and held up her face smiling. I slipped my hand into my pocket and drawing out a gold chain with a cross attached, dropped it over her head.

"It's yours, Tessie."

"Mine?" she faltered.

"Yours. Now go and pose." Then with a radiant smile she ran behind the screen and presently re-appeared with a little box on which was written my name.

"I had intended to give it to you when I went home to-night," she said, "but I can't wait now."

I opened the box. On the pink cotton inside lay a clasp of black onyx, on which was inlaid a curious symbol or letter in gold. It was neither Arabic or Chinese, nor as I found afterwards did it belong to any human script.

"It's all I had to give you for a keepsake," she said, timidly.

I was annoyed, but I told her how much I should prize it, and promised to wear it always. She fastened in on my coat beneath the lapel.

"How foolish, Tess, to go and buy me such a beautiful thing as this," I said.

"I did not buy it," she laughed.

"Where did you get it?"

Then she told me how she found it one day while coming from the Aquarium in the Battery, how she had advertised it and watched the papers, but at last gave up all hopes of finding the owner.

"That was last winter," she said, "the very day I had the first horrid dream about the hearse."

I remembered my dream of the previous night but said nothing, and presently my charcoal was flying over a new canvas, and Tessie stood motionless on the model-stand.

III

The day following was a disastrous one for me. While moving a framed canvas from one easel to another my foot slipped on the polished floor and I fell heavily on both wrists. They were so badly sprained that it was useless to attempt to hold a brush, and I was obliged to wander about the studio, glaring at unfinished drawings and sketches until despair seized me and I sat down to smoke and twiddle my thumbs with rage. The rain blew against the windows and rattled on the roof of the church, driving me into a nervous fit with its interminable patter. Tessie sat sewing by the window, and every now and then raised her head and looked at me with such innocent compassion that I began to feel ashamed of my irritation and looked about for something to occupy me. I had read all the papers and all the books in the library, but for the sake of something to do I went to the bookcases and shoved them open with my elbow. I knew every volume by its color and examined them all, passing slowly around the library and whistling to keep up my spirits. I was turning to go into the dining-room when my eye fell upon a book bound in yellow, standing in a corner of the top shelf of the last bookcase. I did not remember it and from the floor could not decipher the pale lettering on the back, so I went to the smoking-room and called Tessie. She came in from the studio and climbed up to reach the book.

"What is it?" I asked.

" 'The King in Yellow.' "

I was dumfounded. Who had placed it there? How came it in my rooms? I had long ago decided that I should never open that book, and nothing on earth could have persuaded me to buy it. Fearful lest curiosity might tempt me to open it, I had never even looked at it in book-stores. If I ever had any curiosity to read it, the awful tragedy of young Castaigne, who I knew, prevented me from exploring its wicked pages. I had refused to listen to any description of it, and indeed, nobody ever ventured to discuss the second part aloud, so I had absolutely no knowledge of what those leaves might reveal. I stared at the poisonous mottled binding as I would at a snake.

"Don't touch it, Tessie," I said; "come down."

Of course my admonition was enough to around her curiosity, and before I could prevent it she took the book and, laughing, danced off into the studio with it. I called to her but she slipped away with a tormenting smile at my helpless hands, and I followed her with some impatience.

"Tessie!" I cried, entering the library, "listen, I am serious. Put that book away. I do not wish you to open it!" The library was empty. I went into both drawing-rooms, then into the bedrooms, laundry, kitchen, and finally returned to the library and began a systematic search. She had hidden herself so well that it was half an hour later when I discovered her crouching white and silent by the latticed window in the store-room above. At the first glance I saw she had been punished for her foolishness. "The King in Yellow" lay at her feet, but the book was open at the second part. I looked at Tessie and saw it was too late. She had opened "The King in

Yellow." Then I took her by the hand and led her into the studio. She seemed dazed, and when I told her to lie down on the sofa she obeyed me without a word. After a while she closed her eyes and her breathing became regular and deep, but I could not determine whether or not she slept. For a long while I sat silently beside her, but she neither stirred nor spoke, and at last I rose and entering the unused store-room took the yellow book in my least injured hand. It seemed heavy as lead, but I carried it into the studio again, and sitting down on the rug beside the sofa, opened it and read it through from beginning to end.

When, faint with the excess of my emotions, I dropped the volume and leaned wearily back against the sofa, Tessie opened her eyes and looked at me.

*   *   *   *   *

We had been speaking for some time in a dull monotonous strain before I realized that we were discussing "The King in Yellow." Oh the sin of writing such words,—words which are clear as crystal, limpid and musical as bubbling springs, words which sparkle and glow like the poisoned diamonds of the Medicis! Oh the wickedness, the hopeless damnation of a soul who could fascinate and paralyze human creatures with such words, —words understood by the ignorant and wise alike, words which are more precious than jewels, more soothing than music, more awful than death!

We talked on, unmindful of the gathering shadows, and she was begging me to throw away the clasp of black onyx quaintly inlaid with what we now knew to be the Yellow Sign. I never shall know why I refused, though even at this hour, here in my bedroom as I write this confession, I should be glad to know *what* it was that prevented me from tearing the Yellow Sign from my breast and casting it into the fire. I am sure I wished to do so, and yet Tessie pleaded with me in vain. Night fell and the hours dragged on, but still we murmured to each other of the King and the Pallid Mask, and midnight sounded from the misty spires in the fog-wrapped city. We spoke of Hastur and of Cassilda, while outside the fog rolled against the blank window-panes as the cloud waves roll and break on the shores of Hali.

The house was very silent and not a sound came up from the misty streets. Tessie lay among the cushions, her face a gray blot in the gloom, but her hands were clasped in mine and I knew that she knew and read my thoughts as I read hers, for we had understood the mystery of the Hyades and the Phantom of the Truth was laid. Then as we answered each other, swiftly, silently, thought on thought, the shadows stirred in the gloom about us, and far in the distant streets we heard a sound. Nearer and nearer it came, the dull crunching of wheels, nearer and yet nearer, and now, outside before the door it ceased, and I dragged myself to the window and saw a black-plumed hearse. The gate below opened and shut, and I crept shaking to my door and bolted it, but I knew no bolts, no locks, could keep that creature out who was coming for the Yellow Sign. And now I heard him moving very softly along the hall. Now he was at the door, and the bolts rotted at his touch. Now he entered. With eyes staring from my head I peered into the darkness, but when he came into the room I did not see him. It was only when I felt him envelop me in his cold soft grasp that I cried out and struggled with deadly fury, but my hands were useless and he tore the onyx clasp from my coat and struck me full in the face. Then, as I fell, I heard Tessie's soft cry and her spirit fled: and even while falling I longed to follow her, for I knew that the King in Yellow had opened his tattered mantle and there was only God to cry to now.

I could tell more, but I cannot see what help it will be to the world. As for me I am past human help or hope. As I lie here, writing, careless even whether or not I die before I finish, I can see the doctor gathering up his powders and phials with a vague gesture to the good priest beside me, which I understand.

They will be very curious to know the tragedy—they of the outside world who write books and print millions of newspapers, but I shall write no more, and the father confessor will seal my last words with the seal of sanctity when his holy office is done. They of the outside world may send their creatures into wrecked homes and death-smitten firesides, and their newspapers will batten on blood and tears, but with me their spies must halt before the confessional. They know that Tessie is dead and that I am dying. They know how the people of the house, aroused by an infernal scream, rushed into my rooms and found one living and two dead, but they do not know what I shall tell them now; they do not know that the doctor said as he pointed to a horrible decomposed heap on the floor—the livid corpse of the watchman from the church: "I have no theory, no explanation. That man must have been dead for months!"

* * * * *

I think I am dying. I wish the priest would—

M. R. JAMES (1862-1936) was a prolific British scholar of medieval studies, palaeography, biblical scholarship, and bibliography. He also wrote four collections of ghost stories. Lovecraft discovered James in December 1925 as he began research for his essay "Supernatural Horror in Literature," in which he wrote: "Dr. James has, it is clear, an intelligent and scientific knowledge of human nerves and feelings; and knows just how to apportion statement, imagery, and subtle suggestions in order to secure the best results with his readers. . . . It is hard to select a favourite or especially typical tale, though each reader will no doubt have such preferences as his temperament may determine. "Count Magnus" is assuredly one of the best, forming as it does a veritable Golconda of suspense and suggestion."

"Count Magnus" comes from James's first collection of tales, *Ghost Stories of an Antiquary* (1904).

COUNT MAGNUS
by M. R. James

By what means the papers out of which I have made a connected story came into my hands is the last point which the reader will learn from these pages. But it is necessary to prefix to my extracts from them a statement of the form in which I possess them.

They consist, then, partly of a series of collections for a book of travels, such a volume as was a common product of the forties and fifties. Horace Marryat's "Journal of a Residence in Jutland and the Danish Isles" is a fair specimen of the class to which I allude. These books usually treated of some unfamiliar district on the Continent. They were illustrated with woodcuts or steel plates. They gave details of hotel accommodation, and of means of communication, such as we now expect to find in any well-regulated guidebook, and they dealt largely in reported conversations with intelligent foreigners, racy innkeepers and garrulous peasants. In a word, they were chatty.

Begun with the idea of furnishing material for such a book, my papers as they progressed assumed the character of a record of one single personal experience, and this record was continued up to the very eve, almost, of its termination.

The writer was a Mr. Wraxall. For my knowledge of him I have to depend entirely on the evidence his writings afford, and from these I deduce that he was a man past middle age, possessed of some private means, and very much alone in the world. He had, it seems, no settled abode in England, but was a denizen of hotels and boarding-houses. It is probable that he entertained the idea of settling down at some future time which never came; and I think it also likely that the Pantechnicon fire in the early seventies must have destroyed a great deal that would have thrown light on his antecedents, for he refers once or twice to property of his that was warehoused at that establishment.

It is further apparent that Mr. Wraxall had published a book, and that it treated of a holiday he had once taken in Brittany. More than this I cannot say about his work, because a diligent search in bibliographical works has convinced me that it must have appeared either anonymously or under a pseudonym.

As to his character, it is not difficult to form some superficial opinion. He must have been an intelligent and cultivated man. It seems that he was near being a Fellow of his college at Oxford—Brasenose, as I judge from the Calendar. His besetting fault was pretty clearly that of over-inquisitiveness, possibly a good fault in a traveller, certainly a fault for which this traveller paid dearly enough in the end.

On what proved to be his last expedition, he was plotting another book. Scandinavia, a region not widely known to Englishmen forty years ago, had struck him as an interesting field. He must have lighted on some old books of Swedish history or memoirs, and the idea had struck him that there was room for a book descriptive of travel in Sweden, interspersed with episodes from the history of some of the great Swedish families. He procured letters of introduction, therefore, to some persons of quality in Sweden, and set out thither in the early summer of 1863.

Of his travels in the North there is no need to speak, nor of his residence of some weeks in Stockholm. I need only mention that some *savant* resident there put him on the track of an important collection of family papers belonging to the proprietors of an ancient manor-house in Vestergothland, and obtained for him permission to examine them.

The manor-house, or *herrgård*, in question is to be called Råbäck (pronounced something like Roebeck), though that is not its name. It is one of the best buildings of its kind in all the country, and the picture of it in Dahlenberg's *Suecia antiqua et moderna*, engraved in 1694, shows it very much as the tourist may see it to-day. It was built soon after 1600, and is, roughly speaking, very much like an English house of that period in respect of material—red-brick with stone facings—and style. The man who built it was a scion of the great house of De la Gardie, and his descendants possess it still. De la Gardie is the name by which I will designate them when mention of them becomes necessary.

They received Mr. Wraxall with great kindness and courtesy, and pressed him to stay in the house as long as his researches lasted. But, preferring to be independent, and mistrusting his powers of conversing in Swedish, he settled himself at the village inn, which turned out quite sufficiently comfortable, at any rate during the summer months. This arrangement would entail a short walk daily to and from the manor-house of something under a mile. The house itself stood in a park, and was protected—we should say grown up—with large old timber. Near it you found the walled garden, and then entered a close wood fringing one of the small lakes with which the whole country is pitted. Then came the wall of the demesne, and you climbed a steep knoll—a knob of rock lightly covered with soil—and on the top of this stood the church, fenced in with tall dark trees. It was a curious building to English eyes. The nave and aisles were low, and filled with pews and galleries. In the western gallery stood the handsome old organ, gaily painted, and with silver pipes. The ceiling was flat, and had been adorned by a seventeenth-century artist with a strange and hideous "Last Judgement", full of lurid flames, falling cities, burning ships, crying souls, and brown and smiling demons. Handsome brass coronæ hung from the roof; the pulpit was like a doll's-house, covered with little painted wooden cherubs and saints; a stand with three hour-glasses was hinged to the preacher's desk. Such sights as these may be seen in many a church in Sweden now, but what distinguished this one was an addition to the original building. At the eastern end of the north aisle the builder of the manor-house had erected a mausoleum for himself and his family. It was a largish eight-sided building, lighted by a series of oval windows, and it had a domed roof, topped by a kind of pumpkin-shaped object rising into a spire, a form in which Swedish architects greatly delighted. The roof was of copper externally, and was painted black, while the walls, in common with those of the church, were staringly white. To this mausoleum there was no access from the church. It had a portal and steps of its own on the northern side.

Past the churchyard the path to the village goes, and not more than three or four minutes bring you to the inn door.

On the first day of his stay at Råbäck Mr. Wraxall found the church door open, and made those notes of the interior which I have epitomized. Into the mausoleum, however, he could not make his way. He could by looking through the keyhole just descry that there were fine marble effigies and sarcophagi of copper, and a wealth of armorial ornament, which made him very anxious to spend some time in investigation.

The papers he had come to examine at the manor-house proved to be of just the kind he wanted for his book. There were family correspondence, journals, and account-books of the earliest owners of the estate, very carefully kept and clearly written, full of amusing and picturesque detail. The first De la Gardie appeared in them as a strong and capable man. Shortly after the building of the mansion there had been a period of distress in the district, and the peasants had risen and attacked several châteaux and done some damage. The owner of Råbäck took a leading part in suppressing the trouble, and there was reference to executions of ringleaders and severe punishments inflicted with no sparing hand.

The portrait of this Magnus de la Gardie was one of the best in the house, and Mr. Wraxall studied it with no little interest after his day's work. He gives no detailed description of it, but I gather that the face impressed him rather by its power than by its beauty or goodness; in fact, he writes that Count Magnus was an almost phenomenally ugly man.

On this day Mr. Wraxall took his supper with the family, and walked back in the late but still bright evening.

"I must remember," he writes, "to ask the sexton if he can let me into the mausoleum at the church. He evidently has access to it himself, for I saw him to-night standing on the steps, and, as I thought, locking or unlocking the door."

I find that early on the following day Mr. Wraxall had some conversation with his landlord. His setting it down at such length as he does surprised me at first; but I soon realized that the papers I was reading were, at least in their beginning, the materials for the book he was meditating, and that it was to have been one of those quasi-journalistic productions which admit of the introduction of an admixture of conversational matter.

His object, he says, was to find out whether any traditions of Count Magnus de la Gardie lingered on in the scenes of that gentleman's activity, and whether the popular estimate of him were favourable or not. He found that the Count was decidedly not a favourite. If his tenants came late to their work on the days which they owed to him as Lord of the Manor, they were set on the wooden horse, or flogged and branded in the manor-house yard. One or two cases there were of men who had occupied lands which encroached on the lord's domain, and whose houses had been mysteriously burnt on a winter's night, with the whole family inside. But what seemed to dwell on the innkeeper's mind most—for he returned to the subject more than once—was that the Count had been on the Black Pilgrimage, and had brought something or someone back with him.

You will naturally inquire, as Mr. Wraxall did, what the Black Pilgrimage may have been. But your curiosity on the point must remain unsatisfied for the time being, just as his did. The landlord was evidently unwilling to give a full answer, or indeed any answer, on the point, and, being called out for a moment, trotted off with obvious alacrity, only putting his head in at the door a few minutes afterwards to say that he was called away to Skara, and should not be back till evening.

So Mr. Wraxall had to go unsatisfied to his day's work at the manor-house. The papers on which he was just then engaged soon put his thoughts into another channel, for he had to occupy himself with glancing over the correspondence between Sophia Albertina in Stockholm and her married cousin Ulrica Leonora at Råbäck in the years 1705-1710. The letters were of exceptional interest from the light they threw upon the culture of that period in Sweden, as anyone can testify who has read the full edition of them in the publications of the Swedish Historical Manuscripts Commission.

In the afternoon he had done with these, and after returning the boxes in which they were kept to their places on the shelf, he proceeded, very naturally, to take down some of the volumes nearest to them, in order to determine which of them had best be his principal subject of investigation next day. The shelf he had hit upon was occupied mostly by a collection of account-books in the writing of the first Count Magnus. But one among them was not an account-book, but a book of alchemical and other tracts in another sixteenth-century hand. Not being very familiar with alchemical literature, Mr. Wraxall spends much space which he might have spared in setting out the names and beginnings of the various treatises: The book of the Phœnix, book of the Thirty Words, book of the Toad, book of

Miriam, Turba philosophorum, and so forth; and then he announces with a good deal of circumstance his delight at finding, on a leaf originally left blank near the middle of the book, some writing of Count Magnus himself headed "Liber nigræ peregrinationis." It is true that only a few lines were written, but there was quite enough to show that the landlord had that morning been referring to a belief at least as old as the time of Count Magnus, and probably shared by him. This is the English of what was written:

"If any man desires to obtain a long life, if he would obtain a faithful messenger and see the blood of his enemies, it is necessary that he should first go into the city of Chorazin, and there salute the prince...." Here there was an erasure of one word, not very thoroughly done, so that Mr Wraxall felt pretty sure that he was right in reading it as *aëris* ("of the air"). But there was no more of the text copied, only a line in Latin: "Quære reliqua hujus materiei inter secretiora" (See the rest of this matter among the more private things).

It could not be denied that this threw a rather lurid light upon the tastes and beliefs of the Count; but to Mr. Wraxall, separated from him by nearly three centuries, the thought that he might have added to his general forcefulness alchemy, and to alchemy something like magic, only made him a more picturesque figure; and when, after a rather prolonged contemplation of his picture in the hall, Mr. Wraxall set out on his homeward way, his mind was full of the thought of Count Magnus. He had no eyes for his surroundings, no perception of the evening scents of the woods or the evening light on the lake; and when all of a sudden he pulled up short, he was astonished to find himself already at the gate of the churchyard, and within a few minutes of his dinner. His eyes fell on the mausoleum.

"Ah," he said, "Count Magnus, there you are. I should dearly like to see you."

"Like many solitary men," he writes, "I have a habit of talking to myself aloud; and, unlike some of the Greek and Latin particles, I do not expect an answer. Certainly, and perhaps fortunately in this case, there was neither voice nor any that regarded: only the woman who, I suppose, was cleaning up the church, dropped some metallic object on the floor, whose clang startled me. Count Magnus, I think, sleeps sound enough."

That same evening the landlord of the inn, who had heard Mr. Wraxall say that he wished to see the clerk or deacon (as he would be called in Sweden) of the parish, introduced him to that official in the inn parlour.

A visit to the De la Gardie tomb-house was soon arranged for the next day, and a little general conversation ensued.

Mr. Wraxall, remembering that one function of Scandinavian deacons is to teach candidates for Confirmation, thought he would refresh his own memory on a Biblical point.

"Can you tell me," he said, "anything about Chorazin?"

The deacon seemed startled, but readily reminded him how that village had once been denounced.

"To be sure," said Mr. Wraxall; "it is, I suppose, quite a ruin now?"

"So I expect," replied the deacon. "I have heard some of our old priests say that Antichrist is to be born there; and there are tales—"

"Ah! what tales are those?" Mr. Wraxall put in.

"Tales, I was going to say, which I have forgotten," said the deacon; and soon after that he said good-night.

The landlord was now alone, and at Mr. Wraxall's mercy; and that inquirer was not inclined to spare him.

"Herr Nielsen," he said, "I have found out something about the Black Pilgrimage. You may as well tell me what you know. What did the Count bring back with him?"

Swedes are habitually slow, perhaps, in answering, or perhaps the landlord was an exception. I am not sure; but Mr. Wraxall notes that the landlord spent at least one minute in looking at him before he said anything at all. Then he came close up to his guest, and with a good deal of effort he spoke:

"Mr. Wraxall, I can tell you this one little tale, and no more—not any more. You must not ask anything when I have done. In my grandfather's time—that is, ninety-two years ago—there were two men who said: 'The Count is dead; we do not care for him. We will go to-night and have a free hunt in his wood'—the long wood on the hill that you have seen behind Råbäck. Well, those that heard them say this, they said: 'No, do not go; we are sure you will meet with persons walking who should not be walking. They should be resting, not walking.' These men laughed. There were no forest-men to keep the wood, because no one wished to hunt there. The family were not here at the house. These men could do what they wished.

"Very well, they go to the wood that night. My grandfather was sitting here in this room. It was the summer, and a light night. With the window open, he could see out to the wood, and hear.

"So he sat there, and two or three men with him, and they listened. At first they hear nothing at all; then they hear someone—you know how far away it is—they hear someone scream, just as if the most inside part of his soul was twisted out of him. All of them in the room caught hold of each other, and they sat so for three-quarters of an hour. Then they hear someone else, only about three hundred ells off. They hear him laugh out loud: it was not one of those two men that laughed, and, indeed, they have all of them said that it was not any man at all. After that they hear a great door shut.

"Then, when it was just light with the sun, they all went to the priest. They said to him:

" 'Father, put on your gown and your ruff, and come to bury these men, Anders Bjornsen and Hans Thorbjorn.'

"You understand that they were sure these men were dead. So they went to the wood—my grandfather never forgot this. He said they were all like so many dead men themselves. The priest, too, he was in a white fear. He said when they came to him:

" 'I heard one cry in the night, and I heard one laugh afterwards. If I cannot forget that, I shall not be able to sleep again.'

"So they went to the wood, and they found these men on the edge of the wood. Hans Thorbjorn was standing with his back against a tree, and all the time he was pushing with his hands—pushing something away from him which was not there. So he was not dead. And they led him away, and took him to the house at Nykjoping, and he died before the winter; but he went on pushing with his hands. Also Anders Bjornsen was there; but he was dead. And I tell you this about Anders Bjornsen, that he was once a beautiful man, but now his face was not there, because the flesh of it was sucked away off the bones. You understand that? My grandfather did not forget that. And they laid him on the bier which they brought, and they put a cloth over his head, and the priest walked before; and they began to sing the psalm for the dead as well as they could. So, as they were singing the end of the first verse, one fell down, who was carrying the head of the bier, and the others looked back, and they saw that the cloth had fallen off, and the eyes of Anders Bjornsen were looking up, because there was nothing to close over them. And this they could not bear. Therefore the priest laid the cloth upon him, and sent for a spade, and they buried him in that place."

The next day Mr. Wraxall records that the deacon called for him soon after his breakfast, and took him to the church and mausoleum. He noticed that the key of the latter was hung on a nail just by the pulpit, and it occurred to him that, as the church door seemed to be left unlocked as a rule, it would not be difficult for him to pay a second and more private visit to the monuments if there proved to be more of interest among them than could be digested at first. The building, when he entered it, he found not unimposing. The monuments, mostly large erections of the seventeenth and eighteenth centuries, were dignified if luxuriant, and the epitaphs and heraldry were copious. The central space of the domed room was occupied by three copper sarcophagi, covered with finely-engraved ornament. Two of them had, as is commonly the case in Denmark and Sweden, a large metal crucifix on the lid. The third, that of Count Magnus, as it appeared, had, instead of that, a full-length effigy engraved upon it, and round the edge were several bands of similar ornament representing various scenes. One was a battle, with cannon belching out smoke, and walled towns, and troops of pikemen. Another showed an execution. In a third, among trees, was a man running at full speed, with flying hair and outstretched hands. After him followed a strange form; it would be hard to say whether the artist had intended it for a man, and was unable to give the requisite similitude, or whether it was intentionally made as monstrous as it looked. In view of the skill with which the rest of the drawing was done, Mr. Wraxall felt inclined to adopt the latter idea. The figure was unduly short, and was for the most part muffled in a hooded garment which swept the ground. The only part of the form which projected from that shelter was not shaped like any hand or arm. Mr. Wraxall compares it to the tentacle of a devil-fish, and continues: "On seeing this, I said to myself, 'This, then, which is evidently an allegorical representation of some kind—a fiend pursuing a hunted soul—may be the origin of the story of Count Magnus and his mysterious companion. Let us see how the huntsman is pictured: doubtless it will be a demon blowing his horn.'" But, as it turned out, there was no such sensational figure, only the semblance of a cloaked man on a hillock, who stood leaning on a stick, and watching the hunt with an interest which the engraver had tried to express in his attitude.

Mr. Wraxall noted the finely-worked and massive steel padlocks— three in number—which secured the sarcophagus. One of them, he saw, was detached, and lay on the pavement. And then, unwilling to delay the deacon longer or to waste his own working-time, he made his way onward to the manor-house.

"It is curious," he notes, "how on retracing a familiar path one's thoughts engross one to the absolute exclusion of surrounding objects. To-night, for the second time, I had entirely failed to notice where I was going

(I had planned a private visit to the tomb-house to copy the epitaphs), when I suddenly, as it were, awoke to consciousness, and found myself (as before) turning in at the churchyard gate, and, I believe, singing or chanting some such words as, 'Are you awake, Count Magnus? Are you asleep, Count Magnus?' and then something more which I have failed to recollect. It seemed to me that I must have been behaving in this nonsensical way for some time."

He found the key of the mausoleum where he had expected to find it, and copied the greater part of what he wanted; in fact, he stayed until the light began to fail him.

"I must have been wrong," he writes, "in saying that one of the padlocks of my Count's sarcophagus was unfastened; I see to-night that two are loose. I picked both up, and laid them carefully on the window-ledge, after trying unsuccessfully to close them. The remaining one is still firm, and, though I take it to be a spring lock, I cannot guess how it is opened. Had I succeeded in undoing it, I am almost afraid I should have taken the liberty of opening the sarcophagus. It is strange, the interest I feel in the personality of this, I fear, somewhat ferocious and grim old noble."

The day following was, as it turned out, the last of Mr. Wraxall's stay at Råbäck. He received letters connected with certain investments which made it desirable that he should return to England; his work among the papers was practically done, and travelling was slow. He decided, therefore, to make his farewells, put some finishing touches to his notes, and be off.

These finishing touches and farewells, as it turned out, took more time than he had expected. The hospitable family insisted on his staying to dine with them—they dined at three—and it was verging on half-past six before he was outside the iron gates of Råbäck. He dwelt on every step of his walk by the lake, determined to saturate himself, now that he trod it for the last time, in the sentiment of the place and hour. And when he reached the summit of the churchyard knoll, he lingered for many minutes, gazing at the limitless prospect of woods near and distant, all dark beneath a sky of liquid green. When at last he turned to go, the thought struck him that surely he must bid farewell to Count Magnus as well as the rest of the De la Gardies. The church was but twenty yards away, and he knew where the key of the mausoleum hung. It was not long before he was standing over the great copper coffin, and, as usual, talking to himself aloud. "You may have been a bit of a rascal in your time, Magnus," he was saying, "but for all that I should like to see you, or, rather—"

128

"Just at that instant," he says, "I felt a blow on my foot. Hastily enough I drew it back, and something fell on the pavement with a clash. It was the third, the last of the three padlocks which had fastened the sarcophagus. I stooped to pick it up, and—Heaven is my witness that I am writing only the bare truth—before I had raised myself there was a sound of metal hinges creaking, and I distinctly saw the lid shifting upwards. I may have behaved like a coward, but I could not for my life stay for one moment. I was outside that dreadful building in less time than I can write—almost as quickly as I could have said—the words; and what frightens me yet more, I could not turn the key in the lock. As I sit here in my room noting these facts, I ask myself (it was not twenty minutes ago) whether that noise of creaking metal continued, and I cannot tell whether it did or not. I only know that there was something more than I have written that alarmed me, but whether it was sound or sight I am not able to remember. What is this that I have done?"

Poor Mr. Wraxall! He set out on his journey to England on the next day, as he had planned, and he reached England in safety; and yet, as I gather from his changed hand and inconsequent jottings, a broken man. One of several small notebooks that have come to me with his papers gives, not a key to, but a kind of inkling of, his experiences. Much of his journey was made by canal-boat, and I find not less than six painful attempts to enumerate and describe his fellow-passengers. The entries are of this kind:

"24. Pastor of village in Skåne. Usual black coat and soft black hat.

"25. Commercial traveller from Stockholm going to Trollhättan. Black cloak, brown hat.

"26. Man in long black cloak, broad-leafed hat, very old-fashioned."

This entry is lined out, and a note added: "Perhaps identical with No. 13. Have not yet seen his face." On referring to No. 13, I find that he is a Roman priest in a cassock.

The net result of the reckoning is always the same. Twenty-eight people appear in the enumeration, one being always a man in a long black cloak and broad hat, and the other a "short figure in dark cloak and hood". On the other hand, it is always noted that only twenty-six passengers appear at meals, and that the man in the cloak is perhaps absent, and the short figure is certainly absent.

On reaching England, it appears that Mr. Wraxall landed at Harwich, and that he resolved at once to put himself out of the reach of some person or persons whom he never specifies, but whom he had evidently come to regard as his pursuers. Accordingly he took a vehicle—it was a closed fly—not trusting the railway, and drove across country to the village of Belchamp St. Paul. It was about nine o'clock on a moonlight August night when he neared the place. He was sitting forward, and looking out of the window at the fields and thickets—there was little else to be seen—racing past him. Suddenly he came to a cross-road. At the corner two figures were standing motionless; both were in dark cloaks; the taller one wore a hat, the shorter a hood. He had no time to see their faces, nor did they make any motion that he could discern. Yet the horse shied violently and broke into a gallop, and Mr. Wraxall sank back into his seat in something like desperation. He had seen them before.

Arrived at Belchamp St. Paul, he was fortunate enough to find a decent furnished lodging, and for the next twenty-four hours he lived, comparatively speaking, in peace. His last notes were written on this day. They are too disjointed and ejaculatory to be given here in full, but the substance of them is clear enough. He is expecting a visit from his pursuers—how or when he knows not—and his constant cry is "What has he done?" and "Is there no hope?" Doctors, he knows, would call him mad, policemen would laugh at him. The parson is away. What can he do but lock his door and cry to God?

People still remembered last year at Belchamp St. Paul how a strange gentleman came one evening in August years back; and how the next morning but one he was found dead, and there was an inquest; and the jury that viewed the body fainted, seven of 'em did, and none of 'em wouldn't speak to what they see, and the verdict was visitation of God; and how the people as kep' the 'ouse moved out that same week, and went away from that part. But they do not, I think, know that any glimmer of light has ever been thrown, or could be thrown, on the mystery. It so happened that last year the little house came into my hands as part of a legacy. It had stood empty since 1863, and there seemed no prospect of letting it; so I had it pulled down, and the papers of which I have given you an abstract were found in a forgotten cupboard under the window in the best bedroom.

In a letter to Wilfred Blanch Talman of November 1936, Lovecraft described "The White People" as a close second to being the greatest weird story ever written. In "Supernatural Horror in Literature" he noted that "Mr. Machen's narrative, a triumph of skilful selectiveness and restraint, accumulates enormous power as it flows on in a stream of innocent childish prattle." "The White People" first appeared in *Horlick's Magazine*, January 1904, and was collected in *The House of Souls* (1906).

THE WHITE PEOPLE
by Arthur Machen

Prologue

"Sorcery and sanctity," said Ambrose, "these are the only realities. Each is an ecstasy, a withdrawal from the common life."

Cotgrave listened, interested. He had been brought by a friend to this mouldering house in a northern suburb, through an old garden to the room where Ambrose the recluse dozed and dreamed over his books.

"Yes," he went on, "magic is justified of her children. There are many, I think, who eat dry crusts and drink water, with a joy infinitely sharper than anything within the experience of the 'practical' epicure."

"You are speaking of the saints?"

"Yes, and of the sinners, too. I think you are falling into the very general error of confining the spiritual world to the supremely good; but the supremely wicked, necessarily, have their portion in it. The merely carnal, sensual man can no more be a great sinner than he can be a great saint. Most of us are just indifferent, mixed-up creatures; we muddle through the world without realizing the meaning and the inner sense of things, and, consequently, our wickedness and our goodness are alike second-rate, unimportant."

"And you think the great sinner, then, will be an ascetic, as well as the great saint?"

"Great people of all kinds forsake the imperfect copies and go to the perfect originals. I have no doubt but that many of the very highest among the saints have never done a 'good action' (using the words in their ordinary sense). And, on the other hand, there have been those who have sounded the very depths of sin, who all their lives have never done an 'ill deed.' "

He went out of the room for a moment, and Cotgrave, in high delight, turned to his friend and thanked him for the introduction.

"He's grand," he said. "I never saw that kind of lunatic before."

Ambrose returned with more whisky and helped the two men in a liberal manner. He abused the teetotal sect with ferocity, as he handed the seltzer, and pouring out a glass of water for himself, was about to resume his monologue, when Cotgrave broke in—

"I can't stand it, you know," he said, "your paradoxes are too monstrous. A man may be a great sinner and yet never do anything sinful! Come!"

"You're quite wrong," said Ambrose. "I never make paradoxes; I wish I could. I merely said that a man may have an exquisite taste in Romanée Conti, and yet never have even smelt four ale. That's all, and it's more like a truism than a paradox, isn't it? Your surprise at my remark is due to the fact that you haven't realized what sin is. Oh, yes, there is a sort of connexion between Sin with the capital letter, and actions which are commonly called sinful: with murder, theft, adultery, and so forth. Much the same connexion that there is between the A, B, C and fine literature. But I believe that the misconception—it is all but universal—arises in great measure from our looking at the matter through social spectacles. We think that a man who does evil to *us* and to his neighbours must be very evil. So he is, from a social standpoint; but can't you realize that Evil in its essence is a lonely thing, a passion of the solitary, individual soul? Really, the average murderer, *quâ* murderer, is not by any means a sinner in the true sense of the word. He is simply a wild beast that we have to get rid of to save our own necks from his knife. I should class him rather with tigers than with sinners."

"It seems a little strange."

"I think not. The murderer murders not from positive qualities, but from negative ones; he lacks something which non-murderers possess. Evil, of course, is wholly positive—only it is on the wrong side. You may believe me that sin in its proper sense is very rare; it is probable that there have been far fewer sinners than saints. Yes, your standpoint is all very well for practical, social purposes; we are naturally inclined to think that a person who is very disagreeable to us must be a very great sinner! It is very disagreeable to have one's pocket picked, and we pronounce the thief to be a very great sinner. In truth, he is merely an undeveloped man. He cannot be a saint, of course; but he may be, and often is, an infinitely better creature than thousands who have never broken a single commandment. He is a great nuisance to *us*, I admit, and we very properly lock him up if we catch him; but between his troublesome and unsocial action and evil—Oh, the connexion is of the weakest."

It was getting very late. The man who had brought Cotgrave had probably heard all this before, since he assisted with a bland and judicious smile, but Cotgrave began to think that his "lunatic" was turning into a sage.

"Do you know," he said, "you interest me immensely? You think, then, that we do not understand the real nature of evil?"

"No, I don't think we do. We over-estimate it and we under-estimate it. We take the very numerous infractions of our social 'bye-laws'—the very necessary and very proper regulations which keep the human company together—and we get frightened at the prevalence of 'sin' and 'evil.' But this is really nonsense. Take theft, for example. Have you any *horror* at the thought of Robin Hood, of the Highland caterans of the seventeenth century, of the moss-troopers, of the company promoters of our day?

"Then, on the other hand, we underrate evil. We attach such an enormous importance to the 'sin' of meddling with our pockets (and our wives) that we have quite forgotten the awfulness of real sin."

"And what is sin?" said Cotgrave.

"I think I must reply to your question by another. What would your feelings be, seriously, if your cat or your dog began to talk to you, and to dispute with you in human accents? You would be overwhelmed with horror. I am sure of it. And if the roses in your garden sang a weird song, you would go mad. And suppose the stones in the road began to swell and grow before your eyes, and if the pebble that you noticed at night had shot out stony blossoms in the morning?

"Well, these examples may give you some notion of what sin really is."

"Look here," said the third man, hitherto placid, "you two seem pretty well wound up. But I'm going home. I've missed my tram, and I shall have to walk."

Ambrose and Cotgrave seemed to settle down more profoundly when the other had gone out into the early misty morning and the pale light of the lamps.

"You astonish me," said Cotgrave. "I had never thought of that. If that is really so, one must turn everything upside down. Then the essence of sin really is—"

"In the taking of heaven by storm, it seems to me," said Ambrose. "It appears to me that it is simply an attempt to penetrate into another and higher sphere in a forbidden manner. You can understand why it is so rare. There are few, indeed, who wish to penetrate into other spheres, higher or lower, in ways allowed or forbidden. Men, in the mass, are amply content with life as they find it. Therefore there are few saints, and sinners (in the proper sense) are fewer still, and men of genius, who partake sometimes of each character, are rare also. Yes; on the whole, it is, perhaps, harder to be a great sinner than a great saint."

"There is something profoundly unnatural about sin? Is that what you mean?"

"Exactly. Holiness requires as great, or almost as great, an effort; but holiness works on lines that were natural once; it is an effort to recover the ecstasy that was before the Fall. But sin is an effort to gain the ecstasy and the knowledge that pertain alone to angels and in making this effort man becomes a demon. I told you that the mere murderer is not therefore a sinner; that is true, but the sinner is sometimes a murderer. Gilles de Raiz is an instance. So you see that while the good and the evil are unnatural to man as he now is—to man the social, civilized being—evil is unnatural in a much deeper sense than good. The saint endeavours to recover a gift which he has lost; the sinner tries to obtain something which was never his. In brief, he repeats the Fall."

"But are you a Catholic?" said Cotgrave.

"Yes; I am a member of the persecuted Anglican Church."

"Then, how about those texts which seem to reckon as sin that which you would set down as a mere trivial dereliction?"

"Yes; but in one place the word 'sorcerers' comes in the same sentence, doesn't it? That seems to me to give the key-note. Consider: can you imagine for a moment that a false statement which saves an innocent man's life is a sin? No; very good, then, it is not the mere liar who is excluded by those words; it is, above all, the 'sorcerers' who use the material life, who use the failings incidental to material life as instruments to obtain their infinitely wicked ends. And let me tell you this: our higher senses are so blunted, we are so drenched with materialism, that we should probably fail to recognize real wickedness if we encountered it."

"But shouldn't we experience a certain horror—a terror such as you hinted we would experience if a rose tree sang—in the mere presence of an evil man?"

"We should if we were natural: children and women feel this horror you speak of, even animals experience it. But with most of us convention and civilization and education have blinded and deafened and obscured the natural reason. No, sometimes we may recognize evil by its hatred of the good—one doesn't need much penetration to guess at the influence which dictated, quite unconsciously, the 'Blackwood' review of Keats—but this is purely incidental; and, as a rule, I suspect that the Hierarchs of Tophet pass quite unnoticed, or, perhaps, in certain cases, as good but mistaken men."

"But you used the word 'unconscious' just now, of Keats' reviewers. Is wickedness ever unconscious?"

"Always. It must be so. It is like holiness and genius in this as in other points; it is a certain rapture or ecstasy of the soul; a transcendent effort to surpass the ordinary bounds. So, surpassing these, it surpasses also the understanding, the faculty that takes note of that which comes before it. No, a man may be infinitely and horribly wicked and never suspect it But I tell you, evil in this, its certain and true sense, is rare, and I think it is growing rarer."

"I am trying to get hold of it all," said Cotgrave. "From what you say, I gather that the true evil differs generically from that which we call evil?"

"Quite so. There is, no doubt, an analogy between the two; a resemblance such as enables us to use, quite legitimately, such terms as the 'foot of the mountain' and the 'leg of the table.' And, sometimes, of course, the two speak, as it were, in the same language. The rough miner, or 'puddler,' the untrained, undeveloped 'tiger-man,' heated by a quart or two above his usual measure, comes home and kicks his irritating and injudicious wife to death. He is a murderer. And Gilles de Raiz was a murderer. But you see the gulf that separates the two? The 'word,' if I may so speak, is accidentally the same in each case, but the 'meaning' is utterly different. It is flagrant 'Hobson Jobson' to confuse the two, or rather, it is as if one supposed that Juggernaut and the Argonauts had something to do etymologically with one another. And no doubt the same weak likeness, or analogy, runs between all the 'social' sins and the real spiritual sins, and in some cases, perhaps, the lesser may be 'schoolmasters' to lead one on to the greater—from the shadow to the reality. If you are anything of a Theologian, you will see the importance of all this."

"I am sorry to say," remarked Cotgrave, "that I have devoted very little of my time to theology. Indeed, I have often wondered on what grounds theologians have claimed the title of Science of Sciences for their favourite study; since the 'theological' books I have looked into have always seemed to me to be concerned with feeble and obvious pieties, or with the kings of Israel and Judah. I do not care to hear about those kings."

Ambrose grinned.

"We must try to avoid theological discussion," he said. "I perceive that you would be a bitter disputant. But perhaps the 'dates of the kings' have as much to do with theology as the hobnails of the murderous puddler with evil."

"Then, to return to our main subject, you think that sin is an esoteric, occult thing?"

"Yes. It is the infernal miracle as holiness is the supernal. Now and then it is raised to such a pitch that we entirely fail to suspect its existence; it is like the note of the great pedal pipes of the organ, which is so deep that we cannot hear it. In other cases it may lead to the lunatic asylum, or to still stranger issues. But you must never confuse it with mere social misdoing. Remember how the Apostle, speaking of the 'other side,' distinguishes between 'charitable' actions and charity. And as one may give all one's goods to the poor, and yet lack charity; so, remember, one may avoid every crime and yet be a sinner."

"Your psychology is very strange to me," said Cotgrave, "but I confess I like it, and I suppose that one might fairly deduce from your premises the conclusion that the real sinner might very possibly strike the observer as a harmless personage enough?"

"Certainly; because the true evil has nothing to do with social life or social laws, or if it has, only incidentally and accidentally. It is a lonely passion of the soul—or a passion of the lonely soul—whichever you like. If, by chance, we understand it, and grasp its full significance, then, indeed, it will fill us with horror and with awe. But this emotion is widely distinguished from the fear and the disgust with which we regard the ordinary criminal, since this latter is largely or entirely founded on the regard which we have for our own skins or purses. We hate a murder, because we know that we should hate to be murdered, or to have any one that we like murdered. So, on the 'other side,' we venerate the saints, but we don't 'like' them as well as our friends. Can you persuade yourself that you would have 'enjoyed' St. Paul's company? Do you think that you and I would have 'got on' with Sir Galahad?

"So with the sinners, as with the saints. If you met a very evil man, and recognized his evil; he would, no doubt, fill you with horror and awe; but there is no reason why you should 'dislike' him. On the contrary, it is quite possible that if you could succeed in putting the sin out of your mind you might find the sinner capital company, and in a little while you might have to reason yourself back into horror. Still, how awful it is. If the roses and the lilies suddenly sang on this coming morning; if the furniture began to move in procession, as in De Maupassant's tale!"

"I am glad you have come back to that comparison," said Cotgrave, "because I wanted to ask you what it is that corresponds in humanity to these imaginary feats of inanimate things. In a word—what is sin? You have given me, I know, an abstract definition, but I should like a concrete example."

"I told you it was very rare," said Ambrose, who appeared willing to avoid the giving of a direct answer. "The materialism of the age, which has done a good deal to suppress sanctity, has done perhaps more to suppress evil. We find the earth so very comfortable that we have no inclination either for ascents or descents. It would seem as if the scholar who decided to 'specialize' in Tophet, would be reduced to purely antiquarian researches. No palæontologist could show you a *live* pterodactyl."

"And yet you, I think, have 'specialized,' and I believe that your researches have descended to our modern times."

"You are really interested, I see. Well, I confess, that I have dabbled a little, and if you like I can show you something that bears on the very curious subject we have been discussing."

Ambrose took a candle and went away to a far, dim corner of the room. Cotgrave saw him open a venerable bureau that stood there, and from some secret recess he drew out a parcel, and came back to the window where they had been sitting.

Ambrose undid a wrapping of paper, and produced a green pocket-book.

"You will take care of it?" he said. "Don't leave it lying about. It is one of the choicer pieces in my collection, and I should be very sorry if it were lost."

He fondled the faded binding.

"I knew the girl who wrote this," he said. "When you read it, you will see how it illustrates the talk we have had to-night. There is a sequel, too, but I won't talk of that.

"There was an odd article in one of the reviews some months ago," he began again, with the air of a man who changes the subject. "It was written by a doctor—Dr. Coryn, I think, was the name. He says that a lady, watching her little girl playing at the drawing-room window, suddenly saw the heavy sash give way and fall on the child's fingers. The lady fainted, I think, but at any rate the doctor was summoned, and when he had dressed the child's wounded and maimed fingers he was summoned to the mother. She was groaning with pain, and it was found that three fingers of her hand, corresponding with those that had been injured on the child's hand, were swollen and inflamed, and later, in the doctor's language, purulent sloughing set in."

Ambrose still handled delicately the green volume.

"Well, here it is," he said at last, parting with difficulty, it seemed, from his treasure.

"You will bring it back as soon as you have read it," he said, as they went out into the hall, into the old garden, faint with the odour of white lilies.

There was a broad red band in the east as Cotgrave turned to go, and from the high ground where he stood he saw that awful spectacle of London in a dream.

The Green Book

The morocco binding of the book was faded, and the colour had grown faint, but there were no stains nor bruises nor marks of usage. The book looked as if it had been bought "on a visit to London" some seventy or eighty years ago, and had somehow been forgotten and suffered to lie away out of sight. There was an old, delicate, lingering odour about it, such an odour as sometimes haunts an ancient piece of furniture for a century or more. The end-papers, inside the binding, were oddly decorated with coloured patterns and faded gold. It looked small, but the paper was fine, and there were many leaves, closely covered with minute, painfully formed characters.

I found this book (the manuscript began) in a drawer in the old bureau that stands on the landing. It was a very rainy day and I could not go out, so in the afternoon I got a candle and rummaged in the bureau. Nearly all the drawers were full of old dresses, but one of the small ones looked empty, and I found this book hidden right at the back. I wanted a book like this, so I took it to write in. It is full of secrets. I have a great many other books of secrets I have written, hidden in a safe place, and I am going to write here many of the old secrets and some new ones; but there are some I shall not put down at all. I must not write down the real names of the days and months which I found out a year ago, nor the way to make the Aklo letters, or the Chian language, or the great beautiful Circles, nor the Mao Games, nor the chief songs. I may write something about all these things but not the way to do them, for peculiar reasons. And I must not say who the Nymphs are, or the Dôls, or Jeelo, or what voolas mean. All these are most secret secrets, and I am glad when I remember what they are, and how many wonderful languages I know, but there are some things that I call the secrets of the secrets of the secrets that I dare not think of unless I am quite alone, and then I shut my eyes, and put my hands over them and whisper the word, and the Alala comes. I only do this at night in my room or in certain woods that I know, but I must not describe them, as they are secret woods. Then there are the Ceremonies, which are all of them important, but some are more delightful than others—there are the White Ceremonies, and the Green Ceremonies, and the Scarlet Ceremonies. The Scarlet Ceremonies are the best, but there is only one place where they can be performed properly, though there is a very nice imitation which I have done in other places. Besides these, I have the dances, and the Comedy, and I have done the Comedy sometimes when the others were looking, and they didn't understand anything about it. I was very little when I first knew about these things.

When I was very small, and mother was alive, I can remember remembering things before that, only it has all got confused. But I remember when I was five or six I heard them talking about me when they thought I was not noticing. They were saying how queer I was a year or two before, and how nurse had called my mother to come and listen to me talking all to myself, and I was saying words that nobody could understand. I was speaking the Xu language, but I only remember a very few of the words, as it was about the little white faces that used to look at me when I was lying in my cradle. They used to talk to me, and I learnt their language and talked to them in it about some great white place where they lived, where the trees and the grass were all white, and there were white hills as high up as the moon, and a cold wind. I have often dreamed of it afterwards, but the faces went away when I was very little. But a wonderful thing happened when I was about five. My nurse was carrying me on her shoulder; there was a field of yellow corn, and we went through it, it was very hot. Then we came to a path through a wood, and a tall man came after

139

us, and went with us till we came to a place where there was a deep pool, and it was very dark and shady. Nurse put me down on the soft moss under a tree, and she said: "She can't get to the pond now." So they left me there, and I sat quite still and watched, and out of the water and out of the wood came two wonderful white people, and they began to play and dance and sing. They were a kind of creamy white like the old ivory figure in the drawing-room; one was a beautiful lady with kind dark eyes, and a grave face, and long black hair, and she smiled such a strange sad smile at the other, who laughed and came to her. They played together, and danced round and round the pool, and they sang a song till I fell asleep. Nurse woke me up when she came back, and she was looking something like the lady had looked, so I told her all about it, and asked her why she looked like that. At first she cried, and then she looked very frightened, and turned quite pale. She put me down on the grass and stared at me, and I could see she was shaking all over. Then she said I had been dreaming, but I knew I hadn't. Then she made me promise not to say a word about it to anybody, and if I did I should be thrown into the black pit. I was not frightened at all, though nurse was, and I never forgot about it, because when I shut my eyes and it was quite quiet, and I was all alone, I could see them again, very faint and far away, but very splendid; and little bits of the song they sang came into my head, but I couldn't sing it.

I was thirteen, nearly fourteen, when I had a very singular adventure, so strange that the day on which it happened is always called the White Day. My mother had been dead for more than a year, and in the morning I had lessons, but they let me go out for walks in the afternoon. And this afternoon I walked a new way, and a little brook led me into a new country, but I tore my frock getting through some of the difficult places, as the way was through many bushes, and beneath the low branches of trees, and up thorny thickets on the hills, and by dark woods full of creeping thorns. And it was a long, long way. It seemed as if I was going on for ever and ever, and I had to creep by a place like a tunnel where a brook must have been, but all the water had dried up, and the floor was rocky, and the bushes had grown overhead till they met, so that it was quite dark. And I went on and on through that dark place; it was a long, long way. And I came to a hill that I never saw before. I was in a dismal thicket full of black twisted boughs that tore me as I went through them, and I cried out because I was smarting all over, and then I found that I was climbing, and I went up and up a long way, till at last the thicket stopped and I came out crying just under the top of a big bare place, where there were ugly grey stones lying all about on the grass, and here and there a little twisted, stunted tree came out from under a stone, like a snake. And I went up, right to the top, a long way. I never saw such big ugly stones before; they came out of the earth some of them, and some looked as if they had been rolled to where they were, and they went on and on as far as I could see, a long, long way. I looked out from them and saw the country, but it was strange. It was winter time, and there were black terrible woods hanging from the hills all round; it was like seeing a large room hung with black curtains, and the shape of the trees seemed quite different from any I had ever seen before. I was afraid. Then beyond the woods there were other hills round in a great ring, but I had never seen any of them; it all looked black, and everything had a voor over it. It was all so still and silent, and the sky was heavy and grey and sad, like a wicked voorish dome in Deep Dendo. I went on into the dreadful rocks. There were hundreds and hundreds of them. Some were like horrid-grinning men; I could see their faces as if they would jump at me out of the stone, and catch hold of me, and drag me with them back into the rock, so that I should always be there. And there were other rocks that were like animals, creeping, horrible animals, putting out their tongues, and others were like words that I could not say, and others like dead people lying on the grass. I went on among them, though they frightened me, and my heart was full of wicked songs that they put into it; and I wanted to make faces and twist myself about in the way they did, and I went on and on a long way till at last I liked the rocks, and they didn't frighten me any more. I sang the songs I thought of; songs full of words that must not be spoken or written down. Then I made faces like the faces on the rocks, and I twisted myself about like the twisted ones, and I lay down flat on the ground like the dead ones, and I went up to one that was grinning, and put my arms round him and hugged him. And so I went on and on through the rocks till I came to a round mound in the middle of them. It was higher than a mound, it was nearly as high as our house, and it was like a great basin turned upside down, all smooth and round and green, with one stone, like a post, sticking up at the top. I climbed up the sides, but they were so steep I had to stop or I should have rolled all the way down again, and I should have knocked against the stones at the bottom, and perhaps been killed. But I wanted to get up to the very top of the big round mound, so I lay down flat on my face, and took hold of the grass with my hands and drew myself up, bit by bit, till I was at the top. Then I sat down on the stone in the middle, and looked all round about. I felt I had come such a long, long way, just as if I were a hundred miles from home, or in some other country, or in one of the strange places I had read about in the "Tales of the Genie" and the "Arabian Nights," or as if I had gone across the sea, far away, for years and I had found another world that nobody had ever seen or heard of before, or as if I had somehow flown through the sky and fallen on one of the stars I had read about where everything is dead and cold and grey, and there is no air, and the wind doesn't blow. I sat on the stone and looked all round and down and round about me. It was just as if I was sitting on a tower in the middle of a great empty town, because I could see nothing all around but the grey rocks on the ground. I couldn't make out their shapes any more, but I could see them on and on for a long way, and I looked at them, and they seemed as if they had been arranged into patterns, and shapes, and figures. I knew they couldn't be because I had seen a lot of them coming right out of the earth, joined to the deep rocks below, so I looked again, but still I saw nothing but circles, and small circles inside big ones, and pyramids, and domes, and spires, and they seemed all to go round and round the place where I was sitting, and the more I looked, the more I saw great big rings of rocks, getting bigger and bigger, and I stared so long that it felt as if they were all moving and turning, like a great wheel, and I was turning, too, in the middle. I got quite dizzy and queer in the head, and everything began to be hazy and not clear, and I saw little sparks of blue light, and the stones looked as if they were springing and dancing and twisting as they went round and round and round. I was frightened again, and I cried out loud, and jumped up from the stone I was sitting on, and fell down. When I got up I was so glad they all looked still, and I sat down on the top and slid down the mound, and went on again. I danced as I went in the peculiar way the rocks had danced when I got giddy, and I was so glad I could do it quite well, and I danced and danced along, and sang extraordinary songs that came into my head. At last I came to the edge of that great flat hill, and there were no more rocks, and the way went again through a dark thicket in a hollow. It was just as bad as the other one I went through climbing up, but I didn't mind this one, because I was so glad I had seen those singular dances and could imitate them. I went down, creeping through the bushes, and a tall nettle stung me on my leg, and made me burn, but I didn't mind it, and I tingled with the boughs and the thorns, but I only laughed and sang. Then I got out of the thicket into a close valley, a little secret place like a dark passage that nobody ever knows of, because it was so narrow and deep and the woods were so thick round it. There is a steep bank with trees hanging over it, and there the ferns keep green all through the winter, when they are dead and brown upon the hill, and the ferns there have a sweet, rich smell like what oozes out of fir trees. There was a little stream of water running down this valley, so small that I could easily step across it. I drank the water with my hand, and it tasted like bright, yellow wine, and it sparkled and bubbled as it ran down over beautiful red and yellow and green stones, so that it seemed alive and all colours at once. I drank it, and I drank more with my hand, but I couldn't drink enough, so I lay down and bent my head and sucked the water up with my lips. It tasted much better, drinking it that way, and a ripple would come up to my mouth and give me a kiss, and I laughed, and drank again, and pretended there was a nymph, like the one in the old picture at home, who lived in the water and was kissing me. So I bent low down to the water, and put my lips softly to it, and whispered to the nymph that I would come again. I felt sure it could not be common water, I was so glad when I got up and went on; and I danced again and went up and up the valley, under hanging hills. And when I came to the top, the ground rose up in front of me, tall and steep as a wall, and there was nothing but the green wall and the sky. I thought of "for ever and for ever, world without end, Amen"; and I thought I must have really found the end of the world, because it was like the end of everything, as if there could be nothing at all beyond, except the kingdom of Voor, where the light goes when it is put out, and the water goes when the sun takes it away. I began to think of all the long, long way I had journeyed, how I had found a brook and followed it, and followed it on, and gone through bushes and thorny thickets, and dark woods full of creeping thorns. Then I had crept up a tunnel under trees, and climbed a thicket, and seen all the grey rocks, and sat in the middle of them when they turned round, and then I had gone on through the grey rocks and come down the hill through the stinging thicket and up the dark valley, all a long, long way. I wondered how I should get home again, if I could ever find the way, and if my home was there any more, or if it were turned and everybody in it into grey rocks, as in the "Arabian Nights." So I sat down on the grass and thought what I should do next. I was tired, and my feet were hot with walking, and as I looked about I saw there was a wonderful well just under the high, steep wall of grass. All the ground round it was covered with bright, green, dripping moss; there was every kind of moss there, moss like beautiful little ferns, and like palms and fir trees, and it was all green as jewellery, and drops of water hung on it like diamonds. And in the middle was the great well, deep and shining and beautiful, so clear that it looked as if I could touch the red sand at the bottom, but it was far below. I stood by it and looked in, as if I were looking in a glass. At the bottom of the well, in the middle of it, the red grains of sand were moving and stirring all the time, and I saw how the water bubbled up, but at the top it was quite smooth, and full and brimming. It was a great well, large like a bath, and with the shining, glittering green moss about it, it looked like a great white jewel, with green jewels all round. My feet were so hot and tired that I took off my boots and stockings, and let my feet down into the water, and the water was soft and cold, and when I got up I wasn't tired any more, and I felt I must go on, farther and farther, and see what was on the other side of the wall. I climbed up it very slowly, going sideways all the time, and when I got to the top and looked over, I was in the queerest country I had seen, stranger even than the hill of the grey rocks. It looked as if earth-children had been playing there with their spades, as it was all hills and hollows, and castles and walls made of earth and covered with grass. There were two mounds like big beehives, round and great and solemn, and then hollow basins, and then a steep mounting wall like the ones I saw once by the seaside where the big guns and the soldiers were. I nearly fell into one of the round hollows, it went away from under my feet so suddenly, and I ran fast down the side and stood at the bottom and looked up. It was strange and solemn to look up. There was nothing but the grey, heavy sky and the sides of the hollow; everything else had gone away, and the hollow was the whole world, and I thought that at night it must be full of ghosts and moving shadows and pale things when the moon shone down to the bottom at the dead of the night, and the wind wailed up above. It was so strange and solemn and lonely, like a hollow temple of dead heathen gods. It reminded me of a tale my nurse had told me when I was quite little; it was the same nurse that took me into the wood where I saw the beautiful white people. And I remembered how nurse had told me the story one winter night, when the wind was beating the trees against the wall, and crying and moaning in the nursery chimney. She said there was, somewhere or other, a hollow pit, just like the one I was standing in, everybody was afraid to go into it or near it, it was such a bad place. But once upon a time there was a poor girl who said she would go into the hollow pit, and everybody tried to stop her, but she would go. And she went down into the pit and came back laughing, and said there was nothing there at all, except green grass and red stones, and white stones and yellow flowers. And soon after people saw she had most beautiful emerald earrings, and they asked how she got them, as she and her mother were quite poor. But she laughed, and said her earrings were not made of emeralds at all, but only of green grass. Then, one day, she wore on her breast the reddest ruby that any one had ever seen, and it was as big as a hen's egg, and glowed and sparkled like a hot burning coal of fire. And they asked how she got it, as she and her mother were quite poor. But she laughed, and said it was not a ruby at all, but only a red stone. Then one day she wore round her neck the loveliest necklace that any one had ever seen, much finer than the queen's finest, and it was made of great bright diamonds, hundreds of them, and they shone like all the stars on a night in June. So they asked her how she got it, as she and her mother were quite poor. But she laughed, and said they were not diamonds at all, but only white stones. And one day she went to the Court, and she wore on her head a crown of pure angel-gold, so nurse said, and it shone like the sun, and it was much more splendid than the crown the king was wearing himself, and in her ears she wore the emeralds, and the big ruby was the brooch on her breast, and the great diamond necklace was sparkling on her neck. And the king and queen thought she was some great princess from a long way off, and got down from their thrones and went to meet her, but somebody told the king and queen who she was, and that she was quite poor. So the king asked why she wore a gold crown, and how she got it, as she and her mother were so poor. And she laughed, and said it wasn't a gold crown at all, but only some yellow flowers she had put in her hair. And the king thought it was very strange, and said she should stay at the Court, and they would see what would happen next. And she was so lovely that everybody said that her eyes were greener than the emeralds, that her lips were redder than the ruby, that her skin was whiter than the diamonds, and that her hair was brighter than the golden crown. So the king's son said he would marry her, and the king said he might. And the bishop married them, and there was a great supper, and afterwards the king's son went to his wife's room. But just when he had his hand on the door, he saw a tall, black man, with a dreadful face, standing in front of the door, and a voice said—

Venture not upon your life,
This is mine own wedded wife.

Then the king's son fell down on the ground in a fit. And they came and tried to get into the room, but they couldn't, and they hacked at the door with hatchets, but the wood had turned hard as iron, and at last everybody ran away, they were so frightened at the screaming and laughing and shrieking and crying that came out of the room. But next day they went

145

in, and found there was nothing in the room but thick black smoke, because the black man had come and taken her away. And on the bed there were two knots of faded grass and a red stone, and some white stones, and some faded yellow flowers. I remembered this tale of nurse's while I was standing at the bottom of the deep hollow; it was so strange and solitary there, and I felt afraid. I could not see any stones or flowers, but I was afraid of bringing them away without knowing, and I thought I would do a charm that came into my head to keep the black man away. So I stood right in the very middle of the hollow, and I made sure that I had none of those things on me, and then I walked round the place, and touched my eyes, and my lips, and my hair in a peculiar manner, and whispered some queer words that nurse taught me to keep bad things away. Then I felt safe and climbed up out of the hollow, and went on through all those mounds and hollows and walls, till I came to the end, which was high above all the rest, and I could see that all the different shapes of the earth were arranged in patterns, something like the grey rocks, only the pattern was different. It was getting late, and the air was indistinct, but it looked from where I was standing something like two great figures of people lying on the grass. And I went on, and at last I found a certain wood, which is too secret to be described, and nobody knows of the passage into it, which I found out in a very curious manner, by seeing some little animal run into the wood through it. So I went after the animal by a very narrow dark way, under thorns and bushes, and it was almost dark when I came to a kind of open place in the middle. And there I saw the most wonderful sight I have ever seen, but it was only for a minute, as I ran away directly, and crept out of the wood by the passage I had come by, and ran and ran as fast as ever I could, because I was afraid, what I had seen was so wonderful and so strange and beautiful. But I wanted to get home and think of it, and I did not know what might not happen if I stayed by the wood. I was hot all over and trembling, and my heart was beating, and strange cries that I could not help came from me as I ran from the wood. I was glad that a great white moon came up from over a round hill and showed me the way, so I went back through the mounds and hollows and down the close valley, and up through the thicket over the place of the grey rocks, and so at last I got home again. My father was busy in his study, and the servants had not told about my not coming home, though they were frightened, and wondered what they ought to do, so I told them I had lost my way, but I did not let them find out the real way I had been. I went to bed and lay awake all through the night, thinking of what I had seen. When I came out of the narrow way, and it looked all shining, though the air was dark, it seemed so certain, and all the way home I was quite sure that I had seen it, and I wanted to be alone in my room, and be glad over it all to myself, and shut my eyes and pretend it was there, and do all the things I would have done if I had not been so afraid. But when I shut my eyes the sight would not come, and I began to think about my adventures all over again, and I remembered how dusky and queer it was at the end, and I was afraid it must be all a mistake, because it seemed impossible it could happen. It seemed like one of nurse's tales, which I didn't really believe in, though I was frightened at the bottom of the hollow; and the stories she told me when I was little came back into my head, and I wondered whether it was really there what I thought I had seen, or whether any of her tales could have happened a long time ago. It was so queer; I lay awake there in my room at the back of the house, and the moon was shining on the other side towards the river, so the bright light did not fall upon the wall. And the house was quite still. I had heard my father come upstairs, and just after the clock struck twelve, and after the house was still and empty, as if there was nobody alive in it. And though it was all dark and indistinct in my room, a pale glimmering kind of light shone in through the white blind, and once I got up and looked out, and there was a great black shadow of the house covering the garden, looking like a prison where men are hanged; and then beyond it was all white; and the wood shone white with black gulfs between the trees. It was still and clear, and there were no clouds on the sky. I wanted to think of what I had seen but I couldn't, and I began to think of all the tales that nurse had told me so long ago that I thought I had forgotten, but they all came back, and mixed up with the thickets and the grey rocks and the hollows in the earth and the secret wood, till I hardly knew what was new and what was old, or whether it was not all dreaming. And then I remembered that hot summer afternoon, so long ago, when nurse left me by myself in the shade, and the white people came out of the water and out of the wood, and played, and danced, and sang, and I began to fancy that nurse told me about something like it before I saw them, only I couldn't recollect exactly what she told me. Then I wondered whether she had been the white lady, as I remembered she was just as white and beautiful, and had the same dark eyes and black hair; and sometimes she smiled and looked like the lady had looked, when she was telling me some of her stories, beginning with "Once on a time," or "In the time of the fairies." But I thought she couldn't be the lady, as she seemed to have gone a different way into the wood, and I didn't think the man who came after us could be the other, or I couldn't have seen that wonderful secret in the secret wood. I thought of the moon: but it was afterwards when I was in the middle of the wild land, where the earth was made into the shape of great figures, and it was all walls, and mysterious hollows, and smooth round mounds, that I saw the great white moon come up over a round hill. I was wondering about all these things, till at last I got quite frightened, because I was afraid something had happened to me, and I remembered nurse's tale of the poor girl who went into the hollow pit, and was carried away at last by the black man. I knew I had gone into a hollow pit too, and perhaps it was the same, and I had done something dreadful. So I did the charm over again, and touched my eyes and my lips and my hair in a peculiar manner, and said the old words from the fairy language, so that I might be sure I had not been carried away. I tried again to see the secret wood, and to creep up the passage and see what I had seen there, but somehow I couldn't, and I kept on thinking of nurse's stories. There was one I remembered about a young man who once upon a time went hunting, and all the day he and his hounds hunted everywhere, and they crossed the rivers and went into all the woods, and went round the marshes, but they couldn't find anything at all, and they hunted all day till the sun sank down and began to set behind the mountain. And the young man was angry because he couldn't find anything, and he was going to turn back, when just as the sun touched the mountain, he saw come out of a brake in front of him a beautiful white stag. And he cheered to his hounds, but they whined and would not follow, and he cheered to his horse, but it shivered and stood stock still, and the young man jumped off the horse and left the hounds and began to follow the white stag all alone. And soon it was quite dark, and the sky was black, without a single star shining in it, and the stag went away into the darkness. And though the man had brought his gun with him he never shot at the stag, because he wanted to catch it, and he was afraid he would lose it in the night. But he never lost it once, though the sky was so black and the air was so dark, and the stag went on and on till the young man didn't know a bit where he was. And they went through enormous woods where the air was full of whispers and a pale, dead light came out from the rotten trunks that were lying on the ground, and just as the man thought he had lost the stag, he would see it all white and shining in front of him, and he would run fast to catch it, but the stag always ran faster, so he did not catch it. And they went through the enormous woods, and they swam across rivers, and they waded through black marshes where the ground bubbled, and the air was full of will-o'-the-wisps, and the stag fled away down into rocky narrow valleys, where the air was like the smell of a vault, and the man went after it. And they went over the great mountains and the man heard the wind come down from the sky, and the stag went on and the man went after. At last the sun rose and the young man found he was in a country that he had never seen before; it was a beautiful valley with a bright stream running through it, and a great, big round hill in the middle. And the stag went down the valley, towards the hill, and it seemed to be getting tired and went slower and slower, and though the man was tired, too, he began to run faster, and he was sure he would catch the stag at last. But just as they got to the bottom of the hill, and the man stretched out his hand to catch the stag, it vanished into the earth, and the man began to cry; he was so sorry that he had lost it after all his long hunting. But as he was crying he saw there was a door in the hill, just in front of him, and he went in, and it was quite dark, but he went on, as he thought he would find the white stag. And all of a sudden it got light, and there was the sky, and the sun shining, and birds singing in the trees, and there was a beautiful fountain. And by the fountain a lovely lady was sitting, who was the queen of the fairies, and she told the man that she had changed herself into a stag to bring him there because she loved him so much. Then she brought out a great gold cup, covered with jewels, from her fairy palace, and she offered him wine in the cup to drink. And he drank, and the more he drank the more he longed to drink, because the wine was enchanted. So he kissed the lovely lady, and she became his wife, and he stayed all that day and all that night in the hill where she lived, and when he woke he found he was lying on the ground, close to where he had seen the stag first, and his horse was there and his hounds were there waiting, and he looked up, and the sun sank behind the mountain. And he went home and lived a long time, but he would never kiss any other lady because he had kissed the queen of the fairies, and he would never drink common wine any more, because he had drunk enchanted wine. And sometimes nurse told me tales that she had heard from her great-grandmother, who was very old, and lived in a cottage on the mountain all alone, and most of these tales were about a hill where people used to meet at night long ago, and they used to play all sorts of strange games and do queer things that nurse told me of, but I couldn't understand, and now, she said, everybody but her great-grandmother had forgotten all about it, and nobody knew where the hill was, not even her great-grandmother. But she told me one very strange story about the hill, and I trembled when I remembered it. She said that people always went there in summer, when it was very hot, and they had to dance a good deal. It would be all dark at first, and there were trees there, which made it much darker, and people would come, one by one, from all directions, by a secret path which nobody else knew, and two persons would keep the gate, and every one as they came up had to give a very curious sign, which nurse showed me as well as she could, but she said she couldn't show me properly. And all kinds of people would come; there would be gentle folks and village folks, and some old people and boys and girls, and quite small children, who sat and watched. And it would all be dark as they came in, except in one corner where some one was burning something that smelt strong and sweet, and made them laugh, and there one would see a glaring of coals, and the smoke mounting up red. So they would all come in, and when the last had come there was no door any more, so that no one else could get in, even if they knew there was anything beyond. And once a gentleman who was a stranger and had ridden a long way, lost his path at night, and his horse took him into the very middle of the wild country, where everything was upside down, and there were dreadful marshes and great stones everywhere, and holes underfoot, and the trees looked like gibbet-posts, because they had great black arms that stretched out across the way. And this strange gentleman was very frightened, and his horse began to shiver all over, and at last it stopped and wouldn't go any farther, and the gentleman got down and tried to lead the horse, but it wouldn't move, and it was all covered with a sweat, like death. So the gentleman went on all alone, going farther and farther into the wild country, till at last he came to a dark place, where he heard shouting and singing and crying, like nothing he had ever heard before. It all sounded quite close to him, but he couldn't get in, and so he began to call, and while he was calling, something came behind him, and in a minute his mouth and arms and legs were all bound up, and he fell into a swoon. And when he came to himself, he was lying by the roadside, just where he had first lost his way, under a blasted oak with a black trunk, and his horse was tied beside him. So he rode on to the town and told the people there what had happened, and some of them were amazed; but others knew. So when once everybody had come, there was no door at all for anybody else to pass in by. And when they were all inside, round in a ring, touching each other, some one began to sing in the darkness, and some one else would make a noise like thunder with a thing they had on purpose, and on still nights people would hear the thundering noise far, far away beyond the wild land, and some of them, who thought they knew what it was, used to make a sign on their breasts when they woke up in their beds at dead of night and heard that terrible deep noise, like thunder on the mountains. And the noise and the singing would go on and on for a long time, and the people who were in a ring swayed a little to and fro; and the song was in an old, old language that nobody knows now, and the tune was queer. Nurse said her great-grandmother had known some one who remembered a little of it, when she was quite a little girl, and nurse tried to sing some of it to me, and it was so strange a tune that I turned all cold and my flesh crept as if I had put my hand on something dead. Sometimes it was a man that sang and sometimes it was a woman, and sometimes the one who sang it did it so well that two or three of the people who were there fell to the ground shrieking and tearing with their hands. The singing went on, and the people in the ring kept swaying to and fro for a long time, and at last the moon would rise over a place they called the Tole Deol, and came up and showed them swinging and swaying from side to side, with the sweet thick smoke curling up from the burning coals, and floating in circles all around them. Then they had their supper. A boy and a girl brought it to them; the boy carried a great cup of wine, and the girl carried a cake of bread, and they passed the bread and the wine round and round, but they tasted quite different from common bread and common wine, and changed everybody that tasted them. Then they all rose up and danced, and secret things were brought out of some hiding place, and they played extraordinary games, and danced round and round and round in the moonlight, and sometimes people would suddenly disappear and never be heard of afterwards, and nobody knew what had happened to them. And they drank more of that curious wine, and they made images and worshipped them, and nurse showed me how the images were made one day when we were out for a walk, and we passed by a place where there was a lot of wet clay. So nurse asked me if I would like to know what those things were like that they made on the hill, and I said yes. Then she asked me if I would promise never to tell a living soul a word about it, and if I did I was to be thrown into the black pit with the dead people, and I said I wouldn't tell anybody, and she said the same thing again and again, and I promised. So she took my wooden spade and dug a big lump of clay and put it in my tin bucket, and told me to say if any one met us that I was going to make pies when I went home. Then we went on a little way till we came to a little brake growing right down into the road, and nurse stopped, and looked up the road and down it, and then peeped through the hedge into the field on the other side, and then she said, "Quick!" and we ran into the brake, and crept in and out among the bushes till we had gone a good way from the road. Then we sat down under a bush, and I wanted so much to know what nurse was going to make with the clay, but before she would begin she made me promise again not to say a word about it, and she went again and peeped through the bushes on every side, though the lane was so small and deep that hardly anybody ever went there. So we sat down, and nurse took the clay out of the bucket, and began to knead it with her hands, and do queer things with it, and turn it about. And she hid it under a big dock-leaf for a minute or two and then she brought it out again, and then she stood up and sat down, and walked round the clay in a peculiar manner, and all the time she was softly singing a sort of rhyme, and her face got very red. Then she sat down again, and took the clay in her hands and began to shape it into a doll, but not like the dolls I have at home, and she made the queerest doll I had ever seen, all out of the wet clay, and hid it under a bush to get dry and hard, and all the time she was making it she was singing these rhymes to herself, and her face got redder and redder. So we left the doll there, hidden away in the bushes where nobody would ever find it. And a few days later we went the same walk, and when we came to that narrow, dark part of the lane where the brake runs down to the bank, nurse made me promise all over again, and she looked about, just as she had done before, and we crept into the bushes till we got to the green place where the little clay man was hidden. I remember it all so well, though I was only eight, and it is eight years ago now as I am writing it down, but the sky was a deep violet blue, and in the middle of the brake where we were sitting there was a great elder tree covered with blossoms, and on the other side there was a clump of meadowsweet, and when I think of that day the smell of the meadowsweet and elder blossom seems to fill the room, and if I shut my eyes I can see the glaring blue sky, with little clouds very white floating across it, and nurse who went away long ago sitting opposite me and looking like the beautiful white lady in the wood. So we sat down and nurse took out the clay doll from the secret place where she had hidden it, and she said we must "pay our respects," and she would show me what to do, and I must watch her all the time. So she did all sorts of queer things with the little clay man, and I noticed she was all streaming with perspiration, though we had walked so slowly, and then she told me to "pay my respects," and I did everything she did because I liked her, and it was such an odd game. And she said that if one loved very much, the clay man was very good, if one did certain things with it, and if one hated very much, it was just as good, only one had to do different things, and we played with it a long time, and pretended all sorts of things. Nurse said her great-grandmother had told her all about these images, but what we did was no harm at all, only a game. But she told me a story about these images that frightened me very much, and that was what I remembered that night when I was lying awake in my room in the pale, empty darkness, thinking of what I had seen and the secret wood. Nurse said there was once a young lady of the high gentry, who lived in a great castle. And she was so beautiful that all the gentlemen wanted to marry her, because she was the loveliest lady that anybody had ever seen, and she was kind to everybody, and everybody thought she was very good. But though she was polite to all the gentlemen who wished to marry her, she put them off, and said she couldn't make up her mind, and she wasn't sure she wanted to marry anybody at all. And her father, who was a very great lord, was angry, though he was so fond of her, and he asked her why she wouldn't choose a bachelor out of all the handsome young men who came to the castle. But she only said she didn't love any of them very much, and she must wait, and if they pestered her, she said she would go and be a nun in a nunnery. So all the gentlemen said they would go away and wait for a year and a day, and when a year and a day were gone, they would come back again and ask her to say which one she would marry. So the day was appointed and they all went away; and the lady had promised that in a year and a day it would be her wedding day with one of them. But the truth was, that she was the queen of the people who danced on the hill on summer nights, and on the proper nights she would lock the door of her room, and she and her maid would steal out of the castle by a secret passage that only they knew of, and go away up to the hill in the wild land. And she knew more of the secret things than any one else, and more than any one knew before or after, because she would not tell anybody the most secret secrets. She knew how to do all the awful things, how to destroy young men, and how to put a curse on people, and other things that I could not understand. And her real name was the Lady Avelin, but the dancing people called her Cassap, which meant somebody very wise, in the old language. And she was whiter than any of them and taller, and her eyes shone in the dark like burning rubies; and she could sing songs that none of the others could sing, and when she sang they all fell down on their faces and worshipped her. And she could do what they called shib-show, which was a very wonderful enchantment. She would tell the great lord, her father, that she wanted to go into the woods to gather flowers, so he let her go, and she and her maid went into the woods where nobody came, and the maid would keep watch.

Then the lady would lie down under the trees and begin to sing a particular song, and she stretched out her arms, and from every part of the wood great serpents would come, hissing and gliding in and out among the trees, and shooting out their forked tongues as they crawled up to the lady. And they all came to her, and twisted round her, round her body, and her arms, and her neck, till she was covered with writhing serpents, and there was only her head to be seen. And she whispered to them, and she sang to them, and they writhed round and round, faster and faster, till she told them to go. And they all went away directly, back to their holes, and on the lady's breast there would be a most curious, beautiful stone, shaped something like an egg, and coloured dark blue and yellow, and red, and green, marked like a serpent's scales. It was called a glame stone, and with it one could do all sorts of wonderful things, and nurse said her great-grandmother had seen a glame stone with her own eyes, and it was for all the world shiny and scaly like a snake. And the lady could do a lot of other things as well, but she was quite fixed that she would not be married. And there were a great many gentlemen who wanted to marry her, but there were five of them who were chief, and their names were Sir Simon, Sir John, Sir Oliver, Sir Richard, and Sir Rowland. All the others believed she spoke the truth, and that she would choose one of them to be her man when a year and a day was done; it was only Sir Simon, who was very crafty, who thought she was deceiving them all, and he vowed he would watch and try if he could find out anything. And though he was very wise he was very young, and he had a smooth, soft face like a girl's, and he pretended, as the rest did, that he would not come to the castle for a year and a day, and he said he was going away beyond the sea to foreign parts. But he really only went a very little way, and came back dressed like a servant girl, and so he got a place in the castle to wash the dishes. And he waited and watched, and he listened and said nothing, and he hid in dark places, and woke up at night and looked out, and he heard things and he saw things that he thought were very strange. And he was so sly that he told the girl that waited on the lady that he was really a young man, and that he had dressed up as a girl because he loved her so very much and wanted to be in the same house with her, and the girl was so pleased that she told him many things, and he was more than ever certain that the Lady Avelin was deceiving him and the others. And he was so clever, and told the servant so many lies, that one night he managed to hide in the Lady Avelin's room behind the curtains. And he stayed quite still and never moved, and at last the lady came. And she bent down under the bed, and raised up a stone, and there was a hollow place underneath, and out of it she took a waxen image, just like the clay one that I and nurse had made in the brake. And all the time her eyes were burning like rubies. And she took the little wax doll up in her arms and held it to her breast, and she whispered and she murmured, and she took it up and she laid it down again, and she held it high, and she held it low, and she laid it down again. And she said, "Happy is he that begat the bishop, that ordered the clerk, that married the man, that had the wife, that fashioned the hive, that harboured the bee, that gathered the wax that my own true love was made of." And she brought out of an aumbry a great golden bowl, and she brought out of a closet a great jar of wine, and she poured some of the wine into the bowl, and she laid her mannikin very gently in the wine, and washed it in the wine all over. Then she went to a cupboard and took a small round cake and laid it on the image's mouth, and then she bore it softly and covered it up. And Sir Simon, who was watching all the time, though he was terribly frightened, saw the lady bend down and stretch out her arms and whisper and sing, and then Sir Simon saw beside her a handsome young man, who kissed her on the lips. And they drank wine out of the golden bowl together, and they ate the cake together. But when the sun rose there was only the little wax doll, and the lady hid it again under the bed in the hollow place. So Sir Simon knew quite well what the lady was, and he waited and he watched, till the time she had said was nearly over, and in a week the year and a day would be done. And one night, when he was watching behind the curtains in her room, he saw her making more wax dolls. And she made five, and hid them away. And the next night she took one out, and held it up, and filled the golden bowl with water, and took the doll by the neck and held it under the water. Then she said—

Sir Dickon, Sir Dickon, your day is done,
You shall be drowned in the water wan.

And the next day news came to the castle that Sir Richard had been drowned at the ford. And at night she took another doll and tied a violet cord round its neck and hung it up on a nail. Then she said—

Sir Rowland, your life has ended its span,
High on a tree I see you hang.

And the next day news came to the castle that Sir Rowland had been hanged by robbers in the wood. And at night she took another doll, and drove her bodkin right into its heart. Then she said—

155

> Sir Noll, Sir Noll, so cease your life,
> Your heart piercèd with the knife.

And the next day news came to the castle that Sir Oliver had fought in a tavern, and a stranger had stabbed him to the heart. And at night she took another doll, and held it to a fire of charcoal till it was melted. Then she said—

> Sir John, return, and turn to clay,
> In fire of fever you waste away.

And the next day news came to the castle that Sir John had died in a burning fever. So then Sir Simon went out of the castle and mounted his horse and rode away to the bishop and told him everything. And the bishop sent his men, and they took the Lady Avelin, and everything she had done was found out. So on the day after the year and a day, when she was to have been married, they carried her through the town in her smock, and they tied her to a great stake in the market-place, and burned her alive before the bishop with her wax image hung round her neck. And people said the wax man screamed in the burning of the flames. And I thought of this story again and again as I was lying awake in my bed, and I seemed to see the Lady Avelin in the market-place, with the yellow flames eating up her beautiful white body. And I thought of it so much that I seemed to get into the story myself, and I fancied I was the lady, and that they were coming to take me to be burnt with fire, with all the people in the town looking at me. And I wondered whether she cared, after all the strange things she had done, and whether it hurt very much to be burned at the stake. I tried again and again to forget nurse's stories, and to remember the secret I had seen that afternoon, and what was in the secret wood, but I could only see the dark and a glimmering in the dark, and then it went away, and I only saw myself running, and then a great moon came up white over a dark round hill. Then all the old stories came back again, and the queer rhymes that nurse used to sing to me; and there was one beginning "Halsy cumsy Helen musty," that she used to sing very softly when she wanted me to go to sleep. And I began to sing it to myself inside of my head, and I went to sleep.

The next morning I was very tired and sleepy, and could hardly do my lessons, and I was very glad when they were over and I had had my dinner, as I wanted to go out and be alone. It was a warm day, and I went to a nice turfy hill by the river, and sat down on my mother's old shawl that I had brought with me on purpose. The sky was grey, like the day before, but there was a kind of white gleam behind it, and from where I was sitting I could look down on the town, and it was all still and quiet and white, like a picture. I remembered that it was on that hill that nurse taught me to play an old game called "Troy Town," in which one had to dance, and wind in and out on a pattern in the grass, and then when one had danced and turned long enough the other person asks you questions, and you can't help answering whether you want to or not, and whatever you are told to do you feel you have to do it. Nurse said there used to be a lot of games like that that some people knew of, and there was one by which people could be turned into anything you liked and an old man her great-grandmother had seen had known a girl who had been turned into a large snake. And there was another very ancient game of dancing and winding and turning, by which you could take a person out of himself and hide him away as long as you liked, and his body went walking about quite empty, without any sense in it. But I came to that hill because I wanted to think of what had happened the day before, and of the secret of the wood. From the place where I was sitting I could see beyond the town, into the opening I had found, where a little brook had led me into an unknown country. And I pretended I was following the brook over again, and I went all the way in my mind, and at last I found the wood, and crept into it under the bushes, and then in the dusk I saw something that made me feel as if I were filled with fire, as if I wanted to dance and sing and fly up into the air, because I was changed and wonderful. But what I saw was not changed at all, and had not grown old, and I wondered again and again how such things could happen, and whether nurse's stories were really true, because in the daytime in the open air everything seemed quite different from what it was at night, when I was frightened, and thought I was to be burned alive. I once told my father one of her little tales, which was about a ghost, and asked him if it was true, and he told me it was not true at all, and that only common, ignorant people believed in such rubbish. He was very angry with nurse for telling me the story, and scolded her, and after that I promised her I would never whisper a word of what she told me, and if I did I should be bitten by the great black snake that lived in the pool in the wood. And all alone on the hill I wondered what was true. I had seen something very amazing and very lovely, and I knew a story, and if I had really seen it, and not made it up out of the dark, and the black bough, and the bright shining that was mounting up to the sky from over the great

157

round hill, but had really seen it in truth, then there were all kinds of wonderful and lovely and terrible things to think of, so I longed and trembled, and I burned and got cold. And I looked down on the town, so quiet and still, like a little white picture, and I thought over and over if it could be true. I was a long time before I could make up my mind to anything; there was such a strange fluttering at my heart that seemed to whisper to me all the time that I had not made it up out of my head, and yet it seemed quite impossible, and I knew my father and everybody would say it was dreadful rubbish. I never dreamed of telling him or anybody else a word about it, because I knew it would be of no use, and I should only get laughed at or scolded, so for a long time I was very quiet, and went about thinking and wondering; and at night I used to dream of amazing things, and sometimes I woke up in the early morning and held out my arms with a cry. And I was frightened, too, because there were dangers, and some awful thing would happen to me, unless I took great care, if the story were true. These old tales were always in my head, night and morning, and I went over them and told them to myself over and over again, and went for walks in the places where nurse had told them to me; and when I sat in the nursery by the fire in the evenings I used to fancy nurse was sitting in the other chair, and telling me some wonderful story in a low voice, for fear anybody should be listening. But she used to like best to tell me about things when we were right out in the country, far from the house, because she said she was telling me such secrets, and walls have ears. And if it was something more than ever secret, we had to hide in brakes or woods; and I used to think it was such fun creeping along a hedge, and going very softly, and then we would get behind the bushes or run into the wood all of a sudden, when we were sure that none was watching us; so we knew that we had our secrets quite all to ourselves, and nobody else at all knew anything about them. Now and then, when we had hidden ourselves as I have described, she used to show me all sorts of odd things. One day, I remember, we were in a hazel brake, overlooking the brook, and we were so snug and warm, as though it was April; the sun was quite hot, and the leaves were just coming out. Nurse said she would show me something funny that would make me laugh, and then she showed me, as she said, how one could turn a whole house upside down, without anybody being able to find out, and the pots and pans would jump about, and the china would be broken, and the chairs would tumble over of themselves. I tried it one day in the kitchen, and I found I could do it quite well, and a whole row of plates on the dresser fell off it, and cook's little work-table tilted up and turned right over "before her eyes," as she said, but she was so frightened and turned so white that I didn't do it again, as I liked her. And afterwards, in the hazel copse, when she had shown me how to make things tumble about, she showed me how to make rapping noises, and I learnt how to do that, too. Then she taught me rhymes to say on certain occasions, and peculiar marks to make on other occasions, and other things that her great-grandmother had taught her when she was a little girl herself. And these were all the things I was thinking about in those days after the strange walk when I thought I had seen a great secret, and I wished nurse were there for me to ask her about it, but she had gone away more than two years before, and nobody seemed to know what had become of her, or where she had gone. But I shall always remember those days if I live to be quite old, because all the time I felt so strange, wondering and doubting, and feeling quite sure at one time, and making up my mind, and then I would feel quite sure that such things couldn't happen really, and it began all over again. But I took great care not to do certain things that might be very dangerous. So I waited and wondered for a long time, and though I was not sure at all, I never dared to try to find out. But one day I became sure that all that nurse said was quite true, and I was all alone when I found it out. I trembled all over with joy and terror, and as fast as I could I ran into one of the old brakes where we used to go—it was the one by the lane, where nurse made the little clay man—and I ran into it, and I crept into it; and when I came to the place where the elder was, I covered up my face with my hands and lay down flat on the grass, and I stayed there for two hours without moving, whispering to myself delicious, terrible things, and saying some words over and over again. It was all true and wonderful and splendid, and when I remembered the story I knew and thought of what I had really seen, I got hot and I got cold, and the air seemed full of scent, and flowers, and singing. And first I wanted to make a little clay man, like the one nurse had made so long ago, and I had to invent plans and stratagems, and to look about, and to think of things beforehand, because nobody must dream of anything that I was doing or going to do, and I was too old to carry clay about in a tin bucket. At last I thought of a plan, and I brought the wet clay to the brake, and did everything that nurse had done, only I made a much finer image than the one she had made; and when it was finished I did everything that I could imagine and much more than she did, because it was the likeness of something far better. And a few days later, when I had done my lessons early, I went for the second time by the way of the little brook that had led me into a strange country. And I followed the brook, and went through the bushes, and beneath the low branches of trees, and up thorny thickets on the hill, and by dark woods full of creeping thorns, a long, long way. Then I crept through the dark tunnel where the brook had been and the ground was stony, till at last I came to the thicket that climbed up the hill, and though the leaves were coming out upon the trees, everything looked almost as black as it was on the first day that I went there. And the thicket was just the same, and I went up slowly till I came out on the big bare hill, and began to walk among the wonderful rocks. I saw the terrible voor again on everything, for though the sky was brighter, the ring of wild hills all around was still dark, and the hanging woods looked dark and dreadful, and the strange rocks were as grey as ever; and when I looked down on them from the great mound, sitting on the stone, I saw all their amazing circles and rounds within rounds, and I had to sit quite still and watch them as they began to turn about me, and each stone danced in its place, and they seemed to go round and round in a great whirl, as if one were in the middle of all the stars and heard them rushing through the air. So I went down among the rocks to dance with them and to sing extraordinary songs; and I went down through the other thicket, and drank from the bright stream in the close and secret valley, putting my lips down to the bubbling water; and then I went on till I came to the deep, brimming well among the glittering moss, and I sat down. I looked before me into the secret darkness of the valley, and behind me was the great high wall of grass, and all around me there were the hanging woods that made the valley such a secret place. I knew there was nobody here at all besides myself, and that no one could see me. So I took off my boots and stockings, and let my feet down into the water, saying the words that I knew. And it was not cold at all, as I expected, but warm and very pleasant, and when my feet were in it I felt as if they were in silk, or as if the nymph were kissing them. So when I had done, I said the other words and made the signs, and then I dried my feet with a towel I had brought on purpose, and put on my stockings and boots. Then I climbed up the steep wall, and went into the place where there are the hollows, and the two beautiful mounds, and the round ridges of land, and all the strange shapes. I did not go down into the hollow this time, but I turned at the end, and made out the figures quite plainly, as it was lighter, and I had remembered the story I had quite forgotten before, and in the story the two figures are called Adam and Eve, and only those who know the story understand what they mean. So I went on and on till I came to the secret wood which must not be described, and

I crept into it by the way I had found. And when I had gone about halfway I stopped, and turned round, and got ready, and I bound the handkerchief tightly round my eyes, and made quite sure that I could not see at all, not a twig, nor the end of a leaf, nor the light of the sky, as it was an old red silk handkerchief with large yellow spots, that went round twice and covered my eyes, so that I could see nothing. Then I began to go on, step by step, very slowly. My heart beat faster and faster, and something rose in my throat that choked me and made me want to cry out, but I shut my lips, and went on. Boughs caught in my hair as I went, and great thorns tore me; but I went on to the end of the path. Then I stopped, and held out my arms and bowed, and I went round the first time, feeling with my hands, and there was nothing. I went round the second time, feeling with my hands, and there was nothing. Then I went round the third time, feeling with my hands, and the story was all true, and I wished that the years were gone by, and that I had not so long a time to wait before I was happy for ever and ever.

Nurse must have been a prophet like those we read of in the Bible. Everything that she said began to come true, and since then other things that she told me of have happened. That was how I came to know that her stories were true and that I had not made up the secret myself out of my own head. But there was another thing that happened that day. I went a second time to the secret place. It was at the deep brimming well, and when I was standing on the moss I bent over and looked in, and then I knew who the white lady was that I had seen come out of the water in the wood long ago when I was quite little. And I trembled all over, because that told me other things. Then I remembered how sometime after I had seen the white people in the wood, nurse asked me more about them, and I told her all over again, and she listened, and said nothing for a long, long time, and at last she said, "You will see her again." So I understood what had happened and what was to happen. And I understood about the nymphs; how I might meet them in all kinds of places, and they would always help me, and I must always look for them, and find them in all sorts of strange shapes and appearances. And without the nymphs I could never have found the secret, and without them none of the other things could happen. Nurse had told me all about them long ago, but she called them by another name, and I did not know what she meant, or what her tales of them were about, only that they were very queer. And there were two kinds, the bright and the dark, and both were very lovely and very wonderful, and some people saw only one kind, and some only the other, but some saw them both. But usually the dark appeared first, and the bright ones came afterwards, and there were extraordinary tales about them. It was a day or two after I had come home from the secret place that I first really knew the nymphs. Nurse had shown me how to call them, and I had tried, but I did not know what she meant, and so I thought it was all nonsense. But I made up my mind I would try again, so I went to the wood where the pool was, where I saw the white people, and I tried again. The dark nymph, Alanna, came, and she turned the pool of water into a pool of fire. . . .

Epilogue

"That's a very queer story," said Cotgrave, handing back the green book to the recluse, Ambrose. "I see the drift of a good deal, but there are many things that I do not grasp at all. On the last page, for example, what does she mean by 'nymphs'?"

"Well, I think there are references throughout the manuscript to certain 'processes' which have been handed down by tradition from age to age. Some of these processes are just beginning to come within the purview of science, which has arrived at them—or rather at the steps which lead to them—by quite different paths. I have interpreted the reference to 'nymphs' as a reference to one of these processes."

"And you believe that there are such things?"

"Oh, I think so. Yes, I believe I could give you convincing evidence on that point. I am afraid you have neglected the study of alchemy? It is a pity, for the symbolism, at all events, is very beautiful, and moreover if you were acquainted with certain books on the subject, I could recall to your mind phrases which might explain a good deal in the manuscript that you have been reading."

"Yes; but I want to know whether you seriously think that there is any foundation of fact beneath these fancies. Is it not all a department of poetry; a curious dream with which man has indulged himself?"

"I can only say that it is no doubt better for the great mass of people to dismiss it all as a dream. But if you ask my veritable belief—that goes quite the other way. No; I should not say belief, but rather knowledge. I may tell you that I have known cases in which men have stumbled quite by accident on certain of these 'processes,' and have been astonished by wholly unexpected results. In the cases I am thinking of there could have been no possibility of 'suggestion' or sub-conscious action of any kind. One might as well suppose a schoolboy 'suggesting' the existence of

Æschylus to himself, while he plods mechanically through the declen-sions.

"But you have noticed the obscurity," Ambrose went on, "and in this particular case it must have been dictated by instinct, since the writer never thought that her manuscripts would fall into other hands. But the practice is universal, and for most excellent reasons. Powerful and sovereign medicines, which are, of necessity, virulent poisons also, are kept in a locked cabinet. The child may find the key by chance, and drink herself dead; but in most cases the search is educational, and the phials contain precious elixirs for him who has patiently fashioned the key for himself."

"You do not care to go into details?"

"No, frankly, I do not. No, you must remain unconvinced. But you saw how the manuscript illustrates the talk we had last week?"

"Is this girl still alive?"

"No. I was one of those who found her. I knew the father well; he was a lawyer, and had always left her very much to herself. He thought of nothing but deeds and leases, and the news came to him as an awful surprise. She was missing one morning; I suppose it was about a year after she had written what you have read. The servants were called, and they told things, and put the only natural interpretation on them—a perfectly erroneous one.

"They discovered that green book somewhere in her room, and I found her in the place that she described with so much dread, lying on the ground before the image."

"It was an image?"

"Yes, it was hidden by the thorns and the thick undergrowth that had surrounded it. It was a wild, lonely country; but you know what it was like by her description, though of course you will understand that the colours have been heightened. A child's imagination always makes the heights higher and the depths deeper than they really are; and she had, unfortu-nately for herself, something more than imagination. One might say, perhaps, that the picture in her mind which she succeeded in a measure in putting into words, was the scene as it would have appeared to an imaginative artist. But it is a strange, desolate land."

"And she was dead?"

"Yes. She had poisoned herself—in time. No; there was not a word to be said against her in the ordinary sense. You may recollect a story I told you the other night about a lady who saw her child's fingers crushed by a window?"

"And what was this statue?"

"Well, it was of Roman workmanship, of a stone that with the centuries had not blackened, but had become white and luminous. The thicket had grown up about it and concealed it, and in the Middle Ages the followers of a very old tradition had known how to use it for their own purposes. In fact it had been incorporated into the monstrous mythology of the Sabbath. You will have noted that those to whom a sight of that shining whiteness had been vouchsafed by chance, or rather, perhaps, by apparent chance, were required to blindfold themselves on their second approach. That is very significant."

"And is it there still?"

"I sent for tools, and we hammered it into dust and fragments."

"The persistence of tradition never surprises me," Ambrose went on after a pause. "I could name many an English parish where such traditions as that girl had listened to in her childhood are still existent in occult but unabated vigour. No, for me, it is the 'story' not the 'sequel,' which is strange and awful, for I have always believed that wonder is of the soul."

ALGERNON BLACKWOOD (1869-1951) was a British novelist, short story writer, and mystic who specialized in exploring mankind's relation with the cosmos—that is, within the natural or supernatural world. "The Willows" is one of his most famous tales. In "Supernatural Horror in Literature," Lovecraft wrote of it: "Here art and restraint in narrative reach their very highest development, and an impression of lasting poignancy is produced without a single strained passage or a single false note." In an October 1930 letter to Robert E. Howard, Lovecraft referred to "The Willows" as "the greatest horror-tale ever written," a sentiment he reiterated in a November 1936 letter to Wilfred Blanch Talman when he called it "the greatest weird story ever written." "The Willows" was first published in Blackwood's collection *The Listener and Other Stories* (1907).

THE WILLOWS
by Algernon Blackwood

After leaving Vienna, and long before you come to Buda-Pesth, the Danube enters a region of singular loneliness and desolation, where its waters spread away on all sides regardless of a main channel, and the country becomes a swamp for miles upon miles, covered by a vast sea of low willow-bushes. On the big maps this deserted area is painted in a fluffy blue, growing fainter in colour as it leaves the banks, and across it may be seen in large straggling letters the word *Sümpfe*, meaning marshes.

In high flood this great acreage of sand, shingle-beds, and willow-grown islands is almost topped by the water, but in normal seasons the bushes bend and rustle in the free winds, showing their silver leaves to the sunshine in an ever-moving plain of bewildering beauty. These willows never attain to the dignity of trees; they have no rigid trunks; they remain humble bushes, with rounded tops and soft outline, swaying on slender stems that answer to the least pressure of the wind; supple as grasses, and so continually shifting that they somehow give the impression that the entire plain is moving and *alive*. For the wind sends waves rising and falling over the whole surface, waves of leaves instead of waves of water, green swells like the sea, too, until the branches turn and lift, and then silvery white as their under-side turns to the sun.

Happy to slip beyond the control of the stern banks, the Danube here wanders about at will among the intricate network of channels intersecting the islands everywhere with broad avenues down which the waters pour with a shouting sound; making whirlpools, eddies, and foaming rapids; tearing at the sandy banks; carrying away masses of shore and willow-clumps; and forming new islands innumerably which shift daily in size and shape and possess at best an impermanent life, since the flood-time obliterates their very existence.

Properly speaking, this fascinating part of the river's life begins soon after leaving Pressburg, and we, in our Canadian canoe, with gipsy tent and frying-pan on board, reached it on the crest of a rising flood about mid-July. That very same morning, when the sky was reddening before sunrise, we had slipped swiftly through still-sleeping Vienna, leaving it a couple of hours later a mere patch of smoke against the blue hills of the Wienerwald on the horizon; we had breakfasted below Fischeramend under a grove of birch trees roaring in the wind; and had then swept on the tearing current past Orth, Hainburg, Petronell (the old Roman Carnuntum of Marcus Aurelius), and so under the frowning heights of Thelsen on a spur of the Carpathians, where the March steals in quietly from the left and the frontier is crossed between Austria and Hungary.

Racing along at twelve kilometres an hour soon took us well into Hungary, and the muddy waters—sure sign of flood—sent us aground on many a shingle-bed, and twisted us like a cork in many a sudden belching whirlpool before the towers of Pressburg (Hungarian, Poszóny) showed against the sky; and then the canoe, leaping like a spirited horse, flew at top speed under the grey walls, negotiated safely the sunken chain of the Fliegende Brücke ferry, turned the corner sharply to the left, and plunged on yellow foam into the wilderness of islands, sand-banks, and swamp-land beyond—the land of the willows.

The change came suddenly, as when a series of bioscope pictures snaps down on the streets of a town and shifts without warning into the scenery of lake and forest. We entered the land of desolation on wings, and in less than half an hour there was neither boat nor fishing-hut nor red roof, nor any single sign of human habitation and civilisation within sight. The sense of remoteness from the world of human kind, the utter isolation, the fascination of this singular world of willows, winds, and waters, instantly laid its spell upon us both, so that we allowed laughingly to one another that we ought by rights to have held some special kind of passport to admit us, and that we had, somewhat audaciously, come without asking leave into a separate little kingdom of wonder and magic—a kingdom that was reserved for the use of others who had a right to it, with everywhere unwritten warnings to trespassers for those who had the imagination to discover them.

Though still early in the afternoon, the ceaseless buffetings of a most tempestuous wind made us feel weary, and we at once began casting about for a suitable camping-ground for the night. But the bewildering character of the islands made landing difficult; the swirling flood carried us in-shore and then swept us out again; the willow branches tore our hands as we seized them to stop the canoe, and we pulled many a yard of sandy bank into the water before at length we shot with a great sideways blow from the wind into a backwater and managed to beach the bows in a cloud of spray. Then we lay panting and laughing after our exertions on the hot yellow sand, sheltered from the wind, and in the full blaze of a scorching sun, a cloudless blue sky above, and an immense army of dancing, shouting willow bushes, closing in from all sides, shining with spray and clapping their thousand little hands as though to applaud the success of our efforts.

"What a river!" I said to my companion, thinking of all the way we had travelled from the source in the Black Forest, and how he had often been obliged to wade and push in the upper shallows at the beginning of June.

"Won't stand much nonsense now, will it?" he said, pulling the canoe a little farther into safety up the sand, and then composing himself for a nap.

I lay by his side, happy and peaceful in the bath of the elements—water, wind, sand, and the great fire of the sun—thinking of the long journey that lay behind us, and of the great stretch before us to the Black Sea, and how lucky I was to have such a delightful and charming travelling companion as my friend, the Swede.

We had made many similar journeys together, but the Danube, more than any other river I knew, impressed us from the very beginning with its *aliveness*. From its tiny bubbling entry into the world among the pinewood gardens of Donaueschingen, until this moment when it began to play the great river-game of losing itself among the deserted swamps, unobserved, unrestrained, it had seemed to us like following the growth of some living creature. Sleepy at first, but later developing violent desires as it became conscious of its deep soul, it rolled, like some huge fluid being, through all the countries we had passed, holding our little craft on its mighty shoulders, playing roughly with us sometimes, yet always friendly and well-meaning, till at length we had come inevitably to regard it as a Great Personage.

How, indeed, could it be otherwise, since it told us so much of its secret life? At night we heard it singing to the moon as we lay in our tent, uttering that odd sibilant note peculiar to itself and said to be caused by the rapid tearing of the pebbles along its bed, so great is its hurrying speed. We knew, too, the voice of its gurgling whirlpools, suddenly bubbling up on a surface previously quite calm; the roar of its shallows and swift rapids; its constant steady thundering below all mere surface sounds; and that ceaseless tearing of its icy waters at the banks. How it stood up and shouted when the rains fell flat upon its face! And how its laughter roared out when the wind blew upstream and tried to stop its growing speed! We knew all its sounds and voices, its tumblings and foamings, its unnecessary splashing against the bridges; that self-conscious chatter when there were hills to look on; the affected dignity of its speech when it passed through the little towns, far too important to laugh; and all these faint, sweet whisperings when the sun caught it fairly in some slow curve and poured down upon it till the steam rose.

It was full of tricks, too, in its early life before the great world knew it. There were places in the upper reaches among the Swabian forests, when yet the first whispers of its destiny had not reached it, where it elected to disappear through holes in the ground, to appear again on the other side of the porous limestone hills and start a new river with another name; leaving, too, so little water in its own bed that we had to climb out and wade and push the canoe through miles of shallows.

And a chief pleasure, in those early days of its irresponsible youth, was to lie low, like Brer Fox, just before the little turbulent tributaries came to join it from the Alps, and to refuse to acknowledge them when in, but to run for miles side by side, the dividing line well marked, the very levels different, the Danube utterly declining to recognize the newcomer. Below Passau, however, it gave up this particular trick, for there the Inn comes in with a thundering power impossible to ignore, and so pushes and incommodes the parent river that there is hardly room for them in the long twisting gorge that follows, and the Danube is shoved this way and that against the cliffs, and forced to hurry itself with great waves and mush dashing to and fro in order to get through in time. And during the fight our canoe slipped down from its shoulder to its breast, and had the time of its life among the struggling waves. But the Inn taught the old river a lesson, and after Passau it no longer pretended to ignore new arrivals.

This was many days back, of course, and since then we had come to know other aspects of the great creature, and across the Bavarian wheat plain of Straubing she wandered so slowly under the blazing June sun that we could well imagine only the surface inches were water, while below there moved, concealed as by a silken mantle, a whole army of Undines, passing silently and unseen down to the sea, and very leisurely too, lest they be discovered.

Much, too, we forgave her because of her friendliness to the birds and animals that haunted the shores. Cormorants lined the banks in lonely places in rows like short black palings; grey crows crowded the shingle-beds; storks stood fishing in the vistas of shallower water that opened up between the islands, and hawks, swans, and marsh birds of all sorts filled the air with glinting wings and singing, petulant cries. It was impossible to feel annoyed with the river's vagaries after seeing a deer leap with a splash into the water at sunrise and swim past the bows of the canoe; and often we saw fawns peering at us from the underbrush, or looked straight into the brown eyes of a stag as we charged full tilt round a corner and entered another reach of the river. Foxes, too, everywhere haunted the banks, tripping daintily among the driftwood and disappearing so suddenly that it was impossible to see how they managed it.

But now, after leaving Pressburg, everything changed a little, and the Danube became more serious. It ceased trifling. It was half-way to the Black Sea, within scenting distance almost of other, stranger countries where no tricks would be permitted or understood. It became suddenly grown-up, and claimed our respect and even our awe. It broke out into three arms, for one thing, that only met again a hundred kilometres farther down, and for a canoe there were no indications which one was intended to be followed.

"If you take a side channel," said the Hungarian officer we met in the Pressburg shop while buying provisions, "you may find yourselves, when the flood subsides, forty miles from anywhere, high and dry, and you may easily starve. There are no people, no farms, no fishermen. I warn you not to continue. The river, too, is still rising, and this wind will increase."

The rising river did not alarm us in the least, but the matter of being left high and dry by a sudden subsidence of the waters might be serious, and we had consequently laid in an extra stock of provisions. For the rest, the officer's prophecy held true, and the wind, blowing down a perfectly clear sky, increased steadily till it reached the dignity of a westerly gale.

It was earlier than usual when we camped, for the sun was a good hour or two from the horizon, and leaving my friend still asleep on the hot sand, I wandered about in desultory examination of our hotel. The island, I found, was less than an acre in extent, a mere sandy bank standing some two or three feet above the level of the river. The far end, pointing into the sunset, was covered with flying spray which the tremendous wind drove off the crests of the broken waves. It was triangular in shape, with the apex up stream.

I stood there for several minutes, watching the impetuous crimson flood bearing down with a shouting roar, dashing in waves against the bank as though to sweep it bodily away, and then swirling by in two foaming streams on either side. The ground seemed to shake with the shock and rush, while the furious movement of the willow bushes as the wind poured over them increased the curious illusion that the island itself actually moved. Above, for a mile or two, I could see the great river descending upon me: it was like looking up the slope of a sliding hill, white with foam, and leaping up everywhere to show itself to the sun.

The rest of the island was too thickly grown with willows to make walking pleasant, but I made the tour, nevertheless. From the lower end the light, of course, changed, and the river looked dark and angry. Only the backs of the flying waves were visible, streaked with foam, and pushed forcibly by the great puffs of wind that fell upon them from behind. For a short mile it was visible, pouring in and out among the islands, and then disappearing with a huge sweep into the willows, which closed about it like a herd of monstrous antediluvian creatures crowding down to drink. They made me think of gigantic sponge-like growths that sucked the river up into themselves. They caused it to vanish from sight. They herded there together in such overpowering numbers.

Altogether it was an impressive scene, with its utter loneliness, its bizarre suggestion; and as I gazed, long and curiously, a singular emotion began to stir somewhere in the depths of me. Midway in my delight of the wild beauty, there crept, unbidden and unexplained, a curious feeling of disquietude, almost of alarm.

A rising river, perhaps, always suggests something of the ominous: many of the little islands I saw before me would probably have been swept away by the morning; this resistless, thundering flood of water touched the sense of awe. Yet I was aware that my uneasiness lay deeper far than the emotions of awe and wonder. It was not that I felt. Nor had it directly to do with the power of the driving wind—this shouting hurricane that might almost carry up a few acres of willows into the air and scatter them like so much chaff over the landscape. The wind was simply enjoying itself, for nothing rose out of the flat landscape to stop it, and I was conscious of sharing its great game with a kind of pleasurable excitement. Yet this novel emotion had nothing to do with the wind. Indeed, so vague was the sense of distress I experienced, that it was impossible to trace it to its source and deal with it accordingly, though I was aware somehow that it had to do with my realisation of our utter insignificance before this unrestrained power of the elements about me. The huge-grown river had something to do with it too—a vague, unpleasant idea that we had somehow trifled with these great elemental forces in whose power we lay helpless every hour of the day and night. For here, indeed, they were gigantically at play together, and the sight appealed to the imagination.

But my emotion, so far as I could understand it, seemed to attach itself more particularly to the willow bushes, to these acres and acres of willows, crowding, so thickly growing there, swarming everywhere the eye could reach, pressing upon the river as though to suffocate it, standing in dense array mile after mile beneath the sky, watching, waiting, listening. And, apart quite from the elements, the willows connected themselves subtly with my malaise, attacking the mind insidiously somehow by reason of their vast numbers, and contriving in some way or other to represent to the imagination a new and mighty power, a power, moreover, not altogether friendly to us.

Great revelations of nature, of course, never fail to impress in one way or another, and I was no stranger to moods of the kind. Mountains overawe and oceans terrify, while the mystery of great forests exercises a spell peculiarly its own. But all these, at one point or another, somewhere link on intimately with human life and human experience. They stir comprehensible, even if alarming, emotions. They tend on the whole to exalt.

With this multitude of willows, however, it was something far different, I felt. Some essence emanated from them that besieged the heart. A sense of awe awakened, true, but of awe touched somewhere by a vague terror. Their serried ranks, growing everywhere darker about me as the shadows deepened, moving furiously yet softly in the wind, woke in me the curious and unwelcome suggestion that we had trespassed here upon the borders of an alien world, a world where we were intruders, a world where we were not wanted or invited to remain—where we ran grave risks perhaps!

The feeling, however, though it refused to yield its meaning entirely to analysis, did not at the time trouble me by passing into menace. Yet it never left me quite, even during the very practical business of putting up the tent in a hurricane of wind and building a fire for the stew-pot. It remained, just enough to bother and perplex, and to rob a most delightful camping-ground of a good portion of its charm. To my companion, however, I said nothing, for he was a man I considered devoid of imagination. In the first place, I could never have explained to him what I meant, and in the second, he would have laughed stupidly at me if I had.

There was a slight depression in the centre of the island, and here we pitched the tent. The surrounding willows broke the wind a bit.

"A poor camp," observed the imperturbable Swede when at last the tent stood upright; "no stones and precious little firewood. I'm for moving on early to-morrow—eh? This sand won't hold anything."

But the experience of a collapsing tent at midnight had taught us many devices, and we made the cosy gipsy house as safe as possible, and then set about collecting a store of wood to last till bed-time. Willow bushes drop no branches, and driftwood was our only source of supply. We hunted the shores pretty thoroughly. Everywhere the banks were crumbling as the rising flood tore at them and carried away great portions with a splash and a gurgle.

"The island's much smaller than when we landed," said the accurate Swede. "It won't last long at this rate. We'd better drag the canoe close to the tent, and be ready to start at a moment's notice. *I* shall sleep in my clothes."

He was a little distance off, climbing along the bank, and I heard his rather jolly laugh as he spoke.

"By Jove!" I heard him call, a moment later, and turned to see what had caused his exclamation. But for the moment he was hidden by the willows, and I could not find him.

"What in the world's this?" I heard him cry again, and this time his voice had become serious.

I ran up quickly and joined him on the bank. He was looking over the river, pointing at something in the water.

"Good heavens, it's a man's body!" he cried excitedly. "Look!"

A black thing, turning over and over in the foaming waves, swept rapidly past. It kept disappearing and coming up to the surface again. It was about twenty feet from the shore, and just as it was opposite to where we stood it lurched round and looked straight at us. We saw its eyes reflecting the sunset, and gleaming an odd yellow as the body turned over. Then it gave a swift, gulping plunge, and dived out of sight in a flash.

"An otter, by gad!" we exclaimed in the same breath, laughing.

It *was* an otter, alive, and out on the hunt; yet it had looked exactly like the body of a drowned man turning helplessly in the current. Far below it came to the surface once again, and we saw its black skin, wet and shining in the sunlight.

Then, too, just as we turned back, our arms full of driftwood, another thing happened to recall us to the river bank. This time it really was a man, and what was more, a man in a boat. Now a small boat on the Danube was an unusual sight at any time, but here in this deserted region, and at flood time, it was so unexpected as to constitute a real event. We stood and stared.

Whether it was due to the slanting sunlight, or the refraction from the wonderfully illuminated water, I cannot say, but, whatever the cause, I found it difficult to focus my sight properly upon the flying apparition. It seemed, however, to be a man standing upright in a sort of flat-bottomed boat, steering with a long oar, and being carried down the opposite shore at a tremendous pace. He apparently was looking across in our direction, but the distance was too great and the light too uncertain for us to make out very plainly what he was about. It seemed to me that he was gesticulating and making signs at us. His voice came across the water to us shouting something furiously, but the wind drowned it so that no single word was audible. There was something curious about the whole appearance—man, boat, signs, voice—that made an impression on me out of all proportion to its cause.

"He's crossing himself!" I cried. "Look, he's making the sign of the Cross!"

"I believe you're right," the Swede said, shading his eyes with his hand and watching the man out of sight. He seemed to be gone in a moment, melting away down there into the sea of willows where the sun caught them in the bend of the river and turned them into a great crimson wall of beauty. Mist, too, had begun to ruse, so that the air was hazy.

"But what in the world is he doing at night-fall on this flooded river?" I said, half to myself. "Where is he going at such a time, and what did he mean by his signs and shouting? D'you think he wished to warn us about something?"

"He saw our smoke, and thought we were spirits probably," laughed my companion. "These Hungarians believe in all sorts of rubbish: you remember the shopwoman at Pressburg warning us that no one ever landed here because it belonged to some sort of beings outside man's world! I suppose they believe in fairies and elementals, possibly demons, too. That peasant in the boat saw people on the islands for the first time in his life," he added, after a slight pause, "and it scared him, that's all."

The Swede's tone of voice was not convincing, and his manner lacked something that was usually there. I noted the change instantly while he talked, though without being able to label it precisely.

"If they had enough imagination," I laughed loudly—I remember trying to make as much *noise* as I could—"they might well people a place like this with the old gods of antiquity. The Romans must have haunted all this region more or less with their shrines and sacred groves and elemental deities."

The subject dropped and we returned to our stew-pot, for my friend was not given to imaginative conversation as a rule. Moreover, just then I remember feeling distinctly glad that he was not imaginative; his stolid, practical nature suddenly seemed to me welcome and comforting. It was an admirable temperament, I felt; he could steer down rapids like a red Indian, shoot dangerous bridges and whirlpools better than any white man I ever saw in a canoe. He was a grand fellow for an adventurous trip, a tower of strength when untoward things happened. I looked at his strong face and light curly hair as he staggered along under his pile of driftwood (twice the size of mine!), and I experienced a feeling of relief. Yes, I was distinctly glad just then that the Swede was—what he was, and that he never made remarks that suggested more than they said.

"The river's still rising, though," he added, as if following out some thoughts of his own, and dropping his load with a gasp. "This island will be under water in two days if it goes on."

"I wish the *wind* would go down," I said. "I don't care a fig for the river."

The flood, indeed, had no terrors for us; we could get off at ten minute's notice, and the more water the better we liked it. It meant an increasing current and the obliteration of the treacherous shingle-beds that so often threatened to tear the bottom out of our canoe.

Contrary to our expectations, the wind did not go down with the sun. It seemed to increase with the darkness, howling overhead and shaking the willows round us like straws. Curious sounds accompanied it sometimes, like the explosion of heavy guns, and it fell upon the water and the island in great flat blows of immense power. It made me think of the sounds a planet must make, could we only hear it, driving along through space.

But the sky kept wholly clear of clouds, and soon after supper the full moon rose up in the east and covered the river and the plain of shouting willows with a light like the day.

We lay on the sandy patch beside the fire, smoking, listening to the noises of the night round us, and talking happily of the journey we had already made, and of our plans ahead. The map lay spread in the door of the tent, but the high wind made it hard to study, and presently we lowered the curtain and extinguished the lantern. The firelight was enough to smoke and see each other's faces by, and the sparks flew about overhead like fireworks. A few yards beyond, the river gurgled and hissed, and from time to time a heavy splash announced the falling away of further portions of the bank.

Our talk, I noticed, had to do with the far-away scenes and incidents of our first camps in the Black Forest, or of other subjects altogether remote from the present setting, for neither of us spoke of the actual moment more than was necessary—almost as though we had agreed tacitly to avoid discussion of the camp and its incidents. Neither the otter nor the boatman, for instance, received the honour of a single mention, though ordinarily these would have furnished discussion for the greater part of the evening. They were, of course, distinct events in such a place.

The scarcity of wood made it a business to keep the fire going, for the wind, that drove the smoke in our faces wherever we sat, helped at the same time to make a forced draught. We took it in turn to make foraging expeditions into the darkness, and the quantity the Swede brought back always made me feel that he took an absurdly long time finding it; for the fact was I did not care much about being left alone, and yet it always seemed to be my turn to grub about among the bushes or scramble along the slippery banks in the moonlight. The long day's battle with wind and water—such wind and such water!—had tired us both, and an early bed was the obvious programme. Yet neither of us made the move for the tent. We lay there, tending the fire, talking in desultory fashion, peering about us into the dense willow bushes, and listening to the thunder of wind and river. The loneliness of the place had entered our very bones, and silence seemed natural, for after a bit the sound of our voices became a trifle unreal and forced; whispering would have been the fitting mode of communication, I felt, and the human voice, always rather absurd amid the roar of the elements, now carried with it something almost illegitimate. It was like talking out loud in church, or in some place where it was not lawful, perhaps not quite *safe*, to be overheard.

The eeriness of this lonely island, set among a million willows, swept by a hurricane, and surrounded by hurrying deep waters, touched us both, I fancy. Untrodden by man, almost unknown to man, it lay there beneath he moon, remote from human influence, on the frontier of another world, an alien world, a world tenanted by willows only and the souls of willows. And we, in our rashness, had dared to invade it, even to make use of it! Something more than the power of its mystery stirred in me as I lay on the sand, feet to fire, and peered up through the leaves at the stars. For the last time I rose to get firewood.

"When this has burnt up," I said firmly, "I shall turn in," and my companion watched me lazily as I moved off into the surrounding shadows.

For an unimaginative man I thought he seemed unusually receptive that night, unusually open to suggestion of things other than sensory. He too was touched by the beauty and loneliness of the place. I was not altogether pleased, I remember, to recognise this slight change in him, and instead of immediately collecting sticks, I made my way to the far point of the island where the moonlight on plain and river could be seen to better advantage. The desire to be alone had come suddenly upon me; my former dread returned in force; there was a vague feeling in me I wished to face and probe to the bottom.

When I reached the point of sand jutting out among the waves, the spell of the place descended upon me with a positive shock. No mere "scenery" could have produced such an effect. There was something more here, something to alarm.

I gazed across the waste of wild waters; I watched the whispering willows; I heard the ceaseless beating of the tireless wind; and, one and all, each in its own way, stirred in me this sensation of a strange distress. But the *willows* especially; for ever they went on chattering and talking among themselves, laughing a little, shrilly crying out, sometimes sighing—but what it was they made so much to-do about belonged to the secret life of the great plain they inhabited. And it was utterly alien to the world I knew, or to that of the wild yet kindly elements. They made me think of a host of beings from another plane of life, another evolution altogether, perhaps, all discussing a mystery known only to themselves. I watched them moving busily together, oddly shaking their big bushy heads, twirling their myriad leaves even when there was no wind. They moved of their own will as though alive, and they touched, by some incalculable method, my own keen sense of the *horrible*.

There they stood in the moonlight, like a vast army surrounding our camp, shaking their innumerable silver spears defiantly, formed all ready for an attack.

The psychology of places, for some imaginations at least, is very vivid; for the wanderer, especially, camps have their "note" either of welcome or rejection. At first it may not always be apparent, because the busy preparations of tent and cooking prevent, but with the first pause—after supper usually—it comes and announces itself. And the note of this willow-camp now became unmistakably plain to me; we were interlopers, trespassers; we were not welcomed. The sense of unfamiliarity grew upon me as I stood there watching. We touched the frontier of a region where our presence was resented. For a night's lodging we might perhaps be tolerated; but for a prolonged and inquisitive stay—No! by all the gods of the trees and wilderness, no! We were the first human influences upon this island, and we were not wanted. *The willows were against us.*

Strange thoughts like these, bizarre fancies, borne I know not whence, found lodgment in my mind as I stood listening. What, I thought, if, after all, these crouching willows proved to be alive; if suddenly they should rise up, like a swarm of living creatures, marshalled by the gods whose territory we had invaded, sweep towards us off the vast swamps, booming overhead in the night—and then *settle down*! As I looked it was so easy to imagine they actually moved, crept nearer, retreated a little, huddled together in masses, hostile, waiting for the great wind that should finally start them a-running. I could have sworn their aspect changed a little, and their ranks deepened and pressed more closely together.

The melancholy shrill cry of a night-bird sounded overhead, and suddenly I nearly lost my balance as the piece of bank I stood upon fell with a great splash into the river, undermined by the flood. I stepped back just in time, and went on hunting for firewood again, half laughing at the odd fancies that crowded so thickly into my mind and cast their spell upon me. I recalled the Swede's remark about moving on next day, and I was just thinking that I fully agreed with him, when I turned with a start and saw the subject of my thoughts standing immediately in front of me. He was quite close. The roar of the elements had covered his approach.

"You've been gone so long," he shouted above the wind, "I thought something must have happened to you."

But there was that in his tone, and a certain look in his face as well, that conveyed to me more than his usual words, and in a flash I understood the real reason for his coming. It was because the spell of the place had entered his soul too, and he did not like being alone.

"River still rising," he cried, pointing to the flood in the moonlight, "and the wind's simply awful."

He always said the same things, but it was the cry for companionship that gave the real importance to his words.

"Lucky," I cried back, "our tent's in the hollow. I think it'll hold all right." I added something about the difficulty of finding wood, in order to explain my absence, but the wind caught my words and flung them across the river, so that he did not hear, but just looked at me through the branches, nodding his head.

"Lucky if we get away without disaster!" he shouted, or words to that effect; and I remember feeling half angry with him for putting the thought into words, for it was exactly what I felt myself. There was disaster impending somewhere, and the sense of presentiment lay unpleasantly upon me.

We went back to the fire and made a final blaze, poking it up with our feet. We took a last look round. But for the wind the heat would have been unpleasant. I put this thought into words, and I remember my friend's reply struck me oddly: that he would rather have the heat, the ordinary July weather, than this "diabolical wind".

Everything was snug for the night; the canoe lying turned over beside the tent, with both yellow paddles beneath her; the provision sack hanging from a willow-stem, and the washed-up dishes removed to a safe distance from the fire, all ready for the morning meal.

We smothered the embers of the fire with sand, and then turned in. The flap of the tent door was up, and I saw the branches and the stars and the white moonlight. The shaking willows and the heavy buffetings of the wind against our taut little house were the last things I remembered as sleep came down and covered all with its soft and delicious forgetfulness.

II

Suddenly I found myself lying awake, peering from my sandy mattress through the door of the tent. I looked at my watch pinned against the canvas, and saw by the bright moonlight that it was past twelve o'clock—the threshold of a new day—and I had therefore slept a couple of hours.

The Swede was asleep still beside me; the wind howled as before; something plucked at my heart and made me feel afraid. There was a sense of disturbance in my immediate neighbourhood.

I sat up quickly and looked out. The trees were swaying violently to and fro as the gusts smote them, but our little bit of green canvas lay snugly safe in the hollow, for the wind passed over it without meeting enough resistance to make it vicious. The feeling of disquietude did not pass, however, and I crawled quietly out of the tent to see if our belongings were safe. I moved carefully so as not to waken my companion. A curious excitement was on me.

I was half-way out, kneeling on all fours, when my eye first took in that the tops of the bushes opposite, with their moving tracery of leaves, made shapes against the sky. I sat back on my haunches and stared. It was incredible, surely, but there, opposite and slightly above me, were shapes of some indeterminate sort among the willows, and as the branches swayed in the wind they seemed to group themselves about these shapes, forming a series of monstrous outlines that shifted rapidly beneath the moon. Close, about fifty feet in front of me, I saw these things.

My first instinct was to waken my companion, that he too might see them, but something made me hesitate—the sudden realisation, probably, that I should not welcome corroboration; and meanwhile I crouched there staring in amazement with smarting eyes. I was wide awake. I remember saying to myself that I was *not* dreaming.

They first became properly visible, these huge figures, just within the tops of the bushes—immense, bronze-coloured, moving, and wholly independent of the swaying of the branches. I saw them plainly and noted, now I came to examine them more calmly, that they were very much larger than human, and indeed that something in their appearance proclaimed them to be *not human* at all. Certainly they were not merely the moving tracery of the branches against the moonlight. They shifted independently. They rose upwards in a continuous stream from earth to sky, vanishing utterly as soon as they reached the dark of the sky. They were interlaced one with another, making a great column, and I saw their limbs and huge bodies melting in and out of each other, forming this serpentine line that bent and swayed and twisted spirally with the contortions of the wind-tossed trees. They were nude, fluid shapes, passing up the bushes, *within* the leaves almost—rising up in a living column into the heavens. Their faces I never could see. Unceasingly they poured upwards, swaying in great bending curves, with a hue of dull bronze upon their skins.

I stared, trying to force every atom of vision from my eyes. For a long time I thought they *must* every moment disappear and resolve themselves into the movements of the branches and prove to be an optical illusion. I searched everywhere for a proof of reality, when all the while I understood quite well that the standard of reality had changed. For the longer I looked the more certain I became that these figures were real and living, though perhaps not according to the standards that the camera and the biologist would insist upon.

Far from feeling fear, I was possessed with a sense of awe and wonder such as I have never known. I seemed to be gazing at the personified elemental forces of this haunted and primeval region. Our intrusion had stirred the powers of the place into activity. It was we who were the cause of the disturbance, and my brain filled to bursting with stories and legends of the spirits and deities of places that have been acknowledged and worshipped by men in all ages of the world's history. But, before I could arrive at any possible explanation, something impelled me to go farther out, and I crept forward on the sand and stood upright. I felt the ground still warm under my bare feet; the wind tore at my hair and face; and the sound of the river burst upon my ears with a sudden roar. These things, I knew, were real, and proved that my senses were acting normally. Yet the figures still rose from earth to heaven, silent, majestically, in a great spiral of grace and strength that overwhelmed me at length with a genuine deep emotion of worship. I felt that I must fall down and worship—absolutely worship.

Perhaps in another minute I might have done so, when a gust of wind swept against me with such force that it blew me sideways, and I nearly stumbled and fell. It seemed to shake the dream violently out of me. At least it gave me another point of view somehow. The figures still remained, still ascended into heaven from the heart of the night, but my reason at last began to assert itself. It must be a subjective experience, I argued—none the less real for that, but still subjective. The moonlight and the branches combined to work out these pictures upon the mirror of my imagination, and for some reason I projected them outwards and made them appear objective. I knew this must be the case, of course. I was the subject of a vivid and interesting hallucination. I took courage, and began to move forward across the open patches of sand. By Jove, though, was it all hallucination? Was it merely subjective? Did not my reason argue in the old futile way from the little standard of the known?

I only know that great column of figures ascended darkly into the sky for what seemed a very long period of time, and with a very complete measure of reality as most men are accustomed to gauge reality. Then suddenly they were gone!

And, once they were gone and the immediate wonder of their great presence had passed, fear came down upon me with a cold rush. The esoteric meaning of this lonely and haunted region suddenly flamed up within me, and I began to tremble dreadfully. I took a quick look round— a look of horror that came near to panic—calculating vainly ways of escape; and then, realising how helpless I was to achieve anything really effective, I crept back silently into the tent and lay down again upon my sandy mattress, first lowering the door-curtain to shut out the sight of the willows in the moonlight, and then burying my head as deeply as possible beneath the blankets to deaden the sound of the terrifying wind.

III

As though further to convince me that I had not been dreaming, I remember that it was a long time before I fell again into a troubled and restless sleep; and even then only the upper crust of me slept, and underneath there was something that never quite lost consciousness, but lay alert and on the watch.

But this second time I jumped up with a genuine start of terror. It was neither the wind nor the river that woke me, but the slow approach of something that caused the sleeping portion of me to grow smaller and smaller till at last it vanished altogether, and I found myself sitting bolt upright—listening.

Outside there was a sound of multitudinous little patterings. They had been coming, I was aware, for a long time, and in my sleep they had first become audible. I sat there nervously wide awake as though I had not slept at all. It seemed to me that my breathing came with difficulty, and that there was a great weight upon the surface of my body. In spite of the hot night, I felt clammy with cold and shivered. Something surely was pressing steadily against the sides of the tent and weighing down upon it from above. Was it the body of the wind? Was this the pattering rain, the dripping of the leaves? The spray blown from the river by the wind and gathering in big drops? I thought quickly of a dozen things.

Then suddenly the explanation leaped into my mind: a bough from the poplar, the only large tree on the island, had fallen with the wind. Still half caught by the other branches, it would fall with the next gust and crush us, and meanwhile its leaves brushed and tapped upon the tight canvas surface of the tent. I raised a loose flap and rushed out, calling to the Swede to follow.

But when I got out and stood upright I saw that the tent was free. There was no hanging bough; there was no rain or spray; nothing approached.

A cold, grey light filtered down through the bushes and lay on the faintly gleaming sand. Stars still crowded the sky directly overhead, and the wind howled magnificently, but the fire no longer gave out any glow, and I saw the east reddening in streaks through the trees. Several hours must have passed since I stood there before watching the ascending figures, and the memory of it now came back to me horribly, like an evil dream. Oh, how tired it made me feel, that ceaseless raging wind! Yet, though the deep lassitude of a sleepless night was on me, my nerves were tingling with the activity of an equally tireless apprehension, and all idea of repose was out of the question. The river I saw had risen further. Its thunder filled the air, and a fine spray made itself felt through my thin sleeping shirt.

Yet nowhere did I discover the slightest evidence of anything to cause alarm. This deep, prolonged disturbance in my heart remained wholly unaccounted for.

My companion had not stirred when I called him, and there was no need to waken him now. I looked about me carefully, noting everything; the turned-over canoe; the yellow paddles—two of them, I'm certain; the provision sack and the extra lantern hanging together from the tree; and, crowding everywhere about me, enveloping all, the willows, those endless, shaking willows. A bird uttered its morning cry, and a string of duck passed with whirring flight overhead in the twilight. The sand whirled, dry and stinging, about my bare feet in the wind.

I walked round the tent and then went out a little way into the bush, so that I could see across the river to the farther landscape, and the same profound yet indefinable emotion of distress seized upon me again as I saw the interminable sea of bushes stretching to the horizon, looking ghostly and unreal in the wan light of dawn. I walked softly here and there, still puzzling over that odd sound of infinite pattering, and of that pressure upon the tent that had wakened me. It *must* have been the wind, I reflected—the wind bearing upon the loose, hot sand, driving the dry particles smartly against the taut canvas—the wind dropping heavily upon our fragile roof.

Yet all the time my nervousness and malaise increased appreciably. I crossed over to the farther shore and noted how the coast-line had altered in the night, and what masses of sand the river had torn away. I dipped my hands and feet into the cool current, and bathed my forehead. Already there was a glow of sunrise in the sky and the exquisite freshness of coming day. On my way back I passed purposely beneath the very bushes where I had seen the column of figures rising into the air, and midway among the clumps I suddenly found myself overtaken by a sense of vast terror. From the shadows a large figure went swiftly by. Someone passed me, as sure as ever man did. . . .

It was a great staggering blow from the wind that helped me forward again, and once out in the more open space, the sense of terror diminished strangely. The winds were about and walking, I remember saying to myself, for the winds often move like great presences under the trees. And altogether the fear that hovered about me was such an unknown and immense kind of fear, so unlike anything I had ever felt before, that it woke a sense of awe and wonder in me that did much to counteract its worst effects; and when I reached a high point in the middle of the island from which I could see the wide stretch of river, crimson in the sunrise, the whole magical beauty of it all was so overpowering that a sort of wild yearning woke in me and almost brought a cry up into the throat.

But this cry found no expression, for as my eyes wandered from the plain beyond to the island round me and noted our little tent half hidden among the willows, a dreadful discovery leaped out at me, compared to which my terror of the walking winds seemed as nothing at all.

For a change, I thought, had somehow come about in the arrangement of the landscape. It was not that my point of vantage gave me a different view, but that an alteration had apparently been effected in the relation of the tent to the willows, and of the willows to the tent. Surely the bushes now crowded much closer—unnecessarily, unpleasantly close. *They had moved nearer.*

Creeping with silent feet over the shifting sands, drawing imperceptibly nearer by soft, unhurried movements, the willows had come closer during the night. But had the wind moved them, or had they moved of themselves? I recalled the sound of infinite small patterings and the pressure upon the tent and upon my own heart that caused me to wake in terror. I swayed for a moment in the wind like a tree, finding it hard to keep my upright position on the sandy hillock. There was a suggestion here of personal agency, of deliberate intention, of aggressive hostility, and it terrified me into a sort of rigidity.

Then the reaction followed quickly. The idea was so bizarre, so absurd, that I felt inclined to laugh. But the laughter came no more readily than the cry, for the knowledge that my mind was so receptive to such dangerous imaginings brought the additional terror that it was through our minds and not through our physical bodies that the attack would come, and was coming.

The wind buffeted me about, and, very quickly it seemed, the sun came up over the horizon, for it was after four o'clock, and I must have stood on that little pinnacle of sand longer than I knew, afraid to come down to close quarters with the willows. I returned quietly, creepily, to the tent, first taking another exhaustive look round and—yes, I confess it—making a few measurements. I paced out on the warm sand the distances between the willows and the tent, making a note of the shortest distance particularly.

I crawled stealthily into my blankets. My companion, to all appearances, still slept soundly, and I was glad that this was so. Provided my experiences were not corroborated, I could find strength somehow to deny them, perhaps. With the daylight I could persuade myself that it was all a subjective hallucination, a fantasy of the night, a projection of the excited imagination.

Nothing further came in to disturb me, and I fell asleep almost at once, utterly exhausted, yet still in dread of hearing again that weird sound of multitudinous pattering, or of feeling the pressure upon my heart that had made it difficult to breathe.

IV

The sun was high in the heavens when my companion woke me from a heavy sleep and announced that the porridge was cooked and there was just time to bathe. The grateful smell of frizzling bacon entered the tent door.

"River still rising," he said, "and several islands out in mid-stream have disappeared altogether. Our own island's much smaller."

"Any wood left?" I asked sleepily.

"The wood and the island will finish to-morrow in a dead heat," he laughed, "but there's enough to last us till then."

I plunged in from the point of the island, which had indeed altered a lot in size and shape during the night, and was swept down in a moment to the landing place opposite the tent. The water was icy, and the banks flew by like the country from an express train. Bathing under such conditions was an exhilarating operation, and the terror of the night seemed cleansed out of me by a process of evaporation in the brain. The sun was blazing hot; not a cloud showed itself anywhere; the wind, however, had not abated one little jot.

Quite suddenly then the implied meaning of the Swede's words flashed across me, showing that he no longer wished to leave post-haste, and had changed his mind. "Enough to last till to-morrow"—he assumed we should stay on the island another night. It struck me as odd. The night before he was so positive the other way. How had the change come about?

Great crumblings of the banks occurred at breakfast, with heavy splashings and clouds of spray which the wind brought into our frying-pan, and my fellow-traveller talked incessantly about the difficulty the Vienna-Pesth steamers must have to find the channel in flood. But the state of his mind interested and impressed me far more than the state of the river or the difficulties of the steamers. He had changed somehow since the evening before. His manner was different—a trifle excited, a trifle shy, with a sort of suspicion about his voice and gestures. I hardly know how to describe it now in cold blood, but at the time I remember being quite certain of one thing—that he had become frightened!

He ate very little breakfast, and for once omitted to smoke his pipe. He had the map spread open beside him, and kept studying its markings.

"We'd better get off sharp in an hour," I said presently, feeling for an opening that must bring him indirectly to a partial confession at any rate. And his answer puzzled me uncomfortably: "Rather! If they'll let us."

"Who'll let us? The elements?" I asked quickly, with affected indifference.

"The powers of this awful place, whoever they are," he replied, keeping his eyes on the map. "The gods are here, if they are anywhere at all in the world."

"The elements are always the true immortals," I replied, laughing as naturally as I could manage, yet knowing quite well that my face reflected my true feelings when he looked up gravely at me and spoke across the smoke:

"We shall be fortunate if we get away without further disaster."

This was exactly what I had dreaded, and I screwed myself up to the point of the direct question. It was like agreeing to allow the dentist to extract the tooth; it had to come anyhow in the long run, and the rest was all pretence.

"Further disaster! Why, what's happened?"

185

"For one thing—the steering paddle's gone," he said quietly.

"The steering paddle gone!" I repeated, greatly excited, for this was our rudder, and the Danube in flood without a rudder was suicide. "But what—"

"And there's a tear in the bottom of the canoe," he added, with a genuine little tremor in his voice.

I continued staring at him, able only to repeat the words in his face somewhat foolishly. There, in the heat of the sun, and on this burning sand, I was aware of a freezing atmosphere descending round us. I got up to follow him, for he merely nodded his head gravely and led the way towards the tent a few yards on the other side of the fireplace. The canoe still lay there as I had last seen her in the night, ribs uppermost, the paddles, or rather, *the* paddle, on the sand beside her.

"There's only one," he said, stooping to pick it up. "And here's the rent in the base-board."

It was on the tip of my tongue to tell him that I had clearly noticed *two* paddles a few hours before, but a second impulse made me think better of it, and I said nothing. I approached to see.

There was a long, finely made tear in the bottom of the canoe where a little slither of wood had been neatly taken clean out; it looked as if the tooth of a sharp rock or snag had eaten down her length, and investigation showed that the hole went through. Had we launched out in her without observing it we must inevitably have foundered. At first the water would have made the wood swell so as to close the hole, but once out in midstream the water must have poured in, and the canoe, never more than two inches above the surface, would have filled and sunk very rapidly.

"There, you see an attempt to prepare a victim for the sacrifice," I heard him saying, more to himself than to me, "two victims rather," he added as he bent over and ran his fingers along the slit.

I began to whistle—a thing I always do unconsciously when utterly nonplussed—and purposely paid no attention to his words. I was determined to consider them foolish.

"It wasn't there last night," he said presently, straightening up from his examination and looking anywhere but at me.

"We must have scratched her in landing, of course," I stopped whistling to say. "The stones are very sharp—"

I stopped abruptly, for at that moment he turned round and met my eye squarely. I knew just as well as he did how impossible my explanation was. There were no stones, to begin with.

"And then there's this to explain too," he added quietly, handing me the paddle and pointing to the blade.

A new and curious emotion spread freezingly over me as I took and examined it. The blade was scraped down all over, beautifully scraped, as though someone had sand-papered it with care, making it so thin that the first vigorous stroke must have snapped it off at the elbow.

"One of us walked in his sleep and did this thing," I said feebly, "or— or it has been filed by the constant stream of sand particles blown against it by the wind, perhaps."

"Ah," said the Swede, turning away, laughing a little, "you can explain everything!"

"The same wind that caught the steering paddle and flung it so near the bank that it fell in with the next lump that crumbled," I called out after him, absolutely determined to find an explanation for everything he showed me.

"I see," he shouted back, turning his head to look at me before disappearing among the willow bushes.

Once alone with these perplexing evidences of personal agency, I think my first thoughts took the form of "One of us must have done this thing, and it certainly was not I." But my second thought decided how impossible it was to suppose, under all the circumstances, that either of us had done it. That my companion, the trusted friend of a dozen similar expeditions, could have knowingly had a hand in it, was a suggestion not to be entertained for a moment. Equally absurd seemed the explanation that this imperturbable and densely practical nature had suddenly become insane and was busied with insane purposes.

Yet the fact remained that what disturbed me most, and kept my fear actively alive even in this blaze of sunshine and wild beauty, was the clear certainty that some curious alteration had come about in his *mind*—that the was nervous, timid, suspicious, aware of goings on he did not speak about, watching a series of secret and hitherto unmentionable events—waiting, in a word, for a climax that he expected, and, I thought, expected very soon. This grew up in my mind intuitively—I hardly knew how.

I made a hurried examination of the tent and its surroundings, but the measurements of the night remained the same. There were deep hollows formed in the sand I now noticed for the first time, basin-shaped and of various depths and sizes, varying from that of a tea-cup to a large bowl. The wind, no doubt, was responsible for these miniature craters, just as it was for lifting the paddle and tossing it towards the water. The rent in the canoe was the only thing that seemed quite inexplicable; and, after all, it *was* conceivable that a sharp point had caught it when we landed. The examination I made of the shore did not assist this theory, but all the same I clung to it with that diminishing portion of my intelligence which I called my "reason". An explanation of some kind was an absolute necessity, just as some working explanation of the universe is necessary—however absurd—to the happiness of every individual who seeks to do his duty in the world and face the problems of life. The simile seemed to me at the time an exact parallel.

I at once set the pitch melting, and presently the Swede joined me at the work, though under the best conditions in the world the canoe could not be safe for travelling till the following day. I drew his attention casually to the hollows in the sand.

"Yes," he said, "I know. They're all over the island. But *you* can explain them, no doubt!"

"Wind, of course," I answered without hesitation. "Have you never watched those little whirlwinds in the street that twist and twirl everything into a circle? This sand's loose enough to yield, that's all."

He made no reply, and we worked on in silence for a bit. I watched him surreptitiously all the time, and I had an idea he was watching me. He seemed, too, to be always listening attentively to something I could not hear, or perhaps for something that he expected to hear, for he kept turning about and staring into the bushes, and up into the sky, and out across the water where it was visible through the openings among the willows. Sometimes he even put his hand to his ear and held it there for several minutes. He said nothing to me, however, about it, and I asked no questions. And meanwhile, as he mended that torn canoe with the skill and address of a red Indian, I was glad to notice his absorption in the work, for there was a vague dread in my heart that he would speak of the changed aspect of the willows. And, if he had noticed *that*, my imagination could no longer be held a sufficient explanation of it.

At length, after a long pause, he began to talk.

"Queer thing," he added in a hurried sort of voice, as though he wanted to say something and get it over. "Queer thing, I mean, about that otter last night."

I had expected something so totally different that he caught me with surprise, and I looked up sharply.

"Shows how lonely this place is. Otters are awfully shy things—"

"I don't mean that, of course," he interrupted. "I mean—do you think—did you think it really *was* an otter?"

"What else, in the name of Heaven, what else?"

"You know, I saw it before you did, and at first it seemed—so *much* bigger than an otter."

"The sunset as you looked up-stream magnified it, or something," I replied.

He looked at me absently a moment, as though his mind were busy with other thoughts.

"It had such extraordinary yellow eyes," he went on half to himself.

"That was the sun too," I laughed, a trifle boisterously. "I suppose you'll wonder next if that fellow in the boat—"

I suddenly decided not to finish the sentence. He was in the act again of listening, turning his head to the wind, and something in the expression of his face made me halt. The subject dropped, and we went on with our caulking. Apparently he had not noticed my unfinished sentence. Five minutes later, however, he looked at me across the canoe, the smoking pitch in his hand, his face exceedingly grave.

"I *did* rather wonder, if you want to know," he said slowly, "what that thing in the boat was. I remember thinking at the time it was not a man. The whole business seemed to rise quite suddenly out of the water."

I laughed again boisterously in his face, but this time there was impatience, and a strain of anger too, in my feeling.

"Look here now," I cried, "this place is quite queer enough without going out of our way to imagine things! That boat was an ordinary boat, and the man in it was an ordinary man, and they were both going down stream as fast as they could lick. And that otter *was* an otter, so don't let's play the fool about it!"

He looked steadily at me with the same grave expression. He was not in the least annoyed. I took courage from his silence.

"And, for Heaven's sake," I went on, "don't keep pretending you hear things, because it only gives me the jumps, and there's nothing to hear but the river and this cursed old thundering wind."

"You *fool!*" he answered in a low, shocked voice, "you utter fool. That's just the way all victims talk. As if you didn't understand just as well as I do!" he sneered with scorn in his voice, and a sort of resignation. "The best thing you can do is to keep quiet and try to hold your mind as firm as possible. This feeble attempt at self-deception only makes the truth harder when you're forced to meet it."

My little effort was over, and I found nothing more to say, for I knew quite well his words were true, and that *I* was the fool, not *he*. Up to a certain stage in the adventure he kept ahead of me easily, and I think I felt annoyed to be out of it, to be thus proved less psychic, less sensitive than himself to these extraordinary happenings, and half ignorant all the time of what was going on under my very nose. *He knew* from the very beginning, apparently. But at the moment I wholly missed the point of his words about the necessity of there being a victim, and that we ourselves were destined to satisfy the want. I dropped all pretence thenceforward, but thenceforward likewise my fear increased steadily to the climax.

"But you're quite right about one thing," he added, before the subject passed, "and that is that we're wiser not to talk about it, or even to think about it, because what one *thinks* finds expression in words, and what one *says*, happens."

That afternoon, while the canoe dried and hardened, we spent trying to fish, testing the leak, collecting wood, and watching the enormous flood of rising water. Masses of driftwood swept near our shores sometimes, and we fished for them with long willow branches. The island grew perceptibly smaller as the banks were torn away with great gulps and splashes. The weather kept brilliantly fine till about four o'clock, and then for the first time for three days the wind showed signs of abating. Clouds began to gather in the south-west, spreading thence slowly over the sky.

This lessening of the wind came as a great relief, for the incessant roaring, banging, and thundering had irritated our nerves. Yet the silence that came about five o'clock with its sudden cessation was in a manner quite as oppressive. The booming of the river had everything in its own way then; it filled the air with deep murmurs, more musical than the wind noises, but infinitely more monotonous. The wind held many notes, rising, falling, always beating out some sort of great elemental tune; whereas the river's song lay between three notes at most—dull pedal notes, that held a lugubrious quality foreign to the wind, and somehow seemed to me, in my then nervous state, to sound wonderfully well the music of doom.

It was extraordinary, too, how the withdrawal suddenly of bright sunlight took everything out of the landscape that made for cheerfulness; and since this particular landscape had already managed to convey the suggestion of something sinister, the change of course was all the more unwelcome and noticeable. For me, I know, the darkening outlook became distinctly more alarming, and I found myself more than once calculating how soon after sunset the full moon would get up in the east, and whether the gathering clouds would greatly interfere with her lighting of the little island.

With this general hush of the wind—though it still indulged in occasional brief gusts—the river seemed to me to grow blacker, the willows to stand more densely together. The latter, too, kept up a sort of independent movement of their own, rustling among themselves when no wind stirred, and shaking oddly from the roots upwards. When common objects in this way be come charged with the suggestion of horror, they stimulate the imagination far more than things of unusual appearance; and these bushes, crowding huddled about us, assumed for me in the darkness a bizarre *grotesquerie* of appearance that lent to them somehow the aspect of purposeful and living creatures. Their very ordinariness, I felt, masked what was malignant and hostile to us. The forces of the region drew nearer with the coming of night. They were focusing upon our island, and more particularly upon ourselves. For thus, somehow, in the terms of the imagination, did my really indescribable sensations in this extraordinary place present themselves.

I had slept a good deal in the early afternoon, and had thus recovered somewhat from the exhaustion of a disturbed night, but this only served apparently to render me more susceptible than before to the obsessing spell of the haunting. I fought against it, laughing at my feelings as absurd and childish, with very obvious physiological explanations, yet, in spite of every effort, they gained in strength upon me so that I dreaded the night as a child lost in a forest must dread the approach of darkness.

The canoe we had carefully covered with a waterproof sheet during the day, and the one remaining paddle had been securely tied by the Swede to the base of a tree, lest the wind should rob us of that too. From five o'clock onwards I busied myself with the stew-pot and preparations for dinner, it being my turn to cook that night. We had potatoes, onions, bits of bacon fat to add flavour, and a general thick residue from former stews at the bottom of the pot; with black bread broken up into it the result was most excellent, and it was followed by a stew of plums with sugar and a brew of strong tea with dried milk. A good pile of wood lay close at hand, and the absence of wind made my duties easy. My companion sat lazily watching me, dividing his attentions between cleaning his pipe and giving useless advice—an admitted privilege of the off-duty man. He had been very quiet all the afternoon, engaged in re-caulking the canoe, strengthening the tent ropes, and fishing for driftwood while I slept. No more talk about undesirable things had passed between us, and I think his only remarks had to do with the gradual destruction of the island, which he declared was now fully a third smaller than when we first landed.

The pot had just begun to bubble when I heard his voice calling to me from the bank, where he had wandered away without my noticing. I ran up.

"Come and listen," he said, "and see what you make of it." He held his hand cupwise to his ear, as so often before.

"*Now* do you hear anything?" he asked, watching me curiously.

. We stood there, listening attentively together. At first I heard only the deep note of the water and the hissings rising from its turbulent surface. The willows, for once, were motionless and silent. Then a sound began to reach my ears faintly, a peculiar sound—something like the humming of a distant gong. It seemed to come across to us in the darkness from the waste of swamps and willows opposite. It was repeated at regular intervals, but it was certainly neither the sound of a bell nor the hooting of a distant steamer. I can liken it to nothing so much as to the sound of an immense gong, suspended far up in the sky, repeating incessantly its muffled metallic note, soft and musical, as it was repeatedly struck. My heart quickened as I listened.

"I've heard it all day," said my companion. "While you slept this afternoon it came all round the island. I hunted it down, but could never get near enough to see—to localise it correctly. Sometimes it was overhead, and sometimes it seemed under the water. Once or twice, too, I could have sworn it was not outside at all, but *within myself*—you know—the way a sound in the fourth dimension is supposed to come."

I was too much puzzled to pay much attention to his words. I listened carefully, striving to associate it with any known familiar sound I could think of, but without success. It changed in the direction, too, coming nearer, and then sinking utterly away into remote distance. I cannot say that it was ominous in quality, because to me it seemed distinctly musical, yet I must admit it set going a distressing feeling that made me wish I had never heard it.

"The wind blowing in those sand-funnels," I said, determined to find an explanation, "or the bushes rubbing together after the storm perhaps."

"It comes off the whole swamp," my friend answered. "It comes from everywhere at once." He ignored my explanations. "It comes from the willow bushes somehow—"

"But now the wind has dropped," I objected. "The willows can hardly make a noise by themselves, can they?"

His answer frightened me, first because I had dreaded it, and secondly, because I knew intuitively it was true.

"It is *because* the wind has dropped we now hear it. It was drowned before. It is the cry, I believe, of the—"

I dashed back to my fire, warned by the sound of bubbling that the stew was in danger, but determined at the same time to escape further conversation. I was resolute, if possible, to avoid the exchanging of views. I dreaded, too, that he would begin about the gods, or the elemental forces, or something else disquieting, and I wanted to keep myself well in hand for what might happen later. There was another night to be faced before we escaped from this distressing place, and there was no knowing yet what it might bring forth.

"Come and cut up bread for the pot," I called to him, vigorously stirring the appetising mixture. That stew-pot held sanity for us both, and the thought made me laugh.

He came over slowly and took the provision sack from the tree, fumbling in its mysterious depths, and then emptying the entire contents upon the ground-sheet at his feet.

"Hurry up!" I cried; "it's boiling."

The Swede burst out into a roar of laughter that startled me. It was forced laughter, not artificial exactly, but mirthless.

"There's nothing here!" he shouted, holding his sides.

"Bread, I mean."

"It's gone. There is no bread. They've taken it!"

I dropped the long spoon and ran up. Everything the sack had contained lay upon the ground-sheet, but there was no loaf.

The whole dead weight of my growing fear fell upon me and shook me. Then I burst out laughing too. It was the only thing to do: and the sound of my laughter also made me understand his. The stain of psychical pressure caused it—this explosion of unnatural laughter in both of us; it was an effort of repressed forces to seek relief; it was a temporary safety-valve. And with both of us it ceased quite suddenly.

"How criminally stupid of me!" I cried, still determined to be consistent and find an explanation. "I clean forgot to buy a loaf at Pressburg. That chattering woman put everything out of my head, and I must have left it lying on the counter or—"

"The oatmeal, too, is much less than it was this morning," the Swede interrupted.

Why in the world need he draw attention to it? I thought angrily.

"There's enough for to-morrow," I said, stirring vigorously, "and we can get lots more at Komorn or Gran. In twenty-four hours we shall be miles from here."

"I hope so—to God," he muttered, putting the things back into the sack, "unless we're claimed first as victims for the sacrifice," he added with a foolish laugh. He dragged the sack into the tent, for safety's sake, I suppose, and I heard him mumbling to himself, but so indistinctly that it seemed quite natural for me to ignore his words.

Our meal was beyond question a gloomy one, and we ate it almost in silence, avoiding one another's eyes, and keeping the fire bright. Then we washed up and prepared for the night, and, once smoking, our minds unoccupied with any definite duties, the apprehension I had felt all day long became more and more acute. It was not then active fear, I think, but the very vagueness of its origin distressed me far more that if I had been able to ticket and face it squarely. The curious sound I have likened to the note of a gong became now almost incessant, and filled the stillness of the night with a faint, continuous ringing rather than a series of distinct notes. At one time it was behind and at another time in front of us. Sometimes I fancied it came from the bushes on our left, and then again from the clumps on our right. More often it hovered directly overhead like the whirring of wings. It was really everywhere at once, behind, in front, at our sides and over our heads, completely surrounding us. The sound really defies description. But nothing within my knowledge is like that ceaseless muffled humming rising off the deserted world of swamps and willows.

We sat smoking in comparative silence, the strain growing every minute greater. The worst feature of the situation seemed to me that we did not know what to expect, and could therefore make no sort of preparation by way of defence. We could anticipate nothing. My explanations made in the sunshine, moreover, now came to haunt me with their foolish and wholly unsatisfactory nature, and it was more and more clear to us that some kind of plain talk with my companion was inevitable, whether I liked it or not. After all, we had to spend the night together, and to sleep in the same tent side by side. I saw that I could not get along much longer without the support of his mind, and for that, of course, plain talk was imperative. As long as possible, however, I postponed this little climax, and tried to ignore or laugh at the occasional sentences he flung into the emptiness.

Some of these sentences, moreover, were confoundedly disquieting to me, coming as they did to corroborate much that I felt myself; corroboration, too—which made it so much more convincing—from a totally different point of view. He composed such curious sentences, and hurled them at me in such an inconsequential sort of way, as though his main line of thought was secret to himself, and these fragments were the bits he found it impossible to digest. He got rid of them by uttering them. Speech relieved him. It was like being sick.

"There are things about us, I'm sure, that make for disorder, disintegration, destruction, *our* destruction," he said once, while the fire blazed between us. "We've strayed out of a safe line somewhere."

And, another time, when the gong sounds had come nearer, ringing much louder than before, and directly over our heads, he said as though talking to himself:

"I don't think a phonograph would show any record of that. The sound doesn't come to me by the ears at all. The vibrations reach me in another manner altogether, and seem to be within me, which is precisely how a fourth dimensional sound might be supposed to make itself heard."

I purposely made no reply to this, but I sat up a little closer to the fire and peered about me into the darkness. The clouds were massed all over the sky, and no trace of moonlight came through. Very still, too, everything was, so that the river and the frogs had things all their own way.

"It has that about it," he went on, "which is utterly out of common experience. It is *unknown*. Only one thing describes it really: it is a non-human sound; I mean a sound outside humanity."

Having rid himself of this indigestible morsel, he lay quiet for a time, but he had so admirably expressed my own feeling that it was a relief to have the thought out, and to have confined it by the limitation of words from dangerous wandering to and fro in the mind.

The solitude of that Danube camping-place, can I ever forget it? The feeling of being utterly alone on an empty planet! My thoughts ran incessantly upon cities and the haunts of men. I would have given my soul, as the saying is, for the "feel" of those Bavarian villages we had passed through by the score; for the normal, human commonplaces: peasants drinking beer, tables beneath the trees, hot sunshine, and a ruined castle on the rocks behind the red-roofed church. Even the tourists would have been welcome.

Yet what I felt of dread was no ordinary ghostly fear. It was infinitely greater, stranger, and seemed to arise from some dim ancestral sense of terror more profoundly disturbing than anything I had known or dreamed of. We had "strayed", as the Swede put it, into some region or some set of conditions where the risks were great, yet unintelligible to us; where the frontiers of some unknown world lay close about us. It was a spot held by the dwellers in some outer space, a sort of peep-hole whence they could spy upon the earth, themselves unseen, a point where the veil between had worn a little thin. As the final result of too long a sojourn here, we should be carried over the border and deprived of what we called "our lives," yet by mental, not physical, processes. In that sense, as he said, we should be the victims of our adventure—a sacrifice.

It took us in different fashion, each according to the measure of his sensitiveness and powers of resistance. I translated it vaguely into a personification of the mightily disturbed elements, investing them with the horror of a deliberate and malefic purpose, resentful of our audacious intrusion into their breeding-place; whereas my friend threw it into the unoriginal form at first of a trespass on some ancient shrine, some place where the old gods still held sway, where the emotional forces of former worshippers still clung, and the ancestral portion of him yielded to the old pagan spell.

At any rate, here was a place unpolluted by men, kept clean by the winds from coarsening human influences, a place where spiritual agencies were within reach and aggressive. Never, before or since, have I been so attacked by indescribable suggestions of a "beyond region", of another scheme of life, another evolution not parallel to the human. And in the end our minds would succumb under the weight of the awful spell, and we should be drawn across the frontier into *their* world.

Small things testified to the amazing influence of the place, and now in the silence round the fire they allowed themselves to be noted by the mind. The very atmosphere had proved itself a magnifying medium to distort every indication: the otter rolling in the current, the hurrying boatman making signs, the shifting willows, one and all had been robbed of its natural character, and revealed in something of its other aspect—as it existed across the border to that other region. And this changed aspect I felt was now not merely to me, but to the race. The whole experience whose verge we touched was unknown to humanity at all. It was a new order of experience, and in the true sense of the word *unearthly*.

"It's the deliberate, calculating purpose that reduces one's courage to zero," the Swede said suddenly, as if he had been actually following my thoughts. "Otherwise imagination might count for much. But the paddle, the canoe, the lessening food—"

"Haven't I explained all that once?" I interrupted viciously.

"You have," he answered dryly; "you have indeed."

He made other remarks too, as usual, about what he called the "plain determination to provide a victim"; but, having now arranged my thoughts better, I recognised that this was simply the cry of his frightened soul against the knowledge that he was being attacked in a vital part, and that he would be somehow taken or destroyed. The situation called for a courage and calmness of reasoning that neither of us could compass, and I have never before been so clearly conscious of two persons in me—the one that explained everything, and the other that laughed at such foolish explanations, yet was horribly afraid.

Meanwhile, in the pitchy night the fire died down and the wood pile grew small. Neither of us moved to replenish the stock, and the darkness consequently came up very close to our faces. A few feet beyond the circle of firelight it was inky black. Occasionally a stray puff of wind set the willows shivering about us, but apart from this not very welcome sound a deep and depressing silence reigned, broken only by the gurgling of the river and the humming in the air overhead.

We both missed, I think, the shouting company of the winds.

At length, at a moment when a stray puff prolonged itself as though the wind were about to rise again, I reached the point for me of saturation, the point where it was absolutely necessary to find relief in plain speech, or else to betray myself by some hysterical extravagance that must have been far worse in its effect upon both of us. I kicked the fire into a blaze, and turned to my companion abruptly. He looked up with a start.

"I can't disguise it any longer," I said; "I don't like this place, and the darkness, and the noises, and the awful feelings I get. There's something here that beats me utterly. I'm in a blue funk, and that's the plain truth. If the other shore was—different, I swear I'd be inclined to swim for it!"

The Swede's face turned very white beneath the deep tan of sun and wind. He stared straight at me and answered quietly, but his voice betrayed his huge excitement by its unnatural calmness. For the moment, at any rate, he was the strong man of the two. He was more phlegmatic, for one thing.

"It's not a physical condition we can escape from by running away," he replied, in the tone of a doctor diagnosing some grave disease; "we must sit tight and wait. There are forces close here that could kill a herd of elephants in a second as easily as you or I could squash a fly. Our only chance is to keep perfectly still. Our insignificance perhaps may save us."

I put a dozen questions into my expression of face, but found no words. It was precisely like listening to an accurate description of a disease whose symptoms had puzzled me.

"I mean that so far, although aware of our disturbing presence, they have not *found* us—not 'located' us, as the Americans say," he went on. "They're blundering about like men hunting for a leak of gas. The paddle and canoe and provisions prove that. I think they *feel* us, but cannot actually see us. We must keep our minds quiet—it's our minds they feel. We must control our thoughts, or it's all up with us."

"Death, you mean?" I stammered, icy with the horror of his suggestion.

"Worse—by far," he said. "Death, according to one's belief, means either annihilation or release from the limitations of the senses, but it involves no change of character. *You* don't suddenly alter just because the body's gone. But this means a radical alteration, a complete change, a horrible loss of oneself by substitution—far worse than death, and not even annihilation. We happen to have camped in a spot where their region touches ours, where the veil between has worn thin"—horrors! he was using my very own phrase, my actual words—"so that they are aware of our being in their neighbourhood."

"But *who* are aware?" I asked.

I forgot the shaking of the willows in the windless calm, the humming overhead, everything except that I was waiting for an answer that I dreaded more than I can possibly explain.

He lowered his voice at once to reply, leaning forward a little over the fire, an indefinable change in his face that made me avoid his eyes and look down upon the ground.

"All my life," he said, "I have been strangely, vividly conscious of another region—not far removed from our own world in one sense, yet wholly different in kind—where great things go on unceasingly, where immense and terrible personalities hurry by, intent on vast purposes compared to which earthly affairs, the rise and fall of nations, the destinies of empires, the fate of armies and continents, are all as dust in the balance; vast purposes, I mean, that deal directly with the soul, and not indirectly with mere expressions of the soul—"

"I suggest just now—" I began, seeking to stop him, feeling as though

198

I was face to face with a madman. But he instantly overbore me with his torrent that *had* to come.

"You think," he said, "it is the spirit of the elements, and I thought perhaps it was the old gods. But I tell you now it is—*neither*. These would be comprehensible entities, for they have relations with men, depending upon them for worship or sacrifice, whereas these beings who are now about us have absolutely nothing to do with mankind, and it is mere chance that their space happens just at this spot to touch our own."

The mere conception, which his words somehow made so convincing, as I listened to them there in the dark stillness of that lonely island, set me shaking a little all over. I found it impossible to control my movements.

"And what do you propose?" I began again.

"A sacrifice, a victim, might save us by distracting them until we could get away," he went on, "just as the wolves stop to devour the dogs and give the sleigh another start. But—I see no chance of any other victim now."

I stared blankly at him. The gleam in his eye was dreadful. Presently he continued.

"It's the willows, of course. The willows *mask* the others, but the others are feeling about for us. If we let our minds betray our fear, we're lost, lost utterly." He looked at me with an expression so calm, so determined, so sincere, that I no longer had any doubts as to his sanity. He was as sane as any man ever was. "If we can hold out through the night," he added, "we may get off in the daylight unnoticed, or rather, *undiscovered*."

"But you really think a sacrifice would—"

That gong-like humming came down very close over our heads as I spoke, but it was my friend's scared face that really stopped my mouth.

"Hush!" he whispered, holding up his hand. "Do not mention them more than you can help. Do not refer to them *by name*. To name is to reveal: it is the inevitable clue, and our only hope lies in ignoring them, in order that they may ignore us."

"Even in thought?" He was extraordinarily agitated.

"Especially in thought. Our thoughts make spirals in their world. We must keep them *out of our minds* at all costs if possible."

I raked the fire together to prevent the darkness having everything its own way. I never longed for the sun as I longed for it then in the awful blackness of that summer night.

"Were you awake all last night?" he went on suddenly.

"I slept badly a little after dawn," I replied evasively, trying to follow his instructions, which I knew instinctively were true, "but the wind, of course—"

"I know. But the wind won't account for all the noises."

"Then you heard it too?"

"The multiplying countless little footsteps I heard," he said, adding, after a moment's hesitation, "and that other sound—"

"You mean above the tent, and the pressing down upon us of something tremendous, gigantic?"

He nodded significantly.

"It was like the beginning of a sort of inner suffocation?" I said.

"Partly, yes. It seemed to me that the weight of the atmosphere had been altered—had increased enormously, so that we should have been crushed."

"And *that*," I went on, determined to have it all out, pointing upwards where the gong-like note hummed ceaselessly, rising and falling like wind. "What do you make of that?"

"It's *their* sound," he whispered gravely. "It's the sound of their world, the humming in their region. The division here is so thin that it leaks through somehow. But, if you listen carefully, you'll find it's not above so much as around us. It's in the willows. It's the willows themselves humming, because here the willows have been made symbols of the forces that are against us."

I could not follow exactly what he meant by this, yet the thought and idea in my mind were beyond question the thought and idea in his. I realised what he realised, only with less power of analysis than his. It was on the tip of my tongue to tell him at last about my hallucination of the ascending figures and the moving bushes, when he suddenly thrust his face again close into mine across the firelight and began to speak in a very earnest whisper. He amazed me by his calmness and pluck, his apparent control of the situation. This man I had for years deemed unimaginative, stolid!

"Now listen," he said. "The only thing for us to do is to go on as though nothing had happened, follow our usual habits, go to bed, and so forth; pretend we feel nothing and notice nothing. It is a question wholly of the mind, and the less we think about them the better our chance of escape. Above all, don't *think*, for what you think happens!"

"All right," I managed to reply, simply breathless with his words and the strangeness of it all; "all right, I'll try, but tell me one more thing first. Tell me what you make of those hollows in the ground all about us, those sand-funnels?"

"No!" he cried, forgetting to whisper in his excitement. "I dare not, simply dare not, put the thought into words. If you have not guessed I am glad. Don't try to. *They* have put it into my mind; try your hardest to prevent their putting it into yours."

He sank his voice again to a whisper before he finished, and I did not press him to explain. There was already just about as much horror in me as I could hold. The conversation came to an end, and we smoked our pipes busily in silence.

Then something happened, something unimportant apparently, as the way is when the nerves are in a very great state of tension, and this small thing for a brief space gave me an entirely different point of view. I chanced to look down at my sand-shoe—the sort we used for the canoe—and something to do with the hole at the toe suddenly recalled to me the London shop where I had bought them, the difficulty the man had in fitting me, and other details of the uninteresting but practical operation. At once, in its train, followed a wholesome view of the modern sceptical world I was accustomed to move in at home. I thought of roast beef, and ale, motor-cars, policemen, brass bands, and a dozen other things that proclaimed the soul of ordinariness or utility. The effect was immediate and astonishing even to myself. Psychologically, I suppose, it was simply a sudden and violent reaction after the strain of living in an atmosphere of things that to the normal consciousness must seem impossible and incredible. But, whatever the cause, it momentarily lifted the spell from my heart, and left me for the short space of a minute feeling free and utterly unafraid. I looked up at my friend opposite.

"You damned old pagan!" I cried, laughing aloud in his face. "You imaginative idiot! You superstitious idolator! You—"

I stopped in the middle, seized anew by the old horror. I tried to smother the sound of my voice as something sacrilegious. The Swede, of course, heard it too—the strange cry overhead in the darkness—and that sudden drop in the air as though something had come nearer.

He had turned ashen white under the tan. He stood bolt upright in front of the fire, stiff as a rod, staring at me.

"After that," he said in a sort of helpless, frantic way, "we must go! We can't stay now; we must strike camp this very instant and go on—down the river."

He was talking, I saw, quite wildly, his words dictated by abject terror—the terror he had resisted so long, but which had caught him at last.

"In the dark?" I exclaimed, shaking with fear after my hysterical outburst, but still realising our position better than he did. "Sheer madness! The river's in flood, and we've only got a single paddle. Besides, we only go deeper into their country! There's nothing ahead for fifty miles but willows, willows, willows!"

He sat down again in a state of semi-collapse. The positions, by one of those kaleidoscopic changes nature loves, were suddenly reversed, and the control of our forces passed over into my hands. His mind at last had reached the point where it was beginning to weaken.

"What on earth possessed you to do such a thing?" he whispered with the awe of genuine terror in his voice and face.

I crossed round to his side of the fire. I took both his hands in mine, kneeling down beside him and looking straight into his frightened eyes.

"We'll make one more blaze," I said firmly, "and then turn in for the night. At sunrise we'll be off full speed for Komorn. Now, pull yourself together a bit, and remember your own advice about *not thinking fear!*"

He said no more, and I saw that he would agree and obey. In some measure, too, it was a sort of relief to get up and make an excursion into the darkness for more wood. We kept close together, almost touching, groping among the bushes and along the bank. The humming overhead never ceased, but seemed to me to grow louder as we increased our distance from the fire. It was shivery work!

We were grubbing away in the middle of a thickish clump of willows where some driftwood from a former flood had caught high among the branches, when my body was seized in a grip that made me half drop upon the sand. It was the Swede. He had fallen against me, and was clutching me for support. I heard his breath coming and going in short gasps.

"Look! By my soul!" he whispered, and for the first time in my experience I knew what it was to hear tears of terror in a human voice. He was pointing to the fire, some fifty feet away. I followed the direction of his finger, and I swear my heart missed a beat.

There, in front of the dim glow, *something was moving.*

I saw it through a veil that hung before my eyes like the gauze drop-curtain used at the back of a theatre—hazily a little. It was neither a human figure nor an animal. To me it gave the strange impression of being as large as several animals grouped together, like horses, two or three, moving slowly. The Swede, too, got a similar result, though expressing it differently, for he thought it was shaped and sized like a clump of willow bushes, rounded at the top, and moving all over upon its surface—"coiling upon itself like smoke," he said afterwards.

"I watched it settle downwards through the bushes," he sobbed at me. "Look, by God! It's coming this way! Oh, oh!"—he gave a kind of whistling cry. *"They've found us."*

I gave one terrified glance, which just enabled me to see that the shadowy form was swinging towards us through the bushes, and then I collapsed backwards with a crash into the branches. These failed, of course, to support my weight, so that with the Swede on top of me we fell in a struggling heap upon the sand. I really hardly knew what was happening. I was conscious only of a sort of enveloping sensation of icy fear that plucked the nerves out of their fleshly covering, twisted them this way and that, and replaced them quivering. My eyes were tightly shut; something in my throat choked me; a feeling that my consciousness was expanding, extending out into space, swiftly gave way to another feeling that I was losing it altogether, and about to die.

An acute spasm of pain passed through me, and I was aware that the Swede had hold of me in such a way that he hurt me abominably. It was the way he caught at me in falling.

But it was the pain, he declared afterwards, that saved me; it caused me to *forget them* and think of something else at the very instant when they were about to find me. It concealed my mind from them at the moment of discovery, yet just in time to evade their terrible seizing of me. He himself, he says, actually swooned at the same moment, and that was what saved him.

I only know that at a later time, how long or short is impossible to say, I found myself scrambling up out of the slippery network of willow branches, and saw my companion standing in front of me holding out a hand to assist me. I stared at him in a dazed way, rubbing the arm he had twisted for me. Nothing came to me to say, somehow.

"I lost consciousness for a moment or two," I heard him say. "That's what saved me. It made me stop thinking about them."

"You nearly broke my arm in two," I said, uttering my only connected thought at the moment. A numbness came over me.

"That's what saved *you!*" he replied. "Between us, we've managed to set them off on a false tack somewhere. The humming has ceased. It's gone—for the moment at any rate!"

A wave of hysterical laughter seized me again, and this time spread to my friend too—great healing gusts of shaking laughter that brought a tremendous sense of relief in their train. We made our way back to the fire and put the wood on so that it blazed at once. Then we saw that the tent had fallen over and lay in a tangled heap upon the ground.

We picked it up, and during the process tripped more than once and caught our feet in sand.

"It's those sand-funnels," exclaimed the Swede, when the tent was up again and the firelight lit up the ground for several yards about us. "And look at the size of them!"

All round the tent and about the fireplace where we had seen the moving shadows there were deep funnel-shaped hollows in the sand, exactly similar to the ones we had already found over the island, only far bigger and deeper, beautifully formed, and wide enough in some instances to admit the whole of my foot and leg.

Neither of us said a word. We both knew that sleep was the safest thing we could do, and to bed we went accordingly without further delay, having first thrown sand on the fire and taken the provision sack and the paddle inside the tent with us. The canoe, too, we propped in such a way at the end of the tent that our feet touched it, and the least motion would disturb and wake us.

In case of emergency, too, we again went to bed in our clothes, ready for a sudden start.

V

It was my firm intention to lie awake all night and watch, but the exhaustion of nerves and body decreed otherwise, and sleep after a while came over me with a welcome blanket of oblivion. The fact that my companion also slept quickened its approach. At first he fidgeted and constantly sat up, asking me if I "heard this" or "heard that." He tossed about on his cork mattress, and said the tent was moving and the river had risen over the point of the island; but each time I went out to look I returned with the report that all was well, and finally he grew calmer and lay still. Then at length his breathing became regular and I heard unmistakable sounds of snoring—the first and only time in my life when snoring has been a welcome and calming influence.

This, I remember, was the last thought in my mind before dozing off.

A difficulty in breathing woke me, and I found the blanket over my face. But something else besides the blanket was pressing upon me, and my first thought was that my companion had rolled off his mattress on to my own in his sleep. I called to him and sat up, and at the same moment it

204

came to me that the tent was *surrounded*. That sound of multitudinous soft pattering was again audible outside, filling the night with horror.

I called again to him, louder than before. He did not answer, but I missed the sound of his snoring, and also noticed that the flap of the tent was down. This was the unpardonable sin. I crawled out in the darkness to hook it back securely, and it was then for the first time I realised positively that the Swede was not there. He had gone.

I dashed out in a mad run, seized by a dreadful agitation, and the moment I was out I plunged into a sort of torrent of humming that surrounded me completely and came out of every quarter of the heavens at once. It was that same familiar humming—gone mad! A swarm of great invisible bees might have been about me in the air. The sound seemed to thicken the very atmosphere, and I felt that my lungs worked with difficulty.

But my friend was in danger, and I could not hesitate.

The dawn was just about to break, and a faint whitish light spread upwards over the clouds from a thin strip of clear horizon. No wind stirred. I could just make out the bushes and river beyond, and the pale sandy patches. In my excitement I ran frantically to and fro about the island, calling him by name, shouting at the top of my voice the first words that came into my head. But the willows smothered my voice, and the humming muffled it, so that the sound only travelled a few feet round me. I plunged among the bushes, tripping headlong, tumbling over roots, and scraping my face as I tore this way and that among the preventing branches.

Then, quite unexpectedly, I came out upon the island's point and saw a dark figure outlined between the water and the sky. It was the Swede. And already he had one foot in the river! A moment more and he would have taken the plunge.

I threw myself upon him, flinging my arms about his waist and dragging him shorewards with all my strength. Of course he struggled furiously, making a noise all the time just like that cursed humming, and using the most outlandish phrases in his anger about "going *inside* to Them", and "taking the way of the water and the wind", and God only knows what more besides, that I tried in vain to recall afterwards, but which turned me sick with horror and amazement as I listened. But in the end I managed to get him into the comparative safety of the tent, and flung him breathless and cursing upon the mattress where I held him until the fit had passed.

I think the suddenness with which it all went and he grew calm, coinciding as it did with the equally abrupt cessation of the humming and pattering outside—I think this was almost the strangest part of the whole business perhaps. For he had just opened his eyes and turned his tired face up to me so that the dawn threw a pale light upon it through the doorway, and said, for all the world just like a frightened child:

"My life, old man—it's my life I owe you. But it's all over now anyhow. They've found a victim in our place!"

Then he dropped back upon his blankets and went to sleep literally under my eyes. He simply collapsed, and began to snore again as healthily as though nothing had happened and he had never tried to offer his own life as a sacrifice by drowning. And when the sunlight woke him three hours later—hours of ceaseless vigil for me—it became so clear to me that he remembered absolutely nothing of what he had attempted to do, that I deemed it wise to hold my peace and ask no dangerous questions.

He woke naturally and easily, as I have said, when the sun was already high in a windless hot sky, and he at once got up and set about the preparation of the fire for breakfast. I followed him anxiously at bathing, but he did not attempt to plunge in, merely dipping his head and making some remark about the extra coldness of the water.

"River's falling at last," he said, "and I'm glad of it."

"The humming has stopped too," I said.

He looked up at me quietly with his normal expression. Evidently he remembered everything except his own attempt at suicide.

"Everything has stopped," he said, "because—"

He hesitated. But I knew some reference to that remark he had made just before he fainted was in his mind, and I was determined to know it.

"Because 'They've found another victim'?" I said, forcing a little laugh.

"Exactly," he answered, "exactly! I feel as positive of it as though—as though—I feel quite safe again, I mean," he finished.

He began to look curiously about him. The sunlight lay in hot patches on the sand. There was no wind. The willows were motionless. He slowly rose to feet.

"Come," he said; "I think if we look, we shall find it."

He started off on a run, and I followed him. He kept to the banks, poking with a stick among the sandy bays and caves and little back-waters, myself always close on his heels.

"Ah!" he exclaimed presently, "ah!"

The tone of his voice somehow brought back to me a vivid sense of the horror of the last twenty-four hours, and I hurried up to join him. He was pointing with his stick at a large black object that lay half in the water and half on the sand. It appeared to be caught by some twisted willow roots so that the river could not sweep it away. A few hours before the spot must have been under water.

"See," he said quietly, "the victim that made our escape possible!"

And when I peered across his shoulder I saw that his stick rested on the body of a man. He turned it over. It was the corpse of a peasant, and the face was hidden in the sand. Clearly the man had been drowned, but a few hours before, and his body must have been swept down upon our island somewhere about the hour of the dawn—*at the very time the fit had passed.*

"We must give it a decent burial, you know."

"I suppose so," I replied. I shuddered a little in spite of myself, for there was something about the appearance of that poor drowned man that turned me cold.

The Swede glanced up sharply at me, an undecipherable expression on his face, and began clambering down the bank. I followed him more leisurely. The current, I noticed, had torn away much of the clothing from the body, so that the neck and part of the chest lay bare.

Half-way down the bank my companion suddenly stopped and held up his hand in warning; but either my foot slipped, or I had gained too much momentum to bring myself quickly to a halt, for I bumped into him and sent him forward with a sort of leap to save himself. We tumbled together on to the hard sand so that our feet splashed into the water. And, before anything could be done, we had collided a little heavily against the corpse.

The Swede uttered a sharp cry. And I sprang back as if I had been shot.

At the moment we touched the body there rose from its surface the loud sound of humming—the sound of several hummings—which passed with a vast commotion as of winged things in the air about us and disappeared upwards into the sky, growing fainter and fainter till they finally ceased in the distance. It was exactly as though we had disturbed some living yet invisible creatures at work.

My companion clutched me, and I think I clutched him, but before either of us had time properly to recover from the unexpected shock, we saw that a movement of the current was turning the corpse round so that it became released from the grip of the willow roots. A moment later it had turned completely over, the dead face uppermost, staring at the sky. It lay on the edge of the main stream. In another moment it would be swept away.

The Swede started to save it, shouting again something I did not catch about a "proper burial"—and then abruptly dropped upon his knees on the sand and covered his eyes with his hands. I was beside him in an instant.

I saw what he had seen.

For just as the body swung round to the current the face and the exposed chest turned full towards us, and showed plainly how the skin and flesh were indented with small hollows, beautifully formed, and exactly similar in shape and kind to the sand-funnels that we had found all over the island.

"Their mark!" I heard my companion mutter under his breath. "Their awful mark!"

And when I turned my eyes again from his ghastly face to the river, the current had done its work, and the body had been swept away into midstream and was already beyond our reach and almost out of sight, turning over and over on the waves like an otter.

M. P. SHIEL (1865-1947) was a British writer, an eccentric prose stylist best remembered for his apocalyptic novel *The Purple Cloud* (1901). Lovecraft discovered Shiel in 1923, and upon reading "The House of Sounds" wrote of it to his friend Frank Belknap Long: "This last is the masterpiece! How can I describe its poison-grey 'insidious madness'? If I say it is very like 'The Fall of the House of Usher' . . . I shall not even have suggested the utterly unique delirium of arctic wastes, titan seas, insane brazen towers, centuried malignancy, frenzied waves and cataracts, and above all hideous, insistent, brain-petrifying, Pan-accursed cosmic SOUND . . . I am left breathless and inarticulate." "The House of Sounds" was originally entitled "Vaila" when it was first published in *Shapes in the Fire* (1896). Shiel rewrote it (considerably lessening the fin de siècle prose of the original) and retitled it for inclusion in *The Pale Ape and Other Pulses* (1911).

THE HOUSE OF SOUNDS
by M. P. Shiel

"E caddi come l'uom cui sonno piglia,"—Dante.

A good many years ago, when a young man, a student in Paris, I knew the great Carot, and witnessed by his side many of those cases of mind-malady, in the analysis of which he was such a master. I remember one little maid of the Marais who, until the age of nine, did not differ from her playmates; but one night, lying abed she whispered into her mother's ear: "Mama, can you not hear *the sound of the world?*" It appears that her geography had just taught her that our globe reels with an enormous velocity on an orbit about the sun; and this *sound of the world* of hers was merely a murmur in the ear, heard in the silence of night. Within six months she was as mad as a March-hare.

I mentioned the case to my friend, Haco Harfager, then occupying with me an old mansion in St. Germain, shut in by a wall and jungle of shrubbery. He listened with singular interest, and during a good while sat wrapped in gloom.

Another case which I gave made a great impression upon my friend: A young man, a toy-maker of St. Antoine, suffering from consumption— but sober, industrious—returning one gloaming to his garret, happened to purchase one of those factious journals which circulate by lamplight over the Boulevards. This simple act was the beginning of his doom. He had never been a reader: knew little of the reel and turmoil of the world. But the next night he purchased another journal. Soon he acquired a knowledge of politics, the huge movements, the tumult of life. And this interest grew absorbing. Till late into the night, every night, he lay poring over the roar of action, the printed passion. He would awake sick, but brisk in spirit—and bought a morning paper. And the more his teeth gnashed, the less they ate. He grew negligent, irregular at work, turning on his bed through the day. Rags overtook him. As the grand interest grew upon his frail soul so every lesser interest failed in him. There came a day when he no more cared for his own life; and another day when he tore the hairs from his head.

As to this man the great Carot said to me:

"Really, one does not know whether to chuckle or to weep over such a business. Observe, for one thing, how diversely men are made! There are minds precisely so sensitive as a thread of melted lead: *every* breath will fret and trouble them: and how about the hurricane? For such this scheme of things is clearly no fit habitation, but a Machine of Death, a baleful Immense. *Too* cruel to some is the rushing shriek of Being—they *cannot* stand the world. Let each look well to his own little shred of existence, I say, and leave the monstrous Automaton alone! Here in this poor toy-maker you have a case of the ear: it is only the neurosis, Oxyecoia. Grand was that Greek myth of 'the Harpies'—by *them* was this creature snatched away—or say, caught by a limb in the wheels of the universe, and so perished. It is quite a ravishing exit—translation in a chariot of flame! Only remember that the member first seized was *the pinna*—he bent *ear* to the howl of the world, and ended by himself howling. Between chaos and our shoes swings, I assure you, the thinnest film! I knew a man who had this aural peculiarity: that every sound brought him some knowledge of the matter causing the sound: a rod for instance, of mixed copper and tin striking upon a rod of mixed iron and lead, conveyed to him not merely the proportion of each metal in each rod, but some knowledge of the essential meaning and spirit, as it were, of copper, of tin, of iron and of lead. Him also did the Harpies snatch aloft!"

I have mentioned that I related some of these cases to my friend, Harfager: and I was astonished at the obvious pains which he gave himself to hide his interest, his gaping nostrils. . . .

From first days when we happened to attend the same seminary in Stockholm an intimacy had sprung up between us. But it was not an intimacy accompanied by the ordinary signs of friendship. Harfager was the shyest, most isolated, of beings. Though our joint housekeeping (brought about by a chance meeting at a midnight *séance*) had now lasted some months, I knew nothing of his plans. Through the day we read together, he rapt back into the past, I engrossed with the present; late at night we reclined on sofas within the vast cave of a hearth-place *Louis Onze*, and smoked over the dying fire in silence. Occasionally a *soirée* or lecture might draw me from the house; except once, I never understood that Harfager left it. On that occasion I was hurrying through the Rue St. Honoré, where a rush of traffic rattles over the old pavers retained there, when I came upon him. In this tumult he stood in a listening attitude; and for a moment did not know me.

Even as a boy I had seen in my friend the genuine patrician—not that his personality gave any impression of loftiness or opulence: on the contrary. He did, however, suggest an incalculable *ancientness*; and I have known no nobleman who so bore in his expression the assurance of the essential Prince, whose pale blossom is of yesterday, and will perish to-morrow, but whose root shoots through the ages. This much I knew of Harfager; also that on one or other of his islands north of Zetland lived his mother and an aunt; that he was somewhat deaf; but liable to a thousand torments or delights at certain sounds, the whine of a door, the note of a bird. . . .

He was somewhat under the middle height; and inclined to portliness. His nose rose highly aquiline from that sort of brow called "the musical"— that is, with temples which incline *outward* to the cheek-bones, making breadth for the base of the brain; while the direction of the heavy-lidded eyes and of the eyebrows was a downward *droop* from the nose of their outer ends. He wore a thin chin-beard. But the feature of his face were the ears, which were nearly circular, very small and flat, without that outer curve called "the helix." I came to understand that this had long been a trait of his race. Over the whole wan face of my friend was engraved an air of woeful inability, utter gravity of sorrow: one said "Sardanapalus," frail last of the race of Nimrod.

After a year I found it necessary to mention to Harfager my intention of leaving Paris, as we reclined one night in our nooks within the fireplace. He replied to my tidings with a polite "Indeed!" and continued to gloat over the grate: but after an hour turned to me and observed: "Well, it seems to be a hard world."

Truisms uttered in just such a tone of discovery I occasionally heard from him; but his earnest gaze, his despondency now, astonished me.

"Apropos of what?" I asked.

"My friend, do not leave me!" He spread his arms.

I learned that he was the object of a devilish malice; that he was the prey of a horrible temptation. That a lure, a becking hand, a lurking lust, which it was the effort of his life to escape (and to which he was especially liable in solitude) perpetually enticed him; and that so it had been almost from the day when, at the age of five, he had been sent by his father from his desolate home in the ocean.

And whose was this malice?

He told me his mother's and aunt's.

And what was this temptation?

He said it was the temptation to go back—to hurry with the very frenzy of hunger—back to that home.

I demanded with what motives, and in what way, the malice of his mother and aunt manifested itself. He answered that there was, he fancied, no definite motive, but only a fated malevolence; and that the respect in which it manifested itself was the prayers and commands with which they plagued him to go again to the hold of his ancestors.

All this I could not understand, and said so. In what consisted this magnetism, and this peril, of his home? To this Harfager did not reply, but rising from his seat, disappeared behind the hearth-curtains, and left the apartment. When he returned, it was with a quarto tome bound in hide, which proved to be Hugh Gascoigne's "Chronicle of Norse Families" in English black-letter. The passage to which he pointed I read as follows:

"Now of these two brothers the older, Harold, being of seemly personage and prowess, did go a pilgrimage into Danemark, wherefrom he repaired again home to Hjaltland (Zetland), and with him fetched the amiable Thronda for his wife, who was a daughter of the sank (blood) royal of Danemark. And his younger brother, Sweyn, that was sad and debonair, but far surpassed the other in cunning, received him with all good cheer.

"But eftsoons (soon after) fell Sweyn sick for all his love that he had of Thronda, his brother's wife. And while the worthy Harold ministered about the bed where Sweyn lay sick, lo, Sweyn fastened on him a violent stroke with a sword, and with no longer tarrying enclosed his hands in bonds, and cast him in the bottom of a deep hold. And because Harold would not deprive himself of the governance of Thronda his wife, Sweyn cut off both his ear[s], and put out one of his eyes, and after divers such torment was ready to slay him. But on a day the valiant Harold, breaking his bonds, and embracing his adversary, did by the sleight of wrestling overthrow him, and escaped. Notwithstanding, he faltered when he came to the Somburg Head, not far from the Castle, and, albeit that he was swift-foot, could no farther run, by reason that he was faint with the long plagues of his brother. And whilst he there lay in a swoon, did Sweyn come upon him, and when he had stricken him with a dart, cast him from Somburg Head into the sea.

"Not long hereafterward did the lady Thronda (though she knew not the manner of her lord's death, nor, verily, if he was dead or alive) receive Sweyn into favour, and with great gaudying and blowing of beamous (trumpets) did become his wife. And right soon they two went thence to sojourn in far parts.

"Now, it befell that Sweyn was minded by a dream to have built a great mansion in Hjaltland for the home-coming of the lady Thronda; wherefore he called to him a cunning Master-workman, and sent him to England to gather men for the building of this lusty House, while he himself remained with his lady at Rome. Then came this Architect to London, but passing thence to Hjaltland was drowned, he and his feers (mates), all and some.

"And after two years, which was the time assigned, Sweyn Harfager sent a letter to Hjaltland to understand how his great House did: for he knew not of the drowning of the Architect: and soon after he received answer that the House *did well*, and was building on the Isle of Rayba. But that was not the Isle where Sweyn had appointed the building to be: and he was afeard, and near fell down dead for dread, because, in the letter, he saw before him the manner of writing of his brother Harold. And he said in this form: 'Surely Harold is alive, else be this letter writ with ghostly hand.' And he was wo many days, seeing that this was a deadly stroke.

"Thereafter he took himself back to Hjaltland to know how the matter

213

was, and there the old Castle on Somburg Head was break down to the earth. Then Sweyn was wode-wroth, and cried: 'Jhesu mercy, where is all the great house of my fathers gone? alas! this wicked day of destiny!' And one of the people told him that a host of workmen from far parts had break it down. And he said: 'Who hath bid them?' but that could none answer. Then he said again: 'nis (is not) my brother Harold alive? for I have behold his writing': and that, too, could none answer. So he went to Rayba, and saw there a great House stand, and when he looked on it, he said: 'This, sooth, was y-built by my brother Harold, be he dead or be he on-live: And there he dwelt, and his lady, and his sons' sons until now: for that the House is ruthless and without pity; wherefore 'tis said that upon all who dwell there falleth a wicked madness and a lecherous anguish; and that by way of the ears do they drinck the cup of the furie of the earless Harold, till the time of the House be ended."

After I had read the narrative half-aloud, I smiled, saying: "This, Harfager, is very tolerable romance on the part of the good Gascoigne, but has the look of indifferent history:'

"It is, nevertheless, *history*," he replied.

"You believe that?"

"The house stands solidly on Rayba."

"But you believe that mediæval ghosts superintended the building of their family mansions?"

"Gascoigne nowhere says that," he answered: "for to be 'stricken with a darte,' is not necessarily to die; nor, if he did say it, have I any knowledge on the subject."

"And what, Harfager, is the nature of that 'wicked madness,' that 'lecherous anguish,' of which Gascoigne speaks?"

"Do you ask me?"—he spread his arms—"what do I know? I know nothing! I was banished from the place at the age of five. Yet the cry of it still rings in my mind. And have I not *told* you of anguishes—even in myself—of inherited longing and loathing. . . ."

Anyway, I *had* to go to Heidelberg just then: so I said I would compromise by making my absence short, and rejoin him in a few weeks. I took his moody silence to mean assent; and soon afterwards left him.

But I was detained: and when I got back to our old house found it empty. Harfager was gone.

It was only after twelve years that a letter was forwarded me—a rather wild letter, an awfully long one—in the writing of my friend. It was dated at Rayba. From the writing I understood that it had been dashed off *with furious haste*, so that I was the more astonished at the very trivial nature of the contents. On the first half page he spoke of our old friendship, and asked if I would see his mother, who was dying; the rest of the epistle consisted of an analysis of his mother's family-tree, the apparent aim being to show that she was a genuine Harfager, and a distant cousin of his father. He then went on to comment on the great prolificness of his race, stating that since the fourteenth century over *four millions* of its members had lived; three only of them, he believed, being now left. This settled, the letter ended.

Influenced by this, I travelled northward; reached Caithness; passed the stormy Orkneys; reached Lerwick; and from Unst, the most bleak and northerly of the Zetlands, contrived, by dint of bribes, to pit the weather-worthiness of a lug-sailed "sixern" (identical with the "langschips" of the Vikings) against a flowing sea and an ugly sky. The trip, I was told, was at such a season of some risk. It was the sombre December of those seas; and the weather, they said, although never cold, is seldom other than tempes-tuous. A mist now lay over the billows, enclosing our boat in a dome of doleful gloaming; and there was a ghostly something in the look of the silent sea and brooding sky which produced upon my nerves the mood of a journey out of nature, a cruise beyond the world. Occasionally, however, we ran past one of those "skerries," or sea-stacks, whose craggy sea-walls, disintegrated by the struggles of the Gulf Stream with the North Sea, had a look of awful ruin and havoc. But I only noticed three of these: for before the dun day had well run half its course, sudden darkness was upon us; and with it one of those storms of which the winter of this semi-Arctic sea is one succession. During the haggard glimpses of the following day the rain did not stop; but before darkness had quite fallen, my skipper (who talked continuously to a mate of seal-maidens, and water-horses, and *grülies*), paused to point me out a mound of gloomier grey on the weather-bow, which, he said, should be Rayba.

Rayba, he said, was the centre of quite a nest of those *rösts* (eddies) and cross-currents which the tidal wave hurls with complicated swirlings among all the islands: but at Rayba they ran with more than usual angriness, owing to the row of sea-crags which garrisoned the land around: approach was therefore at all times difficult, and at night foolhardy. With a running sea, however, we came sufficiently close to see the mane of foam which railed round the coast-wall. Its shock, according to the captain, had often more than all the efficiency of artillery, tossing tons of rock to heights of six hundred feet upon the island.

When the sun next pried above the horizon, we had closely approached the coast; and it was then that for the first time the impression of some *spinning* motion of the island (due probably to the swirling movements of the water) was produced upon me. We affected a landing at a *voe*, or sea-arm, on the west coast—the east, though the point of my aim, was out of the question on account of the swell. Here I found in two *skeoes* (or sheds), thatched with feal, five or six seamen, who gained a livelihood by trading for the groceries of the great house on the east: and, taking one of them for a guide, I began the climb of the island.

Now, during the night in the boat, I had been aware of a booming in the ears for which even the roar of the sea round the coast seemed insufficient to account; and this now, as we went on, became immensely augmented—and with it, once more, that conviction within me of *spinning* motions. Rayba I found to be a land of precipices of flaggy gneiss; at about the centre, however, we came upon a table-land, sloping from west to east, and covered by a lot of lochs, which sullenly flowed into one another. I could see no shore eastward to this chain of waters, and by dint of shouting to my leader, and bending ear to his shoutings, I came to know that there *was* no such shore—I say *shout*, for nothing less could have sounded through the steady bellowing as of ten thousand bisons that now resounded on every side. A certain trembling, too, of the earth became distinct. In vain, mean-time, did the eye in its dreary survey seek a tree or shrub—for no kind of vegetation, save peat, could brave for a day the perennial tempest of this benighted island. Darkness, half an hour after noon, commenced to fall upon us: and it was soon afterwards that my guide, pointing down a defile near the east coast, hurriedly started back upon the way he had come. I bawled a question after him, as he went: but at this point the voice of mortals had ceased to be in the least audible.

Down this defile, with a sinking of the heart, and a singular sickness of giddiness, I passed; and, on reaching its end, emerged upon a ledge of rock which shuddered to the immediate onsets of the sea—though all this part of the island was, besides, in the grip of an ague not due to the great guns of the sea. Hugging a crag of cliff for steadiness from the gusts, I gazed forth upon a scene not less eerily dismal than some drear district of the dreams of Dante. Three "skerries," flanked by stacks as fantastic and twisted as a witch's finger, and giving a home to hosts of osprey and scart, seal and walrus, lay at some fathoms distance; and from its rush among them, the sea in blanched, tumultuous, but inaudible wrath, like an army with banners, ranted toward the land. Letting go my crag, I staggered some distance to the left: and now all at once an amphitheatre opened before me, and there broke upon my view a panorama of such appalling majesty as had never entered my heart to fancy.

"An amphitheatre," I said: but it was rather the form of a Norman door that I saw. Fancy such a door, half a mile wide, flat on the ground, the rounded part farthest from the sea; and all round it let a wall of rock tower perpendicular forty yards: and now down this rounded door-shape, and *over its whole extent*, let a roaring ocean roll its tonnage in hoary fury—and the stupor with which I looked, and then the shrinking, and then the instinct of flight, will find comprehension.

This was the disemboguement of the lochs of Rayba.

And within the curve of this Norman cataract, robed in the world of its smokes and far-excursive surfs, stood a fabric of brass.

The last beam of the day had now nearly passed; but I could still see through the mist which bleakly nimbused it as in tears, that the building was low in proportion to the hugeness of its circumference; that it was roofed with a dome; and that round it ran two rows of Norman windows, the upper smaller than the lower. Certain indications led me to infer that the house had been founded upon a bed of rock which lay, circular and detached, within the curve of the cataract; but this nowhere emerged above the flood: for the whole floor which I had before me dashed one reeking deep river to the beachless sea—passage to the mansion being made possible by a massive causeway-bridge, with arches, all bearded with sea-weed.

Descending from my ledge, I passed along it, now drenched in spray; and, as I came nearer, could see that the house, too, was to half its height more thickly bearded than an old hull with barnacles and every variety of bright sea-weed; also—what was very surprising—that from many spots near the top of the brazen wall ponderous chains, dropping beards, reached out in rays: so that the fabric had the aspect of a many-anchored ark. But without pausing to look closely, I pushed forward, and rushing through the smooth waterfall which poured all round from the roof, by one of its many porches I entered the dwelling.

Darkness now was around me—and sound. I seemed to stand in the centre of some yelling planet, the row resembling the resounding of many thousands of cannon, punctuated by strange crashing and breaking uproars. And a sadness descended on me; I was near to tears. "Here," I

said, "is the place of weeping; not elsewhere is the vale of sighing."
However, I passed forward through a succession of halls, and was wondering where to go next, when a hideous figure, with a lamp in his hand, stamped towards me. I shrank from him! It seemed the skeleton of a lank man wrapped in a winding-sheet, till the light of one tiny eye, and a film of skin over a portion of the face reassured one. Of ears he showed no sign. His name, I afterwards learned, was Aith; and his appearance was explained by his pretence (true or false), that he had once suffered *burning*, almost to the cinder-stage, but had somehow recovered. With an expression of malice, and agitated gestures, he led the way to a chamber on the upper stage, where, having struck light to a taper, he made signs toward a spread table, and left me.

For a long time I sat in solitude, conscious of the shaking of the mansion, though every sense was swallowed up and confounded in the one impression of sound. Water, water, was the world—a nightmare on my breast, a desire to gasp for breath, a tingling on my nerves, a sense of being infinitely drowned and buried in boundless deluges; and when the feeling of giddiness, too, increased, I sprang up and paced—but suddenly stopped, angry, I scarce knew why, with myself. I had, in fact, caught myself walking with a certain *hurry*, not usual with me, not natural to me. So I forced myself to stand and take note of the hall. It was large, and damp with mists, so that its tattered, but rich, furniture looked lost in it, its centre occupied by a tomb bearing the name of a Harfager of the fourteenth century, and its walls old panels of oak. Having drearily seen these things, I waited on with an intolerable consciousness of solitude; but a little after midnight the tapestry parted, and Harfager with a rapid stalk walked in.

In twelve years my friend had grown old. He showed, it is true, a tendency to portliness: yet, to a knowing eye he was in reality tabid, ill-nourished. And his neck stuck forward from his chest; and the lower part of his back had quite a forward bend of age; and his hair floated about his face and shoulders in a wildness of awful whiteness, while a white chin-beard hung to his chest. His dress was a robe of bauge, which, as he went, waved aflaunt from his bare and hairy shins; and he was shod in those soft slippers called *rivlins*.

To my astonishment, he spoke. When I passionately shouted that I could gather no fragment of sound from his moving mouth, he clapped both his palms to his ears, and then anew besieged mine: but again without result: and now, with an angry throw of the hand, he caught up his taper, and walked from the apartment.

218

There was something strikingly unnatural in his manner—something which reminded me of the skeleton, Aith: an excess of zeal, a fever, a rage, *a loudness*, an eagerness of gait, a great extravagance of gesture. His hand constantly dashed wiffs of hair from a face which, though of the saffron of death, had red eyes—thick-lidded eyes, fixed in a downward and sideward gaze. When he came back to me, it was with a leaf of ivory, and a piece of graphite, hanging from the cord tied round his garment; and he rapidly wrote a petition that, if not too tired, I would take part with him in the funeral of his mother.

I shouted assent.

Once more he clapped his palms to his ears; then wrote: "Do not shout: no whisper in any part of the building is inaudible to me."

I remembered that in early life he had been slightly *deaf*.

We passed together through many apartments, he shading the taper with his hand—a necessary action, for, as I quickly discovered, in no nook of the quivering building was the air in a state of rest, but was for ever commoved by a curious agitation, a faint windiness, like an echo of tempests, which communicated a universal nervousness to the curtains. Everywhere I met the same past grandeur, present raggedness and decay. In many of the rooms were tombs; one was a museum thronged with bronzes, but broken, grown with fungoids, dripping with moisture—it was as if the mansion, in ardour of travail, sweated; and a miasma of decomposition tainted all the air.

I followed Harfager through the maze of his way with some difficulty, for he went headlong—only once stopping, when with a face ungainly wild over the glare of the light, he tossed up his fingers, and gave out a single word: from the form of his lips I guessed the word "*Hark!*"

Presently we entered a very long chamber, in which, on chairs beside a bed, lay a coffin flanked by a file of candles. The coffin was very deep, and had this singularity—that the foot-piece was absent, so that the soles of the corpse could be seen as we approached. I saw, too, three upright rods secured to a side of the coffin, each rod fitted at its top with a little silver bell of the sort called *morrice*, pendent from a flexible spring. And at the head of the bed, Aith, with an air of irascibility, was stamping to and fro within a narrow area.

Harfager deposited the taper upon a stone table, and stood poring with a crazy intentness over the body. I, too, stood and looked at death so grim and rigorous as I think I never saw. The coffin looked angrily full of tangled grey locks, the lady being of great age, bony and hook-nosed; and

her face shook with solemn constancy to the quivering of the building. I
noticed that over the body had been fixed three bridges, like the bridge of
a violin, their sides fitting into grooves in the coffin's sides, and their tops
of a shape to fit the slope of the two coffin-lids when closed. One of these
bridges passed over the knees of the dead lady; another bridged her
stomach; the third her neck. In each of them was a hole, and across each
of the three holes passed a string from the morrice-bell above it—the three
holes being thus divided by the three tight strings into six semi-circles.
Before I could guess the significance of all this, Harfager closed the folding
coffin-lids, which had little holes for the passage of the three strings. He
then turned the key in the lock, and uttered a word which I took to be
"come."

Aith now took hold of the handle at the coffin's head; and out of the
dark parts of the hall a lady in black walked forward. She was tall, pallid,
of imposing aspect; and from the curvature of her nose, and her circular
ears, I guessed her the lady Swertha, aunt of Harfager. Her eyes were quite
red—if with crying I could not tell.

Harfager and I taking each a handle near the coffin-foot, and the lady
bearing before us one of the black candlesticks, the obsequies began.
When I got to the doorway, I noticed in a corner there two more coffins,
engraved with the names Harfager and his aunt. Thence we wound our
way down a wide stairway winding to a lower floor; and descending thence
still lower by narrow brass steps, came to a portal of metal, where the lady,
depositing the candlestick, left us.

The chamber of death into which we now bore the body had for its
outer wall the brazen outer wall of the whole house at a spot where this
closely approached the cataract, and was no doubt profoundly drowned in
the world of surge without: so that the earthquake there was urgent. On
every side the place was piled with coffins, ranged high and wide upon
shelves; and the huge rush and scampering which ensued on our entrance
proved it the paradise of troops of rats. As it was inconceivable that these
could have eaten a way through sixteen brazen feet—for even the floor here
was brazen—I assumed that some fruitful pair must have found in the
house, on its building, an ark from the waters. Even this guess, though,
seemed wild; and Harfager afterwards confided to me his suspicion that
they had for some reason been *placed* there by the original builder.

We deposited our load upon a stone bench in the centre; whereupon
Aith made haste to be away. Harfager then repeatedly walked from end to
end of the place, scrutinising with many a stoop and peer and upward

stretch, the shelves and their props. Could he, I was led to wonder, have any doubts as to their soundness? Damp, in fact, and decay pervaded everything. A bit of timber which I touched crumbled to dust under my thumb.

He presently beckoned to me, and, with yet one halt and "*Hark!*" from him, we passed through the house to my chamber; where, left alone, I paced about, agitated with a vague anger; then tumbled to an agony of slumber.

In the far interior of the mansion even the bleared day of this land of bleakness never rose upon our gloom; but I was able to regulate my gettings-up by a clock which stood in my chamber; or I was called by Harfager, with whom in a short time I renewed more than all our former friendship. That I should say *more* is curious: but so it *was*: and this was proved by the fact that we grew to take, and to excuse, freedoms of speech and of manner which, as two persons of more than usual reserve, we had once never dreamed of permitting to ourselves in respect of each other. Once, for example, in our pacings of aimless haste down passages that vanished in shadow and length of perspective remoteness, he wrote that my step was very slow. I replied that it was just such a step as suited my then mood. He wrote: "You have developed a tendency to *fret*." I was very offended, and said: "Certainly, there are more fingers than one in the world which *that* ring will fit!"

Another day he was no less than rude to me for seeking to reveal to him the secret of the unhuman keenness of his hearing—and of mine! For I, too, to my dismay, began, as time passed, to catch hints of shouted sounds. The cause might be found, I asserted, in a fervour of the auditory nerve, which, if the cataract were absent, the roar of the ocean, and the row of the perpetual tempest round us, might by themselves be sufficient to bring about; his own ear-interior, I said, must be inflamed to an exquisite pitch of fever; and I named the disease to him as the "Paracusis Wilisü." When he frowned dissent, I, quite undeterred, proceeded to relate the case (that had occurred within my own experience) of a very deaf lady who could hear the drop of a pin in a railway-train[†]; and now he made me the reply: "Of ignorant people I am accustomed to consider the mere scientist the most ignorant!"

[†]Such cases are known to many medical men. The concussion on the deaf nerve is the cause of the acquired sensitiveness; nor is there any limit to that sensitiveness when the tumult is immensely augmented.

But I, for my part, regarded it as merely far-fetched that he should pretend to be in the dark as to the morbid state of his hearing! He himself, indeed, confessed to me his own, Aith's, and the lady Swertha's proneness to paroxysms of *vertigo*. I was startled! for I had myself shortly previously been roused out of sleep by feelings of reeling and nausea, and an assurance that the room furiously flew round with me. The impression passed away, and I attributed it, perhaps hastily, to some disturbance in the nerve-endings of "the labyrinth," or inner ear. In Harfager, however, the conviction of whirling motions in the house, in the world, got to so horrible a degree of certainty, that its effects sometimes resembled those of lunacy or energumenal possession. Never, he said, was the sensation of giddiness altogether dead in him; seldom the sensation that he gazed with stretched-out arms over the brink of abysms which wooed his half-consenting foot. Once, as we walked, he was hurled as by unearthly powers to the ground, and there for an hour sprawled, bathed in sweat, with distraught bedazzlement and amaze in his stare, which watched the racing walls. He was constantly racked, moreover, with the consciousness of sounds so peculiar in their character, that I could account for them on no other supposition than that of a *tinnitus* infinitely sick. Through the roar there sometimes visited him, he told me, the lullaby of some bird, from the burden of whose song he had the consciousness that she derived from a very remote country, was of the whiteness of foam, and crested with a comb of mauve. Or else he knew of accumulated human tones, distant, yet articulate, busily contending in volubility, and in the end melting into a medley of musical movements. Or, anon, he was shocked by an infinite and imminent crashing, like the monstrous racket of the crackling of a cosmos of crockery round his ears. He told me, moreover, that he could frequently see, rather than hear, the parti-coloured wheels of a mazy sphere-music deep, deep within the black dark of the cataract's roar. These impressions, which I protested *must* be merely entotic had sometimes a pleasing effect upon him, and he would stand long to listen with a lifted hand to their seduction: others again inflamed him to a mad anger. I guessed that they were the cause of those "*Harks!*" that at intervals of about an hour did not fail to break from him. But in this I was wrong: and it was with a thrill of dismay that I soon came to know the truth.

For, as we were once passing by an iron door on the lower floor, he stopped, and for some minutes stood listening with a leer most keen and cunning. Presently the cry "*Hark!*" escaped him; and he then turned to me and wrote on the tablet: "Did you not hear?" I had heard nothing but the roar; and he howled into my ear in sounds now audible to me as an echo caught far off in dreams: "You shall see."

He took up the candlestick; produced from the pocket of his robe a key; unlocked the iron door; and we passed into a room very loftily domed in proportion to its area, and empty, save that a pair of steps lay against its wall, and that in the centre of its marble floor was a pool, like a Roman "impluvium," only round like the room—a pool evidently profound in depth, full of a thick and inky fluid. I was very perturbed by its present aspect, for as the candle burned upon its surface, I observed that this had been quite recently *disturbed*, in a style for which the shivering of the house could not account, since *ripples* of slime were now rounding out from its middle to its brink. When I glanced at Harfager for explanation, he gave me a signal to wait; and now for about an hour, with his hands behind his back, paced the chamber; but then paused, and we two stood together by the pool's margin, gazing into the water. Suddenly his clutch tightened on my arm, and I saw, with a touch of horror, a tiny ball, probably of lead, but daubed blood-red by some chemical, fall from the roof, and sink into the middle of the pool. It hissed on contact with the water a whiff of mist.

"In the name of all that is sinister," I whispered, "what thing is this?"

Again he made me a busy and confident signal to wait, moved the ladder-steps toward the pool, handed me the taper. When I had mounted, holding high the light, I saw hanging out of the fogs in the dome a globe of old copper, lengthened into balloon-shape by a neck, at the end of which I could spy a tiny hole. Painted over the globe was barely visible in red print-letters:

"HARFAGER-HOUS: 1389-188."

I was down quicker than I went up!

"But the meaning?" I panted.

"Did you see the writing?"

"Yes. The meaning?"

He wrote: "By comparing Gascoigne with Thrunster, I find that the house was *built* about 1389."

"But the last figures?"

"After the last 8," he replied, "there is another figure not quite obliterated by a tarnish-spot:'

"What figure?" I asked.

"It cannot be read, but may be surmised. As the year 1888 is now all but passed, it can only be the figure 9."

"Oh, you are depraved in mind!" I cried, very irritated: "you assume—you *state*—in a manner which no mind trained to base its conclusions on facts can bear with patience."

"And you are irrational," he wrote. "You know, I suppose, the formula of Archimedes by which, the diameter of a globe being known, its volume also is known? Now, the diameter of that globe in the dome I know to be four and a half feet; and the diameter of the leaden balls about the third of an inch. Supposing, then, that 1389 was the year in which the globe was full of balls, you may readily calculate that not many fellows of the four million and odd which have since dropped at the rate of one an hour are now left within. The fall of the balls *cannot* persist another year. The figure 9 is therefore forced upon us."

"But you assume, Harfager!" I cried: "Oh, believe me, my friend, this is the very wantonness of wickedness! By what algebra of despair do you know that each ball represents one of the scions of your house, or that the last date was intended to correspond with the stoppage of the horologe. And, even if so, what is the significance of it? It can have *no significance!*"

"Do you want to madden me?" he shouted. Then furiously writing; "I swear that I know nothing of its significance! But it is not evident to you that the thing is a big hour-glass, intended to count the hours, not of a day, but of a cycle; and of a cycle of five hundred years?"

"But the whole contrivance," I passionately cried, "is a baleful phantasm of our brains! How is the fall of the balls regulated? Ah, my friend, you wander—your mind is debauched in this brawl of waters."

"I have not ascertained," he replied, "by what internal works, or clammy medium, or spiral coil, dependent probably for its action upon the vibration of the mansion, the balls are retarded in their fall: that was a matter well within the skill of the mediæval mechanic, the inventor of the clock; but this at least is clear, that one element of their retardation is the smallness of the aperture through which they have to pass; that this element, by known laws of statics, will cease to operate when no more than three balls remain; and that, consequently, the last three will fall at almost the same instant."

"In Heaven's name!" I exclaimed, careless now what folly I poured out, "but your mother is dead, Harfager! Do you deny that there remain but you and the Lady Swertha?"

A glance of disdain was all the answer he then gave me as to this.

But he confessed to me a day later that the leaden drops were a constant sorrow to his ears; that from hour to hour his life was a keen waiting for their fall; that even from his brief sleeps he infallibly started awake at each descent; that in whatever region of the mansion he chanced to be, they found him out with a crashing loudness; and that each crash tweaked him with a twinge of anguish within the ear. I was therefore shocked at his declaration that these droppings had now become as the life of life to him; had acquired an entwining so close with the tone of his mind, that their ceasing might even mean for him the reeling of Reason: at which confession he sobbed, with his face buried, as he leant upon a column. When this paroxysm was past, I asked him if it was out of the question that he should once for all cast off the fascination of the horologe, and escape with me from the place. He wrote in mysterious reply: "A *three*-fold cord is not easily broken." I started, asking—"How three-fold?" He wrote with a bitter smile: "To be in love with pain—to pine after aching—is not that a wicked madness?" I stood astonished that he had unconsciously quoted Gascoigne! "a wicked madness!" "a lecherous anguish!" "You have seen my aunt's face," he proceeded; "your eyes were dim if you did not see in it an impious calm, the glee of a blasphemous patience, a grin behind her daring smile." He then spoke of a prospect at the terror of which his whole soul trembled, yet which sometimes laughed in his heart in the form of a *hope*. It was the prospect of any considerable increase in the volume of sound about his ears. At *that*, he said, the brain must totter. On the night of my arrival the noise of my boots, and, since then, my voice occasionally raised, had produced acute pain in him. To such an ear, I understood him to say, the luxury of torture involved in a large sound-increase around was an allurement from which no human virtue could turn: and when I said that I could not even conceive such an increase, much less the means by which it could be effected, he brought out from the archives of the mansion some annals kept by the heads of his family. From these it appeared that the tempests that ever lacerated the latitude of Rayba did not fail to give place, at intervals of some years, to one mammoth madness, one Samson among the merry men, and Sirius among the suns. At such periods the rains descended—and the floods came—even as in the first world-deluge; those *rösts*, or eddies, which ever encircled Rayba, spurning then the bands of lateral space, burst aloft into a whirl of water-spouts, to dance about the little land, upon which, converging, some of them discharged their waters: and the locks which flowed to the cataract thus re-doubled their volume, and crashed with redoubled roar. Harfager said it was miraculous that for eighteen years no such grand event had transacted itself at Rayba.

"And what," I asked "in addition to the dropping balls, and the prospect of an increase of sound, is the third strand of that 'three-fold cord' of which you have spoken."

For answer he led me to a circular hall which, he said, he had ascertained to be the centre of the circular mansion. It was a very large hall—so large as I think I never saw—so large that the amount of wall lighted at one time by the candle seemed nearly flat: and nearly the whole of its area, from floor to roof, was occupied by a column of brass, the space between the wall and column being only such as to admit of a stretched-out arm.

"This column," Harfager wrote, "goes up to the dome and passes beyond it; it goes down to the lower floor, and passes through that; it goes down thence to the brazen flooring of the vaults and *passes through that* into the bedrock. Under each floor it spreads out, helping to support the floor. What is the precise quality of the impression which I have made upon your mind by this description?"

"I do not know," I answered, turning from him: "ask me none of your enigmas, Harfager: I feel a giddiness. . . ."

"But answer me," he said: "consider *the strangeness* of that brazen lowest floor, which I have discovered to be some six feet thick, and whose under-surface, I have reason to think, is somewhat *above* the bed-rock; remember that the fabric is at no point *fastened* to the column; think of the *chains* which ray out from the outer wall, apparently *anchoring* the house to the ground. Tell me, what impression have I *now* made?"

"And is it for *this* you wait?" I cried. "Yet there may have been no malevolent intention! You jump at conclusions! Any fixed building in such a land and spot as this would at any time be liable to be broken up by some sovereign tempest! What if it was the intention of the builder that in such a case the chains should break, and the building, by yielding, be saved?"

"You have no lack of charity at least," he replied; and we then went back to the book we were reading together.

He had not wholly lost the old habit of study, although he could no longer get himself to *sit* to read; so with a volume (often tossed down) he would stamp about within the region of the lamplight; or I, unconscious of my voice, might read to him. By a whim of his mood the few books which now lay within the limits of his patience had all for their motive something of the *picaresque*, or the foppishly speculative: Quevedo's "Tacaño"; or the system of Tycho Brahe; above all, George Hakewill's "Power and Providence of God." One day, however, as I read, he interrupted me with the sentence, à propos of nothing: "What I cannot understand is that you, a scientist, should believe that life ceases with the ceasing of breathing"—and from that moment the tone of our reading changed. For he led me to the crypts of the library in the lowest part of the building, and hour after hour, with a *furore* of triumph overwhelmed me with books proving the length of life after "death." What, he asked, was my opinion of Baron Verulam's account of the dead man who was heard to utter words of prayer? or of the bounding bowels of the dead convict? On my expressing unbelief, he seemed surprised, and reminded me of the writhings of dead cobras, of the long beating of a frog's heart after "death." "She is not dead," he quoted, "but *sleepeth*." The idea of Bacon and Paracelsus that the principle of life resides in a spirit or fluid was proof to him that such fluid could not, from its very nature, undergo any *sudden* annihilation, while the organs which it pervades remain. When I asked what limit he, then, set to the persistence of "life" in the "dead," he answered that when decay had so far advanced that the nerves could no longer be called nerves, or when the brain had been disconnected at the neck from the body, as by rats gnawing, then the king of terrors was king verily. With an indiscretion strange to me before my residence at Rayba, I now blurted out the question whether in all this he could be referring to his mother? For a while he stood thoughtful, then wrote: "Even if I had not had reason to believe that my own and Swertha's life in some way hung upon the final cessations of hers, I should still have taken precautions to ascertain the march of the destroyer on her frame: as it is, I shall not lack even the exactest information:" He then explained that the rats which ran riot in the place of death would in time do their full work upon her; but would be unable to reach to the region of the throat without first gnawing their way through the three strings stretched across the holes of the bridges within the coffin, and thus, one by one, liberating the three morrisco-bells to tinklings.

The winter solstice had gone, another year began. I was sleeping a deep sleep by night when Harfager came into my chamber, and shook me. His face was ghastly in the taper's glare. A change within a short time had taken place upon him. He was hardly the same. He was like some poor wight into whose surprised eyes in the night have pried the eyes of Affright.

He said that he was aware of strainings and creakings, which gave him the feeling of being suspended in airy spaces by a thread which must break to his weight; and he begged me, for God's sake, to accompany him to the coffins. We passed together through the house, he craven, haggard, his gait

227

now laggard, into the chamber of the dead, where he stole to and fro examining the shelves. Out of the footless coffin of the dowager trembling on its bench I saw a water-rat crawl; and as Harfager passed beneath one of the shortest of the shelves which bore one coffin, it suddenly dropped from a height to dust at his feet. He screamed the cry of a frighted creature; tottered to my support; and I bore him back to the upper parts of the palace.

He sat, with his face buried, in a corner of a small chamber, doddering, overtaken, as it were, with the extremity of age, no longer marking with his "*Hark!*" the fall of the leaden drops. To my remonstrances he responded only with the moan, "so soon!" Whenever I looked for him, I found him there, his manhood now collapsed in an ague. I do not think that during this time he slept.

On the second night, as I was approaching him, he sprang suddenly upright with the outcry: "The first bell is tinkling!"

And he had scarcely screamed it when, from some long way off, a faint wail, which at its origin must have been a fierce shriek, reached my now feverish ears. Harfager, for his part, clapped his palms to his ears, and dashed from his place, I following in hot chase through the black breadth of the mansion: till we came to a chamber containing a candelabrum, and arrased in faded red. On the floor in swoon lay the lady Swertha, her dark-gray hair in disarray wrapping her like an angry sea; tufts of it scattered, torn from the roots; and on her throat prints of strangling fingers. We bore her to her bed in an alcove; and, having discovered some tincture in a cabinet, I administered it between her fixed teeth. In her rapt countenance I saw that death was not; and, as I found something appalling in her aspect, shortly afterwards left her to Harfager.

When I next saw him his manner had undergone a kind of change which I can only describe as gruesome. It resembled the officious self-importance seen in a person of weak intellect who spurs himself with the thought, "to business! the time is short!" while his walk sickened me with a hint of *ataxie locomotrice*. When I asked him as to his aunt, as to the meaning of the marks of violence on her body, bending ear to his deep and unctuous tones, I could hear: "An attempt has been made upon her life by the skeleton, Aith."

He seemed not to share my astonishment at this thing! nor could give me any clear answer as to his reason for retaining such a servant, or as to the origin of Aith's service. Aith, he told me, had been admitted into the palace during the period of his own absence in youth, and he knew little of him beyond the fact that he was extraordinarily strong. *Whence* he had come, or how, no person except the lady Swertha was aware: and she, it seems, feared, or at least persistently flinched from admitting him into the mystery. He added that, as a matter of fact, the lady, from the day of his coming back to Rayba, had with some object imposed upon herself a dumbness on all subjects, which he had never once known her to break through, except by an occasional note.

With an ataxic strenuousness, with the airs of a drunken man constraining himself to ordered action, Harfager now set himself to the doing of a host of trivial things: he collected chronicles and arranged them in order of date; he docketed or ticketed packets of documents; he insisted upon my assistance in turning the faces of paintings to the wall. He was, however, now constantly stopped by bursts of vertigo, six times in a single hour being hurled to the ground, while blood frequently guttered from his ears. He complained to me in a tone of piteous wail of the wooing of a silver *piccolo* that continually seduced him. As he bent, sweating, over his momentous nothings, his hands fluttered like aspen. I noted the movements of his whimpering lips, the rheum of his sunken eyes: sudden doting had come upon his youth.

On a day he threw it utterly off, and was young anew. He entered my room; roused me from dreams; I observed the lunacy of bliss in his eyes, heard his hiss in my ear:

"Up! *The storm!*"

Ah! I had known it—in the nightmare of the night. I felt it in the air of the room. It had come. I saw it lurid by the lamplight on the hell of Harfager's face.

A glee burst at once into birth within me, as I sprang from my couch, glancing at the clock: it was eight—in the morning. Harfager, with the naked stalk of some maniac prophet, had already taken himself away; and I started out after him. A deepening was clearly felt in the quivering of the edifice; anon for a second it stopped still, as if, breathlessly, to listen; its air was troubled with a vague gustiness. Occasionally there came to me as it were the noising of some far-off lamentation and voice in Ramah, but whether this was in my ear or the screaming of the gale I could not tell; or again I could hear one clear chord of an organ's vaunt. About noon I spied Harfager, lamp in hand, running along a corridor, with naked soles. As we met he looked at me, but hardly with recognition, and passed by; stopped, however, and ran back to howl into my ear the question: "Would you *see*?" He then beckoned before me, and I followed to a very small opening in the outer wall, closed with a slab of brass. As he lifted the latch, the slab dashed inward with instant impetuosity and tossed him a long way, while the breath of the tempest, braying through the brazen tube with a brutal bravura, caught and pinned me upon a corner of a wall, and all down the corridor a long crashing racket of crowds of pictures and couches followed. I nevertheless managed to push my way on the belly to the opening. Hence the sea should have been visible; but my senses were met by nothing but a vision of tumbled tenebrousness, and a general impression of the letter O. The sun of Rayba had gone out. In a moment of opportunity our two forces got the shutter shut again.

"Come!"—he had obtained a fresh glimmer, and beckoned before me—"let's go see how the dead fare in the great desolation:" and we ran, but had hardly got to the middle of the stairway, when I was thrilled by the consciousness of some great shock, the bass of a dull thud, which nothing save the thumping to the floor of the whole lump of the coffins could have caused. I looked for Harfager, and for a moment only saw his heels skedaddling, panic-hounded, his ears stopped, his mouth round! Then, indeed, fear reached me—a tremor in the audacity of my heart, a thought that now at any rate I must desert him in his extremity, and work out my own salvation. Yet it was with hesitancy that I turned to search for him for the last farewell—a hesitancy which I felt to be not unselfish, but selfish, and unhealthy. I rambled through the night, seeking light, and having happened upon a lamp, proceeded to seek for Harfager. Several hours went by in this way, during which I could not doubt from the state of the air in the house that the violence about me was being wildly heightened. Sounds as of screams—unreal, like the shriekings of demons—now reached my ears. As the time of night came on, I began to detect in the greatly augmented baritone of the cataract a fresh character—a shrillness—the whistle of a rapture—a malice—the menace of a rabies blind and deaf. It must have been at about the hour of six that I found Harfager. He sat in an obscure room, with his brow bowed down, his hands on his knees, his face covered with hair, and with blood from the ears. The right sleeve of his robe had been rent away in some renewed attempt, I imagined, to manage a window; and the rather crushed arm hung lank from the shoulder. For some time I stood and eyed him mouthing his mumblings; but now that I had found him uttered nothing as to my departure. Presently he looked sharply up with the call "*Hark!*"—then with impatience, "Hark! Hark!"—then with a shout, "The second bell!" And *again*, in immediate sequence upon his shout, there sounded a wail, vague yet

230

real, through the house. Harfager at the instant dropped reeling with giddiness; but I, snatching up a lamp, dashed out, shivering but eager. For some while the wild wailing went on (either actually, or by reflex action of my ear); and as I ran for the lady's apartment, I saw opposite to it the open door of an armoury, into which I passed, caught up a battle-axe, and was now about to dart in to her aid, when Aith, with a blazing eye, shied out of her chamber. I cast up my axe, and, shouting, dashed forward to down him: but by some chance the lamp fell from me, and before I knew anything more, the axe sprang from my grasp, and I was cast far backward by some most grim vigour. There was, however, enough light shining out of the chamber to show that the skeleton had darted into a door of the armoury, so I instantly slammed and locked the door near me by which I had procured the axe, and hurrying to the other, secured it, too. Aith was thus a prisoner. I then entered the lady's chamber. She lay over the bed in the alcove, and to my bent ear grossly croaked the ruckle of death. A glance at her mangled throat convincing me that her last moments were come, I settled her on the bed, curtained her within the loosened festoons of the hangings of black, and turned from the cursedness of her aspect. On an *escritoire* near I noticed a note, intended apparently for Harfager: "I mean to defy, and fly; not from fear, but for the delight of the defiance itself. *Can you come?*" Taking a flame from the candelabrum, I left her to her loneliness, and throes of her death.

I had passed some way backward when I was startled by a queer sound—a crash—resembling the crash of a tamboureen; and as I could hear it pretty clearly, and from a distance, this meant some prodigious energy. In two minutes it again broke out; and thenceforth at regular intervals—with an effect of pain upon me; and the conviction grew gradually within me that Aith had unhung two of the old brass shields from their pegs, and holding them by their handles, and dashing them viciously together, thus expressed the frenzy that had now overtaken him. When I found my way back to Harfager, very anguish was now stamping in him about the chamber; he shook his head like a tormented horse, brushing and barring from his hearing each crash of the brass shields. "Ah, when—when—" he hoarsely groaned into my ear, "will that ruckle cease in her throat? I will myself, I tell you—*with my own hand*—oh God. . . ." Since the morning his auditory fever (as indeed my own also) appeared to have increased in steady proportion with the roaring and screeching chaos round; and the death-struggle in the lady's throat bitterly filled for him the intervals of the grisly cymbaling of Aith. He presently sent twinkling fingers into the air, and, with his arms cast out, darted into the darkness.

And again I sought him, and long again in vain. As the hours passed, and the day deepened toward its baleful midnight, the cry of the now redoubled cataract, mixed with the mass and majesty of the now climatic tempest, took on too intentional a *shriek* to be longer tolerable to any reason. My own mind escaped my sway, and went its way: for here in the hot-bed of fever I was fevered. I wandered from chamber to chamber, precipitate, dizzy on the upbuoyance of a joy. "As a man upon whom sleep seizes," so I had fallen. Even yet, as I passed near the region of the armoury, the rapturous shields of Aith did not fail to smash faintly upon my ear. Harfager I did not see, for he, too, was doubtless roaming a hurtling Ahasuerus round the world of the house. However, at about midnight, observing light shining from a door on the lower stage, I entered and saw him there—the chamber of the dropping horologe. He sat hugging himself on the ladder-steps, gazing at the gloomy pool. The final lights of the riot of the day seemed dying in his eyes; and he gave me no glance as I ran in. His hands, his bare arm, were all washed with new-shed blood; but of this, too, he looked unconscious; his mouth was hanging open to his pantings. As I eyed him, he suddenly leapt high, smiting his hands with the yell, "The last bell tinkling!" and ran out raving. He therefore did not see (though he may have understood by hearing) the thing which, with cowering awe, I now saw: for a ball slipped from the horologe with a hiss and mist of smoke into the pool; and while the clock once ticked another: and while the clock yet ticked, another! and the smoke of the first had not perfectly thinned, when the smoke of the third, mixing with it, floated toward the dome. Understanding that the sands of the mansion were run, I, too, throwing up my arm, rushed from the spot; but was suddenly stopped in my flight by the sense of some stupendous destiny emptying its vials upon the edifice; and was made aware by a crackling racket, like musketry, above, and the downpour of a world of waters, that some waterspout, in the waltz and whirl, had hurled its broken summit upon us, and burst through the dome. At that moment I beheld Harfager running toward me, his hands buried in his hair; and, as he raced past, I caught him, crying: "Harfager, save yourself! the very fountains, Harfager—by the grand God, man"—I hissed it into his inmost ear—"*the very fountains of the Great Deep. . .!*" He glared at me, and went on his way, while I, whisking myself into a room, closed the door. Here for some time with weak knees I waited; but the eagerness of my frenzy pressed me, and I again stepped out, to find the corridors everywhere thigh-deep with water; while rags of the storm, bragging through the hole in the dome, were now blustering about the house. My light was at once puffed out; but I was surprised by the presence of *another* light—most ghostly, gloomy, bluish—mild, yet wild—which now gloated everywhere through the house. I was standing in wonder at this when a gust of auguster passion galloped up the mansion; and, with it, I was made aware of the *snap* of something somewhere. There was a minute's infinite waiting—and then—quick—ever quicker—came the throb, snap, pop, in spacious succession, of the anchoring chains of the mansion before the hurried shoulder of the hurricane. And *again* a second of breathless stillness—and then—deliberately—its hour came—the house moved. My flesh worked like the flesh of worms which squirm. Slowly moved, and stopped—then there was a sweep—and a swirl—and a pause! then a swirl—and a sweep—and a pause! then steady labour on the brazen axis as the labourer tramps by the harrow; then a heightening of zest—then intensity—then the final light liveliness of flight. And now once again, as, staggering and plunging, I spun, the notion of escape for a moment came to me, but this time I shook an impious fist. "No, but, God, no, no," I gasped, "I will no more go from here: here let me waltzing pass in this carnival of the vortices, anarchy of the thunders!"—and I ran staggering. But memory gropes in a greyer gloaming as to all that followed. I struggled up the stairway, now flowing a river, and for a good while ran staggering and plunging, full of wild rantings, about, amid the downfall of roofs, and the ruins of walls. The air was thick with splashes, the whole roof now, save three rafters, having been snatched by the wind away; and in the blush of that bluish moonshine the tapestries were flapping and trailing wildly out after the flying place, like the streaming hair of some ranting fakir stung reeling by the tarantulas of distraction. At one point, where the largest of the porticoes protruded, the mansion began at every revolution to bump with grum shudderings against some obstruction: it bumped, and while the lips said one-two-three it three times bumped again. It was the mænadism of mass! Swift—still swifter—in an ague of flurry it raced, every portico a sail to the gale, racking its great frame to fragments. I, running by the door of a room littered with the ruins of a wall, saw through that livid moonlight Harfager sitting on a tomb—a drum by him, upon which, with a club in his bloody fist, he feebly, but persistingly, beat. The speed of the leaning house had now attained the *sleeping* stage, that last pitch of the spinning-top; and now all at once Harfager dashed away the mat of hair which wrapped his face, sprang, stretched his arms, and began to spin—

giddily—in the same direction as the mansion—nor less sleep-embathed, with lifted hair, with quivering cheeks. . . . From such a sight I shied with retching; and staggering, plunging, presently found myself on the lower floor opposite a porch, where an outer door chancing to crash before me, the breath of the tempest smote freshly upon me. On this an impulse, partly of madness, more of sanity, spurred in my soul; and I spurted out of the doorway, to be whirled far out into the limbo without.

The river at once rushed me deep-drenched toward the sea—though even there, in that depth of whirlpool, a shrill din, like the splitting of a world, reached my ears. It had hardly passed when my body butted in its course upon one of the arches, cushioned with seaweed, of the not all demolished cause-way. Nor had I utterly lost consciousness. A clutch freed my head from the drench; and in the end I heaved myself to the level of the summit. Hence to the ledge of rock by which I had come, the bridge being intact, I rowed myself on my face under the thumps of the wind, and under a rushing of rain, like a shimmering of silk through the air. Noticing the same wild shining about me which had blushed through the broken dome into the mansion, I glanced backward—and saw that the dwelling of the Harfagers was a memory of the past; then upward—and the whole north heaven, to the zenith, shone one ocean of variegated glories—the *aurora borealis*, which was being fairly brushed and flustered by the gale. At the augustness of which sight, I was touched to a gush of tears. And with them the dream broke! the infatuation passed! a palm seemed to skin back from my brain the films and media of delusion; and on my knees I threw my hands to heaven in thankfulness for the marvel of my rescue from all the temptation, the tribulation, and the breakage, of Rayba.

A. MERRITT (1884-1943) was primarily an editor for the *American Weekly* (a magazine supplement to the Hearst newspapers), but also wrote a number of stories and novels for the pulp magazines. "The Moon Pool," published in *All-Story Weekly* for 22 June 1918, was one of his earliest and best. In 1919, Merritt re-wrote both "The Moon Pool" and its sequel, "The Conquest of the Moon Pool," as a novel, also titled *The Moon Pool*. Lovecraft considered the novel inferior to the original story. In January 1934, Merritt hosted Lovecraft to a dinner at his club in New York, which Lovecraft described in a letter to R. H. Barlow: "Merritt is a stout, sandy, grey-eyed man of about 45 or 50—extremely pleasant & genial, & a brilliant & well-informed conversationalist on all subjects. He is associate editor of Heart's American Weekly, but all his main interests centre in his weird writing. He agrees with me that the original Moon-Pool novelette in the All-Story is his best work." Merritt's reputation has not stood well the test of time, and even his original version of "The Moon Pool" is perhaps better considered as a popular weird tale than as a literary one.

THE MOON POOL
by A. Merritt

To the Editor of All-Story Magazine:

The International Association of Science has directed me to place before you the following narrative with the view, if you are agreeable, of publication as soon as possible. Because of your extraordinarily large circulation and its diffusion not only throughout the United States, but throughout the reading world, it was felt that yours was the ideal medium to bring the facts before the greatest audience and so enable the association to right a wrong which, but for Dr. Goodwin's very understandable and perhaps entirely human hesitation, would never have gained headway.

The association in selecting you as the subject of this request, took into consideration the fact that the space limit of newspapers are such that the complete narrative of Dr. Goodwin could not be published therein, whereas with you this handicap does not exist. It was also convinced that so important and unusual a document could not communicate its unique impression of truth and sincerity unless read in its entirety exactly as it was before the International Association of Science, April 18, 1918.

I have been authorized to announce that we have discovered that Dr. Goodwin is now actually on his way to the Caroline Islands, and that the association is preparing an expedition to follow him speedily; to save him if it can arrive in time; at the least to investigate and to destroy if possible, and if necessary, the cause of his journey.

The maps which Dr. Goodwin received from Dr. Throckmartin accompany this manuscript. It is our desire that they be published with it for the guidance of other scientists or courageous men who may be impelled on reading it to follow us with another expedition. For it is not at all certain that the human expedients planned by the association can cope with phenomena so clearly beyond the range of present human knowledge as that which Dr. Throckmartin describes as emanating from what he calls "the moon pool," and that which Dr. Goodwin saw on board the Southern Queen. Again it may be that this unearthly dweller in the prehistoric island ruins of the South Seas is only one of many. Further, there is the hint conveyed by the underground chanting heard by Dr. Throckmartin; raising the question of the existence of considerable other forces or creatures possessing powers of knowledge of which we are densely ignorant, and in the exercise of which the world must be deeply concerned.

It is unnecessary to say to you that Dr. Walter T. Goodwin, Ph.D., F.R.G.S., et cetera, though in his early thirties, is known as the foremost of American botanists, and that Dr. David Throckmartin's scientific reputation is so great that even the cloud that has gathered about his memory could not blacken his achievements.

For those who would follow us, full information as to the methods of the expedition can be secured at the office of the president of the association.

Out foremost purpose in asking publication is, however, as I have said, to remove the shadow from the name of Dr. Throckmartin, of his young wife, and of his brilliant young associate, Dr. Charles Stanton, who accompanied him on his ill-fated journey.

The association has entrusted this explanation and the narrative of Dr. Goodwin to Mr. A. Merritt, who has courteously volunteered to set it before you together with other facts which we have asked him to communicate to you verbally.

Respectfully yours,
THE INTERNATIONAL ASSOCIATION OF SCIENCE,
Per J. B. K., President.

I. The Throckmartin Mystery

I break a silence of three years to clear the name of Dr. David Throckmartin and to lift the shadow of scandal from that of his wife and of Dr. Charles Stanton, his assistant. That I have not found the courage to do so before, all men who are jealous of their scientific reputations will understand when they have heard what I have written. How strongly I attest to my belief in the truth of what I am about to lay before you will be equallly clear as you listen and realize, as I do, the storm of ridicule and disbelief it is sure to bring upon me. Yet I hope that you will also believe before this narrative is finished.

Let me recapitulate what, until now, has actually been known of the Throckmartin expedition to the island of Ponape in the Carolines—the Throckmartin Mystery, as it is called.

Dr. Throckmartin set forth early in 1915 to make some observations of Nan-Matal, that extraordinary group of island ruins, remains of a high and prehistoric civilization, that are clustered along the vast shore of Ponape. With him went his wife to whom he had been wedded less than half a year. The daughter of Professor Frazier-Smith, she was as deeply interested and almost as well informed as he upon these relics of a vanished race that titanically strew certain islands of the Pacific and form the basis for the theory of a submerged Pacific continent.

Mrs. Throckmartin, it will be recalled, was much younger, fifteen years at least, than her husband. Dr. Charles Stanton, who accompanied them as Dr. Throckmartin's assistant, was about her age. These three and a Swedish woman, Thora Helversen, who had been Edith Throckmartin's nurse in babyhood and who was entirely devoted to her, made up the expedition.

Dr. Throckmartin planned to spend a year among the ruins, not only of Ponape, but of Lele—the twin centers of that colossal riddle of humanity whose answer has its roots in immeasurable antiquity; a weird flower of man-made civilization that blossomed ages before the seeds of Egypt were sown; of whose arts we know little and of whose science and secret knowledge of nature nothing.

He carried with him complete equipment for his work and gathered at Ponape a dozen or so natives for laborers. They went straight to Metalanim harbor and set up their camp on the island called Uschen-Tau in the group known as the Nan-Matal. You will remember that these islands are entirely uninhabited and are shunned by the people on the main island.

Three months later Dr. Throckmartin appeared at Port Moresby, Papua. He came on a schooner manned by Solomon Islanders and commanded by a Chinese half-breed captain. He reported that he was on his way to Melbourne for additional scientific equipment and whites to help him in his excavations, saying that the superstition of the natives made their aid negligible. He went immediately on board the steamer Southern Queen which was sailing that same morning. Three nights later he disappeared from the Southern Queen and it was officially reported that he had met death either by being swept overboard or by casting himself into the sea.

A relief-boat sent with the news to Ponape found the Throckmartin camp on the island Uschen-Tau and a smaller camp on the island called Nan-Tanach. All the equipment, clothing, supplies were intact. But of Mrs. Throckmartin, of Dr. Stanton, or of Thora Helversen they could find not a single trace!

The natives who had been employed by the archeologist were questioned. They said that the ruins were the abode of great spirits—*ani*—who were particularly powerful when the moon was at the full. On these nights all the islanders were doubly careful to give the ruins wide berth. Upon being employed, they had demanded leave from the day before full moon until it was on the wane and this had been granted them by Dr. Throckmartin. Thrice they had left the expedition alone on these nights. On their third return they had found the four white people gone and they "knew that the *ani* had eaten them." They were afraid and had fled.

That was all.

The Chinese half caste was found and reluctantly testified at last that he had picked Dr. Throckmartin up from a small boat about fifty miles off Ponape. The scientist had seemed half mad, but he had given the seaman a large sum of money to bring him to Port Moresby and to say, if questioned, that he had boarded the boat at Ponape harbor.

That, gentlemen, is all that has been known to anyone of the fate of the Throckmartin expedition.

Why, you will ask, do I break silence now; and how came I in possession of the facts I am about to set forth?

To the first I answer: I was at the Geographical Club recently and I overheard two members talking. They mentioned the name of Throckmartin and I became an eavesdropper. One said:

"Of course what probably happened was that Throckmartin killed them all. It's a dangerous thing for a man to marry a woman so much younger than himself and then throw her into the necessarily close company of exploration with a man as young and as agreeable as Stanton was. The inevitable happened, no doubt. Throckmartin discovered; avenged himself. Then followed remorse and suicide."

"Throckmartin didn't seem to be that kind," said the other thoughtfully.

"No, he didn't," agreed the first.

"Isn't there another story?" went on the second speaker. "Something about Mrs. Throckmartin running away with Stanton and taking the woman, Thora, with her? Somebody told me they had been recognized in Singapore recently."

"You can take your pick of the two stories," replied his vis-à-vis. "It's one or the other I suppose."

It was neither one nor the other, gentlemen. I know—and I will answer now the second question—because I was with Throckmartin when he—vanished. I know what he told me and I know what my own eyes saw. Incredible, abnormal, against all the known facts of our science as it was, I testify to it. And it is my intention, after sending you this, to sail to Ponape, to go to the Nan-Matal and to the islet beneath whose frowning walls dwells the mystery that Throckmartin sought and found—and that at the last sought and found Throckmartin!

I attach herewith a copy of the map of the islands that he gave me. I attach also his sketch of the great courtyard of Nan-Tanach, the location of the moon door, his indication of the probable location of the moon pool and the passage to it and his approximation of the position of the shining globes. If I do not return and there are any with enough belief, scientific curiosity and courage to follow, these will furnish a plain trail.

I will now proceed straightforwardly with my narrative.

For six months I had been on the d'Entrecasteaux Islands gathering data for the concluding chapters of my book upon "Flora of the Volcanic

Islands of the South Pacific." The day before, I had reached Port Moresby and had seen my specimens safely stored on board the Southern Queen. As I sat on the upper deck that morning I thought, with homesick mind, of the long leagues between me and Melbourne and the longer ones between Melbourne and New York.

It was one of Papua's yellow mornings, when she shows herself in her most somber, most baleful mood. The sky was a smoldering ocher. Over the island brooded a spirit sullen, implacable and alien; filled with the threat of latent, malefic forces waiting to be unleashed. It seemed an emanation from the untamed, sinister heart of Papua herself—sinister even when she smiles. And now and then, on the wind, came a breath from unexplored jungles, filled with unfamiliar odors, mysterious, and menacing.

It is on such mornings that Papua speaks to you of her immemorial ancientness and of her power. I am not unduly imaginative but it is a mood that makes me shrink—I mention it because it bears directly upon Dr. Throckmartin's fate. Nor is the mood Papua's alone. I have felt it in New Guinea, in Australia, in the Solomons and in the Carolines. But it is in Papua that it seems most articulate. It is as though she said: "I am the ancient of days; I have seen the earth in the throes of its shaping; I am the primeval; I have seen races born and die and, lo, in my breast are secrets that would blast you by the telling, you pale babes of a puling age. You and I ought not be in the same world; yet I am and I shall be! Never will you fathom me and you I hate though I tolerate! I tolerate—but how long?"

And then I seem to see a giant paw that reaches from Papua toward the outer world, stretching and sheathing monstrous claws.

All feel this mood of hers. Her own people have it woven in them, part of their web and woof; flashing into light unexpectedly like a soul from another universe; masking itself as swiftly.

I fought against Papua as every white man must on one of her yellow mornings. And as I fought I saw a tall figure come striding down the pier. Behind him came a Kapa-Kapa boy swinging a new valise. There was something familiar about the tall man. As he reached the gangplank he looked up straight into my eyes, stared at me for a moment and waved his hand. It was Dr. Throckmartin!

Coincident with my recognition of him there came a shock of surprise that was definitely—unpleasant. It was Throckmartin—but there was something disturbingly different about him and the man I had known so well and had bidden farewell less than a year before. He was then, as you know, just turned forty, lithe, erect, muscular; the face of a student and of a seeker. His controlling expression was one of enthusiasm, of intellectual keenness, of—what shall I say—expectant search. His ever eagerly questioning brain had stamped itself upon his face.

I sought in my mind for an explanation of that which I had felt on the flash of his greeting. Hurrying down to the lower deck I found him with the purser. As I spoke he turned and held out to me an eager hand—and then I saw what the change was that had come over him!

He knew, of course, by my face the uncontrollable shock that my closer look had given me. His eyes filled and he turned briskly to the purser; then hurried off to his stateroom, leaving me standing, half dazed.

At the stair he half turned.

"Oh, Goodwin," he said. "I'd like to see you later. Just now there's something I must write before we start—"

He went up swiftly.

" 'E looks rather queer—eh?" said the purser. "Know 'im well, sir? Seems to 'ave given you quite a start, sir."

I made some reply and went slowly to my chair. I tried to analyze what it was that had disturbed me so; what profound change in Throckmartin that had so shaken me. Now it came to me. It was as though the man had suffered some terrific soul searing shock of rapture and horror combined; some soul cataclysm that in its climax had remolded his face deep from within, setting on it the seal of wedded joy and fear. As though indeed ecstasy supernal and terror infernal had once come to him hand in hand, taken possession of him, looked out of his eyes and, departing, left behind upon him ineradicably their shadow.

Gone was Throckmartin's old eager look, utterly gone, and in its place was this—something—I had never seen before on any face. I caught myself wondering what his face must have been when the seal was stamped freshly upon it. And what in the name of all knowledge was the agency that had done this thing! For it came to me suddenly that the true reason for this distress, the deep perturbation and amaze that he stirred in me was that the two expressions were mingled, inextricably, lay side by side, not contending but in some frightful fashion—harmonious! That was what shocked. For how could hate and love, ecstasy and horror, heaven and hell mix, join hands—kiss? Yet these were what close embraced, lay on Throckmartin's face.

If I seem to dwell on this, have patience; it is necessary indeed.

Alternately I looked out over the port and paced about the deck, striving to read the riddle; to banish it from my mind. And all the time still over Papua brooded its baleful spirit of ancient evil, unfathomable, not to be understood; nor had it lifted when the Southern Queen lifted anchor and steamed out into the gulf.

II. Down the Moon Path

I watched with relief the shores sink down behind us; welcomed the touch of the free sea wind. We seemed to be drawing away from something malefic; something that lurked within the island spell I have described, and the thought crept into my mind, spoke—whispered rather—from Throckmartin's face.

I had hoped—and within the hope was an inexplicable shrinking, an unexpressed dread—that I would meet Throckmartin at lunch. He did not come down and I was sensible of a distinct relief within my disappointment. All that afternoon I lounged about uneasily but still he kept to his cabin. Nor did he appear at dinner.

Dusk and night fell swiftly. I was warm and went back to my deckchair. The Southern Queen was rolling to a disquieting swell and I had the place to myself. I had looked my fellow passengers over while we were at table. They were a scant dozen. A couple of English officials and their wives, engrossed in "shop" and bulwarked by the English unapproachableness of the first night out; a clerk or two; a shoe salesman from Brisbane; a scattering of others—none of them worth breaking my solitude for, I decided.

Over the heavens was a canopy of cloud, glowing faintly and testifying to the moon riding behind it. There was much phosphorescence. Now and then, before the ship and at the sides, arose those strange little swirls of mist that steam up from the Southern Ocean like the breath of sea monsters, whirl for a moment and disappear. I lighted a cigarette and tried once more to banish from my mind Throckmartin's face—and unsuccessfully as ever.

Suddenly the deck door opened and through it came Throckmartin himself. He paused uncertainly, looked up at the sky with a curiously eager, intent gaze, hesitated, then closed the door behind him.

"Throckmartin," I called. "Come sit with me. It's Goodwin."

Immediately he made his way to me, sitting beside me with a gasp of relief that I noted curiously. His hand touched mine and gripped it with tenseness that hurt. His hand was icelike. I puffed up my cigarette and by its glow scanned him closely. He was watching a large swirl of the mist that was passing before the ship. The phosphorescence beneath it illumined it with a fitful opalescence. I saw fear in his eyes. The swirl passed; he sighed; his grip relaxed and he sank back.

"Throckmartin," I said, wasting no time in preliminaries. "What's wrong? Can I help you?"

He was silent.

"Is your wife all right and what are you doing here when I heard you had gone to the Carolines for a year?" I went on.

I felt his body grow tense again. He did not speak for a moment and then:

"I'm going to Melbourne, Goodwin," he said. "I need a few things— need them urgently. And more men—white men."

His voice was low; preoccupied. It was as though the brain that dictated the words did so perfunctorily, half impatiently; aloof, watching, strained to catch the first hint of approach of something dreaded.

"You are making progress then?" I asked. It was a banal question, put forth in a blind effort to claim his attention.

"Progress?" he repeated. "Progress—"

He stopped abruptly; rose from his chair, gazed intently toward the north. I followed his gaze. Far, far away the moon had broken through the clouds. Almost on the horizon, you could see the faint luminescence of it upon the quiet sea. The distant patch of light quivered and shook. The clouds thickened again and it was gone. The ship raced southward, swiftly.

Throckmartin dropped into his chair. He lighted a cigarette with a hand that trembled. The flash of the match fell on his face and I noted with a queer thrill of apprehension that its unfamiliar expression had deepened; become curiously intensified as though a faint acid had passed over it, etching its lines faintly deeper.

"It's the full moon tonight, isn't it?" he asked, palpably with studied inconsequence.

"The first night of full moon," I answered. He was silent again. I sat silent too, waiting for him to make up his mind to speak. He turned to me as though he had made a sudden resolution.

"Goodwin," he said. "I do need help. If ever man needed it, I do. Goodwin—can you imagine yourself in another world, alien, unfamiliar, a world of terror, whose unknown joy is its greatest terror of all; you all alone there; a stranger! As such a man would need help, so I need—"

243

He paused abruptly and arose to his feet stiffly; the cigarette dropped from his fingers. I saw that the moon had again broken through the clouds, and this time much nearer. Not a mile away was the patch of light that it threw upon the waves. Back of it, to the rim of the sea was a lane of moonlight; it was a gleaming gigantic serpent racing over the rim of the world straight and surely toward the ship.

Throckmartin gazed at it as though turned to stone. He stiffened to it as a pointer does to a hidden covey. To me from him pulsed a thrill of terror—but terror tinged with an unfamiliar, an infernal joy. It came to me and passed away—leaving me trembling with its shock of bitter sweet.

He bent forward, all his soul in his eyes. The moon path swept closer, closer still. It was now less than half a mile away. From it the ship fled; almost it came to me, as though pursued. Down upon it, swift and straight, a radiant torrent cleaving the waves, raced the moon stream. And then—

"Good God!" breathed Throckmartin, and if ever the words were a prayer and an invocation they were.

And then, for the first time—I saw—*it!*

The moon path, as I have said, stretched to the horizon and was bordered by darkness. It was as though the clouds above had been parted to form a lane—drawn aside like curtains or as the waters of the Red Sea were held back to let the hosts of Israel through. On each side of the stream was the black shadow cast by the folds of the high canopies. And straight as a road between the opaque walls gleamed, shimmered and danced the shining, racing, rapids of moonlight.

Far, it seemed immeasurably far, along this stream of silver fire I sensed, rather than saw, something coming. It drew into sight as a deeper glow within the light. On and on it sped toward us—an opalescent mistiness that swept on with the suggestion of some winged creature in darting flight. Dimly there crept into my mind memory of the Dyak legend of the winged messenger of Buddha—the Akla bird whose feathers are woven of the moon rays, whose heart is a living opal, whose wings in flight echo the crystal clear music of the white stars—but whose beak is of frozen flame and shreds the souls of the unbelievers. Still it sped on, and now there came to me sweet, insistent tinklings—like a pizzicati on violins of glass, crystalline, as purest, clearest glass transformed to sound. And again the myth of the Akla bird came to me.

But now it was close to the end of the white path; close up to the barrier of darkness still between the ship and the sparkling head of the moon stream. And now it beat up against the barrier as a bird against the bars of its cage. And I knew that this was no mist born of sea and air. It whirled with shimmering plumes, with swirls of lacy light, with spirals of living vapor. It held within it odd, unfamiliar gleams as of shifting mother-of-pearl. Coruscations and glittering atoms drifted through it as though it drew them from the rays that bathed it.

Nearer and nearer it came, borne on the sparkling waves, and less and less grew the protecting wall of shadow between it and us. The crystalline sounds were louder—rhythmic as music from another planet.

Now I saw that within the mistiness was a core, a nucleus of intenser light—veined, opaline, effulgent, intensely alive. And above it, tangled in the plumes and spirals that throbbed and whirled were seven glowing lights.

Through all the incessant but strangely ordered movement of the—*thing*—these lights held firm and steady. They were seven—like seven little moons. One was of a pearly pink, one of delicate nacreous blue, one of lambent saffron, one of the emerald you see in the shallow waters of tropic isles; a deathly white; a ghostly amethyst; and one of the silver that is seen only when the flying fish leap beneath the moon. There they shone—these seven little varicolored orbs within the opaline mistiness of whatever it was that, poised and expectant, waited to be drawn to us on the light filled waves.

The tinkling music was louder still. It pierced the ears with a shower of tiny lances; it made the heart beat jubilantly—and checked it dolorously. It closed your throat with a throb of rapture and gripped it tight like the hand of infinite sorrow!

Came to me now a murmuring cry, stilling the crystal clear notes, it was articulate—but as though from something utterly foreign to this world. The ear took the cry and translated with conscious labor into the sounds of earth. And even as it compassed, the brain shrank from it irresistibly and simultaneously it seemed, reached toward it with irresistible eagerness.

"Av-o-lo-ha! Av-o-lo-ha!" So the cry seemed to throb.

The grip of Throckmartin's hand relaxed. He walked stiffly toward the front of the deck, straight toward the vision, now but a few yards away from the bow. I ran toward him and gripped him—and fell back. For now his face had lost all human semblance. Utter agony and utter ecstasy—there they were side by side, not resisting each other; unholy inhuman companions blending into a look that none of God's creatures should wear—and deep, deep as his soul! A devil and a God dwelling harmoniously side by side! So must Satan, newly fallen, still divine, seeing heaven and contemplating hell, have looked.

And then—swiftly the moon path faded! The clouds swept over the sky as though a hand had drawn them together. Up from the south came a roaring squall. As the moon vanished what I had seen vanished with it—blotted out as an image on a magic lantern; the tinkling ceased abruptly—leaving a silence like that which follows an abrupt and stupendous thunder clap. There was nothing about us but silence and blackness!

Through me there passed a great trembling as one who had stood on the very verge of the gulf wherein the men of the Louisades say lurks the fisher of the souls of men, and has been plucked back by sheerest chance.

Throckmartin passed an arm around me.

"It is as I thought," he said. In his voice was a new note; of the calm certainty that has swept aside a waiting terror of the unknown. "Now I know! Come with me to my cabin, old friend. For now that you too have seen I can tell you"—he hesitated—"what it was you saw," he ended.

As we passed through the door we came face to face with the ship's first officer. Throckmartin turned quickly, but not soon enough for the mate not to see and stare with amazement. His eyes turned questioningly to me.

With a strong effort of will Throckmartin composed his face into at least a semblance of normality.

"Are we going to have much of a storm?" he asked.

"Yes," said the mate. Then the seaman, getting the better of his curiosity, added, profanely: "We'll probably have it all the way to Melbourne."

Throckmartin straightened as though with a new thought. He gripped the officer's sleeve eagerly.

"You mean at least cloudy weather—for"—he hesitated—"for the next three nights, say?"

"And for three more," replied the mate.

"Thank God!" cried Throckmartin, and I think I never heard such relief and hope as was in his voice.

The sailor stood amazed. "Thank God?" he repeated. "Thank—what d'ye mean?"

But Throckmartin was moving onward to his cabin. I started to follow. The first officer stopped me.

"Your friend," he said, "is he ill?"

"The sea!" I answered hurriedly. "He's not used to it. I am going to look after him."

I saw doubt and disbelief in the seaman's eyes but I hurried on. For I knew now that Throckmartin was ill indeed—but that it was a sickness neither the ship's doctor nor any other could heal.

III. "Dead! All Dead!"

Throckmartin was sitting on the side of his berth as I entered. He had taken off his coat. He was leaning over, face in hands.

"Lock the door," he said quietly, not raising his head. "Close the portholes and draw the curtains—and—have you an electric flash in your pocket—a good, strong one?"

He glanced at the small pocket flash I handed him and clicked it on. "Not big enough I'm afraid," he said. "And after all"—he hesitated—"it's only a theory."

"What's only a theory?" I asked in astonishment.

"Thinking of it as a weapon against—what you saw," he said, with a wry smile.

"Throckmartin," I cried. "What was it? Did I really see—that thing—there in the moon path? Did I really hear—"

"This for instance," he interrupted.

Softly he whispered: "Av-o-lo-ha!" With the murmur I seemed to hear again the crystalline unearthly music; an echo of it, faint, sinister, mocking, jubilant.

"Throckmartin," I said. "What was it? What are you flying from, man? Where is your wife—and Stanton?"

"Dead!" he said monotonously. "Dead! All dead!" Then as I re-coiled in horror—"All dead. Edith, Stanton, Thora—dead—or worse. And Edith in the moon pool—with them—drawn by what you saw on the moon path—and that wants me—and that has put its brand upon me—and pursues me."

With a vicious movement he ripped open his shirt.

"Look at this," he said. I gazed. Around his chest, an inch above his heart, the skin was white as pearl. The whiteness was sharply de-fined against the healthy tint of the body. He turned and I saw it ran around his back. It circled him. The band made a perfect cincture about two inches wide.

"Burn it!" he said, and offered me his cigarette. I drew back. He gestured—peremptorily. I pressed the glowing end of the cigarette into the ribbon of white flesh. He did not flinch nor was there odor of burning nor, as I drew the little cylinder away, any mark upon the whiteness.

"Feel it!" he commanded again. I placed my fingers upon the band. It was cold—like frozen marble.

He handed me a small penknife.

"Cut!" he ordered. This time, my scientific interest fully aroused, I did so without reluctance. The blade cut into flesh. I waited for the blood to come. None appeared. I drew out the knife and thrust it in again, fully a quarter of an inch deep. I might have been cutting paper so far as any evidence followed that what I was piercing was human skin and muscle.

Another thought came to me and I drew back, revolted.

"Throckmartin," I whispered. "Not leprosy!"

"Nothing so easy," he said. "Look again and find the places you cut."

I looked, as he bade me, and in the white ring there was not a single mark. Where I had pressed the blade there was no trace. It was as though the skin had parted to make way for the blade and closed.

Throckmartin arose and drew his shirt about him.

"Two things you have seen," he said. "*It*—and its mark—the seal it placed on me that gives it, I think, the power to follow me. Seeing, you must believe my story. Goodwin, I tell you again that my wife is dead—or worse—I do not know; the prey of—what you saw; so, too, is Stanton; so Thora. How—" He stopped for a moment. Then continued:

"And I am going to Melbourne for the things to empty its den and its shrine; for dynamite to destroy it and its lair—if anything made on earth will destroy it; and for white men with courage to use them. Perhaps—perhaps after you have heard, you will be one of these men?" He looked at me a bit wistfully. "And now—do not interrupt me, I beg of you, till I am through—for"—he smiled wanly—"the mate may be wrong. And if he is"—he arose and paced twice about the room—"if he is I may not have time to tell you."

"Throckmartin," I answered, "I have no closed mind. Tell me and if I can I will help."

He took my hand and pressed it.

"Goodwin," he began, "if I have seemed to take the death of my wife lightly—or rather"—his face contorted—"or rather—if I have seemed to pass it by as something not of first importance to me—believe me it is not so. If the rope is long enough—if what the mate says is so—if there is cloudy weather until the moon begins to wane—I can conquer—that I know. But if it does not—if the dweller in the moon pool gets me—then must you or some one avenge my wife—and me—and Stanton. Yet I cannot believe that God would let a thing like that conquer! But why did He then let it take my Edith? And why does He allow it to exist? Are there things stronger than God, do you think, Goodwin?"

He turned to me feverishly. I hesitated.

"I do not know just how you define God," I said. "If you mean the will to know, working through science—"

He waved me aside impatiently.

"Science," he said. "What is our science against—that? Or against the science of whatever cursed, vanished race that made it—or made the way for it to enter this world of ours?"

With an effort he regained control of himself.

"Goodwin," he said, "do you know at all of the ruins on the Carolines; the cyclopean, megolithic cities and harbors of Ponape and Lele, of Kusaie, of Ruk and Hogolu, and a score of other islets there? Particularly, do you know of the Nan-Matal and Metalanim?"

"Of the Metalanim I have heard and seen photographs," I said. "They call it don't they, the Lost Venice of the Pacific?"

"Look at this map," said Throckmartin. He handed me the map. "That," he went on, "is Christian's map of Metalanim harbor and the Nan-Matal. Do you see the rectangles marked Nan-Tanach?"

"Yes," I said.

"There," he said, "under those walls is the moon pool and the seven gleaming lights that raise the dweller in the pool and the altar and shrine of the dweller. And there in the moon pool with it lie Edith and Stanton and Thora."

"The dweller in the moon pool?" I repeated half-incredulously.

"The thing you saw," said Throckmartin solemnly.

A solid sheet of rain swept the ports, and the Southern Queen began to roll on the rising swells. Throckmartin drew another deep breath of relief, and drawing aside a curtain peered out into the night. Its blackness seemed to reassure him. At any rate, when he sat again he was calm.

"There are no more wonderful ruins in the world than those of the island Venice of Metalanim on the east shore of Ponape," he said al-most casually. "They take in some fifty islets and cover with their intersecting canals and lagoons about twelve square miles. Who built them? None knows! When were they built? Ages before the memory of present man, that is sure. Ten thousand, twenty thousand, a hundred thousand years ago—the last more likely.

"All these islets, Goodwin, are squared, and their shores are frowning sea-walls of gigantic basalt blocks hewn and put in place by the hands of ancient man. Each inner water-front is faced with a terrace of those basalt blocks which stand out six feet above the shallow canals that meander between them. On the islets behind these walls are cyclopean and time-shattered fortresses, palaces, terraces, pyramids; immense courtyards, strewn with ruins—and all so old that they seem to wither the eyes of those who look on them.

"There has been a great subsidence. You can stand out of Metalanim harbor for three miles and look down upon the tops of similar monolithic structures and walls twenty feet below you in the water.

"And all about, strung on their canals, are the bulwarked islets with their enigmatic giant walls peering through the dense growths of mangroves—dead, deserted for incalculable ages; shunned by those who live near.

"You as a botanist are familiar with the evidence that a vast shadowy continent existed in the Pacific—a continent that was not rent asunder by volcanic forces as was that legendary one of Atlantis in the Eastern Ocean. My work in Java, in Papua, and in the Ladrones had set my mind upon this Pacific lost land. Just as the Azores are believed to be the last high peaks of Atlantis, so evidence came to me steadily that Ponape and Lele and their basalt bulwarked islets were the last points of the slowly sunken western land clinging still to the sunlight, and had been the last refuge and sacred places of the rulers of that race which had lost their immemorial home under the rising waters of the Pacific.

"I believed that under these ruins I might find the evidence of what I sought. Time and again I had encountered legends of subterranean networks beneath the Nan-Matal, of passages running back into the main island itself; basalt corridors that followed the lines of the shallow canals and ran under them to islet after islet, linking them in mysterious chains.

"My—my wife and I had talked before we were married of making this our great work. After the honeymoon we prepared for the expedition. It was to be my monument. Stanton was as enthusiastic as ourselves. We sailed, as you know, last May in fulfilment of our dreams.

"At Ponape we selected, not without difficulty, workmen to help us—diggers. I had to make extraordinary inducements before I could get together my force. Their beliefs are gloomy, these Ponapeans. They people their swamps, their forests, their mountains and shores with malignant spirits—ani they call them. And they are afraid—bitterly afraid of the isles of ruins and what they think the ruins hide. I do not wonder—now! For their fear has come down to them, through the ages, from the people

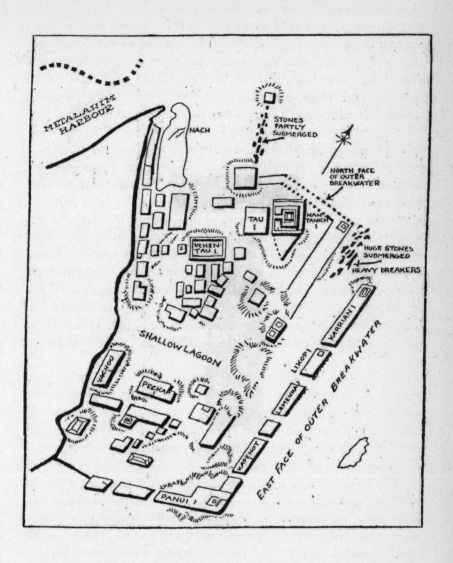

A copy of the map of the islets of the Nan-Matal, which Dr. Throckmartin gave Dr. Goodwin. It in its turn is a copy of the official sketch plan by F. W. Christian, the first explorer to map the Caroline Islands' mysterious maze.

'before their fathers,' as they call them, who, they say, made these mighty spirits their slaves and messengers.

"When they were told where they were to go, and how long we expected to stay, they murmured. Those who, at last, were tempted made what I thought then merely a superstitious proviso that they were to be allowed to go away on the three nights of the full moon. Would to God I had heeded them and gone, too!"

He stopped and again over his face the lines etched deep.

"We passed," he went on, "into Metalanim harbor. Off to our left—a mile away arose a massive quadrangle. Its walls were all of forty feet high and hundreds of feet on each side. As we passed it our natives grew very silent; watched it furtively, fearfully. I knew it for the ruins that are called Nan-Tanach, the 'place of frowning walls.' And at the silence of my men I recalled what Christian had written of this place; of how he had come upon its 'ancient platforms and tetragonal enclosures of stonework; its wonder of tortuous alleyways and labyrinth of shallow canals; grim masses of stonework peering out from behind verdant screens; cyclopean barricades,' and of how, when we had turned into its ghostly shadows, straightaway the merriment of our guides was hushed and conversation died down to whispers. For we were close to Nan-Tanach—the place of lofty walls, the most remarkable of all the Metalanim ruins." He arose and stood over me.

"Nan-Tanach, Goodwin," he said solemnly—"a place where merriment is hushed indeed and words are stifled; Nan-Tanach—where the moon pool lies hidden—lies hidden behind the moon rock, but sends its diabolic soul out—even through the prisoning stone." He raised clenched hands. "Oh, God," he breathed, "grant me that I may blast it from earth!"

He was silent for a little time.

"Of course I wanted to pitch our camp there," he began again quietly, "but I soon gave up that idea. The natives were panic-stricken—threatened to turn back. 'No,' they said, 'too great *ani* there. We go to any other place—but not there.' Although, even then, I felt that the secret of the place was in Nan-Tanach, I found it necessary to give in. The laborers were essential to the success of the expedition, and I told myself that after a little time had passed and I had persuaded them that there was nothing anywhere that could molest them, we would move our tents to it. We finally picked for our base the islet called Uschen-Tau—you see it here—" He pointed to the map. "It was close to the isle of desire, but far enough away from it to satisfy our men. There was an excellent camping-place there and a spring of fresh water. It offered, besides, an excellent field for preliminary work before attacking the larger ruins. We pitched out tents, and in a couple of days the work was in full swing."

IV. The Moon Rock

"I do not intend to tell you now," Throckmartin continued, "the results of the next two weeks, Goodwin, nor of what we found. Later—if I am allowed I will lay all that before you. It is sufficient to say that at the end of those two weeks I had found confirmation of many of my theories, and we were well under way to solve a mystery of humanity's youth—so we thought. But enough. I must hurry on to the first stirrings of the inexplicable thing that was in store for us.

"The place, for all its decay and desolation, had not infected us with any touch of morbidity—that is not Edith, Stanton or myself. My wife was happy—never had she been happier. Stanton and she, while engrossed in the work as much as I, were of the same age, and they frankly enjoyed the companionship that only youth can give youth. I was glad—never jealous.

"But Thora was very unhappy. She was a Swede, as you know, and in her blood ran the beliefs and superstitions of the Northland—some of them so strangely akin to those of this far southern land; beliefs of spirits of mountain and forest and water—werewolves and beings malign. From the first she showed a curious sensitivity to what, I suppose, may be called the 'influences' of the place. She said it 'smelled' of ghosts and warlocks.

"I laughed at her then—but now I believe that this sensitivity of what we call primitive people is perhaps only a clearer perception of the unknown which we, who deny the unknown, have lost. It is a *rapprochement* toward an acknowledgment of other forces which, no doubt, betrays them to the very forces they sense and fear. It was what made Thora first to feel—what was to happen. A prey to these fears, Thora always followed my wife about like a shadow; carried with her always a little sharp hand-ax, and although we twitted her about the futility of chopping fantoms with such a weapon she would not relinquish it.

"Two weeks slipped by, and at their end the spokesman for our natives came to us. The next night was the full of the moon, he said. He reminded me of my promise. They would go back to their village next morning; they would return after the third night, as at that time the power of the *ani* would begin to wane with the moon. They left us sundry charms for our 'protection,' and solemnly cautioned us to keep as far away as possible from Nan-Tanach during their absence—although their leader politely informed us that, no doubt, we were stronger than the spirits. Half-exasperated, half-amused I watched them go.

"No work could be done without them, of course, so we decided to spend the days of their absence junketing about the southern islets of the group. Under the moon the ruins were inexpressibly weird and beautiful. We marked down several spots for subsequent exploration, and on the morning of the third day set forth along the east face of the breakwater for our camp on Uschen-Tau, planning to have everything in readiness for the return of our men the next day.

"We landed just before dusk, tired and ready for our cots. It was only a little after ten o'clock when Edith awakened me.

" 'Listen!' she said. 'Lean over with your ear close to the ground!' I did so, and seemed to hear, far, far below, as though coming up from great distances, a faint chanting. It gathered strength, died down, ended; began, gathered volume, faded away into silence.

" 'It's the waves rolling on rocks somewhere,' I said. 'We're probably over some ledge of rock that carries the sound.'

" 'It's the first time I've heard it,' replied my wife doubtfully. We listened again. Then through the dim rhythms, deep beneath us, another sound came. It drifted across the lagoon that lay between us and Nan-Tanach in little tinkling waves. It was music—of a sort; I won't describe the strange effect it had upon me. You've felt it—"

"You mean on the deck?" I asked. Throckmartin nodded.

"I went to the flap of the tent," he continued, "and peered out. As I did so Stanton lifted his flap and walked out into the moonlight, looking over to the other islet and listening. I called to him.

" 'That's the queerest sound!' he said. He listened again. 'Crystalline! Like little notes of translucent glass. Like the bells of crystal on the sistrums of Isis at Dendarah Temple,' he added half-dreamily. We gazed intently at the island. Suddenly, on the gigantic sea-wall, moving slowly, rhythmically, we saw a little group of lights. Stanton laughed.

" 'The beggars!' he exclaimed. 'That's why they wanted to get away, is it? Don't you see, Dave, it's some sort of a festival—rites of some kind that they hold during the full moon! That's why they were so eager to have us *keep* away, too.'

"I felt a curious sense of relief, although I had not been sensible of any oppression. The explanation seemed good. It explained the tinkling music and also the chanting—worshipers, no doubt, in the ruins—their voices carried along passages I now knew honeycombed the whole Nan-Matal.

" 'Let's slip over,' suggested Stanton—but I would not.

" 'They're a difficult lot as it is,' I said. 'If we break into one of their religious ceremonies they'll probably never forgive us. Let's keep out of any family party where we haven't been invited.'

" 'That's so,' agreed Stanton.

"The strange tinkling music, if music it can be called, rose and fell, rose and fell—now laden with sorrow, now filled with joy.

" 'There's something—something very unsettling about it,' said Edith at last soberly. 'I wonder what they make those sounds with. They frighten me half to death, and, at the same time, they make me feel as though some enormous rapture was just around the corner.'

"I had noted this effect, too, although I had said nothing of it. And at the same time there came to me a clear perception that the chanting which had preceded it had seemed to come from a vast multitude—thousands more than the place we were contemplating could possibly have held. Of course, I thought, this might be due to some acoustic property of the basalt; an amplification of sound by some gigantic sounding-board of rock; still—

" 'It's devilish uncanny!' broke in Stanton, answering my thought.

"And as he spoke the flap of Thora's tent was raised and out into the moonlight strode the old Swede. She was the great Norse type—tall, deep-breasted, molded on the old Viking lines. Her sixty years had slipped from her. She looked like some ancient priestess of Odin." He hesitated. "She knew," he said slowly, "something more far-seeing than my science had given her sight. She warned me—she warned me! Fools and mad that we are to pass such things by without heed!" He brushed a hand over his eyes.

"She stood there," he went on. "Her eyes were wide, brilliant, staring. She thrust her head forward toward Nan-Tanach, regarding the moving lights; she listened. Suddenly she raised her arms and made a curious gesture to the moon. It was—an archaic—movement; she seemed to drag it from remote antiquity—yet in it was a strange suggestion of power. Twice she repeated this gesture and—the tinkling died away! She turned to us.

" 'Go!' she said, and her voice seemed to come from far distances. 'Go from here—and quickly! Go while you may. They have called—' She pointed to the islet. 'They know you are here. They wait.' Her eyes widened further. 'It is there,' she wailed. 'It beckons—the—the—'

"She fell at Edith's feet, and as she fell over the lagoon came again the tinklings, now with a quicker note of jubilance—almost of triumph.

"We ran to Thora, Stanton and I, and picked her up. Her head rolled and her face, eyes closed, turned as though drawn full into the moonlight. I felt in my heart a throb of unfamiliar fear—for her face had changed again. Stamped upon it was a look of mingled transport and horror—alien, terrifying, strangely revolting. It was"—he thrust his face close to my eyes—"what you see in mine!"

For a dozen heart-beats I stared at him, fascinated; then he sank back again into the half-shadow of the berth.

"I managed to hide her face from Edith," he went on. "I thought she had suffered some sort of a nervous seizure. We carried her into her tent. Once within the unholy mask dropped from her, and she was again only the kindly, rugged old woman. I watched her throughout the night. The sounds from Nan-Tanach continued until about an hour before moon-set. In the morning Thora awoke, none the worse, apparently. She had had bad dreams, she said. She could not remember what they were—except that they had warned her of danger. She was oddly sullen, and I noted that throughout the morning her gaze returned again half-fascinatedly, half-wonderingly to the neighboring isles.

"That afternoon the natives returned. They were so exuberant in their apparent relief to find us well and intact that Stanton's suspicions of them were confirmed. He slyly told their leader that 'from the noise they had made on Nan-Tanach the night before they must have thoroughly enjoyed themselves.'

"I think I never saw such stark terror as the Ponapean manifested at the remark! Stanton himself was so plainly startled that he tried to pass it over as a jest. He met poor success! The men seemed panic-stricken, and for a time I thought they were about to abandon us—but they did not. They pitched their camp at the western side of the island—out of sight of Nan-Tanach. I noticed that they built large fires, and whenever I awoke that night I heard their voices in slow, minor chant—one of their song 'charms,' I thought drowsily, against evil *ani*. I heard nothing else; the place of frowning walls was wrapped in silence—no lights showed. The next morning the men were quiet, a little depressed, but as the hours wore on they regained their spirits, and soon life at the camp was going on just as it had before.

"You will understand, Goodwin, how the occurrences I have related would excite the scientific curiosity. We rejected immediately, of course, any explanation admitting the supernatural. Why not? Except the curiously disquieting effects of the tinkling music and Thora's behavior there was nothing to warrant any such fantastic theories—even if our minds had been the kind to harbor them.

"Our—symptoms let me call them—could all very easily be accounted for. It is unquestionable that the vibrations created by certain musical instruments have definite and sometimes extraordinary effect upon the nervous system. We accepted this as the explanation of the reactions we had experienced in hearing the unfamiliar sounds. Thora's nervousness, her superstitious apprehensions, had wrought her up to a condition of semisomnambulistic hysteria. Science could readily explain her part in the night's scene.

"We came to the conclusion that there must be a passageway between Ponape and Nan-Tanach, known to the natives—and used by them during their rites. Ceremonies were probably held in great vaults or caverns beneath the ruins—for certainly a race which could have cut and set into place the enormous basalt blocks that formed them would have had little difficulty in hollowing out caverns, even had none existed before. Evidence of such subterranean passages we had already discovered. We decided at last that on the next departure of our laborers we would set forth immediately to Nan-Tanach. We would investigate during the day, and at evening my wife and Thora would go back to camp, leaving Stanton and me to spend the night on the island, observing from some safe hiding-place what might occur.

"The moon waned; appeared crescent in the west; waxed slowly toward the full. Before the men left us they literally prayed us to accompany them. Their importunities only made us more eager to see what it was that, we were now convinced, they wanted to conceal from us. At least that was true of Stanton and myself. It was not true of Edith. She was thoughtful, abstracted—reluctant. Thora, on the other hand, showed an unusual restlessness, almost an eagerness to go. Goodwin"—he paused— "Goodwin, I know now that the poison was working in Thora—and that women have perceptions that we men lack—forebodings, sensings. Would to God I had known it then—Edith!" he cried suddenly. "Edith—come back to me! Forgive me!"

I stretched the decanter out to him. He drank deeply. Soon he had regained control of himself.

"When the men were out of sight around the turn of the harbor," he went on, "we took our boat and made straight for Nan-Tanach. Soon its mighty sea-wall towered above us. We passed through the water-gate with its gigantic hewn prisms of basalt and landed beside a half-submerged pier. In front of us stretched a series of giant steps leading into a vast court strewn with fragments of fallen pillars. In the center of the court, beyond the shattered pillars, rose another terrace of basalt blocks, concealing, I knew, still another enclosure.

"And now, Goodwin, for the better understanding of what follows and to guide you, should I—not be able—to accompany you when you go there, listen carefully to my description of this place: Nan-Tanach is literally three rectangles. The first rectangle is the sea-wall, built up of monoliths—hewn and squared, twenty feet wide at the top. To get to the gateway in the sea-wall you pass along the canal marked on the map between Nan-Tanach and the islet named Tau. The entrance to the canal is hidden by dense thickets of mangroves; once through these the way is clear. The gigantic steps lead up from the landing of the sea-gate through the entrance to the courtyard.

"This courtyard is surrounded by another basalt wall, rectangular, following with mathematical exactness the march of the outer barricades. The sea-wall is from thirty to forty feet high—originally it must have been much higher, but there has been subsidence in parts. The wall of the first enclosure is fifteen feet across the top and its height varies from twenty to fifty feet—here, too, the gradual sinking of the land has caused portions of it to fall.

"Between the terrace of the enclosure and the sea-wall is, on each side, a considerable space. It is covered with little thickets of fern, of eucalyptus, shrubs; hibiscus vines run riot, covering the fragments with their flowers.

"Within the courtyard is the second enclosure. Its terrace, of the same basalt as the outer walls, is about twenty feet high. Entrance is gained to it by many breaches which time has made in its stonework. This is the inner court, the heart of Nan-Tanach! There lies the great central vault with which is associated the one name of living being that has come to us out of the mists of the past. The natives say it was the treasure-house of Chau-te-leur, a mighty king who reigned long 'before their fathers.' As Chau is the ancient Ponapean word both for sun and king, the name means, without doubt, 'place of the sun king.' It is a memory of a dynastic name of the race that ruled the Pacific continent, now vanished—just as the rulers of ancient Crete took the name of Minos and the rulers of Egypt the name of Pharaoh.

"And opposite this place of the sun king is the moon rock that hides the moon pool.

"It was Stanton who first found what I call the moon rock. We had been inspecting the inner courtyard; Edith and Thora were getting together our lunch. I forgot to say that we had previously gone all over the islet and had found not a trace of living thing. I came out of the vault of Chau-te-leur to find Stanton before a part of the terrace studying it wonderingly.

" 'What do you make of this?' he asked me as I came up. He pointed to the wall. I followed his finger and saw a slab of stone about fifteen feet high and ten wide. At first all I noticed was the exquisite nicety with which its edges joined the blocks about it. Then I realized that its color was subtly different—tinged with gray and of a smooth, peculiar—deadness.

" 'Looks more like calcite than basalt,' I said. I touched it and withdrew my hand quickly, for at the contact every nerve in my arm tingled, as though a shock of frozen electricity had passed through it. It was not cold as we know cold that I felt. It was a chill force—the phrase I have used—frozen electricity—describes it better than anything else. Stanton looked at me oddly.

" 'So you felt it, too,' he said. 'I was wondering whether I was developing hallucinations like Thora. Notice, by the way, that the blocks beside it are quite warm beneath the sun.'

"I felt them and touched the grayish stone again. The same faint shock ran through my hand—a tingling chill that had in it a suggestion of substance, of force. We examined the slab more closely. Its edges were cut as though by an engraver of jewels. They fitted against the neighboring blocks in almost a hair-line. Its base, we saw, was slightly curved, and fitted as closely as top and sides upon the huge stones on which it rested. And then we noted that these stones had been hollowed to follow the line of the gray stone's foot. There was a semicircular depression running from one side of the slab to the other. It was as though the gray rock stood in the center of a shallow cup—revealing half, covering half. Something about this hollow attracted me. I reached down and felt it. Goodwin, although the balance of the stones that formed it, like all the stones of the courtyard, were rough and age-worn—this was as smooth, as even surfaced as though it just left the hands of the polisher.

" 'It's a door!' exclaimed Stanton. 'It swings around in that little cup. That's what makes the hollow so smooth.'

" 'Maybe you're right,' I replied. 'But how the devil can we open it?'

"We went over the slab again—pressing upon its edges, thrusting against its sides. During one of those efforts I happened to look up—and cried out. For a foot above and on each side of the corner of the gray rock's lintel I had seen a slight convexity, visible only from the angle at which my gaze struck it. These bosses on the basalt were circular, eighteen inches in diameter, as we learned later, and at the center extended two inches only beyond the face of the terrace. Unless one looked directly up at them while leaning against the moon rock—for this slab, Goodwin, is the moon rock—they were invisible. And none would dare stand there!

"We carried with us a small scaling-ladder, and up this I went. The bosses were apparently nothing more than chiseled curvatures in the stone. I laid my hand on the one I was examining, and drew it back so sharply I almost threw myself from the ladder. In my palm, at the base of my thumb, I had felt the same shock that I had in touching the slab below. I put my hand back. The impression came from a spot not more than an inch wide. I went carefully over the entire convexity, and six times more the chill ran through my arm. There were, Goodwin, seven circles an inch wide in the curved place, each of which communicated the precise sensation I have described. The convexity on the opposite side of the slab gave precisely the same results. But no amount of touching or of pressing these spots singly or in any combination gave the slightest promise of motion to the slab itself.

" 'And yet—they're what open it,' said Stanton positively.

" 'Why do you say that?' I asked.

" 'I—don't know,' he answered hesitating. 'But something tells me so. Throck,' he went on half earnestly, half laughingly, 'the purely scientific part of me is fighting the purely human part of me. The scientific part is urging me to find some way to get that slab either down or open. The human part is just as strongly urging me to do nothing of the sort and get away while I can!'

"He laughed again—shamefacedly.

" 'Which will it be?' he asked—and I thought that in his tone the human side of him was ascendant.

" 'It will probably stay as it is—unless we blow it to bits,' I said.

" 'I thought of that,' he answered, 'and—I wouldn't dare,' he added somberly enough. And even as I had spoken there came to me the same feeling that he had expressed. It was as though something passed out of the gray rock that struck my heart as a hand strikes an impious lip. We turned away—uneasily, and faced Thora coming through a breach in the terrace.

" 'Miss Edith wants you quick,' she began—and stopped. I saw her eyes go past me and widen. She was looking at the gray rock. Her body grew suddenly rigid; she took a few stiff steps forward and ran straight to it. We saw her cast herself upon its breast, hands and face pressed against it; heard her scream as though her very soul was being drawn from her—and watched her fall at its foot. As we picked her up I saw steal from her face the look I had observed when I first heard the crystal music of Nan-Tanach—that unhuman mingling of opposites!"

V. Av-o-lo-ha

"We carried Thora back, down to where Edith was waiting. We told her what had happened and what we had found. She listened gravely, and as we finished Thora sighed and opened her eyes.

" 'I would like to see the stone,' she said. 'Charles, you stay here with Thora.' We passed through the outer court silently—and stood before the rock. She touched it, drew back her hand as I had; thrust it forward again resolutely and held it there. She seemed to be listening. Then she turned to me.

" 'David,' said my wife, and the wistfulness in her voice hurt me—'David, would you be very, very disappointed if we went from here—without trying to find out any more about it—would you?'

"Goodwin, I never wanted anything so much in my life as I wanted to learn what that rock concealed. You will understand—the cumulative curiosity that all the happenings had caused; the certainty that before me was an entrance to a place that, while known to the natives—for I still clung to that theory—was utterly unknown to any man of my race; that within, ready for my finding, was the answer to the stupendous riddle of these islands and a lost chapter in the history of humanity. There before me—and was I asked to turn away, leaving it unread!

"Nevertheless, I tried to master my desire, and I answered—'Edith, not a bit if you want us to do it.'

"She read my struggle in my eyes. She looked at me searchingly for a moment and then turned back toward the gray rock. I saw a shiver pass through her. I felt a tinge of remorse and pity!

" 'Edith,' I exclaimed, 'we'll go!'

"She looked at me hard. 'Science is a jealous mistress,' she quoted. 'No, after all it may be just fancy. At any rate, you can't run away. No! But, Dave, I'm going to stay too!'

" 'You are not!' I exclaimed. 'You're going back to the camp with Thora. Stanton and I will be all right.'

"'I'm going to stay,' she repeated. And there was no changing her decision. As we neared the others she laid a hand on my arm.

" 'Dave,' she said, 'If there should be something—well—inexplicable tonight—something that seems—too dangerous—will you promise to go back to our own islet tomorrow, or, while we can, and wait until the natives return?'

"I promised eagerly—for the desire to stay and see what came with the night was like a fire within me.

"And would to God I had not waited another moment, Goodwin; would to God I had gathered them all together then and sailed back on the instant through the mangroves to Uschen-Tau!

"We found Thora on her feet again and singularly composed. She claimed to have no more recollection of what had happened after she had spoken to Stanton and to me in front of the gray rock than she had after the seizure on Uschen-Tau. She grew sullen under our questioning, precisely as she had before. But to my astonishment, when she heard of our arrangements for the night, she betrayed a febrile excitement that had in it something of exultance.

"We had picked a place about five hundred feet away from the steps leading into the outer court. I would have preferred going into the inner enclosure, but I feared for Edith. Besides, it was better to go slowly until we knew what was opposed to us. And there was no place in the heart of the ruins where we could hide—except in the vault, and none of us liked to think of that. The spot we had selected was well hidden. We could not be seen, and yet we had a clear view of the stairs and the gateway. We settled down just before dusk to wait for whatever might come. I was nearest the giant steps; next to me Edith; then Thora, and last Stanton. Each of us had with us automatic pistols, and all, except Thora, had rifles.

"Night fell. After a time the eastern sky began to lighten, and we knew that the moon was rising; grew lighter still, and the orb peeped over the sea; swam suddenly into full sight. Edith gripped my hand, for, as though the full emergence into the heavens had been a signal, we heard begin beneath us the deep chanting. It came from illimitable depths.

"The moon poured her rays down upon us, and I saw Stanton start. On the instant I caught the sound that had roused him. It came from the inner enclosure. It was like a long, soft sighing. It was not human; seemed in some way—mechanical. I glanced at Edith and then at Thora. My wife was intently listening. Thora sat, as she had since we had placed ourselves, elbows on knees, her hands covering her face.

"And then suddenly from the moonlight flooding us there came to me a great drowsiness. Sleep seemed to drip from the rays and fall upon my eyes, closing them—closing them inexorably. I felt Edith's hand relax in mine, and under my own heavy lids saw her nodding. I saw Stanton's head fall upon his breast and his body sway drunkenly. I tried to rise—to fight against the profound desire for slumber that pressed in on me.

"And as I fought I saw Thora raise her head as though listening; saw her rise and turn her face toward the gateway. For a moment she gazed, and my drugged eyes seemed to perceive within it a deeper, stronger radiance. Thora looked at us. There was infinite despair in her face—and expectancy. I tried again to rise—and a surge of sleep rushed over me. Dimly, as I sank within it, I heard a crystalline chiming; raised my lids once more with a supreme effort, saw Thora, bathed in light, standing at the top of the stairs, and then—sleep took me for its very own—swept me into the very heart of oblivion!

"Dawn was breaking when I wakened. Recollection rushed back on me and I thrust a panic-stricken hand out toward Edith; touched her and felt my heart give a great leap of thankfulness. She stirred, sat up, rubbing dazed eyes. I glanced toward Stanton. He lay on his side, back toward us, head in arms.

"Edith looked at me laughingly. 'Heavens! What sleep!' she said. Memory came to her. Her face paled. 'What happened?' she whispered. 'What made us sleep like that?' She looked over to Stanton, sprang to her feet, ran to him, shook him. He turned over with a mighty yawn, and I saw relief lighten her face as it had lightened my heart.

"Stanton raised himself stiffly. He looked at us. 'What's the matter?' he exclaimed. 'You look as though you've seen ghosts!'

"Edith caught my hands. 'Where's Thora?' she cried. Before I could answer she ran out into the open calling: 'Thora! Thora!'

"Stanton stared at me. 'Taken!' was all I could say. Together we went to my wife, now standing beside the great stone steps, looking up fearfully at the gateway into the terraces. There I told them what I had seen before sleep had drowned me. And together then we ran up the stairs, through the court and up to the gray rock.

"The gray rock was closed as it had been the day before, nor was there trace of its having opened. No trace! Even as I thought this Edith dropped to her knees before it and reached toward something lying at its foot. It was a little piece of gray silk. I knew it for part of the kerchief Thora wore about her hair. Edith took the fragment; hesitated. I saw then that it had been *cut* from the kerchief as though by a razor-edge; I saw, too, that a few threads ran from it—down toward the base of the slab; ran to the base of the gray rock and—under it! The gray rock was a door! And it had opened and Thora had passed through it!

"I think, Goodwin, that for the next few minutes we all were a little insane. We beat upon that diabolic entrance with our hands, with stones and clubs. At last reason came back to us. Stanton set forth for the camp to bring back blasting powder and tools. While he was gone Edith and I searched the whole islet for any other clue. We found not a trace of Thora nor any indication of any living being save ourselves. We went back to the gateway to find Stanton returned.

"Goodwin, during the next two hours we tried every way in our power to force entrance through the slab. The rock within effective blasting radius of the cursed door resisted our drills. We tried explosions at the base of the slab with charges covered by rock. They made not the slightest impression on the surface beneath, expending their force, of course, upon the slighter resistance of their coverings.

"Afternoon found us hopeless, so far as breaking through the rock was concerned. Night was coming on and before it came we would have to decide our course of action. I wanted to go to Ponape for help. But Edith objected that this would take hours and after we had reached there it would be impossible to persuade our men to return with us that night, if at all. What then was left? Clearly only one of two choices: to go back to our camp and wait for our men to return and on their return try to persuade them to go with us to Nan-Tanach. But this would mean the abandonment of Thora for at least two days. We could not do it; it would have been too cowardly.

"The other choice was to wait where we were for night to come; to wait for the rock to open as it had the night before, and to make a sortie through it for Thora before it could close again. With the sun had come confidence; at least a shattering of the mephitic mists of superstition with which the strangeness of the things that had befallen us had clouded for a time our minds. In that brilliant light there seemed no place for fantoms.

"The evidence that the slab had opened was unmistakable, but might not Thora simply have *found* it open through some mechanism, still working after ages, and dependent for its action upon laws of physics unknown to us upon the full light of the moon? The assertion of the natives that the *ani* had greatest power at this time might be a far-flung reflection of knowledge which had found ways to use forces contained in moonlight, as we have found ways to utilize the forces in the sun's rays. If so, Thora was probably behind the slab, sending out prayers to us for help.

"But how explain the sleep that had descended upon us? Might it not have been some emanation from plants or gaseous emanations from the island itself? Such things were far from uncommon, we agreed. In some way, the period of their greatest activity might coincide with the period of the moon, but if this were so why had not Thora also slept?

"There, indeed, we faced an impasse. It might be, of course, that Thora had been resistant to such emanations as certain of us are resistant and immune from various bacteria. It was possible. And it might still be that our first theory was correct and that Nan-Tanach was a sacred place; a gathering point for priests possessing fragments of the ancient secrets, vanished knowledge, and the resented intruders. We knew the command certain primitive folk have of sleep sounds and vapors. It might be that here was the true explanation.

"But whatever the truth, our path lay clear before us. We had to spend that night on Nan-Tanach!

"As dusk fell we looked over our weapons. Edith was an excellent shot with both rifle and pistol. With the idea that the impulse toward sleep was the result either of emanations such as I have described or man made, we constructed rough-and-ready but effective neutralizers, which we placed over our mouths and nostrils. We had decided that my wife was to remain in the hiding place. Stanton would take up a station on the far side of the stairway and I would place myself opposite him on the side near Edith. The place I picked out was less than five hun-dred feet from her, and I could reassure myself now and as to her safety as I looked down upon the hollow wherein she crouched. As the phenomena had previously synchronized with the rising of the moon, we had no reason to think they would occur any earlier this night. From our respective stations Stanton and I could command the gateway entrance. His position gave him also a glimpse of the outer courtyard.

"A faint glow in the sky heralded the moon. I kissed Edith, and Stanton and I took our places. The moon dawn increased rapidly; the disk swam up, and in a moment it seemed was shining in full radiance upon ruins and sea.

"As it rose there came as on the night before the curious little sighing sound from the inner terrace. I saw Stanton straighten up and stare intently through the gateway, rifle ready. Even at the distance he was from me, I discerned amazement in his eyes. The moonlight within the gateway thickened, grew stronger. I watched his amazement grow into sheer wonder.

"I arose.

" 'Stanton, what do you see?' I called cautiously. He waved a silencing hand. I turned my head to look at Edith. A shock ran through me. She lay upon her side. Her face was turned full toward the moon. She was in deepest sleep!

"As I turned again to call to Stanton, my eyes swept the head of the steps and stopped fascinated. For the moonlight had thickened more. It seemed to be—curdled—there; and through it ran little gleams and veins of shimmering white fire. A languor passed through me. It was not the ineffable drowsiness of the preceding night. It was a sapping of all will to move. I tore my eyes away and forced them upon Stanton. I tried to call out to him. I had not the will to make my lips move! I had struggled against this paralysis and as I did so I felt through me a sharp shock. It was like a blow. And with it came utter inability to make a single motion. Goodwin, I could not even move my eyes!

"I saw Stanton leap upon the steps and move toward the gateway. As he did so the light in the courtyard grew dazzlingly brilliant. Through it rained tiny tinklings that set the heart to racing with pure joy and stilled it with terror.

"And now for the first time I heard that cry '*Av-o-lo-ha! Av-o-lo-ha!*' the cry you heard on deck. It murmured with the strange effect of a sound only partly in our own space—as though it were part of a fuller phrase passing through from another dimension and losing much as it came; infinitely caressing, infinitely cruel!

"On Stanton's face I saw come the look I dreaded—and yet knew would appear; that mingled expression of delight and fear. The two lay side by side as they had on Thora, but were intensified. He walked on up the stairs; disappeared beyond the range of my fixed gaze. Again I heard the murmur—'*Av-o-lo-ha!*' There was triumph in it now and triumph in the storm of tinklings that swept over it.

"For another heart-beat there was silence. Then a louder burst of sound and ringing through it Stanton's voice from the court yard—a great cry—a scream—filled with ecstasy insupportable and horror unimaginable! And again there was silence. I strove to burst the invisible bonds that held me. I could not. Even my eyelids were fixed. Within them my eyes, dry and aching, burned.

"Then, Goodwin—I first saw the inexplicable! The crystalline music swelled. Where I sat I could take in the gateway and its basalt portals, rough and broken, rising to the top of the wall forty feet above, shattered, ruined portals—unclimbable. From this gateway an intenser light began to flow. It grew, it gushed, and into it, into my sight, walked Stanton.

"Stanton! But—God! What a vision!"

He ceased. I waited—waited.

VI. Into the Moon Pool

"Goodwin," Throckmartin said at last, "I can describe him only as a thing of living light. He radiated light; was filled with light; overflowed with it. Around him was a shining cloud that whirled through and around him in radiant swirls, shimmering tentacles, luminescent, coruscating spirals.

"I saw his face. It shone with a rapture too great to be borne by living men, and was shadowed with insuperable misery. It was as though his face had been remolded by the hand of God and the hand of Satan, working together and in harmony. You have seen it on my face. But you have never seen it in the degree that Stanton bore it. The eyes were wide open and fixed, as though upon some inward vision of hell and heaven! He walked like the corpse of a man damned who carried within him an angel of light.

"The music swelled again. I heard again the murmuring—'Av-o-lo-ha!' Stanton turned, facing the ragged side of the portal. And then I saw that the light that filled and surrounded him had a nucleus, a core—something shiftingly human shaped—that dissolved and changed, gathered itself, whirled through and beyond him and back again. And as this shining nucleus passed through him Stanton's whole body pulsed with light. As the luminescence moved, there moved with it, still and serene always, seven tiny globes of light like seven little moons.

"So much I saw and then swiftly Stanton seemed to be lifted—levitated—up the unscalable wall and to its top. The glow faded from the moonlight, the tinkling music grew fainter. I tried again to move. The spell still held me fast. The tears were running down now from my rigid lids and brought relief to my tortured eyes.

"I have said my gaze was fixed. It was. But from the side, peripherally, it took in a part of the far wall of the outer enclosure. Ages seemed to pass and I saw a radiance stealing along it. Soon there came into sight the figure that was Stanton. Far away he was—on the gigantic wall. But still I could see the shining spirals whirling jubilantly around and through him; felt rather than saw his tranced face beneath the seven lights. A swirl of crystal notes, and he had passed. And all the time, as though from some opened well of light, the courtyard gleamed and sent out silver fires that dimmed the moon-rays, yet seemed strangely to be a part of them.

"Ten times he passed before me so. The luminescence came with the music; swam for a while along the man-made cliff of basalt and passed away. Between times eternities rolled and still I crouched there, a helpless thing of stone with eyes that would not close!

"At last the moon neared the horizon. There came a louder burst of sound; the second, and last, cry of Stanton, like an echo of the first! Again the soft sigh from the inner terrace. Then—utter silence. The light faded; the moon was setting and with a rush life and power to move returned to me. I made a leap for the steps, rushed up them, through the gateway and straight to the gray rock. It was closed—as I knew it would be. But did I dream it or did I hear, echoing through it as though from vast distances a triumphant shouting—'Av-o-lo-ha! Av-o-lo-ha!'?

"I remembered Edith. I ran back to her. At my touch she wakened; looked at me wonderingly; raised herself on a hand.

"'Dave!' she said, 'I slept—after all.' She saw the despair on my face and leaped to her feet. 'Dave!' she cried. 'What is it? Where's Charles?'

"I lighted a fire before I spoke. Then I told her. And for the balance of that night we sat before the flames, arms around each other—like two frightened children."

Suddenly Throckmartin held his hands out to me appealingly.

"Goodwin, old friend!" he cried. "Don't look at me as though I were mad. It's truth, absolute truth. Wait—" I comforted him as well as I could. After a little time he took up his story.

"Never," he said, "did man welcome the sun as we did that morning. As soon as it was light we went back to the courtyard. The basalt walls whereon I had seen Stanton were black and silent. The terraces were as they had been. The gray slab was in its place. In the shallow hollow at its base was—nothing. Nothing—nothing was there anywhere on the islet of Stanton—not a trace, not a sign on Nan-Tanach to show that he had ever lived.

"What were we to do? Precisely the same arguments that had kept us there the night before held good now—and doubly good. We could not abandon these two; could not go as long as there was the faintest hope of finding them—and yet for love of each other how could we remain? I loved my wife, Goodwin—how much I never knew until that day; and she loved me as deeply.

" 'It takes only one each night,' she said. 'Beloved, let it take me.'

"I wept, Goodwin. We both wept.

" 'We will meet it together,' she said. And it was thus at last that we arranged it."

"That took great courage indeed, Throckmartin," I interrupted. He looked at me eagerly.

"You do believe then?" he exclaimed.

"I believe," I said. He pressed my hand with a grip that nearly crushed it.

"Now," he told me, "I do not fear. If I—fail, you will prepare and carry on the work."

I promised. And—God forgive me—that was three years ago.

"It did take courage," he went on, again quietly. "More than courage. For we knew it was renunciation. Each of us in our hearts felt that one of us would not be there to see the sun rise. And each of us prayed that the death, if death it was, would not come first to the other.

"We talked it all over carefully, bringing to bear all our power of analysis and habit of calm, scientific thought. We considered minutely the time element in the phenomena. Although the deep chanting began at the very moment of moonrise, fully five minutes had passed between its full lifting and the strange sighing sound from the inner terrace. I went back in memory over the happenings of the night before. At least fifteen minutes had intervened between the first heralding sigh and the intensification of the moonlight in the courtyard. And this glow grew for at least ten minutes more before the first burst of the crystal notes. Indeed, more than half an hour must have elapsed, I calculated, between the moment the moon showed above the horizon and the first delicate onslaught of the tinklings.

"The sighing sound—of what had it reminded me? Of course—of a door revolving and swishing softly along its base.

" 'Edith!' I cried. 'I think I have it! The gray rock opens five minutes after upon the moonrise. But whoever or whatever it is that comes through it must wait until the moon has risen higher, or else it must come from a distance. The thing to do is not to wait for it, but to surprise it before it passes out the door. We will go into the inner court early. You will take

269

your rifle and pistol and hide yourself where you can command the opening—if the slab does open. The instant it moves I will enter. It's our best chance, Edith. I think it's our only one.'

"My wife demurred strongly. She wanted to go with me. But I convinced her that it was better for her to stand guard without, prepared to help me if I were forced from what lay behind the rock again into the open.

"The day passed too swiftly. In the face of what we feared our love seemed stronger than ever. Was it the flare of the spark before extinguishment? I wondered. We prepared and ate a good dinner. We tried to keep our minds from anything but the scientific aspect of the phenomena. We agreed that whatever it was its cause must be human, and that we must keep that fact in mind every second. But what kind of men could create such prodigies? We thrilled at the thought of finding perhaps the remnants of a vanished race, living perhaps in cities over whose rocky skies the Pacific rolled; exercising there the lost wisdom of the half-gods of earth's youth.

"At the half-hour before moonrise we two went into the inner courtyard. I took my place at the side of the gray rock. Edith crouched behind a broken pillar twenty feet away, slipped her rifle-barrel over it so that it would cover the opening.

"The minutes crept by. The courtyard was very quiet. The darkness lessened and through the breaches of the terrace I watched the far sky softly lighten. With the first pale flush the stillness became intensified. It deepened—became unbearably—expectant. The moon rose, showed the quarter, the half, then swam up into full sight like a great bubble.

"Its rays fell upon the wall before me and suddenly upon the convexities I have described seven little circles of light sprang out. They gleamed, glimmered, grew brighter—shone. The gigantic slab before me turned as though on a pivot, sighing softly as it moved.

"For a moment I gasped in amazement. It was like a conjurer's trick. And the moving slab I noticed was also glowing, becoming opalescent like the little shining circles above.

"Only for a second I gazed and then with a word to Edith flung myself through the opening which the slab had uncovered. Before me was a platform and from the platform steps led downward into a smooth corridor. This passage was not dark, it glowed with the same faint silvery radiance as the door. Down it I raced. As I ran, plainer than ever before, I heard the chanting. The passage turned abruptly, passed parallel to the walls of the outer courtyard and then once more led abruptly downward. Still I ran, and as I ran I looked at the watch on my wrist. Less than three minutes had elapsed.

"The passage ended. Before me was a high vaulted arch. For a moment I paused. It seemed to open into space; a space filled with lambent, coruscating, many-colored mist whose brightness grew even as I watched. I passed through the arch and stopped in sheer awe!

"In front of me was a pool. It was circular, perhaps twenty feet wide. Around it ran a low, softly curved lip of glimmering silvery stone. Its water was palest blue. The pool with its silvery rim was like a great blue eye staring upward.

"Upon it streamed seven shafts of radiance. They poured down upon the blue eye like cylindrical torrents; they were like shining pillars of light rising from a sapphire floor.

"One was the tender pink of the pearl; one of the aurora's green; a third a deathly white; the fourth the blue in mother-of-pearl; a shimmering column of pale amber; a beam of amethyst; a shaft of molten silver. Such are the colors of the seven lights that stream upon the moon pool. I drew closer, awestricken. The shafts did not illumine the depths. They played upon the surface and seemed there to diffuse, to melt into it. The pool drank them!

"Through the water tiny gleams of phosphorescence began to dart, sparkles and coruscations of pale incandescence. And far, far below I sensed a movement, a shifting glow as of something slowly rising.

"I looked upward, following the radiant pillars to their source. Far above were seven shining globes, and it was from these that the rays poured. Even as I watched their brightness grew. They were like seven moons set high in some caverned heaven. Slowly their splendor increased, and with it the splendor of the seven beams streaming from them. It came to me that they were crystals of some unknown kind set in the roof of the moon pool's vault and that their light was drawn from the moon shining high above them. They were wonderful, those lights—and what must have been the knowledge of those who set them there!

"Brighter and brighter they grew as the moon climbed higher, sending its full radiance down through them. I tore my gaze away and stared at the pool. It had grown milky, opalescent. The rays gushing into it seemed to be filling it; it was alive with sparklings, scintillations, glimmerings. And the luminescence I had seen rising from its depths was larger, nearer!

"A swirl of mist floated up from its surface. It drifted within the embrace of the rosy beam and hung there for a moment. The beam seemed to embrace it, sending through it little shining corpuscles, tiny rosy spiralings. The mist absorbed the rays, was strengthened by it, gained substance. Another swirl sprang into the amber shaft, clung and fed there, moved swiftly toward the first and mingled with it. And now other swirls arose, here and there, too fast to be counted, hung poised in the embrace of the light streams; flashed and pulsed into each other.

"Thicker and thicker still they arose until the surface of the pool was a pulsating pillar of opalescent mist; steadily growing stronger; drawing within it life from the seven beams falling upon it; drawing to it from below the darting, red atoms of the pool. Into its center was passing the luminescence I had sensed rising from the far depths. And the center glowed, throbbed—began to send out questing swirls and tendrils—

"There forming before me was *that* which had walked with Stanton, which had taken Thora—the thing I had come to find!

"With the shock or realization my brain sprang into action. My hand fell to my pistol and I fired shot after shot into its radiance. The place rang with the explosions and there came to me a sense of unforgivable profanation. Devilish as I knew it to be, that chamber of the moon pool seemed also—in some way—holy. As though a god and a demon dwelt there, inextricably commingled.

"As I shot the pillar wavered; the water grew more disturbed. The mist swayed and shook; gathered itself again. I slipped a second clip into the automatic and, another idea coming to me, took careful aim at one of the globes in the roof. From thence I knew came the force that shaped the dweller in the pool. From the pouring rays came its strength. If I could destroy them I could check its forming. I fired again and again. If I hit the globes I did no damage. The little motes in their beams danced with the motes in the mist, troubled. That was all.

"Up from the pool like little bells, like bubbles of crystal notes rose the tinklings. Their notes were higher, had lost their sweetness, were angry, as it were, with themselves.

"And then out from the Inexplicable, hovering over the pool, swept a shining swirl. It caught me above the heart; wrapped itself around me. I felt an icy coldness and then there rushed over me a mingled ecstasy and horror. Every atom of me quivered with delight and at the same time shrank with despair. There was nothing loathsome in it. But it was as though the icy soul of evil and the fiery soul of good had stepped together within me. The pistol dropped from my hand.

"So I stood while the pool gleamed and sparkled; the streams of light grew more intense and the mist glowed and strengthened. I saw that its shining core had shape—but a shape that my eyes and brain could not define. It was as though a being of another sphere should assume what it might of human semblance, but was not able to conceal that what human eyes saw was but a part of it. It was neither man nor woman; it was unearthly and androgynous. Even as I found its human semblance it changed. And still the mingled rapture and terror held me. Only in a little corner of my brain dwelt something untouched; something that held itself apart and watched. Was it the soul? I have never believed—and yet—

"Over the head of the misty body there sprang suddenly out seven little lights. Each was the color of the beam beneath which it rested. I knew now that the dweller was—complete!

"And then—behind me I heard a scream. It was Edith's voice. It came to me that she had heard the shots and followed me. I felt every faculty concentrate into a mighty effort. I wrenched myself free from the gripping tentacle and it swept back. I turned to catch Edith, and as I did so slipped—fell. As I dropped I saw the radiant shape above the pool leap swiftly for me!

"There was the rush past me and as the dweller paused, straight into it raced Edith, arms outstretched to shield me from it!"

He trembled.

"She threw herself squarely within its diabolic splendor," he whispered. "She stopped and reeled as though she had encountered solidity. And as she faltered it wrapped its shining self around her. The crystal tinklings burst forth jubilantly. The light filled her, ran through and around her as it had with Stanton and I saw drop upon her face—the look. From the pillar came the murmur—'*Av-o-lo-ha!*' The vault echoed it.

" 'Edith!' I cried. 'Edith!' I was in agony. She must have heard me, even through the—thing. I saw her try to free herself. Her rush had taken her to the very verge of the moon pool. She tottered; and in an instant—she fell—with the radiance still holding her, still swirling and winding around and through her—into the moon pool! She sank, Goodwin, and with her went—the dweller!

"I dragged myself to the brink. Far down I saw a shining, many-colored nebulous cloud descending; caught a glimpse of Edith's face, disappearing; her eyes stared up to me filled with supernal ecstasy and horror. And—vanished!

"I looked about me stupidly. The seven globes still poured their radiance upon the pool. It was pale-blue again. Its sparklings and coruscations were gone. From far below there came a muffled outburst of triumphant chanting!

" 'Edith!' I cried again. 'Edith, come back to me!' And then a darkness fell upon me. I remember running back through the shimmering corridors and out into the courtyard. Reason had left me. When it returned I was far out at sea in our boat wholly estranged from civilization. A day later I was picked up by the schooner in which I came to Port Moresby.

"I have formed a plan; you must hear it, Goodwin—" He fell upon his berth. I bent over him. Exhaustion and the relief of telling his story had been too much for him. He slept like the dead.

VII. The Dweller Comes

All that night I watched over him. When dawn broke I went to my room to get a little sleep myself. But my slumber was haunted.

The next day the storm was unabated. Throckmartin came to me at lunch. He looked better. His strange expression had waned. He had regained much of his old alertness.

"Come to my cabin," he said. There, he stripped his shirt from him. "Something is happening," he said. "The mark is smaller." It was as he said.

"I'm escaping," he whispered jubilantly. "Just let me get to Melbourne safely, and then we'll see who'll win! For, Goodwin, I'm not at all sure that Edith is dead—as we know death—nor that the others are. There was something outside experience there—some great mystery."

And all that day he talked to me of his plans.

"There's a natural explanation, of course," he said. "My theory is that the moon rock is of some composition sensitive to the action of moon rays; somewhat as the metal selenium is to sun rays. There is a powerful quality in moonlight, as both science and legends can attest. We know of its effect upon the mentality, the nervous system, even upon certain diseases.

"The moon slab is of some material that reacts to moonlight. The circles over the top are, without doubt, its operating agency. When the light strikes them they release the mechanism that opens the slab, just as you can open doors with sunlight by an ingenious arrangement of selenium-cells. Apparently it takes the strength of the full moon to do this.

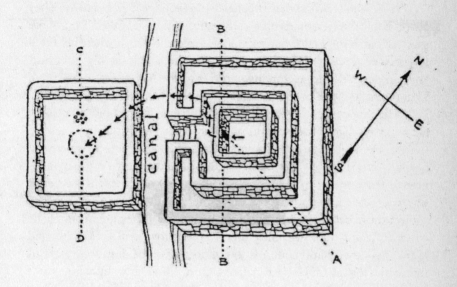

Dr. Throckmartin's sketch of the location of the moon door. The passageways, the probable location of the moon pool deep under Tau Islet, and the conjectured location of the seven lights. A is the moon rock on Nan-Tanach; B B the bosses above it which control its opening: the arrows indicate Dr. Throckmartin's probably course beneath the walls and under the canal. C are the moon lights, and D the cavern of the moon pool on Tau Islet. Proper measurements are not observed in the sketch; the idea being solely to determine position.

We will first try a concentration of the rays of the *nearly* full moon upon these circles to see whether that will open the rock. If it does we will be able to investigate the pool without interruption from—from—what emanates.

"Look, here on the chart are their locations. I have made this in duplicate for you in the event of something happening to me."

He worked upon the chart a little more.

"Here," he said, "is where I believe the seven great globes to be. They are probably hidden somewhere in the ruins of the islet called Tau, where they can catch the first moon rays. I have calculated that when I entered I went so far this way—here is the turn; so far this way, took this other turn and ran down this long, curving corridor to the hall of the moon pool. That ought to make lights, at least approximately, here." He pointed.

"They are certainly cleverly concealed, but they must be open to the air to get the light. They should not be too hard to find. They must be found." He hesitated again. "I suppose it would be safer to destroy them, for it is clearly through them that the phenomenon of the pool is manifested; and yet, to destroy so wonderful a thing! Perhaps the better way would be to have some men up by them, and if it were necessary, to protect those below, to destroy them on signal. Or they might simply be covered. That would neutralize them. To destroy them—" He hesitated again. "No, the phenomenon is too important to be destroyed without fullest investigation." His face clouded again. "But it is *not* human; it can't be," he muttered. He turned to me and laughed. "The old conflict between science and too frail human credulity!" he said.

Again—"We need half a dozen diving-suits. The pool must be entered and searched to its depths. That will indeed take courage, yet in the time of the new moon it should be safe, or perhaps better after the dweller is destroyed or made safe."

We went over plans, accepted them, rejected them, and still the storm raged—and all that day and all that night.

I hurry to the end. That afternoon there came a steady lightening of the clouds which Throckmartin watched with deep uneasiness. Toward dusk they broke away suddenly and soon the sky was clear. The stars came twinkling out.

"It will be to-night," Throckmartin said to me. "Goodwin, friend, stand by me. To-night it will come, and I must fight."

I could say nothing. About an hour before moonrise we went to his cabin. We fastened the port-holes tightly and turned on the electrics. Throckmartin had some queer theory that the electric rays would be a bar to his pursuer. I don't know why. A little later he complained of increasing sleepiness.

"But it's just weariness," he said. "Not at all like that other drowsiness. It's an hour till moonrise still," he yawned at last. "Wake me up a good fifteen minutes before."

He lay upon the berth. I sat thinking. I came to myself with a start. What time was it? I looked at my watch and jumped to the port-hole. It was full moonlight; the orb had been up for fully half an hour. I strode over to Throckmartin and shook him by the shoulder.

"Up, quick, man!" I cried. He rose sleepily. His shirt fell open at the neck and I looked, in amazement, at the white band around his chest. Even under the electric light it shone softly, as though little flecks of light were in it.

Throckmartin seemed only half-awake. He looked down at his breast, saw the glowing cincture, and smiled.

"Oh, yes," he said drowsily, "it's coming—to take me back to Edith! Well, I'm glad."

"Throckmartin!" I cried. "Wake up! Fight."

"Fight!" he said. "No use; keep the maps; come after us."

He went to the port and drowsily drew aside the curtain. The moon traced a broad path of light straight to the ship. Under its rays the band around his chest gleamed brighter and brighter; shot forth little rays; seemed to move.

He peered out intently and, suddenly, before I could stop him, threw open the port. I saw a glimmering presence moving swiftly along the moon path toward us, skimming over the waters.

And with it raced little crystal tinklings and far off I heard a long-drawn murmuring cry.

On the instant the lights went out in the cabin, evidently throughout the ship, for I heard shouting above. I sprang back into a corner and crouched there. At the port-hole was a radiance; swirls and spirals of living white cold fire. It poured into the cabin and it was filled with dancing motes of light, and over the radiant core of it shone seven little lights like tiny moons. It gathered Throckmartin to it. Light pulsed through and from him. I saw his skin turn to a translucent, shimmering whiteness like illumined porcelain. His face became unrecognizable, inhuman with the monstrous twin expressions. So he stood for a moment. The pillar of light seemed to hesitate and the seven lights to contemplate me. I shrank further down into the corner. I saw Throckmartin drawn to the port. The room filled with murmuring. I fainted.

When I awakened the lights were burning again.

But of Throckmartin there was no trace!

Gentlemen, there are some things that we are doomed to regret all our lives. Born in me then was a great fear. I suppose I was unbalanced by what I had seen. I could not think clearly. But there came to me the sheer impossibility of telling the ship's officers what I had seen; what Throckmartin had told me. They would accuse me, I felt, of his murder. At neither appearance of the phenomenon had any save our two selves witnessed it. I was certain of this because they would surely have discussed it. Why none had seen it I do not know.

The next morning when Throckmartin's absence was noted, I merely said that I had left him early in the evening. It occurred to no one to doubt me, or to question me further. His strangeness had caused much comment; all had thought him half-mad. And so it was officially reported that he had fallen or jumped from the ship during the failure of the lights, the cause of which was another mystery of that night.

Afterward, the same inhibition held me back from making his and my story known to my fellow scientists.

But this inhibition is suddenly dead, and I am not sure that its death is not a summons from Throckmartin.

I go to Nan-Tanach, gentlemen, to make amends for my cowardice by seeking out the dweller.

And, gentlemen, I stake all my reputation, all my faith, all that I hold sacred and dear that what I have written here is absolute truth.

LOVECRAFT DESCRIBED THE British poet and short story writer Walter de la Mare (1873-1956) as "a forceful craftsman to whom an unseen mystic world is ever a close and vital reality . . . whose haunting verse and exquisite prose alike bear consistent traces of a strange vision reaching deeply into veiled spheres of beauty and terrible and forbidden dimensions of being." Lovecraft discovered de la Mare in the summer of 1926. He singled out as one of de la Mare's best stories "Seaton's Aunt," which he noted for its "noxious background of malignant vampirism." "Seaton's Aunt" is de la Mare's best-known tale. It was first published in *The London Mercury* in April 1922, and was collected in *The Riddle and Other Stories* (1923).

SEATON'S AUNT
by Walter de la Mare

I had heard rumours of Seaton's Aunt long before I actually encountered her. Seaton, in the hush of confidence, or at any little show of toleration on our part, would remark, "My aunt," or "My old aunt, you know," as if his relative might be a kind of cement to an *entente cordiale*.

He had an unusual quantity of pocket-money; or, at any rate, it was bestowed on him in unusually large amounts; and he spent it freely, though none of us would have described him as an "awfully generous chap." "Hullo, Seaton," we would say, "the old Begum?" At the beginning of term, too, he used to bring back surprising and exotic dainties in a box with a trick padlock that accompanied him from his first appearance at Gummidge's in a billy-cock hat to the rather abrupt conclusion of his schooldays.

From a boy's point of view he looked distastefully foreign, with his yellow skin, and slow chocolate-coloured eyes, and lean weak figure. Merely for his looks he was treated by most of us true-blue Englishmen with condescension, hostility, or con-tempt. We used to call him "Pongo," but without any much better excuse for the nickname than his skin. He was, that is, in one sense of the term what he assuredly was not in the other sense, a sport.

Seaton and I, as I may say, were never in any sense intimate at school; our orbits only intersected in class. I kept deliberately aloof from him. I felt vaguely he was a sneak, and remained quite unmollified by advances on his side, which, in a boy's barbarous fashion, unless it suited me to be magnanimous, I haughtily ignored.

We were both of us quick-footed, and at Prisoner's Base used occasionally to hide together. And so I best remember Seaton—his narrow watchful face in the dusk of a summer evening; his peculiar crouch, and his inarticulate whisperings and mumblings. Otherwise he played all games slackly and limply; used to stand and feed at his locker with a crony or two until his "tuck" gave out; or waste his money on some outlandish fancy or other. He bought, for instance, a silver bangle, which he wore above his left elbow, until some of the fellows showed their masterly contempt of the practice by dropping it nearly red-hot down his neck.

It needed, therefore, a rather peculiar taste, a rather rare kind of schoolboy courage and indifference to criticism, to be much associated with him. And I had neither the taste nor, perhaps, the courage. None the less, he did make advances, and on one memorable occasion went to the length of bestowing on me a whole pot of some outlandish mulberry-coloured jelly that had been duplicated in his term's supplies. In the exuberance of my gratitude I promised to spend the next half-term holiday with him at his aunt's house.

I had clean forgotten my promise when, two or three days before the holiday, he came up and triumphantly reminded me of it.

"Well, to tell you the honest truth, Seaton, old chap—" I began graciously: but he cut me short.

"My aunt expects you," he said; "she is very glad you are coming. She's sure to be quite decent to *you*, Withers."

I looked at him in sheer astonishment; the emphasis was so uncalled for. It seemed to suggest an aunt not hitherto hinted at, and a friendly feeling on Seaton's side that was far more disconcerting than welcome.

We reached his home partly by train, partly by a lift in an empty farm-cart, and partly by walking. It was a whole-day holiday, and we were to sleep the night; he lent me extraordinary night-gear, I remember. The village street was unusually wide, and was fed from a green by two converging roads, with an inn, and a high green sign at the corner. About a hundred yards down the street was a chemist's shop—a Mr. Tanner's. We descended the two steps into his dusky and odorous interior to buy, I remember, some rat poison. A little beyond the chemist's was the forge. You then walked along a very narrow path, under a fairly high wall, nodding here and there with weeds and tufts of grass, and so came to the iron garden-gates, and saw the high flat house behind its huge sycamore. A coach-house stood on the left of the house, and on the right a gate led into a kind of rambling orchard. The lawn lay away over to the left again, and at the bottom (for the whole garden sloped gently to a sluggish and rushy pond-like stream) was a meadow.

We arrived at noon, and entered the gates out of the hot dust beneath the glitter of the dark-curtained windows. Seaton led me at once through the little garden-gate to show me his tadpole pond, swarming with what (being myself not in the least interested in low life) I considered the most horrible creatures—of all shapes, consistencies, and sizes, but with whom Seaton seemed to be on the most intimate of terms. I can see his absorbed face now as he sat on his heels and fished the slimy things out in his sallow palms. Wearying at last of these pets, we loitered about awhile in an aimless fashion. Seaton seemed to be listening, or at any rate waiting, for something to happen or for someone to come. But nothing did happen and no one came.

That was just like Seaton. Anyhow, the first view I got of his aunt was when, at the summons of a distant gong, we turned from the garden, very hungry and thirsty, to go into luncheon. We were approaching the house when Seaton suddenly came to a standstill. Indeed, I have always had the impression that he plucked at my sleeve. Something, at least, seemed to catch me back, as it were, as he cried, "Look out, there she is!"

She was standing at an upper window which opened wide on a hinge, and at first sight she looked an excessively tall and overwhelming figure. This, however, was mainly because the window reached all but to the floor of her bedroom. She was in reality rather an undersized woman, in spite of her long face and big head. She must have stood, I think, unusually still, with eyes fixed on us, though this impression may be due to Seaton's sudden warning and to my consciousness of the cautious and subdued air that had fallen on him at sight of her. I know that without the least reason in the world I felt a kind of guiltiness, as if I had been "caught." There was a silvery star pattern sprinkled on her black silk dress, and even from the ground I could see the immense coils of her hair and the rings on her left hand which was held fingering the small jet buttons of her bodice. She watched our united advance without stirring, until, imperceptibly, her eyes raised and lost themselves in the distance, so that it was out of an assumed reverie that she appeared suddenly to awaken to our presence beneath her when we drew close to the house.

"So this is your friend, Mr. Smithers, I suppose?" she said, bobbing to me.

"Withers, aunt," said Seaton.

"It's much the same," she said, with eyes fixed on me. "Come in, Mr. Withers, and bring him along with you."

She continued to gaze at me—at least, I think she did so. I know that the fixity of her scrutiny and her ironical "Mr." made me feel peculiarly uncomfortable. None the less she was extremely kind and attentive to me, though, no doubt, her kindness and attention showed up more vividly against her complete neglect of Seaton. Only one remark that I have any recollection of she made to him: "When I look on my nephew, Mr. Smithers, I realise that dust we are, and dust shall become. You are hot, dirty, and incorrigible, Arthur."

She sat at the head of the table, Seaton at the foot, and I, before a wide waste of damask tablecloth, between them. It was an old and rather close dining-room, with windows thrown wide to the green garden and a wonderful cascade of fading roses. Miss Seaton's great chair faced this window, so that its rose-reflected light shone full on her yellowish face, and on just such chocolate eyes as my schoolfellow's, except that hers were more than half-covered by unusually long and heavy lids.

There she sat, steadily eating, with those sluggish eyes fixed for the most part on my face; above them stood the deep-lined fork between her eyebrows; and above that the wide expanse of a remarkable brow beneath its strange steep bank of hair. The lunch was copious, and consisted, I remember, of all such dishes as are generally considered too rich and too good for the schoolboy digestion—lobster mayonnaise, cold game sausages, an immense veal and ham pie farced with eggs, truffles, and numberless delicious flavours; besides kickshaws, creams and sweetmeats. We even had wine, a half-glass of old darkish sherry each.

Miss Seaton enjoyed and indulged an enormous appetite. Her example and a natural schoolboy voracity soon overcame my nervousness of her, even to the extent of allowing me to enjoy to the best of my bent so rare a spread. Seaton was singularly modest; the greater part of his meal consisted of almonds and raisins, which he nibbled surreptitiously and as if he found difficulty in swallowing them.

I don't mean that Miss Seaton "conversed" with me. She merely scattered trenchant remarks and now and then twinkled a baited question over my head. But her face was like a dense and involved accompaniment to her talk. She presently dropped the "Mr.," to my intense relief, and called me now Withers, or Wither, now Smithers, and even once towards the close of the meal distinctly Johnson, though how on earth my name suggested it, or whose face mine had reanimated in memory, I cannot conceive.

"And is Arthur a good boy at school, Mr. Wither?" was one of her many questions. "Does he please his masters? Is he first in his class? What does the reverend Dr. Gummidge think of him, eh?"

I knew she was jeering at him, but her face was adamant against the least flicker of sarcasm or facetiousness. I gazed fixedly at a blushing crescent of lobster.

"I think you're eighth, aren't you, Seaton?"

Seaton moved his small pupils towards his aunt. But she continued to gaze with a kind of concentrated detachment at me.

"Arthur will never make a brilliant scholar, I fear," she said, lifting a dexterously-burdened fork to her wide mouth. . . .

After luncheon she preceded me up to my bedroom. It was a jolly little bedroom, with a brass fender and rugs and a polished floor, on which it was possible, I afterwards found, to play "snow-shoes." Over the washstand was a little black-framed water-colour drawing, depicting a large eye with an extremely fishlike intensity in the spark of light on the dark pupil; and in "illuminated" lettering beneath was printed very minutely, "Thou God Seest ME," followed by a long looped monogram, "S.S.," in the corner. The other pictures were all of the sea: brigs on blue water; a schooner overtopping chalk cliffs; a rocky island of prodigious steepness, with two tiny sailors dragging a monstrous boat up a shelf of beach.

"This is the room, Withers, my brother William died in when a boy. Admire the view!"

I looked out of the window across the tree-tops. It was a day hot with sunshine over the green fields, and the cattle were standing swishing their tails in the shallow water. But the view at the moment was only exaggeratedly vivid because I was horribly dreading that she would presently enquire after my luggage, and I had not brought even a toothbrush. I need have had no fear. Hers was not that highly-civilised type of mind that is stuffed with sharp, material details. Nor could her ample presence be described as in the least motherly.

"I would never consent to question a school-fellow behind my nephew's back," she said, standing in the middle of the room, "but tell me, Smithers; why is Arthur so unpopular? You, I understand, are his only close friend." She stood in a dazzle of sun, and out of it her eyes regarded me with such leaden penetration beneath their thick lids that I doubt if my face concealed the least thought from her. "But there, there," she added very suavely, stooping her head a little, "don't trouble to answer me. I never extort an answer. Boys are queer fish. Brains might perhaps have suggested his washing his hands before luncheon; but—not my choice, Smithers. God forbid! And now, perhaps, you would like to go into the garden again. I cannot actually see from here, but I should not be surprised if Arthur is now skulking behind that hedge."

He was. I saw his head come out and take a rapid glance at the windows.

"Join him, Mr. Smithers; we shall meet again, I hope, at the tea-table. The afternoon I spend in retirement."

Whether or not, Seaton and I had not been long engaged with the aid of two green switches in riding round and round a lumbering old grey horse we found in the meadow, before a rather bunched-up figure appeared, walking along the field-path on the other side of the water, with a magenta parasol studiously lowered in our direction throughout her slow progress, as if that were the magnetic needle and we the fixed Pole. Seaton at once lost all nerve in his riding. At the next lurch of the old mare's heels he toppled over into the grass, and I slid off the sleek broad back to join him where he stood, rubbing his shoulder and sourly watching the rather pompous figure till it was out of sight.

"Was that your aunt, Seaton?" I enquired; but not till then.

He nodded.

"Why didn't she take any notice of us, then?"

"She never does."

"Why not?"

"Oh, she knows all right, without; that's the dam awful part of it." Seaton was about the only fellow at Gummidge's who ever had the ostentation to use bad language. He had suffered for it too. But it wasn't, I think, bravado. I believe he really felt certain things more intensely than most of the other fellows, and they were generally things that fortunate and average people do not feel at all—the peculiar quality, for instance, of the British schoolboy's imagination.

"I tell you, Withers," he went on moodily, slinking across the meadow with his hands, covered up in his pockets, "she sees everything. And what she doesn't see she knows without."

"But how?" I said, not because I was much interested, but because the afternoon was so hot and tiresome and purposeless, and it seemed more of a bore to remain silent. Seaton turned gloomily and spoke in a very low voice.

"Don't appear to be talking of her, if you wouldn't mind. It's—because she's in league with the devil. He nodded his head and stooped to pick up a round flat pebble. "I tell you," he said, still stooping, "you fellows don't realise what it is. I know. I'm a bit close and all that. But so would you be if you had that old hag listening to every thought you think,"

I looked at him, then turned and surveyed one by one the windows of the house.

"Where's your *pater*?" I said awkwardly.

"Dead, ages and ages ago, and my mother too. She's not my aunt by rights."

"What is she then?"

"I mean she's not my mother's sister, because my grandmother married twice; and she's one of the first lot. I don't know what you call her, but anyhow she's not my real aunt."

"She gives you plenty of pocket-money."

Seaton looked steadfastly at me out of his flat eyes. "She can't give me what's mine. When I come of age half of the whole lot will be mine; and what's more"—he turned his back on the house—"I'll make her hand over every blessed shilling of it."

I put my hands in my pockets and stared at Seaton; "Is it much?"

He nodded.

"Who told you?" He got suddenly very angry; a darkish red came into his cheeks, his eyes glistened, but he made no answer, and we loitered listlessly about the garden until it was time for tea. . . .

Seaton's aunt was wearing an extraordinary kind of lace jacket when we sidled sheepishly into the drawing-room together. She greeted me with a heavy and protracted smile, and bade me bring a chair close to the little table.

"I hope Arthur has made you feel at home," she said as she handed me my cup in her crooked hand. "He don't talk much to me; but then I'm an old woman. You must come again, Wither, and draw him out of his shell. You old snail!" She wagged her head at Seaton, who sat munching cake and watching her intently.

"And we must correspond, perhaps." She nearly shut her eyes at me. "You must write and tell me everything behind the creature's back." I confess I found her rather disquieting company. The evening drew on. Lamps were brought in by a man with a nondescript face and very quiet footsteps. Seaton was told to bring out the chessmen. And we played a game, she and I, with her big chin thrust over the board at every move as she gloated over the pieces and occasionally croaked "Check!"—after which she would sit back inscrutably staring at me. But the game was never finished. She simply hemmed me defencelessly in with a cloud of men that held me impotent, and yet one and all refused to administer to my poor flustered old king a merciful *coup de grâce.*

"There," she said, as the clock struck ten—"a drawn game, Withers. We are very evenly matched. A very creditable defence, Withers. You know your room. There's supper on a tray in the dining-room. Don't let the creature over-eat himself. The gong will sound three-quarters of an hour *before* a punctual breakfast." She held out her cheek to Seaton, and he kissed it with obvious perfunctoriness. With me she shook hands.

"An excellent game," she said cordially, "but my memory is poor, and"—she swept the pieces helter-skelter into the box—"the result will never be known." She raised her great head far back. "Eh?"

It was a kind of challenge, and I could only murmur: "Oh, I was absolutely in a hole, you know!" when she burst out laughing and waved us both out of the room.

Seaton and I stood and ate our supper, with one candlestick to light us, in a corner of the dining-room. "Well, and how would you like it?" he said very softly, after cautiously poking his head round the doorway.

"Like what?"

"Being spied on—every blessed thing you do and think?"

"I shouldn't like it at all," I said, "if she does."

"And yet you let her smash you up at chess!"

"I didn't let her!" I said, indignantly.

"Well, you funked it, then."

"And I didn't funk it either," I said; "she's so jolly clever with her knights." Seaton stared fixedly at the candle. "You wait, that's all," he said slowly. And we went upstairs to bed.

I had not been long in bed, I think, when I was cautiously awakened by a touch on my shoulder. And there was Seaton's face in the candlelight— and his eyes looking into mine.

"What's up?" I said, rising quickly to my elbow.

"Don't scurry," he whispered, "or she'll hear. I'm sorry for waking you, but I didn't think you'd be asleep so soon."

"Why, what's the time, then?" Seaton wore, what was then rather unusual, a night-suit, and he hauled his big silver watch out of the pocket in his jacket.

"It's a quarter to twelve. I never get to sleep before twelve—not here."

"What do you do, then?"

"Oh, I read and listen."

"Listen?"

Seaton stared into his candle-flame as if he were listening even then. "You can't guess what it is. All you read in ghost stories, that's all rot. You can't see much, Withers, but you know all the same."

"Know what?"

"Why, that they're there."

"Who's there?" I asked fretfully, glancing at the door.

"Why, in the house. It swarms with 'em. Just you stand still and listen outside my bedroom door in the middle of the night. I have, dozens of times; they're all over the place."

"Look here, Seaton," I said, "you asked me to come here, and I didn't mind chucking up a leave just to oblige you and because I'd promised; but don't get talking a lot of rot, that's all, or you'll know the difference when we get back."

"Don't fret," he said coldly, turning away. "I shan't be at school long. And what's more, you're here now, and there isn't anybody else to talk to. I'll chance the other."

"Look here, Seaton," I said, "you may think you're going to scare me with a lot of stuff about voices and all that. But I'll just thank you to clear out; and you may please yourself about pottering about all night."

He made no answer; he was standing by the dressing-table looking across his candle into the looking-glass; he turned and stared slowly round the walls.

"Even this room's nothing more than a coffin. I suppose she told you— 'It's all exactly the same as when my brother William died'—trust her for that that! And good luck to him, say I. Look at that." He raised his candle close to the little water-colour I have mentioned. "There's hundreds of eyes like that in this house; and even if God does see you, He takes precious good care you don't see Him. And it's just the same with them. I tell you what, Withers, I'm getting sick of all this. I shan't stand it much longer."

The house was silent within and without, and even in the yellowish radiance of the candle a faint silver showed through the open window on my blind. I slipped off the bedclothes, wide awake, and sat irresolute on the bedside.

"I know you're only guying me," I said angrily, "but why is the house full of—what you say? Why do you hear—what you *do* hear ? Tell me that, you silly fool!"

Seaton sat down on a chair and rested his candle-stick on his knee. He blinked at me calmly. "She brings them," he said, with lifted eyebrows.

"Who? Your aunt?"

He nodded.

"How?"

"I told you," he answered pettishly. "She's in league. You don't know. She as good as killed my mother; I know that. But it's not only her by a long chalk. She just sucks you dry. I know. And that's what she'll do for me; because I'm like her—like my mother, I mean. She simply hates to see me alive. I wouldn't be like that old she-wolf for a million pounds. And so"— he broke off, with a comprehensive wave of his candlestick—"they're always here. Ah, my boy, wait till she's dead! She'll hear something then, I can tell you. It's all very well now, but wait till then! I wouldn't be in her shoes when she has to clear out—for something. Don't you go and believe I care for ghosts, or whatever you like to call them. We're all in the same box. We're all under her thumb."

He was looking almost nonchalantly at the ceiling at the moment, when I saw his face change, saw his eyes suddenly drop like shot birds and fix themselves on the cranny of the door he had just left ajar. Even from where I sat I could see his colour change; he went greenish. He crouched without stirring, simply fixed. And I, scarcely daring to breathe, sat with creeping skin, simply watching him. His hands relaxed, and he gave a kind of sigh.

"Was that one?" I whispered, with a timid show, of jauntiness. He looked round, opened his mouth, and nodded. "What?" I said. He jerked his thumb with meaningful eyes, and I knew that he meant that his aunt had been there listening at our door cranny.

"Look here, Seaton," I said once more, wriggling to my feet. "You may think I'm a jolly noodle; just as you please. But your aunt has been civil to me and all that, and I don't believe a word you say about her, that's all, and never did. Every fellow's a bit off his pluck at night, and you may think it a fine sport to try your rubbish on me. I heard your aunt come upstairs before I fell asleep. And I'll bet you a level tanner she's in bed now. What's more, you can keep your blessed ghosts to yourself. It's a guilty conscience, I should think."

Seaton looked at me curiously, without answering for a moment. "I'm not a liar, Withers; but I'm not going to quarrel either. You're the only chap I care a button for; or, at any rate, you're the only chap that's ever come here; and it's something to tell a fellow what you feel. I don't care a fig for fifty thousand ghosts, although I swear on my solemn oath that I know they're here. But she"—he turned deliberately—"you laid a tanner she's in bed, Withers; well, I know different. She's never in bed much of the night, and I'll prove it, too, just to show you I'm not such a nolly as you think I am. Come on!"

"Come on where ?"

"Why, to see."

I hesitated. He opened a large cupboard and took out a small dark dressing-gown and a kind of shawl-jacket. He threw the jacket on the bed and put on the gown. His dusky face was colorless, and I could see by the way he fumbled at the sleeves he was shivering. But it was no good showing the white feather now. So I threw the tasselled shawl over my shoulders and, leaving our candle brightly burning on the chair, we went out together and stood in the corridor.

"Now then, listen!" Seaton whispered.

We stood leaning over the staircase. It was like leaning over a well, so still and chill the air was all around us. But presently, as I suppose happens in most old houses, began to echo and answer in my ears a medley of infinite small stirrings and whisperings. Now out of the distance an old timber would relax its fibres, or a scurry die away behind the perishing wainscot. But amid and behind such sounds as these I seemed to begin to be conscious, as it were, of the lightest of footfalls, sounds as faint as the vanishing remembrance of voices in a dream. Seaton was all in obscurity except his face; out of that his eyes gleamed darkly, watching me.

"You'd hear, too, in time, my fine soldier," he muttered. "Come on!"

He descended the stairs, slipping his lean fingers lightly along the balusters. He turned to the right at the loop, and I followed him barefooted along a thickly-carpeted corridor. At the end stood a door ajar. And from here we very stealthily and in complete blackness ascended five narrow stairs. Seaton, with immense caution, slowly pushed open a door, and we stood together looking into a great pool of duskiness, out of which, lit by the feeble clearness of a night-light, rose a vast bed. A heap of clothes lay on the floor; beside them two slippers dozed, with noses each to each, two yards apart. Somewhere a little clock ticked huskily. There was a rather close smell of lavender and *eau de cologne*, mingled with the fragrance of ancient sachets, soap, and drugs. Yet it was a scent even more peculiarly commingled than that.

And the bed! I stared warily in; it was mounded gigantically, and it was empty.

Seaton turned a vague pale face, all shadows: "What did I say?" he muttered. "Who's—who's the fool now, I say? How are we going to get back without meeting her, I say? Answer me that! Oh, I wish to goodness you hadn't come here, Withers."

He stood visibly shivering in his skimpy gown and could hardly speak for his teeth chattering. And very distinctly, in the hush that followed his whisper, I heard approaching a faint unhurried voluminous rustle. Seaton clutched my arm, dragged me to the right across the room to a large cupboard, and drew the door close to on us. And, presently, as with bursting lungs I peeped out into the long, low, curtained bedroom, waddled in that wonderful great head and body. I can see her now, all patched and lined with shadow, her tied-up hair (she must have had enormous quantities of it for so old a woman), her heavy lids above those flat, slow, vigilant eyes. She just passed across my ken in the vague dusk; but the bed was out of sight.

We waited on and on, listening to the clock's muffled ticking. Not the ghost of a sound rose up from the great bed. Either she lay archly listening or slept a sleep serener than an infant's. And when, it seemed, we had been hours in hiding and were cramped, chilled, and half suffocated, we crept out on all fours, with terror knocking at our ribs, and so down the five narrow stairs and back to the little candle-lit blue-and-gold bedroom.

Once there, Seaton gave in. He sat livid on a chair with closed eyes.

"Here," I said, shaking his arm, "I'm going to bed; I've had enough of this foolery; I'm going to bed." His lips quivered, but he made no answer. I poured out some water into my basin and, with that cold pictured azure eye fixed on us, bespattered Seaton's sallow face and forehead and dabbled his hair. He presently sighed and opened fish-like eyes.

"Come on!" I said. "Don't get shamming, there's a good chap. Get on my back, if you like, and I'll carry you into your bedroom."

He waved me away and stood up. So, with my candle in one hand, I took him under the arm and walked him along according to his direction down the corridor. His was a much dingier room than mine, and littered with boxes, paper, cages, and clothes. I huddled him into bed and turned to go. And suddenly, I can hardly explain it now, a kind of cold and deadly terror swept over me. I almost ran out of the room, with eyes fixed rigidly in front of me, blew out my candle, and buried my head under the bedclothes.

When I awoke, roused not by a gong, but by long-continued tapping at my door, sunlight was raying in on cornice and bedpost, and birds were singing in the garden. I got up, ashamed of the night's folly, dressed quickly, and went downstairs. The breakfast room was sweet with flowers and fruit and honey. Seaton's aunt was standing in the garden beside the open French window, feeding a great flutter of birds. I watched her for a moment, unseen. Her face was set in a deep reverie beneath the shadow of a big loose sun-hat. It was deeply lined, crooked, and, in a way I can't describe, fixedly vacant and strange, I coughed, and she turned at once with a prodigious smile to enquire how I had slept. And in that mysterious way by which we learn each other's secret thoughts without a sentence spoken I knew that she had followed every word and movement of the night before, and was triumphing over my affected innocence and ridiculing my friendly and too easy advances.

We returned to school, Seaton and I, lavishly laden, and by rail all the way. I made no reference to the obscure talk we had had, and resolutely refused to meet his eyes or to take up the hints he let fall. I was relieved— and yet I was sorry to be going back, and strode on as fast as I could from the station, with Seaton almost trotting at my heels. But he insisted on buying more fruit and sweets—my share of which I accepted with a very bad grace. It was uncomfortably like a bribe; and, after all, I had no quarrel with his rum old aunt, and hadn't really believed half the stuff he had told me.

I saw as little of him as I could after that. He never referred to our visit or resumed his confidences, though in class I would sometimes catch his eye fixed on mine, full of a mute understanding, which I easily affected not to understand. He left Gummidge's, as I have said, rather abruptly, though I never heard of anything to his discredit. And I did not see him or have any news of him again till by chance we met one summer afternoon in the Strand.

He was dressed rather oddly in a coat too large for him and a bright silky tie. But we instantly recognised one another under the awning of a cheap jeweller's shop. He immediately attached himself to me and dragged me off, not too cheerfully, to lunch with him at an Italian restaurant near by. He chattered about our old school, which he remembered only with dislike and disgust; told me cold-bloodedly of the disastrous fate of one or two of the old fellows who had been among his chief tormentors; insisted on an expensive wine and the whole gamut of the foreign menu; and finally informed me, with a good deal of niggling, that he had come up to town to buy an engagement-ring.

And of course: "How is your aunt?" I enquired, at last.

He seemed to have been awaiting the question. It fell like a stone into a deep pool, so many expressions flitted across his long un-English face.

"She's aged a good deal," he said softly, and broke off.

"She's been very decent," he continued presently after, and paused again. "In a way." He eyed me fleetingly. "I dare say you heard that—she—that is, that we—had lost a good deal of money."

"No," I said.

"Oh, yes!" said Seaton, and paused again.

And somehow, poor fellow, I knew in the clink and clatter of glass and voices that he had lied to me; that he did not possess, and never had possessed, a penny beyond what his aunt had squandered on his too ample allowance of pocket-money.

"And the ghosts?" I enquired quizzically

He grew instantly solemn, and, though it may have been my fancy, slightly yellowed. But "You are making game of me, Withers," was all he said.

He asked for my address, and I rather reluctantly gave him my card.

"Look here, Withers," he said, as we stood together in the sunlight on the kerb, saying good-bye, "here I am, and—and it's all very well. I'm not perhaps as fanciful as I was. But you are practically the only friend I have on earth—except Alice. . . . And there—to make a clean breast of it, I'm not sure that my aunt cares much about my getting married. She doesn't say so, of course. You know her well enough for that." He looked sidelong at the rattling gaudy traffic.

"What I was going to say is this: Would you mind coming down? You needn't stay the night unless you please, though, of course, you know you would be awfully welcome. But I should like you to meet my—to meet

Alice; and then, perhaps, you might tell me your honest opinion of—of the other too."

I vaguely demurred. He pressed me. And we parted with a half promise that I would come. He waved his ball-topped cane at me and ran off in his long jacket after a 'bus.

A letter arrived soon after, in his small weak handwriting, giving me full particulars regarding route and trains. And without the least curiosity, even, perhaps with some little annoyance that chance should have thrown us together again, I accepted his invitation and arrived one hazy midday at his out-of-the-way station to find him sitting on a low seat under a clump of double hollyhocks, awaiting me.

His face looked absent and singularly listless; but he seemed, none the less, pleased to see me.

We walked up the village street, past the little dingy apothecary's and the empty forge, and, as on my first visit, skirted the house together, and, instead of entering by the front door, made our way down the green path into the garden at the back. A pale haze of cloud muffled the sun; the garden lay in a grey shimmer—its old trees, its snap-dragoned faintly glittering walls. But now there was an air of slovenliness where before all had been neat and methodical. In a patch of shallowly-dug soil stood a worn-down spade leaning against a tree. There was an old broken wheelbarrow. The roses had run to leaf and briar; the fruit-trees were unpruned. The goddess of neglect brooded in secret.

"You ain't much of a gardener, Seaton," I said, with a sigh of ease.

"I think, do you know, I like it best like this," said Seaton. "We haven't any man now, of course. Can't afford it." He stood staring at his little dark square of freshly-turned earth. "And it always seems to me," he went on ruminatingly, "that, after all, we are nothing better than interlopers on the earth, disfiguring and staining wherever we go. I know its shocking blasphemy to say so, but then it's different here, you see. We are further away."

"To tell you the truth, Seaton, I *don't* quite see," I said; "but it isn't a new philosophy, is it? Anyhow, it's a precious beastly one."

"It's only what I think," he replied, with all his odd old stubborn meekness.

We wandered on together, talking little, and still with that expression of uneasy vigilance on Seaton's face. He pulled out his watch as we stood gazing idly over the green meadows and the dark motionless bulrushes.

"I think, perhaps, it's nearly time for lunch," he said. "Would you like to come in?"

We turned and walked slowly towards the house, across whose windows I confess my own eyes, too, went restlessly wandering in search of its rather disconcerting inmate. There was a pathetic look of draggledness, of want of means and care, rust and overgrowth and faded paint. Seaton's aunt, a little to my relief, did not share our meal. Seaton carved the cold meat, and dispatched a heaped-up plate by an elderly servant for his aunt's private consumption. We talked little and in half-suppressed tones, and sipped a bottle of Madeira which Seaton had rather heedfully fetched out of the great mahogany side-board.

I played him a dull and effortless game of chess, yawning between the moves he himself made almost at haphazard, and with attention elsewhere engaged. About five o'clock came the sound of a distant ring, and Seaton jumped up, overturning the board, and so ending a game that else might have fatuously continued to this day. He effusively excused himself, and after some little while returned with a slim, dark, rather sallow girl of about nineteen, in a white gown and hat, to whom I was presented with some little nervousness as his "dear old friend and schoolfellow."

We talked on in the pale afternoon light, still, as it seemed to me, and even in spite of a real effort to be clear and gay, in a half-suppressed, lacklustre fashion. We all seemed, if it were not my fancy, to be expectant, to be rather anxiously awaiting an arrival, the appearance of someone who all but filled our collective consciousness. Seaton talked least of all, and in a restless interjectory way, as he continually fidgeted from chair to chair. At last he proposed a stroll in the garden before the sun should have quite gone down.

Alice walked between us. Her hair and eyes were conspicuously dark against the whiteness of her gown. She carried herself not ungracefully, and yet without the least movement of her arms and body, and answered us both without turning her head. There was a curious provocative reserve in that impassive and rather long face, a half-unconscious strength on character.

And yet somehow I knew—I believe we all knew—that this walk, this discussion of their future plans was a futility. I had nothing to base such a cynicism on, except only a vague sense of oppression, the foreboding remembrance of the inert invincible power in the background, to whom optimistic plans and love-making and youth are as chaff and thistledown. We came back, silent, in the last light. Seaton's aunt was there—under an old brass lamp. Her hair was as barbarously massed and curled as ever. Her eyelids, I think, hung even a little heavier in age over their slow-moving inscrutable pupils. We filed in softly out of the evening, and I made my bow.

"In this short interval, Mr. Withers," she remarked amiably, "you have put off youth, put on the man. Dear me, how sad it is to see the young days vanishing! Sit down. My nephew tells me you met by chance—or act of Providence, shall we call it?—and in my beloved Strand! You, I understand, are to be best man—yes, best man, or am I divulging secrets?" She surveyed Arthur and Alice with overwhelming graciousness. They sat apart on two low chairs and smiled in return.

"And Arthur—how do you think Arthur is looking?"

"I think he looks very much in need of a change," I said deliberately.

"A change! Indeed?" She all but shut her eyes at me and with an exaggerated sentimentality shook her head. "My dear Mr. Withers! Are we not *all* in need of a change in this fleeting, fleeting world?" She mused over the remark like a connoisseur. "And you," she continued, turning abruptly to Alice, "I hope you pointed out to Mr. Withers all my pretty bits?"

"We walked round the garden," said Alice, looking out of the window. "It's a very beautiful evening."

"*Is* it?" said the old lady, starting up violently. "Then on this very beautiful evening we will go in to supper. Mr. Withers, your arm; Arthur, bring your bride."

I can scarcely describe with what curious ruminations I led the way into the faded, heavy-aired dining-room, with this indefinable old creature leaning weightily on my arm—the large flat bracelet on the yellow-laced wrist. She fumed a little, breathed rather heavily, as if with an effort of mind rather than of body; for she had grown much stouter and yet little more proportionate. And to talk into that great white face, so close to mine, was a queer experience in the dim light of the corridor, and even in the twinkling crystal of the candles. She was naïve—appallingly naïve; she was sudden and superficial; she was even arch; and all these in the brief, rather puffy passage from one room to the other, with these two tongue-tied children bringing up the rear. The meal was tremendous. I have never seen such a monstrous salad. But the dishes were greasy and over-spiced, and were indifferently cooked. One thing only was quite unchanged—my hostess's appetite was as Gargantuan as ever. The old solid candelabra that lighted us stood before her high-backed chair. Seaton sat a little removed, with his plate almost in darkness.

And throughout this prodigious meal his aunt talked, mainly to me, mainly at Seaton, with an occasional satirical courtesy to Alice and muttered explosions of directions to the servant. She had aged, and yet, if it be not nonsense to say so, seemed no older. I suppose to the Pyramids a decade is but as the rustling down of a handful of dust. And she reminded me of some such unshakable prehistoricism. She certainly was an amazing talker—racy, extravagant, with a delivery that was perfectly overwhelming. As for Seaton—her flashes of silence were for him. On her enormous volubility would suddenly fall a hush: acid sarcasm would be left implied; and she would sit softly moving her great head, with eyes fixed full in a dreamy smile; but with her whole attention, one could see, slowly, joyously absorbing his mute discomfiture.

She confided in us her views on a theme vaguely occupying at the moment, I suppose, all our minds. "We have barbarous institutions, and so must put up, I suppose, with a never-ending procession of fools—of fools *ad infinitum*. Marriage, Mr. Withers, was instituted in the privacy of a garden; *sub rosa*, as it were. Civilization flaunts it in the glare of day. The dull marry the poor; the rich the effete; and so our New Jerusalem is peopled with naturals, plain and coloured, at either end. I detest folly; I detest still more (if I must be frank, dear Arthur) mere cleverness. Mankind has simply become a tailless host of uninstinctive animals. We should never have taken to Evolution, Mr. Withers. 'Natural Selection!' —little gods and fishes!—the deaf for the dumb. We should have used our brains—intellectual pride, the ecclesiastics call it. And by brains I mean—what do I mean, Alice?—I mean, my dear child," and she laid two gross fingers on Alice's narrow sleeve, "I mean courage. Consider it, Arthur. I read that the scientific world is once more beginning to be afraid of spiritual agencies. Spiritual agencies that tap, and actually float, bless their hearts! I think just one more of those mulberries—thank you.

"They talk about 'blind Love,' " she ran inconsequently on as she helped herself, with eyes roving on the dish, "but why blind? I think, do you know, from weeping over its rickets. After all, it is we plain women that triumph, Mr. Withers, beyond the mockery of time. Alice, now! Fleeting, fleeting is youth, my child. What's that you were confiding to your plate, Arthur? Satirical boy. He laughs at his old aunt: nay, but thou didst laugh. He detests all sentiment. He whispers the most acid asides. Come, my love, we will leave these cynics; we will go and commiserate with each other on our sex. The choice of two evils, Mr. Smithers!" I opened the door, and she swept out as if borne on a torrent of unintelligible indignation; and Arthur and I were left in the clear four-flamed light alone.

For a while we sat in silence. He shook his head at my cigarette-case, and I lit a cigarette. Presently he fidgeted in his chair and poked his head forward into the light. He paused to rise and shut again the shut door.

"How long will you be?" he said, standing by the table.

I laughed.

"Oh, it's not that!" he said, in some confusion. "Of course, I like to be with her. But it's not that. The truth is, Withers, I don't care about leaving her too long with my aunt."

I hesitated. He looked at me questioningly.

"Look here, Seaton," I said, "you know well enough that I don't want to interfere in your affairs, or to offer advice where it is not wanted. But don't you think perhaps you may not treat your aunt quite in the right way? As one gets old, you know, a little give and take. I have an old godmother, or something. She talks, too. . . . A little allowance: it does no harm. But hang it all, I'm no talker."

He sat down with his hands in his pockets and still with his eyes fixed almost incredulously on mine. "How?" he said.

"Well, my dear fellow, if I'm any judge—mind, I don't say that I am—but I can't help thinking she thinks you don't care for her; and perhaps takes your silence for—for bad temper. She has been very decent to you, hasn't she?"

" 'Decent'? My God!" said Seaton.

I smoked on in silence; but he continued to look at me with that peculiar concentration I remembered of old.

"I don't think, perhaps, Withers," he began presently, "I don't think you quite understand. Perhaps you are not quite our kind. You always did, just like the other fellows, guy me at school You laughed at me that night you came to stay here—about the voices and all that. But I don't mind being laughed at—because I know."

"Know what?" It was the same old system of dull question and evasive answer.

"I mean I know that what we see and hear is only the smallest fraction of what is. I know she lives quite out of this. She *talks* to you; but it's all make-believe. It's all a 'parlour game.' She's not really with you; only pitting her outside wits against yours and enjoying the fooling. She's living on inside, on what you're rotten without. That's what it is—a cannibal feast. She's a spider. It doesn't much matter what you call it. It means the same kind of thing. I tell you, Withers, she hates me; and you can scarcely dream what that hatred means. I used to think I had an inkling of the reason. It's oceans deeper than that. It just lies behind: herself against myself. Why, after all, how much do we really understand of anything? We don't even know our own histories, and not a tenth, not a tenth of the reasons. What has life been to me?—nothing but a trap. And when one is set free, it only begins again. I thought you might understand; but you are on a different level: that's all."

"What on earth are you talking about?" I said contemptuously, in spite of myself.

"I mean what I say," he said gutturally. "All this outside's only make-believe—but there! what's the good of talking? So far as this is concerned I'm as good as done. You wait."

Seaton blew out three of the candles and, leaving the vacant room in semi-darkness, we groped our way along the corridor to the drawing-room. There a full moon stood shining in at the long garden windows. Alice sat stooping at the door, with her hands clasped, looking out, alone.

"Where is she?" Seaton asked in a low tone.

Alice looked up; their eyes met in a kind of instantaneous understanding, and the door immediately afterwards opened behind us.

"*Such* a moon!" said a voice that, once heard, remained unforgettably on the ear. "A night for lovers, Mr. Withers, if ever there was one. Get a shawl, my dear Arthur, and take Alice for a little promenade. I dare say we old cronies will manage to keep awake. Hasten, hasten, Romeo! My poor, poor Alice, how laggard a lover!"

Seaton returned with a shawl. They drifted out into the moonlight. My companion gazed after them till they were out of hearing, turned to me gravely, and suddenly twisted her white face into such a convulsion of contemptuous amusement that I could only stare blankly in reply.

"Dear innocent children!" she said, with inimitable unctuousness. "Well, well, Mr. Withers, we poor seasoned old creatures must move with the times. Do you sing?"

I scouted the idea.

"Then you must listen to my playing. Chess"—she clasped her forehead with both cramped hands—"chess is now completely beyond my poor wits."

She sat down at the piano and ran her fingers in a flourish over the keys. "What shall it be? How shall we capture them, those passionate hearts? That first fine careless rapture? Poetry itself." She gazed softly into the garden a moment, and presently, with a shake of her body, began to play the opening bars of Beethoven's "Moonlight" Sonata. The piano was old and woolly. She played without music. The lamplight was rather dim. The moon-beams from the window lay across the keys. Her head was in shadow. And whether it was simply due to her personality or to some really occult skill in her playing I cannot say: I only know that she gravely and deliberately set herself to satirise the beautiful music. It brooded on the air, disillusioned, charged with mockery and bitterness. I stood at the window; far down the path I could see the white figure glimmering in that pool of colourless light. A few faint stars shone, and still that amazing woman behind me dragged out of the unwilling keys her wonderful grotesquerie of youth and love and beauty. It came to an end. I knew the player was watching me. "Please, please, go on!" I murmured, without turning. "Please go on playing, Miss Seaton."

No answer was returned to my rather fluttering sarcasm, but I knew in some indefinite way that I was being acutely scrutinised, when suddenly there followed a procession of quiet, plaintive chords which broke at last softly into the hymn, A Few More Years Shall Roll.

I confess it held me spellbound. There is a wistful, strained, plangent pathos in the tune; but beneath those masterly old hands it cried softly and bitterly the solitude and desperate estrangement of the world. Arthur and his lady-love vanished from my thoughts. No one could put into a rather hackneyed old hymn-tune such an appeal who had never known the meaning of the words. Their meaning, anyhow, isn't commonplace."

I turned very cautiously and glanced at the musician. She was leaning forward a little over the keys, so that at the approach of my cautious glance she had but to turn her face into the thin flood of moonlight for every feature to become distinctly visible. And so, with the tune abruptly terminated, we steadfastly regarded one another, and she broke into a chuckle of laughter.

"Not quite so seasoned as I supposed, Mr. Withers. I see you are a real lover of music. To me it is too painful. It evokes too much thought. . . ."

I could scarcely see her little glittering eyes under their penthouse lids.

"And now," she broke off crisply, "tell me, as man of the world, what do you think of my new niece?"

I was not a man of the world, nor was I much flattered in my stiff and dullish way of looking at things by being called one; and I could answer her without the least hesitation.

"I don't think, Miss Seaton, I'm much of a judge of character. She's very charming."

"A brunette?"

"I think I prefer dark women."

"And why? Consider, Mr. Withers; dark hair, dark eyes, dark cloud, dark night, dark vision, dark death, dark grave, dark DARK!"

Perhaps the climax would have rather thrilled Seaton, but I was too thick-skinned. "I don't know much about all that," I answered rather pompously. "Broad daylight's difficult enough for most of us."

"Ah," she said, with a sly inward burst of satirical laughter.

"And I suppose," I went on, perhaps a little nettled, "it isn't the actual darkness one admires, it's the contrast of the skin, and the colour of the eyes, and—and their shining. Just as," I went blundering on, too late to turn back, "just as you only see the stars in the dark. It would be a long day without any evening. As for death and the grave, I don't suppose we shall much notice that." Arthur and his sweetheart were slowly returning along the dewy path. "I believe in making the best of things."

"How very interesting!" came the smooth answer. "I see you are a philosopher, Mr. Withers. H'm! 'As for death and the grave, I don't suppose we shall much notice that.' Very interesting. . . . And I'm sure," she added in a particularly suave voice, "I profoundly hope so." She rose slowly from her stool. "You will take pity on me again, I hope. You and I would get on famously—kindred spirits—elective affinities. And, of course, now that my nephew's going to leave me, now that his affections are centred on another, I shall be a very lonely old woman. . . Shall I not, Arthur?"

Seaton blinked stupidly. "I didn't hear what you said, Aunt."

"I was telling our old friend, Arthur, that when you are gone I shall be a very lonely old woman."

"Oh, I don't think so;" he said in a strange voice.

"He means, Mr. Withers, he means, my dear child," she said, sweeping her eyes over Alice, "he means that I shall have memory for company— heavenly memory—the ghosts of other days. Sentimental boy! And did you enjoy our music, Alice? Did I really stir that youthful heart? . . . O, O, O," continued the horrible old creature, "you billers and cooers, I have been listening to such flatteries, such confessions! Beware, beware, Arthur, there's many a slip." She rolled her little eyes at me, she shrugged her shoulders at Alice, and gazed an instant stonily into her nephew's face.

I held out my hand. "Good night, good night!" she cried. "He that fights and runs away. A good night, Mr. Withers; come again soon!" She thrust out her cheek at Alice, and we all three filed slowly out of the room.

Black shadow darkened the porch and half the spreading sycamore. We walked without speaking up the dusty village street. Here and there a crimson window glowed. At the fork of the high-road I said good-bye. But I had taken hardly more than a dozen paces when a sudden impulse seized me.

"Seaton!" I called.

He turned in the moonlight.

"You have my address; if by any chance, you know, you should care to spend a week or two in town between this and the—the Day, we should be delighted to see you."

"Thank you, Withers, thank you," he said in a low voice.

"I dare say"—I waved my stick gallantly to Alice—"I dare say you will be doing some shopping; we could all meet," I added, laughing.

"Thank you, thank you, Withers—immensely," he repeated.

And so we parted.

But they were out of the jog-trot of my prosaic life. And being of a stolid and incurious nature, I left Seaton and his marriage, and even his aunt, to themselves in my memory, and scarcely gave a thought to them until one day I was walking up the Strand again, and passed the flashing gloaming of the covered-in jeweller's shop where I had accidentally encountered my old schoolfellow in the summer. It was one of those still close autumnal days after a rainy night. I cannot say why, but a vivid recollection returned to my mind of our meeting and of how suppressed Seaton had seemed, and of how vainly he had endeavoured to appear assured and eager. He must be married by now, and had doubtless returned from his honeymoon. And I had clean forgotten my manners, had sent not a word of congratulation, nor—as I might very well have done, and as I knew he would have been immensely pleased at my doing—the ghost of a wedding-present.

On the other hand, I pleaded with myself, I had had no invitation. I paused at the corner of Trafalgar Square, and at the bidding of one of those caprices that seize occasionally on even an unimaginative mind, I suddenly ran after a green 'bus that was passing, and found myself bound on a visit I had not in the least foreseen.

301

The colours of autumn were over the village when I arrived. A beautiful late afternoon sunlight bathed thatch and meadow. But it was close and hot. A child, two dogs, a very old woman with a heavy basket I encountered. One or two incurious tradesmen looked idly up as I passed by. It was all so rural and so still, my whimsical impulse had so much flagged, that for a while I hesitated to venture under the shadow of the sycamore-tree to enquire after the happy pair. I deliberately passed by the faint blue gates and continued my walk under the high green and tufted wall. Hollyhocks had attained their topmost bud and seeded in the little cottage gardens beyond; the Michaelmas daisies were in flower; a sweet warm aromatic smell of fading leaves was in the air. Beyond the cottages lay a field where cattle were grazing, and beyond that I came to a little churchyard. Then the road wound on, pathless and houseless among gorse and bracken. I turned impatiently and walked quickly back to the house and rang the bell.

The rather colourless elderly woman who answered my enquiry informed me that Miss Seaton was at home, as if only taciturnity forbade her adding, "But she doesn't want to see *you*."

"Might I, do you think, have Mr. Arthur's address?" I said.

She looked at me with quiet astonishment, as if waiting for an explanation. Not the faintest of smiles came into her thin face.

"I will tell Miss Seaton," she said after a pause. "Please walk in."

She showed me into the dingy undusted drawing room, filled with evening sunshine and with the green-dyed light that penetrated the leaves overhanging the long French windows. I sat down and waited on and on, occasionally aware of a creaking footfall overhead. At last the door opened a little, and the great face I had once known peered round at me. For it was enormously changed; mainly, I think, because the old eyes had rather suddenly failed, and so a kind of stillness and darkness lay over its calm and wrinkled pallor.

"Who is it?" she asked.

I explained myself and told her the occasion of my visit.

She came in and shut the door carefully after her and, though the fumbling was scarcely perceptible, groped her way to a chair. She had on an old dressing-gown, like a cassock, of a patterned cinnamon colour.

"What is it you want?" she said, seating herself and lifting her blank face to mine.

"Might I just have Arthur's address?" I said deferentially. "I am so sorry to have disturbed you."

"H'm. You have come to see my nephew?"

"Not necessarily to see him, only to hear how he is, and, of course, Mrs. Seaton, too. I am afraid my silence must have appeared. . . ."

"He hasn't noticed your silence," croaked the old voice out of the great mask; "besides, there isn't any Mrs. Seaton."

"Ah, then," I answered, after a momentary pause, "I have not seemed so black as I painted myself! And how is Miss Outram?"

"She's gone into Yorkshire," answered Seaton's aunt.

"And Arthur too?"

She did not reply, but simply sat blinking at me with lifted chin, as if listening, but certainly not for what I might have to say. I began to feel rather at a loss.

"You were no close friend of my nephew's, Mr. Smithers?" she said presently.

"No," I answered, welcoming the cue, "and yet, do you know, Miss Seaton, he is one of the very few of my old schoolfellows I have come across in the last few years, and I suppose as one gets older one begins to value old associations. . . ." My voice seemed to trail off into a vacuum. "I thought Miss Outram," I hastily began again, "a particularly charming girl. I hope they are both quite well."

Still the old face solemnly blinked at me in silence.

"You must find it very lonely, Miss Seaton, with Arthur away?"

"I was never lonely in my life," she said sourly. "I don't look to flesh and blood for my company. When you've got to be my age, Mr. Smithers (which God forbid), you'll find life a very different affair from what you seem to think it is now. You won't seek company then, I'll be bound. It's thrust on you." Her face edged round into the clear green light, and her eyes groped, as it were, over my vacant, disconcerted face. "I dare say, now," she said, composing her mouth, "I dare say my nephew told you a good many tarradiddles in his time. Oh, yes, a good many, eh? He was always a liar. What, now, did he say of me? Tell me, now." She leant forward as far as she could, trembling, with an ingratiating smile.

"I think he is rather superstitious," I said coldly, "but, honestly, I have a very poor memory, Miss Seaton."

"Why?" she said. "*I* haven't."

"The engagement hasn't been broken off, I hope."

"Well, between you and me," she said, shrinking up and with an immensely confidential grimace, "it has."

"I'm sure I'm very sorry to hear it. And where is Arthur?"

303

"Eh?"

"Where is Arthur?"

We faced each other mutely among the dead old bygone furniture. Past all my scrutiny was that large, flat, grey, cryptic countenance. And then, suddenly, our eyes for the first time really met. In some indescribable way out of that thick-lidded obscurity a far small something stooped and looked out at me for a mere instant of time that seemed of almost intolerable protraction. Involuntarily I blinked and shook my head. She muttered something with great rapidity, but quite inarticulately rose and hobbled to the door. I thought I heard mingled in broken mutterings, something about tea.

"Please, please, don't trouble," I began, but could say no more, for the door was already shut between us. I stood and looked out on the long-neglected garden. I could just see the bright greenness of Seaton's old tadpole pond. I wandered about the room. Dusk began to gather, the last birds in that dense shadowiness of trees had ceased to sing. And not a sound was to be heard in the house. I waited on and on, vainly speculating. I even attempted to ring the bell; but the wire was broken, and only jangled loosely at my efforts.

I hesitated, unwilling to call or to venture out, and yet more unwilling to linger on, waiting for a tea that promised to be an exceedingly comfortless supper. And as darkness drew down, a feeling of the utmost unease and disquietude came over me. All my talks with Seaton returned on me with a suddenly enriched meaning. I recalled again his face as we had stood hanging over the staircase, listening in the small hours to the inexplicable stirrings of the night. There were no candles in the room; every minute the autumnal darkness deepened. I cautiously opened the door and listened, and with some little dismay withdrew, for I was uncertain of my way out. I even tried the garden, but was confronted under a veritable thicket of foliage by a padlocked gate. It would be a little too ignominious to be caught scaling a friend's garden fence!

Cautiously returning into the still and musty drawing-room, I took out my watch, and gave the incredible old woman ten minutes in which to reappear. And when that tedious ten minutes had ticked by I could scarcely distinguish its hands. I determined to wait no longer, drew open the door, and, trusting to my sense of direction, groped my way through the corridor that I vaguely remembered led to the front of the house.

I mounted three or four stairs and, lifting a heavy curtain, found myself facing the starry fanlight of the porch. From here I glanced into the gloom of the dining-room. My fingers were on the latch of the outer door when I heard a faint stirring in the darkness above the hall. I looked up and became conscious of, rather than saw, the huddled old figure looking down on me.

There was an immense hushed pause. Then, "Arthur, Arthur," whispered an inexpressibly peevish aspiring voice, "is that you? Is that you, Arthur?"

I can scarcely say why, but the question horribly startled me. No conceivable answer occurred to me. With head craned back, hand clenched on my umbrella, I continued to stare up into the gloom, in this fatuous confrontation.

"Oh, oh;" the voice croaked. "It is you, is it? *That* disgusting man! . . . Go away out. Go away out."

Hesitating no longer I caught open the door and, slamming it behind me, ran out into the garden, under the gigantic old sycamore, and so out at the open gate.

I found myself half up the village street before I stopped running. The local butcher was sitting in his shop reading a piece of newspaper by the light of a small oil-lamp. I crossed the road and enquired the way to the station. And after he had with minute and needless care directed me, I asked casually if Mr. Arthur Seaton still lived with his aunt at the big house just beyond the village. He poked his head in at the little parlour door.

"Here's a gentleman enquiring after young Mr. Seaton, Millie," he said. "He's dead, ain't he?"

"Why, yes, bless you," replied a cheerful voice from within. "Dead and buried these three months or more—young Mr. Seaton. And just before he was to be married, don't you remember, Bob?"

I saw a fair young woman's face peer over the muslin of the little door at me.

"Thank you," I replied, "then I go straight on?"

"That's it, sir; past the pond, bear up the hill a bit to the left, and then there's the station lights before your eyes."

We looked intelligently into each other's faces in the beam of the smoky lamp. But not one of the many questions in my mind could I put into words.

And again I paused irresolutely a few paces further on. It was not, I fancy, merely a foolish apprehension of what the raw-boned butcher might "think" that prevented my going back to see if I could find Seaton's grave in the benighted churchyard. There was precious little use in pottering about in the muddy dark merely to discover where he was buried. And yet I felt a little uneasy. My rather horrible thought was that, so far as I was concerned—one of his extremely few friends—he had never been much better than "buried" in my mind.

II. THE POPULAR WEIRD TALE

AFTER "BEYOND THE DOOR" appeared in the April 1923 issue of *Weird Tales*, Lovecraft wrote a letter to the editor of *Weird Tales* (duly printed in the September issue) remarking that "Most of the stories [in the April issue], of course, are more or less commercial—or should I say conventional?—in technique, but they all have an enjoyable angle. 'Beyond the Door', by Paul Suter, seems to me the most truly touched with the elusive quality of original genius."

[Joseph] Paul Suter (1884-1970) was a short story writer from Ohio. In the 1920s and 1930s he contributed a half dozen or so stories to *Weird Tales*, but published many more in the detective fiction magazines, sometimes bylined J. Paul Suter.

BEYOND THE DOOR
by Paul Suter

"You haven't told me yet how it happened," I said to Mrs. Malkin. She set her lips and eyed me, sharply.

"Didn't you talk with the coroner, sir?"

"Yes, of course," I admitted; "but as I understand you found my uncle, I thought—"

"Well, I wouldn't care to say anything about it," she interrupted, with decision.

This housekeeper of my uncle's was somewhat taller than I, and much heavier—two physical preponderances which afford any woman possessing them an advantage over the inferior male. She appeared a subject for diplomacy rather than argument.

Noting her ample jaw, her breadth of cheek, the unsentimental glint of her eye, I decided on conciliation. I placed a chair for her, there in my Uncle Godfrey's study, and dropped into another, myself.

"At least, before we go over the other parts of the house, suppose we rest a little," I suggested, in my most unctuous manner. "The place rather gets on one's nerves—don't you think so?"

It was sheer luck—I claim no credit for it. My chance reflection found the weak spot in her fortifications. She replied to it with an undoubted smack of satisfaction:

"It's more than seven years that I've been doing for Mr. Sarston, sir. Bringing him his meals regular as clockwork, keeping the house clean—as clean as he'd let me—and sleeping at my own home, o' nights; and in all that time I've said, over and over, there ain't a house in New York the equal of this for queerness."

"Nor anywhere else," I encouraged her, with a laugh; and her confidences opened another notch:

"You're likely right in that, too, sir. As I've said to poor Mr. Sarston, many a time, 'It's all well enough,' says I, 'to have bugs for a hobby. You can afford it; and being a bachelor and by yourself, you don't have to consider other people's likes and dislikes. And it's all well enough if you want to,' says I, 'to keep thousands and thousands o' them in cabinets, all over the place, the way you do. But when it comes to pinnin' them on the walls in regular armies,' I says, 'and on the ceiling of your own study; and even on different parts of the furniture, so that a body don't know what awful things she's agoin' to find under her hand of a sudden when she does the dusting; why then,' I says to him, 'it's drivin' a decent woman too far.' "

"And did he never try to reform his ways when you told him that?" I asked, smiling.

"To be frank with you, Mr. Robinson when I talked like that to him, he generally raised my pay. And what was a body to do then?"

"I can't see how Lucy Lawton stood the place as long as she did," I observed, watching Mrs. Malkin's red face very closely.

She swallowed the bait, and leaned forward, hands on knees.

"Poor girl, it got on her nerves. But she was the quiet kind. You never saw her, sir?"

I shook my head.

"One of them slim, faded girls, with light hair, and hardly a word to say for herself. I don't believe she got to know the next-door neighbor in the whole year she lived with your uncle. She was an orphan, wasn't she, sir?"

"Yes," I said. "Godfrey Sarston and I were her only living relatives. That was why she came from Australia to stay with him, after her father's death."

Mrs. Malkin nodded. I was hoping that, putting a check on my eagerness I could lead her on to a number of things I greatly desired to know. Up to the time I had induced the housekeeper to show me through this strange house of my Uncle Godfrey's, the whole affair had been a mystery of lips which closed and faces which were averted at my approach. Even the coroner seemed unwilling to tell me just how my uncle had died.

"Did you understand she was going to live with him, sir?" asked Mrs. Malkin, looking hard at me.

I confined myself to a nod.

"Well, so did I. Yet, after a year, back she went."

"She went suddenly?" I suggested.

"So suddenly that I never knew a thing about it till after she was gone. I came to do my chores one day, and she was here. I came the next, and she had started back to Australia. That's how sudden she went."

"They must have had a falling out," I conjectured. "I suppose it because of the house."

"Maybe it was and maybe it wasn't."

"You know of other reasons?"

"I have eyes in my head," she said. "But I'm not going to talk about it. Shall we be getting on now, sir?"

I tried another lead:

"I hadn't seen my uncle in five years, you know. He seemed terribly changed. He was not an old man, by any means, yet when I saw him at the funeral—" I paused, expectantly.

To my relief, she responded readily:

"He looked that way for the last few months, especially that last week, I spoke to him about it, two days before—before it happened, sir—and told him he'd do well to see the doctor again. But he cut me off short. My sister took sick the same day, and I was called out of town. The next time I saw him, he was—"

She paused, and then went on, sobbing:

"To think of him lyin' there in that awful place, and callin' and callin' for me, as I know he must, and me not around to hear him!"

As she stopped again, suddenly, and threw a suspicious glance at me, I hastened to insert a matter-of-fact question:

"Did he appear ill on that last day?"

"Not so much ill, as—"

"Yes?" I prompted.

She was silent a long time, while I waited, afraid that some word of mine had brought back her former attitude of hostility. Then she seemed to make up her mind.

"I oughtn't to say another word. I've said too much, already. But you've been liberal with me, sir, and I know somethin' you've a right to be told, which I'm thinkin' no one else is agoin' to tell you. Look at the bottom of his study door a minute, sir."

I followed her direction.

What I saw led me to drop to my hands and knees the better to examine it.

"Why should he put a rubber strip on the bottom of his door?" I asked, getting up.

She replied with another enigmatical suggestion:

"Look at these, if you will, sir. You'll remember that he slept in this study. That was his bed, over there in the alcove."

"Bolts!" I exclaimed. And I reinforced sight with touch by shooting one of them back and forth a few times. "Double bolts on the inside of this bed-room door! An upstairs room, at that. What was the idea?"

Mrs. Malkin portentously shook her head and sighed, as one unburdening her mind.

"Only this can I say, sir; He was afraid of something—*terribly* afraid, sir. Something that came in the night."

"What was it?" I demanded.

"I don't know, sir."

"It was in the night that—it happened?" I asked.

She nodded; then, as if the prologue were over, as if she had prepared my mind sufficiently, she produced something from under her apron. She must have been holding it there all the time.

"It's his diary, sir. It was lying here on the floor. I saved it for you, before the police could get their hands on it."

I opened the little book. One of the sheets near the back was crumpled, and I glanced at it, idly. What I read there impelled me to slap the cover shut again.

"Did you read this?" I demanded.

She met my gaze, frankly.

311

"I looked into it, sir, just as you did—only just *looked* into it. Not for worlds would I do even that again!"

"I noticed some reference here to a slab in the cellar. What slab is that?"

"It covers an old, dried-up well, sir."

"Will you show it to me?"

"You can find it for yourself, sir, if you wish. I'm not goin' down there," she said, decidedly.

"Ah, well, I've seen enough for today," I told her. "I'll take the diary back to my hotel and read it."

I did not return to my hotel, however. In my one brief glance into the little book, I had seen something which had bitten into my soul, only a few words, but they had brought me very near to that queer, solitary man who had been my uncle.

I dismissed Mrs. Malkin, and remained in the study. There was the fitting place to read the diary he had left behind him.

His personality lingered like a vapor in that study. I settled into his deep morris chair, and turned it to catch the light from the single, narrow window—the light, doubtless, by which he had written much of his work on ento-mology .

That same struggling illumination played shadowy tricks with hosts of wall-crucified insects, which seemed engaged in a united effort to crawl upward in sinuous lines. Some of their number, impaled to the ceiling itself, peered quiveringly down on the aspiring multitude. The whole house, with its crisp dead, rustling in any vagrant breeze, brought back to my mind the hand that had pinned them, one by one, on wall and ceiling and furniture. A kindly hand, I reflected, though eccentric; one not to be turned aside from its single hobby.

When quiet, peering Uncle Godfrey went, there passed out another of those scientific enthusiasts, whose passion for exact truth in some one direction has extended the bounds of human knowledge. Could not his unquestioned merits have been balanced against his sin? Was it necessary to even-handed justice that he die face-to-face with Horror, struggling with the thing he most feared? I ponder the question still, though his body—strangely bruised—has been long at rest.

The entries in the little book began with the fifteenth of June. Everything before that date had been torn out. There, in the room where it had been written, I read my Uncle Godfrey's diary.

"It is done. I am trembling so that the words will hardly form under my pen, but my mind is collected. My course was for the best. Suppose I had married her? She would have been unwilling to live in this house. At the outset, her wishes would have come between me and my work, and that would have been only the beginning.

"As a married man, I could not have concentrated properly, I could not have surrounded myself with the atmosphere indispensable to the writing of my book. My scientific message would never have been delivered. As it is, though my heart is sore, I shall stifle these memories in work.

"I wish I had been more gentle with her, especially when she sank to her knees before me, tonight. She kissed my hand. I should not have repulsed her so roughly. In particular, my words could have been better chosen. I said to her, bitterly: 'Get up, and don't nuzzle my hand like a dog.' She rose, without a word, and left me. How was I to know that, within an hour—

"I am largely to blame. Yet, had I taken any other course afterward than the one I did, the authorities would have misunderstood."

Again, there followed a space from which the sheets had been torn; but from the sixteenth of July, all the pages were intact. Something had come over the writing, too. It was still precise and clear—my Uncle Godfrey's characteristic hand—but the letters were less firm. As the entries approached the end, this difference became still more marked.

Here follows, then, the whole of his story; or as much of it as will ever be known. I shall let his words speak for him, without further interruption:

"My nerves are becoming more seriously affected. If certain annoyances do not shortly cease, I shall be obliged to procure medical advice. To be more specific, I find myself, at times, obsessed by an almost uncontrollable desire to descend to the cellar and lift the slab over the old well.

"I never have yielded to the impulse, but it had persisted for minutes together with such intensity that I have had to put work aside; and literally hold myself down in my chair. This insane desire comes only in the dead of night, when its disquieting effect is heightened by the various noises peculiar to the house.

"For instance, there often is a draft of air along the hallways, which causes a rustling among the specimens impaled on the walls. Lately, too, there have been other nocturnal sounds, strongly suggestive of the busy clamor of rats and mice. This calls for investigation. I have been at considerable expense to make the house proof against rodents, which might destroy some of my best specimens. If some structural defect has opened a way for them, the situation must be corrected at once."

"July 17th. The foundations and cellar were examined today by a workman. He states positively that there is no place of ingress for rodents. He contented himself with looking at the slab over the old well, without lifting it."

"July 19th. While I was sitting in this chair, late last night, writing, the impulse to descend to the cellar suddenly came upon me with tremendous insistence. I yielded—which, perhaps, was as well. For at least I satisfied myself that the disquiet which possesses me has no external cause.

"The long journey through the hallways was difficult. Several times, I was keenly aware of the same sounds (perhaps I should say, the same IMPRESSIONS of sounds) that I had erroneously laid to rats. I am convinced now that they are more symptoms of my nervous condition. Further indications of this came in the fact that, as I opened the cellar door, the small noises abruptly ceased. There was no final scamper of tiny footfalls to suggest rats disturbed at their occupations.

"Indeed, I was conscious of a certain impression of expectant silence—as if the thing behind the noises, whatever it was, had paused to watch me enter its domain. Throughout my time in the cellar, I seemed surrounded by this same atmosphere. Sheer 'nerves,' of course.

"In the main, I held myself well under control. As I was about to leave the cellar, however, I unguardedly glanced back over my shoulder at the stone slab covering the old well. At that, a violent tremor came over me, and, losing all command, I rushed back up the cellar stairs, thence to this study. My nerves are playing me sorry tricks."

"July 30th. For more than a week, all has been well. The tone of my nerves seems distinctly better. Mrs. Malkin, who has remarked several times lately upon my paleness, expressed the conviction this afternoon that I am nearly my old self again. This is encouraging. I was beginning to fear that the severe strain of the past few months had left an indelible mark upon me. With continued health, I shall be able to finish my book by spring."

"July 31st. Mrs. Malkin remained rather late tonight in connection with some item of housework, and it was quite dark when I returned to my study from bolting the street door after her. The blackness of the upper hall, which the former owner of the house inexplicably failed to wire for electricity, was profound. As I came to the top of the second flight of stairs, something clutched at my foot, and, for an instant, almost pulled me back. I freed myself and ran to the study."

"August 3rd. Again the awful insistence. I sit here, with this diary upon my knee, and it seems that fingers of iron are tearing at me. I WILL NOT go! My nerves may be utterly unstrung again (I fear they are), but I am still their master."

"August 4th. I did not yield, last night. After a bitter struggle, which must have lasted nearly an hour, the desire to go to the cellar suddenly departed. I must not give in at any time."

"August 5th. Tonight, the rat noises (I shall call them that for want of a more appropriate term) are very noticeable. I went to the length of unbolting my door and stepping into the hallway to listen. After a few minutes, I seemed to be aware of something large and gray watching me from the darkness at the end of the passage. This is a bizarre statement, of course, but it exactly describes my impression. I withdrew hastily into the study, and bolted the door.

"Now that my nervous condition is so palpably affecting the optic nerve, I must not much longer delay seeing a specialist. But—how much shall I tell him?"

"August 8th. Several times, tonight, while sitting here at my work, I have seemed to hear soft footsteps, in the passage. 'Nerves' again, of course, or else some new trick of the wind among the specimens on the walls."

"August 9th. By my watch it is four o'clock in the morning. My mind is made up to record the experience I have passed through. Calmness may come that way.

"Feeling rather fatigued last night, from the strain of a weary day of re- search, I retired early. My sleep was more refreshing than usual, as it is likely to be when one is genuinely tired. I awakened, however (it must have been about an hour ago), with a start of tremendous violence.

"There was moonlight in the room. My nerves were 'on edge', but for a moment, I saw nothing unusual. Then, glancing toward the door, I perceived what appeared to be thin, white fingers, thrust under it—exactly as if some one outside the door were trying to attract my attention in that manner. I rose and turned on the light, but the fingers were gone.

"Needless to say, I did not open the door. I write the occurrence down, just as it took place, or as it seemed; but I can not trust myself to comment upon it."

"August 10th. Have fastened heavy rubber strips on the bottom of my bedroom door."

"August 15th. All quiet, for several nights. I am hoping that the rubber strips, being something definite and tangible, have had a salutary effect upon my nerves. Perhaps I shall not need to see a doctor."

"August 17th. Once more, I have been aroused from sleep. The interruptions seem to come always at the same hour—about three o'clock in the morning. I had been dreaming of the well in the cellar—the same dream, over and over—everything black except the slab, and a figure with bowed head and averted face sitting there. Also, I had vague dreams about a dog. Can it be that my last words to her have impressed that on my mind? I must pull myself together. In particular, I must not, under any pressure, yield, and visit the cellar after nightfall."

"August 18th. Am feeling much more hopeful. Mrs. Malkin remarked on it, while serving dinner. This improvement is due largely to a consultation I have had with Dr. Sartwell, the distinguished specialist in nervous diseases. I went into full details with him, excepting certain reservations. He scouted the idea that my experiences could be other than purely mental.

"When he recommended a change of scene (which I had been expecting), I told him positively that it was out of the question. He said then that, with the aid of a tonic and an occasional sleeping draft, I am likely to progress well enough at home. This is distinctly encouraging. I erred in not going to him at the start. Without doubt, most, if not all, of my hallucinations could have been averted.

"I have been suffering a needless penalty from my nerves for an action I took solely in the interests of science. I have no disposition to tolerate it further. From today, I shall report regularly to Dr. Sartwell."

"August 19th. Used the sleeping draft last night, with gratifying results. The doctor says I must repeat the dose for several nights, until my nerves are well under control again."

"August 21st. All well. It seems that I have found the way out—a very simple and prosaic way. I might have avoided much needless annoyance by seeking expert advice at the beginning. Before retiring, last night, I unbolted my study door and took a turn up and down the passage. I felt no trepidation. The place was as it used to be, before these fancies assailed me. A visit to the cellar after nightfall will be the test for my complete recovery, but I am not yet quite ready for that. Patience!"

"August 22nd. I have just read yesterday's entry, thinking to steady myself. It is cheerful—almost gay; and there are other entries like it in preceding pages. I am a mouse, in the grip of a cat. Let me have freedom for ever so short a time, and I begin to rejoice at my escape. Then the paw descends again.

"It is four in the morning—the usual hour. I retired rather late, last night, after administering the draft. Instead of the dreamless sleep, which heretofore has followed the use of the drug, the slumber into which I fell was punctuated by recurrent visions of the slab, with the bowed figure upon it. Also, I had one poignant dream in which the dog was involved.

"At length, I awakened, and reached mechanically for the light switch beside my bed. When my hand encountered nothing, I suddenly realized the truth. I was standing in my study, with my other hand upon the doorknob. It required only a moment, of course, to find the light and switch it on. I saw then that the bolt had been drawn back.

"The door was quite unlocked. My awakening must have interrupted me in the very act of opening it. I could hear something moving restlessly in the passage outside the door."

"August 23rd. I must beware of sleeping at night. Without confiding the fact to Dr. Sartwell, I have begun to take the drug in the daytime. At first, Mrs. Malkin's views on the subject were pronounced, but my explanations of 'doctor's orders' has silenced her. I am awake for breakfast and supper, and sleep in the hours between. She is leaving me, each evening, a cold lunch to be eaten at midnight."

"August 26th. Several times, I have caught myself nodding in my chair. The last time, I am sure that, on arousing, I perceived the rubber strip under the door bent inward, as if something were pushing it from the other side. I must not, under any circumstances, permit myself to fall asleep."

"September 2nd. Mrs. Malkin is to be away, because of her sister's illness. I can not help dreading her absence. Though she is here only in the daytime, even that companionship is very welcome."

"September 3rd. Let me put this into writing. The mere labor of composition has a soothing influence upon me. God knows, I need such an influence now, as never before!

"In spite of all my watchfulness, I fell asleep, tonight—across my bed. I must have been utterly exhausted. The dream I had was the one about the dog. I was patting the creature's head, over and over.

"I awoke, at last, to find myself in darkness, and in a standing position. There was a suggestion of chill and earthiness in the air. While I was drowsily trying to get my bearings, I became aware that something was muzzling my hand, as a dog might do.

"Still saturated with my dream, I was not greatly astonished. I extended my hand, to pat the dog's head. That brought me to my senses. I was standing in the cellar.

"THE THING BEFORE ME WAS NOT A DOG!

"I can not tell how I fled back up the cellar stairs. I know, however, that, as I turned, the slab was visible, in spite of the darkness, with something sitting upon it. All the way up the stairs, hands snatched at my feet."

This entry seemed to finish this diary, for blank pages followed it; but I remembered the crumpled sheet, near the back of the book. It was partly torn out, as if a hand had clutched it, convulsively. The writing on it, too, was markedly in contrast to the precise, albeit nervous penmanship of even the last entry I had perused. I was forced to hold the scrawl up to the light to decipher it. This is what I read:

"My hand keeps on writing, in spite of myself. What is this? I do not wish to write, but it compels me. Yes, yes, I will tell the truth, I will tell the truth."

A heavy blot followed, partly covering the writing. With difficulty, I made it out:

"The guilt is mine—mine, only. I loved her too well, yet I was unwilling to marry, though she entreated me on her knees—though she kissed my hand. I told her my scientific work came first. She did it, herself. I was not expecting that—I swear I was not expecting it. But I was afraid the authorities would misunderstand. So I took what seemed the best course. She had no friends here who would inquire.

"It is waiting outside my door. I FEEL it. It compels me, through my thoughts. My hand keeps on writing. I must not fall asleep. I must think only of what I am writing. I must—"

Then came the words I had seen when Mrs. Malkin had handed me the book. They were written very large. In places, the pen had dug through the paper. Though they were scrawled, I read them at a glance:

"Not the slab in the cellar! Not that! Oh, my God, anything but that! Anything—"

By what strange compulsion was the hand forced to write down what was in the brain; even to the ultimate thoughts; even to those final words?

The gray light from outside, slanting down through two dull little windows, sank into the sodden hole near the inner wall. The coroner and I stood in the cellar, but not too near the hole.

A small, demonstrative, dark man—the chief of detectives—stood a little apart from us, his eyes intent, his natural animation suppressed. We were watching the stooped shoulders of a police constable, who was angling in the well.

"See anything, Walters?" inquired the detective, raspingly.

The policeman shook his head.

The little man turned his questioning to me.

"You're quite sure?" he demanded.

"Ask the coroner. He saw the diary," I told him.

"I'm afraid there can be no doubt," the coroner confirmed, in his heavy, tired voice.

He was an old man, with lacklustre eyes. It had seemed best to me, on the whole, that he should read my uncle's diary. His position entitled him to all the available facts. What we were seeking in the well might especially concern him.

He looked at me opaquely now, while the policeman bent double again. Then he spoke—like one who reluctantly and at last does his duty. He nodded toward the slab of gray stone, which lay in the shadow to the left of the well.

"It doesn't seem very heavy, does it?" he suggested, in an undertone.

I shook my head. "Still, it's stone," I demurred. "A man would have to be rather strong to lift it."

"To lift it—yes." He glanced about the cellar. "Ah, I forgot," he said, abruptly. "It is in my office, as part of the evidence." He went on, half to himself: "A man—even though not very strong—could take a stick—for instance, the stick that is now in my office—and prop up the slab. If he wished to look into the well," he whispered.

The policeman interrupted, straightening again with a groan, and laying his electric torch beside the well.

"It's breaking my back," he complained. "There's dirt down there. It seems loose, but I can't get through it. Somebody'll have to go down."

The detective cut in:

"I'm lighter than you, Walters."

"I'm not afraid, sir."

"I didn't say you were," the little man snapped. "There's nothing down there, anyway—though we'll have to prove that, I suppose." He glanced truculently at me, but went on talking to the constable: "Rig the rope around me, and don't bungle the knot. I've no intention of falling into the place."

"There *is* something there," whispered the coroner, slowly, to me. His eyes left the little detective and the policeman, carefully tying and testing knots, and turned again to the square slab of stone.

"Suppose—while a man was looking into that hole—with the stone propped up—he should accidentally knock the prop away?" He was still whispering.

"A stone so light that he could prop it up wouldn't be heavy enough to kill him," I objected.

"No." He laid a hand on my shoulder. "Not to *kill* him—to *paralyze* him—if it struck the spine in a certain way. To render him helpless, but not unconscious. The *post mortem* would disclose that, through the bruises on the body."

The policeman and the detective had adjusted the knots to their satisfaction. They were bickering now as to the details of the descent.

"Would that cause death?" I whispered.

"You must remember that the housekeeper was absent for two days. In two days, even that pressure—" He stared at me hard, to make sure that I understood— "with the head down—"

Again the policeman interrupted:

"I'll stand at the well, if you gentlemen will grab the rope behind me. It won't be much of a pull. I'll take the brunt of it."

We let the little man down, with the electric torch strapped to his waist, and some sort of implement—a trowel or a small spade—in his hand. It seemed a long time before his voice, curiously hollow, directed us to stop. The hole must have been deep.

We braced ourselves. I was second, the coroner, last. The policeman relieved his strain somewhat by snagging the rope against the edge of the well, but I marveled, nevertheless, at the ease with which he held the weight. Very little of it came to me.

A noise like muffled scratching reached us from below. Occasionally, the rope shook and shifted slightly at the edge of the hole. At last, the detective's hollow voice spoke.

"What does he say?" the coroner demanded.

The policeman turned his square, dogged face toward us.

"I think he's found something," he explained.

The rope jerked and shifted again. Some sort of struggle seemed to be going on below. The weight suddenly increased, and as suddenly lessened, as if something had been grasped, then had managed to elude the grasp and slip away. I could catch the detective's rapid breathing now; also the sound of inarticulate speech in his hollow voice.

The next words I caught came more clearly. They were a command to pull up. At the same moment, the weight on the rope grew heavier, and remained so.

The policeman's big shoulders began straining, rhythmically.

"All together," he directed. "Take it easy. Pull when I do."

321

Slowly, the rope passed through our hands. With each fresh grip that we took, a small section of it dropped to the floor behind us. I began to feel the strain. I could tell from the coroner's labored breathing that he felt it more, being an old man. The policeman, however, seemed untiring.

The rope tightened suddenly, and there was an ejaculation from below—just below. Still holding fast, the policeman contrived to stoop over and look. He translated the ejaculation for us.

"Let down a little. He's struck with it against the side."

We slackened the rope, until the detective's voice gave us the word again.

The rhythmic tugging continued. Something dark appeared, quite abruptly, at the top of the hole. My nerves leapt in spite of me, but it was merely the top of the detective's head—his dark hair. Something white came next—his pale face, with staring eyes. Then his shoulders, bowed forward, the better to support what was in his arms. Then—

I looked away; but, as he laid his burden down at the side of the well, the detective whispered to us:

"He had her covered up with dirt—covered up . . ."

He began to laugh—a little, high cackle, like a child's—until the coroner took him by the shoulders and deliberately shook him. Then the policeman led him out of the cellar.

It was not then, but afterward, that I put my question to the coroner.

"Tell me," I demanded. "People pass there at all hours. Why didn't my uncle call for help?"

"I have thought of that," he replied. "I believe he did call. I think, probably, he screamed. But his head was down, and he couldn't raise it. His screams must have been swallowed up in the well."

"You are sure he didn't murder her?" He had given me that assurance before but I wished it again.

"Almost sure," he declared. "Though it was on his account, undoubtedly, that she killed herself. Few of us are punished as accurately for our sins as he was."

One should be thankful, even for crumbs of comfort. I am thankful.

But there are times when my uncle's face rises before me. After all, we were the same blood, our sympathies had much in common; under any given circumstances, our thoughts and feelings must have been largely the same. I seem to see him in that final death march along the unlighted passageway—obeying an imperative summons—going on, step by step—down the stairway to the first floor, down the cellar stairs—at last, lifting the slab.

I try not to think of the final expiation. Yet *was* it final? I wonder. Did the last Door of all, when it opened, find him willing to pass through? Or was Something waiting beyond *that* Door?

IN THE OCTOBER 1923 issue of *Weird Tales*, Lovecraft wrote: "I lately read the May *Weird Tales*, and congratulate you on Mr. Humphreys' 'The Floor Above' (for a moment I had a shiver which the author didn't intend— I thought he was going to use an idea which I am planning to use myself!! But it wasn't so, after all)." Nothing is known about M. L. Humphreys, but the byline is probably a pseudonym. It appears only on "The Floor Above" in the May 1923 *Weird Tales*, and not at all in other contemporary magazines. When the story was reprinted in *Weird Tales* in June 1933, the last name is spelled "Humphries." The tale is accomplished enough that one suspects that this story isn't likely to be the only one written by its author.

THE FLOOR ABOVE
by M. L. Humphreys

September 17, 1922.—I sat down to breakfast this morning with a good appetite. The heat seemed over, and a cool wind blew in from my garden, where chrysanthemums were already budding. The sunshine streamed into the room and fell pleasantly on Mrs. O'Brien's broad face as she brought in the eggs and coffee. For a supposedly lonely old bachelor the world seemed to me a pretty good place. I was buttering my third set of waffles when the housekeeper again appeared, this time with the mail.

I glanced carelessly at the three or four letters beside my plate. One of them bore a strangely familiar handwriting. I gazed at it a minute, then seized it with a beating heart. Tears almost came into my eyes. There was no doubt about it—it was Arthur Barker's handwriting! Shaky and changed, to be sure, but ten years have passed since I have seen Arthur, or, rather, since his mysterious disappearance.

For ten years I have not had a word from him. His people know no more than I what has become of him, and long ago we gave him up for dead. He vanished without leaving a trace behind him. It seemed to me, too, that with him vanished the last shreds of my youth. For Arthur was my dearest friend in that happy time. We were boon companions, and many a mad prank we played together.

And now, after ten years of silence, Arthur was writing to me!

The envelope was postmarked Baltimore. Almost reluctantly—for I feared what it might contain—I passed my finger under the flap and opened it. It held a single sheet of paper torn from a pad. But it was Arthur's writing:

> "*Dear Tom:*
> "*Old man, can you run down to see me for a few days? I'm afraid I'm in a bad way.*
>
> > "*Arthur.*"

Scrawled across the bottom was the address, 536 N. Marathon Street.

I have often visited Baltimore, but I can not recall a street of that name.

Of course I shall go. . . . But what a strange letter after ten years! There is something almost uncanny about it.

I shall go tomorrow evening. I can not possibly get off before then.

September 18—I am leaving tonight. Mrs. O'Brien has packed my two suitcases, and everything is in readiness for my departure. Ten minutes ago I handed her the keys and she went off tearfully. She has been sniffling all day and I have been perplexed, for a curious thing occurred this morning.

It was about Arthur's letter. Yesterday, when I had finished reading it, I took it to my desk and placed it in a small compartment together with other personal papers. I remember distinctly that it was on top, with a lavender card from my sister directly underneath. This morning I went to get it. It was gone.

There was the lavender card exactly where I had seen it, but Arthur's letter had completely disappeared. I turned everything upside down, then called Mrs. O'Brien and we both searched, but in vain. Mrs. O'Brien, in spite of all I could say, took it upon herself to feel that I suspected her. . . . But what could have become of it? Fortunately I remembered the address.

September 19—I have arrived. I have seen Arthur. Even now he is in the next room and I am supposed to be preparing for bed. But something tells me I shall not sleep a wink this night. I am strangely wrought up, though there is not the shadow of an excuse for my excitement. I should be rejoicing to have found my friend again. And yet—

I reached Baltimore this morning at eleven o'clock. The day was warm and beautiful, and I loitered outside the station a few minutes before calling a taxi. The driver seemed well acquainted with the street I gave him, and we rolled off across the bridge.

As I drew near my destination, I began to feel anxious and afraid. But the ride lasted longer than I expected—Marathon Street seemed to be located in the suburbs of the city. At last we turned into a dusty street, paved only in patches and lined with linden and aspen trees. The fallen leaves crunched beneath the tires. The September sun beat down with a white intensity. The taxi drew up before a house in the middle of a block that boasted not more than six dwellings. One each side of the house was a vacant lot, and it was set far back at the end of a long narrow yard crowded with trees.

I paid the driver, opened the gate and went in. The trees were so thick that not until I was half-way up the path did I get a good view of the house. It was three stories high, built of brick, in fairly good repair, but lonely and deserted-looking. The blinds were closed in all of the windows with the exception of two, one on the first, one on the second floor. Not a sign of life anywhere, not a cat nor a milk-bottle to break the monotony of leaves that carpeted the porch.

But, overcoming my feeling of uneasiness, I resolutely set my suitcases on the porch, caught at the old-fashioned bell, and gave an energetic jerk. A startling peal jangled through the silence. I waited, but there was no answer.

After a minute I rang again. Then from the interior I heard a queer dragging sound, as if some one was coming slowly down the hall. The knob was turned and the door opened. I saw before me an old woman, wrinkled, withered, and filmy-eyed, who leaned on a crutch.

"Does Mr. Barker live here?" I asked.

She nodded, staring at me in a curious way, but made no move to invite me in.

"Well, I've come to see him," I said. "I'm a friend of his. He sent for me."

At that she drew slightly aside.

"He's upstairs," she said in a cracked voice that was little more than a whisper. "I can't show you up. Hain't been up a stair now in ten years."

"That's all right," I replied, and, seizing my suitcases, I strode down the long hall.

"At the head of the steps," came the whispering voice behind me. "The door at the end of the hall."

I climbed the cold dark stairway, passed along the short hall at the top, and stood before a closed door. I knocked.

"Come in." It was Arthur's voice, and yet—not his.

I opened the door and saw Arthur sitting on a couch, his shoulders hunched over, his eyes raised to mine.

After all, ten years had not changed him so much. As I remembered him, he was of medium height, inclined to be stout, and ruddy-faced, with keen gray eyes. He was still stout; but had lost his color and his eyes had dulled.

"And where have you been all this time?" I demanded, when the first greetings were over.

"Here," he answered.

"In this house?"

"Yes."

"But why didn't you let us hear from you?"

He seemed to be making an effort to speak.

"What did it matter? I didn't suppose anyone cared."

Perhaps it was my imagination, but I could not get rid of the thought that Arthur's pale eyes, fixed tenaciously upon my face, were trying to tell me something, something quite different from what his lips said.

I felt chilled. Although the blinds were open, the room was almost darkened by the branches of the trees that pressed against the window. Arthur had not given me his hand, had seemed troubled to know how to make me welcome. Yet of one thing I was certain: He needed me and he wanted me to know he needed me.

As I took a chair I glanced about the room. It was a typical lodging-house room, medium-sized, with flowered wallpaper, worn matting, nondescript rugs, a wash-stand in one corner, a chiffonier in another, a table in the center, two or three chairs, and the couch which evidently served Arthur as a bed. But it was cold, strangely cold for such a warm day.

Arthur's eyes had wandered uneasily to my suitcases. He made an effort to drag himself to his feet

"Your room is back here," he said, with a motion of his thumb.

"No, wait," I protested "Let's talk about yourself first. What's wrong?"

"I've been sick."

"Haven't you a doctor? If not, I'll get one."

At this he started up with the first sign of animation he had shown.

"No, Tom, don't do it Doctors can't help me now. Besides, I hate them. I'm afraid of them."

His voice trailed away, and I took pity on his agitation. I decided to let the question of doctors drop for the moment.

"As you say," I assented carelessly.

Without more ado, I followed him into my room, which adjoined his and was furnished in much the same fashion. But there were two windows, one on each side, looking out on the vacant lots. Consequently there was more light, for which I was thankful. In a far corner I noticed a door, heavily bolted.

"There's one more room," said Arthur, as I deposited my belongings, "one that you'll like. But we'll have to go through the bathroom."

Groping our way through the musty bathroom, in which a tiny jet of gas was flickering, we stepped into a large, almost luxurious chamber. It was a library, well-furnished, carpeted, and surrounded by shelves fairly bulging with books. But for the chillness and bad light, it was perfect. As I moved about, Arthur followed me with his eyes.

"There are some rare works on botany—"

I had already discovered them, a set of books that I would've given much to own. I could not contain my joy.

"You won't be so bored browsing around in here—"

In spite of my preoccupation, I pricked up my ears. In that monotonous voice there was no sympathy with my joy. It was cold and tired.

When I had satisfied my curiosity we returned to the front room, and Arthur flung himself, or rather fell, upon the couch. It was nearly five o'clock and quite dark. As I lighted the gas, I heard a sound below as of somebody thumping on the wall.

"That's the old woman," Arthur explained. "She cooks my meals, but she's too lame to bring them up."

He made a feeble attempt at rising, but I saw he was worn out.

"Don't stir," I warned him. "I'll bring up your food tonight."

To my surprise, I found the dinner appetizing and well-cooked, and, in spite of the fact that I did not like the looks of the old woman, I ate with relish. Arthur barely touched a few spoonfuls of soup to his lips and absently crumbled some bread in his plate.

Directly I had carried off the dishes, he wrapped his reddish-brown dressing gown about him, stretched out at full length on the couch, and asked me to turn out the gas. When I had complied with his request, I again heard his weak voice asking if I had everything I needed.

"Everything," I assured him, and then there was unbroken silence.

I went to my room, finally, closed the door, and here I am sitting restlessly between the two back windows that look out on the vacant lots.

I have unpacked my clothes and turned down the bed, but I can not make up my mind to retire. If the truth be told, I hate to put out the light. . . . There is something disturbing in the way the dry leaves tap on the panes. And my heart is sad when I think of Arthur.

I have found my old friend, but he is no longer my old friend. Why does he fix his pale eyes so strangely on my face? What does he wish to tell me?

But these are morbid thoughts. I will put them out of my I head. I will go to bed and get a good night's rest. And tomorrow I will wake up finding everything right and as it should be.

September 26—I have been here a week today, and have settled down to this queer existence as if I had never known another. The day after my arrival I discovered that the third volume of the botanical series was done in Latin, which I have set myself the task of translating. It is absorbing work, and when I have buried myself in one of the deep chairs by the library table, the hours fly fast.

For health's sake I force myself to walk a few miles every day. I have tried to prevail on Arthur to do likewise, but he, who used to be so active, now refuses to budge from the house. No wonder he is literally blue! For it is a fact that his complexion, and the shadows about his eyes and temples, are decidedly blue.

What does he do with himself all day? Whenever I enter his room, he is lying on the couch, a book beside him, which he never reads. He does not seem to suffer pain, for he never complains. After several ineffectual attempts to get medical aid for him, I have given up mentioning the subject of doctor. I feel that his trouble is more mental than physical.

September 28—A rainy day. It has been coming down in floods since dawn. And I got a queer turn this afternoon.

As I could not get out for my walk, I spent the morning staging a general house-cleaning. It was time! Dust and dirt everywhere. The bathroom, which has no window and is lighted by gas, was fairly overrun with water-bugs and roaches. Of course I did not penetrate to Arthur's room, but I heard no sound from him as I swept and dusted.

I made a good dinner and settled down in the library, feeling quite cozy. The rain came down steadily and it had grown so cold I decided to make a fire later on. But once I had gathered my tablets and notebooks about me I forgot the cold.

I remember I was on the subject of the *Aster trifolium*, a rare variety seldom found in this country. Turning a page, I came upon a specimen of this very variety, dried, pressed flat, and pasted to the margin. Above it, in Arthur's handwriting, I read: *September 27, 1912*.

I was bending close to examine it, when I felt a vague fear. It seemed to me that some one was in the room and was watching me. Yet I had not heard the door open, nor seen anyone enter. I turned sharply and saw Arthur, wrapped in his reddish-brown dressing-gown, standing at my very elbow.

He was smiling—smiling for the first time since my arrival, and his dun eyes were bright. But I did not like that smile. In spite of myself I jerked away from him. He pointed at the aster.

"It grew in the front yard under a linden tree. I found it yesterday. "

"Yesterday!" I shouted, my nerves on edge. "Good Lord, man! Look! It was ten years ago!"

The smile faded from his face.

"Ten years ago," he repeated thickly. "*Ten years ago?*"

Five o'clock. Dusk is falling. O God! What has come over me? Am I the same man that went out of this house three hours ago? And what has happened? . . .

I had a splendid walk, and was striding homeward in a fine glow. But as I turned the corner and came in sight of the house, it was as if I looked at death itself. I could hardly drag myself up the stairs, and when I peered into the shadowy chamber, and saw the man hunched up on the couch, with his eyes fixed intently on my face, I could have screamed like a woman. I wanted to fly, to rush out into the clear cold air and run—to run and never come back! But I controlled myself, forced my feet to carry me to my room.

There is a weight of hopelessness at my heart. The darkness is advancing, swallowing up everything, but I have not the will to light the gas. . . .

Now there is a flicker in the front room. I am a fool; I must pull myself together. Arthur is lighting up, and downstairs I can hear the thumping that announces dinner. . . .

It is a queer thought that comes to me now, but it is odd I have not noticed it before. We are about to sit down to our evening meal. Arthur will eat practically nothing, for he has no appetite. Yet he remains stout. It can not be healthy fat, but even at that it seems to me that a man who eats as little as he does would become a living skeleton.

October 5—Positively, I must see a doctor about myself, or soon I shall be a nervous wreck. I am acting like a child. Last night I lost all control and played the coward.

I had gone to bed early, tired out from a hard day's work. It was raining again, and as I lay in bed I watched the little rivulets trickling down the panes. Lulled by the sighing of the wind among the leaves, I fell asleep.

I awoke (how long afterward I can not say) to feel a cold hand laid on my arm. For a moment I lay paralyzed with terror. I would have cried aloud, but I had no voice. At last I managed to sit up, to shake the hand off. I reached for the matches and lighted the gas.

It was Arthur who stood by my bed—Arthur wrapped in his eternal reddish- brown dressing-gown. He was excited. His blue face had a yellow tinge, and his eyes gleamed in the light.

"Listen!" he whispered

I listened but heard nothing.

"Don't you hear it?" he gasped, and he pointed upward.

"Upstairs?" I stammered. "Is there somebody upstairs?"

I strained my ears, and at last I fancied I could hear a fugitive sound like the light tapping of footsteps.

"It must be somebody walking about up there," I suggested.

"No!" he cried in a sharp rasping voice. "No! It is nobody walking about up there!"

And he fled into his room.

For a long time I lay trembling, afraid to move. But at last, fearing for Arthur, I got up and crept to his door. He was lying on the couch, with his face in the moonlight, apparently asleep.

October 6—I had a talk with Arthur today. Yesterday I could not bring myself to speak of the previous night's happening, but all of this nonsense must be cleared away.

We were in the library. A fire was burning in the grate, and Arthur had his feet on the fender. The slippers he wears are as objectionable to me as his dressing-gown. They are felt slippers, old and worn, and frayed around the edges as if they had been gnawed by rats. I can not imagine why he does not get a new pair.

"Say, old man," I began abruptly, "do you own this house?"

He nodded.

"Don't you rent any of it?"

"Downstairs—to Mrs. Harlan."

"But upstairs?"

He hesitated, then shook his head.

"No, it's inconvenient. There's only a peculiar way to get upstairs."

I was struck by this.

"By Jove! you're right. Where's the staircase?"

He looked me full in the eyes.

"Don't you remember seeing a bolted door in a corner of your room? The staircase runs from that door."

I did remember it, and somehow the memory made me uncomfortable. I said no more and decided not to refer to what had happened that night. It occurred to me that Arthur might have been walking in his sleep.

October 8—When I went for my walk on Tuesday I dropped in and saw Doctor Lorraine, who is an old friend. He expressed some surprise at my rundown condition and wrote me a prescription.

I am planning to go home next week. How pleasant it will be to walk in my garden and listen to Mrs. O'Brien singing in the kitchen!

October 9—Perhaps I had better postpone my trip. I casually mentioned it to Arthur this morning.

He was lying relaxed on the sofa, but when I spoke of leaving he sat up as straight as a bolt. His eyes fairly blazed.

"No, Tom, don't go!" There was terror in his voice, and such pleading that it wrung my heart.

"You've stood it alone here ten years," I protested. "And now—"

"It's not that," he said. "But if you go, you will never come back."

"Is that all the faith you have in me?"

"I've got faith, Tom. But if you go, you'll never come back."

I decided that I must humor the vagaries of a sick man.

"All right," I agreed. "I'll not go. Anyway, not for some time."

October 12—What is it that hangs over this house like a cloud? For I can no longer deny that there *is* something—something indescribably oppressive. It seems to pervade the whole, neighborhood.

Are all the houses on this block vacant? If not, why do I never see children playing in the street? Why are passers-by so rare? And why, when from the front window I do catch a glimpse of one, is he hastening away as fast as possible?

I am feeling blue again. I know that I need a change, and this morning I told Arthur definitely that I was going.

To my surprise, he made no objection. In fact, he murmured a word of assent and smiled. He smiled as he smiled in the library that morning when he pointed at the *Aster trifolium.* And I don't like that smile. Anyway, it is settled. I shall go next week, Thursday, the 19th.

October 13—I had a strange dream last night. Or was it a dream? It was so vivid. . . . All day long I have been seeing it over and over again.

In my dream I thought that I was lying there in my bed. The moon was shining brightly into the room, so that each piece of furniture stood out distinctly. The bureau is so placed that when I am lying on my back, with my head high on the pillow, I can see full into the mirror.

I thought I was lying in this manner and staring into the mirror. In this way I saw the bolted door in the far corner of the room. I tried to keep my mind off it, to think of something else, but it drew my eyes like a magnet.

It seemed to me that some one was in the room, a vague figure that I could not recognize. It approached the door and caught at the bolts. It dragged at them and struggled, but in vain—they would not give way.

Then it turned and showed me its agonized face. It was Arthur! I recognized his reddish-brown dressing-gown.

I sat up in bed and cried to him, but he was gone. I ran to his room, and there he was, stretched out in the moonlight asleep. It must have been a dream.

October 15—We are having Indian Summer weather now—almost oppressively warm. I have been wandering about all day, unable to settle down to anything. This morning I felt so lonesome that when I took the breakfast dishes down, I tried to strike up a conversation with Mrs. Harlan.

Hitherto I have found her as solemn and uncommunicative as the Sphinx, but as she took the tray from my hands, her wrinkles broke into the semblance of a smile. Positively at that moment it seemed to me that she resembled Arthur. Was it her smile, or the expression of her eyes? Has she, also, something to tell me?

"Don't you get lonesome here?" I asked her sympathetically.

She shook her head. "No, sir, I'm used to it now. I couldn't stand it anywhere else."

"And do you expect to go on living here the rest of your life?"

"That may not be very long, sir," she said, and smiled again.

Her words were simple enough, but the way she looked at me when she uttered them seemed to give them a double meaning. She hobbled away, and I went upstairs and wrote Mrs. O'Brien to expect me early on the morning of the 19th.

October 18—Ten a.m.—Am catching the twelve o'clock train tonight. Thank God, I had the resolution to get away! I believe another week of this life would drive me mad. And perhaps Arthur is right—perhaps I shall never come back.

I ask myself if I have become such a weakling as that, to desert him when he needs me most. I don't know. I don't recognize myself any longer.

. . .

But of course I will be back. There is the translation, for one thing, which is coming along famously. I could never forgive myself for dropping it at the most vital point.

As for Arthur, when I return I intend to give in to him no longer. I will make myself master here and cure him against his will. Fresh air, change of scene, a good doctor, these are the things he needs.

But what is his malady? Is it the influence of this house that has fallen on him like a blight? One might imagine so, since it is having the same effect on me.

Yes, I have reached that point where I no longer sleep. At night I lie awake and try to keep my eyes off the mirror across the room. But in the end I always find myself staring into it—watching the door with the heavy bolts. I long to rise from the bed and draw back the bolts, but I'm afraid.

How slowly the day goes by! The night will never come!

Nine p.m.—Have packed my suitcases and put the room in order. Arthur must be asleep. . . . I'm afraid the parting from him will be painful. I shall leave here at eleven o'clock in order to give myself plenty of time. . . . It is beginning to rain. . . .

October 19—At last! It has come! I am mad! I knew it! I felt it creeping on me all the time! Have I not lived in this house a month? Have I not seen? ... To have seen what I have seen, to have lived for a month as I have lived, one must be mad. . . .

It was ten o'clock. I was waiting impatiently for the last hour to pass. I had seated myself in a rocking-chair by the bed, my suitcases beside me, my back to the mirror. The rain no longer fell. I must have dozed off.

But all at once I was wide awake, my heart beating furiously. Something had touched me. I leapt to my feet, and, as I turned sharply, my eyes fell upon the mirror. In it I saw the door just as I had seen it the other night, and the figure fumbling with the bolt. I wheeled around, but there was nothing there.

I told myself that I was dreaming again, that Arthur was asleep in his bed. But I trembled as I opened the door of his room and peered in. The room was empty, the bed not even crumpled. Lighting a match, I groped my way through the bathroom into the library.

The moon had come from under a cloud and was pouring in a silvery flood through the windows, but Arthur was not there. I stumbled back into my room.

The moon was there, too. . . . And the door, the door in the corner was half open. The bolt had been drawn. In the darkness I could just make out a flight of steps that wound upward.

I could no longer hesitate. Striking another match, I climbed the back stairway.

When I reached the top I found myself in total darkness, for the blinds were tightly closed. Realizing that the room was probably a duplicate of the one below, I felt along the wall until I came to the gas jet. For a moment the flame flickered, then burned bright and clear.

O God! what was it I saw? A table, thick with dust, and something wrapped in a reddish-brown dressing-gown, that sat with its elbows propped upon it.

How long had it been sitting there, that it had grown more dry than the dust upon the table! For how many thousands of days and nights had the flesh rotted from that grinning skull!

In its bony fingers it still clutched a pencil. In front of it lay a sheet of scratched paper, yellow with age. With trembling fingers I brushed away the dust. It was dated October 19, 1912. It read:

"Dear Tom:

"Old man, can you run down to see me for a few days? I'm afraid I'm in a bad way—"

H.F. ARNOLD published only two stories in *Weird Tales*. "The Night Wire" appeared in September 1926, and it was followed by "The City of Iron Cubes," a two-part serial, which appeared in March and April 1929. Arnold also published one science fiction serial, "When Atlantis Was," in *Amazing Stories* in 1937. Biographical information on Arnold has been difficult to obtain, but the writer H. F. Arnold appears to have been Henry Ferris Arnold (1902-1963), an Illinois native who worked as a press agent for the motion picture industry in Los Angeles in the late 1920s and 1930s.

THE NIGHT WIRE
by H. F. Arnold

"New York, September 30 CP FLASH

"Ambassador Holliwell died here today. The end came suddenly as the ambassador was alone in his study. . . . "

There is something ungodly about these night wire jobs. You sit up here on the top floor of a skyscraper and listen in to the whispers of a civilization. New York, London, Calcutta, Bombay, Singapore—they're your next-door neighbors after the street lights go dim and the world has gone to sleep.

Along in the quiet hours between two and four, the receiving operators doze over their sounders and the news comes in. Fires and disasters and suicides. Murders, crowds, catastrophes. Sometimes an earthquake with a casualty list as long as your arm. The night wire man takes it down almost in his sleep, picking it off on his typewriter with one finger.

Once in a long time you prick up your ears and listen. You've heard of some one you knew in Singapore, Halifax or Paris, long ago. Maybe they've been promoted, but more probably they've been murdered or drowned. Perhaps they just decided to quit and took some bizarre way out. Made it interesting enough to get in the news.

But that doesn't happen often. Most of the time you sit and doze and tap, tap on your typewriter and wish you were home in bed.

Sometimes, though, queer things happen. One did the other night, and I haven't got over it yet. I wish I could.

You see, I handle the night manager's desk in a western seaport town; what the name is, doesn't matter.

There is, or rather was, only one night operator on my staff, a fellow named John Morgan, about forty years of age, I should say, and a sober, hard-working sort.

He was one of the best operators I ever knew, what is known as a "double" man. That means he could handle two instruments at once and type the stories on different typewriters at the same time. He was one of the three men I ever knew who could do it consistently, hour after hour, and never make a mistake.

Generally, we used only one wire at night, but sometimes, when it was late and the news was coming fast, the Chicago and Denver stations would open a second wire, and then Morgan would do his stuff. He was a wizard, a mechanical automatic wizard which functioned marvelously but was without imagination.

On the night of the sixteenth he complained of feeling tired. It was the first and last time I had ever heard him say a word about himself, and I had known him for three years.

It was just three o'clock and we were running only one wire. I was nodding over the reports at my desk and not paying much attention to him, when he spoke.

"Jim," he said, "does it feel close in here to you?"

"Why, no, John," I answered, "but I'll open a window if you like."

"Never mind," he said. "I reckon I'm just a little tired."

That was all that was said, and I went on working. Every ten minutes or so I would walk over and take a pile of copy that had stacked up neatly beside the typewriter as the messages were printed out in triplicate.

It must have been twenty minutes after he spoke that I noticed he had opened up the other wire and was using both typewriters. I thought it was a little unusual, as there was nothing very "hot" coming in. On my next trip I picked up the copy from both machines and took it back to my desk to sort out the duplicates.

The first wire was running out the usual sort of stuff and I just looked over it hurridly. Then I turned to the second pile of copy. I remembered it particularly because the story was from a town I had never heard of: "Xebico." Here is the dispatch. I saved a duplicate of it from our files:

"Xebico, Sept 16 CP BULLETIN

"The heaviest mist in the history of the city settled over the town at 4 o'clock yesterday afternoon. All traffic has stopped and the mist hangs like a pall over everything. Lights of ordinary intensity fail to pierce the fog, which is constantly growing heavier.

"Scientists here are unable to agree as to the cause, and the local weather bureau states that the like has never occurred before in the history of the city.

"At 7 p.m. last night the municipal authorities—
(more)"

That was all there was. Nothing out of the ordinary at a bureau headquarters, but, as I say, I noticed the story because of the name of the town.

It must have been fifteen minutes later that I went over for another batch of copy. Morgan was slumped down in his chair and had switched his green electric light shade so that the gleam missed his eyes and hit only the top of the two typewriters.

Only the usual stuff was in the righthand pile, but the lefthand batch carried another story from Xebico. All press dispatches come in "takes," meaning that parts of many different stories are strung along together, perhaps with but a few paragraphs of each coming through at a time. This second story was marked "add fog." Here is the copy:

"At 7 p.m. the fog had increased noticeably. All lights were now invisible and the town was shrouded in pitch darkness.

"As a peculiarity of the phenomenon, the fog is accompanied by a sickly odor, comparable to nothing yet experienced here."

Below that in customary press fashion was the hour, 3:27, and the initials of the operator, JM.

There was only one other story in the pile from the second wire. Here it is:

"2nd add Xebico Fog.

"Accounts as to the origin of the mist differ greatly. Among the most unusual is that of the sexton of the local church, who groped his way to

338

headquarters in a hysterical condition and declared that the fog originated in the village churchyard.

" 'It was first visible as a soft gray blanket clinging to the earth above the graves,' he stated. 'Then it began to rise, higher and higher. A subterranean breeze seemed to blow it in billows, which split up and then joined together again.

" 'Fog phantoms, writhing in anguish, twisted the mist into queer forms and figures. And then, in the very thick midst of the mass, something moved.

" 'I turned and ran from the accursed spot. Behind me I heard screams coming from the houses bordering on the graveyard.'

"Although the sexton's story is generally discredited, a party has left to investigate. Immediately after telling his story, the sexton collapsed and is now in a local hospital, unconscious."

Queer story, wasn't it. Not that we aren't used to it, for a lot of unusual stories come in over the wire. But for some reason or other, perhaps because it was so quiet that night, the report of the fog made a great impression on me.

It was almost with dread that I went over to the waiting piles of copy. Morgan did not move, and the only sound in the room was the tap-tap of the sounders. It was ominous, nerve-racking.

There was another story from Xebico in the pile of copy. I seized on it anxiously.

"New Lead Xebico Fog CP

"The rescue party which went out at 11 p.m. to investigate a weird story of the origin of a fog which, since late yesterday, has shrouded the city in darkness, has failed to return. Another and larger party has been dispatched.

"Meanwhile, the fog has, if possible, grown heavier. It seeps through the cracks in the doors and fills the atmosphere with a depressing odor of decay. It is oppressive, terrifying, bearing with it a subtle impression of things long dead.

"Residents of the city have left their homes and gathered in the local church, where the priests are holding services of prayer. The scene is beyond description. Grown folk and children are alike terrified and many are almost beside themselves with fear.

"Amid the whisps of vapor which partly veil the church auditorium, an old priest is praying for the welfare of his flock. They alternately wail and cross themselves.

"From the outskirts of the city may be heard cries of unknown voices. They echo through the fog in queer uncadenced minor keys. The sounds resemble nothing so much as wind whistling through a gigantic tunnel. But the night is calm and there is no wind. The second rescue party— (more)"

I am a calm man and never in a dozen years spent with the wires, have I been known to become excited, but despite myself I rose from my chair and walked to the window.

Could I be mistaken, or far down in the canyons of the city beneath me did I see a faint trace of fog? Pshaw! It was all imagination.

In the pressroom the click of the sounders seemed to have raised the tempo of their tune. Morgan alone had not stirred from his chair. His head sunk between his shoulders, he tapped the dispatches out on the typewriters with one finger of each hand.

He looked asleep, Maybe he was—but no; endlessly, efficiently, the two machines rattled off line after line, as relentlessly and effortlessly as death itself. There was something about the monotonous movement of the typewriter keys that fascinated me. I walked over and stood behind his chair, reading over his shoulder the type as it came into being, word by word.

Ah, here was another:

"Flash Xebico CP

"There will be no more bulletins from this office. The impossible has happened. No messages have come into this room for twenty minutes. We are cut off from the outside and even the streets below us.

"I will stay with the wire until the end.

"It is the end, indeed. Since 4 p.m. yesterday the fog has hung over the city. Following reports from the sexton of the local church, two rescue parties were sent out to investigate conditions on the outskirts of the city. Neither party has ever returned nor was any word received from them. It is quite certain now that they will never return.

"From my instrument I can gaze down on the city beneath me. From the position of this room on the thirteenth floor, nearly the entire city can be seen. Now I can see only a thick blanket of blackness where customarily are lights and life.

"I fear greatly that the wailing cries heard constantly from the outskirts of the city are the death cries of the inhabitants. They are constantly increasing in volume and are approaching the center of the city.

"The fog yet hangs over everything. If possible, it is even heavier than before, but the conditions have changed. Instead of an opaque, impenetrable wall of odorous vapor, there now swirls and writhes a shapeless mass in contortions of almost human agony. Now and again the mass parts and I catch a brief glimpse of the streets below.

"People are running to and fro, screaming in despair. A vast bedlam of sound flies up to my window, and above all is the immense whistling of unseen and unfelt winds.

"The fog has again swept over the city and the whistling is coming closer and closer.

"It is now directly beneath me.

"God! An instant ago the mist opened and I caught a glimpse of the streets below.

"The fog is not simply vapor—it lives! By the side of each moaning and weeping human is a companion figure, an aura of strange and vari-colored hues. How the shapes cling! Each to a living thing!

"The men and women are down. Flat on their faces. The fog figures caress them lovingly. They are kneeling beside them. They are—but I dare not tell it.

"The prone and writhing bodies have been stripped of their clothing. They are being consumed—piecemeal.

"A merciful wall of hot, steamy vapor has swept over the whole scene. I can see no more.

"Beneath me the wall of vapor is changing colors. It seems to be lighted by internal fires. No, it isn't. I have made a mistake. The colors are from above, reflections from the sky.

"Look up! Look up! The whole sky is in flames. Colors as yet unseen by man or demon. The flames are moving; they have started to intermix; the colors rearrange themselves. They are so brilliant that my eyes burn, yet they are a long way off.

"Now they have begun to swirl, to circle in and out, twisting in intricate designs and patterns. The lights are racing each with each, a kaleidoscope of unearthly brilliance.

"I have made a discovery. There is nothing harmful in the lights. They radiate force and friendliness, almost cheeriness. But by their very strength, they hurt.

"As I look, they are swinging closer and closer, a million miles at each jump. Millions of miles with the speed of light. Aye, it is light of quintessence of all light. Beneath it the fog melts into a jeweled mist radiant, rainbow-colored of a thousand varied spectra.

"I can see the streets. Why, they are filled with people! The lights are coming closer. They are all around me. I am enveloped. I—"

The message stopped abruptly. The wire to Xebico was dead. Beneath my eyes in the narrow circle of light from under the green lamp-shade, the black printing no longer spun itself, letter by letter, across the page.

The room seemed filled with a solemn quiet, a silence vaguely impressive, powerful.

I looked down at Morgan. His hands had dropped nervelessly at his sides, while his body had hunched over peculiarly. I turned the lamp-shade back, throwing light squarely in his face. His eyes were staring, fixed.

Filled with a sudden foreboding, I stepped beside him and called Chicago on the wire. After a second the sounder clicked its answer.

Why? But there was something wrong. Chicago was reporting that Wire Two had not been used throughout the evening.

"Morgan!" I shouted. "Morgan! Wake up, it isn't true. Some one has been hoaxing us. Why—" In my eagerness I grasped him by the shoulder.

His body was quite cold. Morgan had been dead for hours. Could it be that his sensitized brain and automatic fingers had continued to record impressions even after the end?

I shall never know, for I shall never again handle the night shift. Search in a world atlas discloses no town of Xebico. Whatever it was that killed John Morgan will forever remain a mystery.

EVERIL WORRELL MURPHY (1893-1969) wrote under her maiden name, publishing some eighteen stories in *Weird Tales* from 1926 through 1954. "The Canal" was one of her earliest, appearing in the December 1927 issue. It is worth noting here that when "The Canal" was reprinted by August Derleth in his anthology *The Sleeping and the Dead* (1947), the ending was shortened and simplified, making for a less effective and less horrific tale. The version reprinted here is the earlier one—the only one that H. P. Lovecraft knew.

THE CANAL
by Everil Worrell

Past the sleeping city the river sweeps; along its left bank the old canal creeps.

I did not intend that to be poetry, although the scene is poetic—somberly, gruesomely poetic, like the poems of Poe. Too well I know it—too often have I walked over the grass-grown path beside the reflections of black trees and tumble-down shacks and distant factory chimneys in the sluggish waters that moved so slowly, and ceased to move at all.

I shall be called mad, and I shall be a suicide. I shall take no pains to cover up my trail, or to hide the thing that I shall do. What will it matter, afterward, what they say of me? If they knew the truth—if they could vision, even dimly, the beings with whom I have consorted—if the faintest realization might be theirs of the thing I am becoming, and of the fate from which I am saving their city—then they would call me a great hero. But it does not matter what they call me, as I have said before. Let me write down the things I am about to write down, and let them be taken, as they will be taken, for the last ravings of a madman. The city will be in mourning for the thing I shall have done—but its mourning will be of no consequence beside that other fate from which I shall have saved it.

343

I have always had a taste for nocturnal prowling. We as a race have grown too intelligent to take seriously any of the old, instinctive fears that preserved us through preceding generations. Our sole remaining salvation, then, has come to be our tendency to travel in herds. We wander at night—but our objective is somewhere on the brightly lighted streets, or still somewhere where men do not go alone. When we travel far afield, it is in company. Few of my acquaintance, few in the whole city here, would care to ramble at midnight over the grass-grown path I have spoken of, not because they would fear to do so, but because such things are not being done.

Well, it is dangerous to differ individually from one's fellows. It is dangerous to wander from the beaten road. And the fears that guarded the race in the dawn of time and through the centuries were real fears, founded on reality.

A month ago, I was a stranger here. I had just taken my first position— I was graduated from college only three months before, in the spring. I was lonely, and likely to remain so for some time, for I have always been of a solitary nature, making friends slowly.

I had received one invitation out—to visit the camp of a fellow employee in the firm for which I worked, a camp which was located on the farther side of the wide river—the side across from the city and the canal, where the bank was high and steep and heavily wooded, and little tents blossomed all along the water's edge. At night these camps were a string of sparkling lights and tiny, leaping campfires, and the tinkle of music carried faintly far across the calmly flowing water. That far bank of the river was no place for an eccentric, solitary man to love. But the near bank, which would have been an eyesore to the campers had not the river been so wide—the near bank attracted me from my first glimpse of it.

We embarked in a motor-boat at some distance downstream, and swept up along the near bank, and then out and across the current. I turned my eyes backward. The murk of stagnant water that was the canal, the jumble of low buildings beyond it, the lonely, low-lying waste of the narrow strip of land between canal and river, the dark, scattered trees growing there—I intended to see more of these things.

That week-end bored me, but I repaid myself no later than Monday evening, the first evening when I was back in the city, alone and free. I ate a solitary dinner immediately after leaving the office. I went to my room and slept from seven until nearly midnight. I wakened naturally, then, for my whole heart was set on exploring the alluring solitude I had discovered.

I dressed, slipped out of the house and into the street, started the motor in my roadster and drove through the lighted streets.

I left behind that part of town which was thick with vehicles carrying people home from their evening engagements, and began to thread my way through darker and narrower streets. Once I had to back out of a cul-de-sac, and once I had to detour around a closed block. This part of town was not alluring, even to me. It was dismal without being solitary.

But when I had parked my car on a rough, cobbled street that ran directly down into the inky waters of the canal, and crossed a narrow bridge, I was repaid. A few minutes set my feet on the old tow-path where mules had drawn riverboats up and down only a year or so ago. Across the canal now, as I walked upstream at a swinging pace, the miserable shacks where miserable people lived seemed to march with me, and then fell behind. They looked like places in which murders might be committed, every one of them.

The bridge I had crossed was near the end of the city going north, as the canal marked its western extremity. Ten minutes of walking, and the dismal shacks were quite a distance behind, the river was farther away and the strip of waste land much wider and more wooded, and tall trees across the canal marched with me as the evil-looking houses had done before. Far and faint, the sound of a bell in the city reached my ears. It was midnight.

I stopped, enjoying the desolation around me. It had the savor I had expected and hoped for. I stood for some time looking up at the sky, watching the low drift of heavy clouds, which were visible in the dull reflected glow from distant lights in the heart of the city, so that they appeared to have a lurid phosphorescence of their own. The ground under my feet, on the contrary, was utterly devoid of light. I had felt my way carefully, knowing the edge of the canal partly by instinct, partly by the even more perfect blackness of the water in it, and even holding fairly well to the path, because it was perceptibly sunken below the ground beside it.

Now as I stood motionless in this spot, my eyes upcast, my mind adrift with strange fancies, suddenly my feelings of satisfaction and well-being gave way to something different. Fear was an emotion unknown to me—for those things which make men fear, I had always loved. A graveyard at night was to me a charming place for a stroll and meditation. But now the roots of my hair seemed to move upright on my head, and along all the length of my spine I was conscious of a prickling, tingling sensation—such as my forefathers may have felt in the jungle when the hair on their backs stood up as the hair of my head was doing now. Also, I was afraid to move; and I knew that there were eyes upon me, and that that was why I was afraid to move. I was afraid of those eyes—afraid to see them, to look into them.

All this while, I stood perfectly still, my face uptilted toward the sky. But after a terrible mental effort, I mastered myself.

Slowly, slowly, with an attempt to propitiate the owner of the unseen eyes by my casual manner, I lowered my own. I looked straight ahead—at the softly swaying silhouette of the treetops across the canal as they moved gently in the cool night wind; at the mass of blackness that was those trees, and the opposite shore; at the shiny blackness where the reflections of the clouds glinted vaguely and disappeared, that was the canal. And again I raised my eyes a little, for just across the canal where the shadows massed most heavily, there was that at which I must look more closely. And now, as I grew accustomed to the greater blackness and my pupils expanded, I dimly discerned the contours of an old boat or barge, half sunken in water. An old, abandoned canal-boat. But was I dreaming, or was there a white-clad figure seated on the roof of the low cabin aft, a pale, heart-shaped face gleaming strangely at me from the darkness, the glow of two eyes seeming to light up the face, and to detach it from the darkness?

Surely, there could be no doubt as to the eyes. They shone as the eyes of animals shine in the dark, with a phosphorescent gleam, and a glimmer of red! Well, I had heard that some human eyes have that quality at night.

But what a place for a human being to be—a girl, too, I was sure. That daintily heart-shaped face was the face of a girl, surely; I was seeing it clearer and clearer, either because my eyes were growing more accustomed to peering into the deeper shadows, or because of that phosphorescence in the eyes that stared back at me.

I raised my voice softly, not to break too much the stillness of the night. "Hello! who's there? Are you lost, or marooned, and can I help?"

There was a little pause. I was conscious of a soft lapping at my feet. A stronger night wind had sprung up, was ruffling the dark waters. I had been over-warm, and where it struck me the perspiration turned cold on my body, so that I shivered uncontrollably.

"You can stay—and talk a while, if you will. I am lonely, but not lost. I—I live here."

I could hardly believe my ears. The voice was little more than a whisper, but it had carried clearly—a girl's voice, sure enough. And she lived *there*—in an old, abandoned canal-boat, half submerged in the stagnant water.

"You are not *alone* there?"

"No, not alone. My father lives here with me, but he is deaf—and he sleeps soundly."

Did the night wind blow still colder, as though it came to us from some unseen, frozen sea—or was there something in her tone that chilled me, even as a strange attraction drew me toward her? I wanted to draw near to her, to see closely the pale, heart-shaped face, to lose myself in the bright eyes that I had seen shining in the darkness. I wanted—I wanted to hold her in my arms, to find her mouth with mine, to kiss it. . . .

With a start, I realized the nature of my thoughts, and for an instant lost all thought in surprise. Never in my twenty-two years had I felt love before. My fancies had been otherwise directed—a moss-grown, fallen gravestone was a dearer thing to me to contemplate than the fairest face in all the world. Yet, surely, what I felt now was love!

I took a reckless step nearer the edge of the bank.

"Could I come over to you?" I begged. "It's warm, and I don't mind a wetting. It's late, I know—but I would give a great deal to sit beside you and talk, if only for a few minutes before I go back to town. It's a lonely place here for a girl like you to live—your father should not mind if you exchange a few words with someone occasionally."

Was it the unconventionality of my request that made her next words sound like a long-drawn shudder of protest? There was a strangeness in the tones of her voice that held me wondering, every time she spoke.

"No, no. Oh, no! *You must not swim across.*"

"Then—could I come tomorrow, or some day soon, in the daytime; and would you let me come on board then—or would you come on shore and talk to me, perhaps?"

"Not in the daytime—*never* in the daytime!"

Again the intensity of her low-toned negation held me spellbound.

It was not her sense of the impropriety of the hour, then, that had dictated her manner. For surely, any girl with the slightest sense of the fitness of things would rather have a tryst by daytime than after midnight—yet there was an inference in her last words that if I came again it should be again at night.

Still feeling the spell that had enthralled me, as one does not forget the presence of a drug in the air that is stealing one's senses, even when those senses begin to wander and to busy themselves with other things, I yet spoke shortly.

"Why do you say, 'Never in the daytime'? Do you mean that I may come more than this once at night, though now you won't let me cross the canal to you at the expense of my own clothes, and you won't put down your plank or draw-bridge or whatever you come on shore with, and talk to me here for only a moment? I'll come again, if you'll let me talk to you instead of calling across the water. I'll come again, any time you will let me—day or night, I don't care. I want to come to you. But I only ask you to explain. If I came in the daytime and met your father, wouldn't that be the best thing to do? Then we could be really acquainted—we could be friends. "

"In the nighttime, my father sleeps. In the daytime, I sleep. How could I talk to you, or introduce you to my father then? If you came on board this boat in the daytime, you would find my father—and you would be sorry. As for me, I would be sleeping. I could never introduce you to my father, do you see?"

"You sleep soundly, you and your father." Again there was pique in my voice.

"Yes, we sleep soundly."

"And always at different times?"

"Always at different times. We are on guard—one of us is always on guard. We have been hardly used, down there in your city. And we have taken refuge here. And we are always—always—on guard."

The resentment vanished from my breast, and I felt my heart go out to her anew. She was so pale, so pitiful in the night. My eyes were learning better and better how to pierce the darkness; they were giving me a more definite picture of my companion—if I could think of her as a companion, between myself and whom stretched the black water.

The sadness of the lonely scene, the perfection of the solitude itself, these things contributed to her pitifulness. Then there was the strangeness of atmosphere of which, even yet, I had only partly taken note. There was the strange, shivering chill, which yet did not seem like the healthful chill of a cool evening. In fact, it did not prevent me from feeling the oppression of the night, which was unusually sultry. It was like a little breath of deadly cold that came and went, and yet did not alter the temperature of the air itself, as the small ripples on the surface of the water do not concern the water even a foot down.

And even that was not all. There was an unwholesome smell about the night—a dank, moldy smell that might have been the very breath of death and decay. Even I, the connoisseur in all things dismal and unwholesome, tried to keep my mind from dwelling overmuch upon that smell. What it must be to live breathing it constantly in, I could not think. But no doubt the girl and her father were used to it; and no doubt it came from the stagnant water of the canal and from the rotting wood of the old, half-sunken boat that was their refuge.

My heart throbbed with pity again. Their refuge—what a place! And my clearer vision of the girl showed me that she was pitifully thin, even though possessed of the strange face that drew me to her. Her clothes hung around her like old rags, but hers was no scarecrow aspect. Although little flesh clothed her bones, her very bones were beautiful. I was sure the little pale, heart-shaped face would be more beautiful still, if I could only see it closely. I must see it closely—I must establish some claim to consideration as a friend of the strange, lonely crew of the half-sunken wreck.

"This is a poor place to call a refuge," I said finally. "One might have very little money, and yet do somewhat better. Perhaps I might help you—I am sure I could. If your ill-treatment in the city was because of poverty—I am not rich, but I could help that. I could help you a little with money, if you would let me; or, in any case, I could find a position for you. I'm sure I could do that."

The eyes that shone fitfully toward me like two small pools of water intermittently lit by a cloud-swept sky seemed to glow more brightly. She had been half crouching, half sitting on top of the cabin; now she leaped to her feet with one quick, sinuous, abrupt motion, and took a few rapid, restless steps to and fro before she answered.

When she spoke, her voice was little more than a whisper; yet surely rage was in its shrill sibilance.

"Fool! Do you think you would be helping me, to tie me to a desk, to shut me behind doors, away from freedom, away from the delight of doing my own will, of seeking my own way? Never, never would I let you do that. Rather this old boat, rather a deserted grave under the stars, for my home!"

A boundless surprise swept over me, and a positive feeling of kinship with this strange being, whose face I had hardly seen, possessed me. So I myself might have spoken, so I had often felt, though I had never dreamed of putting my thoughts so definitely, so forcibly. My regularized daytime life was a thing I thought little of; I really lived only in my nocturnal prowlings. Why, this girl was right! All of life should be free, and spent in places that interested and attracted.

How little, how little I knew, that night, that dread forces were tugging at my soul, were finding entrance to it and easy access through the morbid weakness of my nature! How little I knew at what a cost I deviated so radically from my kind, who herd in cities and love well-lit ways and the sight of man, and sweet and wholesome places to be solitary in, when the desire for solitude comes over them!

That night it seemed to me that there was but one important thing in life—to allay the angry passion my unfortunate words had aroused in the breast of my beloved, and to win from her some answering feeling.

"I understand—much better than you think," I whispered tremulously. "What I want is to see you again, to come to know you, and to serve you in any way that I may. Surely, there must be something in which I can be of use to you. All you have to do from tonight on for ever, is to command me. I swear it!"

"You swear *that*—you do swear it?"

Delighted at the eagerness of her words, I lifted my hand toward the dark heavens.

"I swear it. From this night on, for ever—I swear it."

"Then listen. Tonight you may not come to me, nor I to you. I do not want you to board this boat—not tonight, not any night. And most of all, not any day. But do not look so sad. I will come to you. No, not tonight, perhaps not for many nights—yet before very long. I will come to you there, on the bank of the canal, when the water in the canal ceases to flow."

I must have made a gesture of impatience, or of despair. It sounded like a way of saying "never"—for why should the water in the canal cease to flow? She read my thoughts in some way, for she answered them.

"You do not understand. I am speaking seriously—I am promising to meet you there on the bank, and soon. For the water within these banks is moving slower, always slower. Higher up, I have heard that the canal has been drained. Between these lower locks, the water still seeps in and drops slowly, slowly downstream. But there will come a night when it will be quite, quite stagnant—and on that night I will come to you. And when I come, I will ask of you a favor. And you will keep your oath."

It was all the assurance I could get that night. She had come back to the side of the cabin where she had sat crouched before, and she resumed again that posture and sat still and silent, watching me. Sometimes I could see her eyes upon me, and sometimes not. But I felt that their gaze was unwavering. The little cold breeze, which I had finally forgotten while I was talking with her, was blowing again, and the unwholesome smell of decay grew heavier before the dawn.

She would not speak again, nor answer me when I spoke to her, and I grew nervous, and strangely ill at ease.

At last I went away. And in the first faint light of dawn I slipped up the stairs of my rooming-house, and into my own room.

I was deadly tired at the office next day. And day after day slipped away and I grew more and more weary; for a man cannot wake day and night without suffering, especially in hot weather, and that was what I was doing. I haunted the old towpath and waited, night after night, on the bank opposite the sunken boat. Sometimes I saw my lady of the darkness, and sometimes not. When I saw her, she spoke little; but sometimes she sat there on the top of the cabin and let me watch her till the dawn, or until the strange uneasiness that was like fright drove me from her and back to my room, where I tossed restlessly in the heat and dreamed strange dreams, half waking, till the sun shone in on my forehead and I tumbled into my clothes and down to the office again.

Once I asked her why she had made the fanciful condition that she would not come ashore to meet me until the waters of the canal had ceased to run. (How eagerly I studied those waters! How I stole away at noontime more than once, not to approach the old boat, but to watch the almost imperceptible downdrift of bubbles, bits of straw, twigs, rubbish!)

My questioning displeased her, and I asked her that no more. It was enough that she chose to be whimsical. My part was to wait.

It was more than a week later that I questioned her again, this time on a different subject. And after that, I curbed my curiosity relentlessly.

"Never speak to me of things you do not understand about me. Never again, or I will not show myself to you again. And when I walk on the path yonder, it will not be with you."

I had asked her what form of persecution she and her father had suffered in the city, that had driven them out to this lonely place, and where in the city they had lived.

Frightened seriously lest I lose the ground I was sure I had gained with her, I was about to speak of something else. But before I could find the words, her low voice came to me again.

"It was horrible, horrible! Those little houses below the bridge, those houses along the canal—tell me, are they not worse than my boat? Life there was shut in, and furtive. I was not free as I am now—and the freedom I will soon have will make me forget the things I have not yet forgotten. The screaming, the reviling and cursing! Fear and flight! As you pass back by those houses, think how you would like to be shut in one of them, and in fear of your life. And then think of them no more; for I would forget them, and I will never speak of them again."

I dared not answer her. I was surprised that she had vouchsafed me so much. But surely her words meant this: that before she had come to live on the decaying, water-rotted old boat, she had lived in one of those horrible houses I passed by on my way to her. Those houses, each of which looked like the predestined scene of a murder!

As I left her that night, I felt that I was very daring.

"One or two nights more and you will walk beside me," I called to her. "I have watched the water at noon, and it hardly moves at all. I threw a scrap of paper into the canal, and it whirled and swung a little where a thin skim of oil lay on the water down there—oil from the big, dirty city you are well out of. But though I watched and watched, I could not see it move downward at all. Perhaps tomorrow night, or the night after, you will walk on the bank with me. I hope it will be clear and moonlit, and I will be near enough to see you clearly—as well as you seem always to see me in darkness or moonlight, equally well. And perhaps I will kiss you—but not unless you let me."

And yet, the next day, for the first time my thoughts were definitely troubled. I had been living in a dream—I began to speculate concerning the end of the path on which my feet were set.

I had conceived, from the first, such a horror of those old houses by the canal! They were well enough to walk past, nursing gruesome thoughts for a midnight treat. But, much as I loved all that was weird and eery about the girl I was wooing so strangely, it was a little too much for my fancy that she had come from them.

By this time, I had become decidedly unpopular in my place of business. Not that I had made enemies, but that my peculiar ways had caused too much adverse comment. It would have taken very little, I think, to have made the entire office force decide that I was mad. After the events of the next twenty-four hours, and after this letter is found and read, they will be sure that they knew it all along! At this time, however, they were punctiliously polite to me, and merely let me alone as much as possible— which suited me perfectly. I dragged wearily through day after day, exhausted from lack of sleep, conscious of their speculative glances, living only for the night to come.

But on this day, I approached the man who had invited me to the camp across the river, who had unknowingly shown me the way that led to my love.

"Have you ever noticed the row of tumble-down houses along the canal on the city side?" I asked him.

He gave me an odd look. I suppose he sensed the significance of my breaking silence after so long to speak of *them*—sensed that in some way I had a deep interest in them.

"You have odd tastes, Morton," he said after a moment. "I suppose you wander into strange places sometimes—I've heard you speak of an enthusiasm for graveyards at night. But my advice to you is to keep away from those houses. They're unsavory, and their reputation is unsavory. Positively, I think you'd be in danger of your life, if you go poking around there. They have been the scene of several murders, and a dope den or two has been cleaned out of them. Why in the world you should want to investigate them—"

"I don't expect to investigate them," I said testily. "I was merely interested in them—from the outside. To tell you the truth, I'd heard a story, a rumor—never mind where. But you say there have been murders there—I suppose this rumor I heard may have had to do with an attempted one. There was a girl who lived there with her father once, and they were set upon there, or something of the sort, and had to run away. Did you ever hear *that* story?"

Barrett gave me an odd look such as one gives in speaking of a past horror so dreadful that the mere speaking of it makes it live terribly again.

"What you say reminds me of a horrible thing that was said to have happened down there once," he said. "It was in all the papers. A little child disappeared in one of those houses, and a couple of poor lodgers who lived there, a girl and her father, were accused of having made away with it. They were accused—they were accused—oh, well, I don't like to talk about such things. It was too dreadful. The child's body was found—*part* of it was found. It was mutilated, and the people in the house seemed to believe it had been mutilated in order to conceal the manner of its death; there was an ugly wound in the throat, it finally came out, and it seemed as if the child might have been bled to death. It was found in the girl's room, hidden away. The old man and his daughter escaped, before the police were called. The countryside was scoured, but they were never found. Why, you must have read it in the papers, several years ago."

I nodded with a heavy heart. I *had* read it in the papers, I remembered now. And again, a terrible questioning came over me. Who was this girl, *what* was this girl, who seemed to have my heart in her keeping?

Why did not a merciful God let me die then?

Befogged with exhaustion, bemused in a dire enchantment, my mind was incapable of thought. And yet, some soul-process akin to that which saves the sleepwalker poised at perilous heights sounded its warning now.

My mind was filled with doleful images. There were women—I had heard and read—who slew to satisfy a blood-lust. There were ghosts, specters—call them what you will, their names have been legion in the dark pages of that lore which dates back to the infancy of the races of the earth— who retained even in death this blood-lust. Vampires—they had been called that. I had read of them. Corpses by day, spirits of evil by night, roaming abroad in their own forms or in the forms of bats or unclean beasts, killing body and soul of their victims—for whoever dies of the repeated "kiss" of the vampire, which leaves its mark on the throat and draws the blood from the body, becomes a vampire also—of such beings I had read.

And, horror of horrors! In that last cursed day at the office, I remembered reading of these vampires—these undead—that in their nocturnal flights they had one limitation—*they could not cross running water.*

That night I went my usual nightly way with tears of weakness on my face—for my weakness was supreme, and I recognized fully at last the misery of being the victim of an enchantment stronger than my feeble will. But I went.

I approached the neighborhood of the canal-boat as the distant city clock chimed the first stroke of twelve. It was the dark of the moon and the sky was overcast. Heat-lightning flickered low in the sky, seeming to come from every point of the compass and circumscribe the horizon, as if unseen fires burned behind the rim of the world. By its fitful glimmer, I saw a new thing: between the old boat and the canal bank stretched a long, slim, solid-looking shadow—a plank had been let down! In that moment, I realized that I had been playing with powers of evil which had no intent now to let me go, which were indeed about to lay hold upon me with an inexorable grasp. Why had I come tonight? Why, but that the spell of the enchantment laid upon me was a thing more potent, and far more unbreakable, than any wholesome spell of love? The creature I sought out—oh, I remembered now, with the cold perspiration beading my brow, the lore hidden away between the covers of the dark old book which I had read so many years ago and half forgotten!—until dim memories of it stirred within me, this last day and night.

My lady of the night! No woman of wholesome flesh and blood and odd perverted tastes that matched my own, but one of the undead! In that moment, I knew it, and knew that the vampires of old legends polluted still, in these latter days, the fair surface of the earth.

And on the instant, behind me in the darkness there was the crackle of a twig, and something brushed against my arm.

This, then, was the fulfillment of my dream. I knew, without turning my head, that the pale, dainty face with its glowing eyes was near my own—that I had only to stretch out my arm to touch the slender grace of the girl I had so longed to draw near. I knew, and should have felt the rapture I had anticipated. Instead, the roots of my hair prickled coldly, unendurably, as they had on the night when I had first sighted the old boat. The miasmic odors of the night, heavy and oppressive with heat and unrelieved by a breath of air, all but overcame me, and I fought with myself to prevent my teeth clicking in my head. The little waves of coldness I had felt often in this spot were chasing over my body, yet they were not from any breeze; the leaves on the trees hung down motionless, as though they were actually wilting on their branches.

With an effort, I turned my head.

Two hands caught me around my neck. The pale face was so near that I felt the warm breath from its nostrils fanning my cheek.

And, suddenly, all that was wholesome in my perverted nature rose upper-most. I longed for the touch of the red mouth, like a dark flower opening before me in the night. I longed for it—and yet more I dreaded it. I shrank back, catching in a powerful grip the fragile wrists of the hands that strove to hold me. I must not—I must not yield to the faintness that I felt stealing over me.

I was facing down the path toward the city. A low rumble of thunder—the first—broke the torrid hush of the summer night. A glare of lightning seemed to tear the night asunder, to light up the universe. Overhead, the clouds were careering madly in fantastic shapes, driven by a wind that swept the upper heavens without causing even a trembling in the air lower down. And far down the canal, that baleful glare seemed to play around and hover over the little row of shanties—murder-cursed, and haunted by the ghost of a dead child.

My gaze was fixed on them, while I held away from me the pallid face and fought off the embrace that sought to overcome my resisting will. And so a long moment passed. The glare faded out of the sky, and a greater darkness took the world. But there was a near, more menacing glare fastened upon my face—the glare of two eyes that watched mine, that had watched me as I, unthinking, stared down at the dark houses.

This girl—this woman who had come to me at my own importunate requests, did not love me, since I had shrunk from her; She did not love me—but it was not only that. She had watched me as I gazed down at the houses that held her dark past, and I was sure that she divined my thoughts. She knew my horror of those houses—she knew my new-born horror of *her*. And she hated me for it, hated me more malignantly than I had believed a human being could hate.

And at that point in my thoughts, I felt my skin prickle and my scalp rise again: could a *human being* cherish such hatred as I read, trembling more and more, in those glowing fires lit with what seemed to me more like the fires of hell than any light that ought to shine in a woman's eyes?

And through all this, not a word had passed between us!

So far I have written calmly. I wish that I could write on so, to the end. If I could do that, there might be one or two of those who will regard this as the document of a maniac, who would believe the horrors of which I am about to write.

But I am only flesh and blood. At this point in the happenings of the awful night, my calmness deserted me—at this point I felt that I had been drawn into the midst of a horrible nightmare from which there was no escape, no waking! As I write, this feeling again overwhelms me, until I can hardly write at all—until, were it not for the thing which I must do, I would rush out into the street and run, screaming, until I was caught and dragged away, to be put behind strong iron bars. Perhaps I would feel safe there—perhaps!

I know that, terrified at the hate I saw confronting me in those redly gleaming eyes, I would have slunk away. The two thin hands that caught my arm again were strong enough to prevent that, however. I had been spared her kiss, but I was not to escape from the oath I had taken to serve her.

"You promised, you swore," she hissed in my ear. "And tonight you are to keep your oath."

I felt my senses reel. My oath—yes, I had an oath to keep. I had lifted my hand toward the dark heavens, and sworn to serve her in any way she chose. Freely, and of my own volition, I had sworn.

I sought to evade her.

"Let me help you back to your boat," I begged. "You have no kindly feeling for me, and—you have seen it—I love you no longer. I will go back to the city—you can go back to your father, and forget that I broke your peace."

The laughter that greeted my speech I shall never forget—not in the depths under the scummy surface of the canal—not in the empty places between the worlds, where my tortured soul may wander.

"So you do not love me, and I hate you! Fool! Have I waited these weary months for the water to stop, only to go back now? After my father and I returned here and found the old boat rotting in the drained canal, and took refuge in it; when the water was turned into the canal while I slept, so that I could never escape until its flow should cease, *because of the thing that I am*—even then I dreamed of tonight.

"When the imprisonment we still shared ceased to matter to my father—come on board the deserted boat tomorrow, and see why, if you dare!—still I dreamed on, of tonight!

"I have been lonely, desolate, starving—now the whole world shall be mine! And by *your* help!"

I asked her, somehow, what she wanted of me, and a madness overcame me so that I hardly heard her reply. Yet somehow, I knew that there was that on the opposite shore of the great river where the pleasure camps were, that she wanted to find. In the madness of my terror, she made me understand and obey her. I must carry her in my arms across the long bridge over the river, deserted in the small hours of the night.

The way back to the city was long tonight—long. She walked behind me, and I turned my eyes neither to right nor left. Only as I passed the tumble-down houses, I saw their reflection in the canal and trembled so that I could have fallen to the ground, at the thoughts of the little child this woman had been accused of slaying there, and at the certainty I felt that she was reading my thoughts.

And now the horror that engulfed me darkened my brain.

I know that we set our feet upon the long, wide bridge that spanned the river. I know the storm broke there, so that I battled for my footing, almost for my life it seemed, against the pelting deluge. And the horror I had invoked was in my arms, clinging to me, burying its head upon my shoulder. So increasingly dreadful had my pale-faced companion become to me, that I hardly thought of her now as a woman at all—only as a demon of the night.

The tempest raged still as she leaped down out of my arms on the other shore. And again I walked with her against my will, while the trees lashed their branches around me, showing the pale under-sides of their leaves in the vivid frequent flashes that rent the heavens.

On and on we went, branches flying through the air and missing us by a miracle of ill fortune. Such as she and I are not slain by falling branches. The river was a welter of whitecaps, flattened down into strange shapes by the pounding rain. The clouds as we glimpsed them were like devils flying through the sky.

Past dark tent after dark tent we stole, and past a few where lights burned dimly behind their canvas walls. And at last we came to an old quarry. Into its artificial ravine she led me, and up to a crevice in the rock wall.

"Reach in your hand and pull out the loose stone you will feel," she whis-pered. "It closes an opening that leads into deep caverns. A human hand must remove that stone—your hand must move it!"

Why did I struggle so to disobey her? Why did I fail? It was as though I *knew*—but my failure was foreordained—I had taken oath!

If you who read have believed that I have set down the truth thus far, the little that is left you will call the ravings of a madman overtaken by his madness. Yet these things happened.

I stretched out my arm, driven by a compulsion I could not resist. At arm's length in the niche in the rock, I felt something move—the loose rock, a long, narrow fragment, much larger than I had expected. Yet it moved easily, seeming to swing on a natural pivot. Outward it swung, toppling toward me—a moment more and there was a swift rush of the ponderous weight I had loosened. I leaped aside and went down, my forehead grazed by the rock.

For a brief moment I must have been unconscious, but only for a moment. My head a stabbing agony of pain, unreal lights flashing before my eyes, I yet knew the reality of the storm that beat me down as I struggled to my feet. I knew the reality of the dark, loathsome shapes that passed me in the dark, crawling out of the orifice in the rock and flapping through the wild night, along the way that led to the pleasure camps.

So the caverns I had laid open to the outer world were infested with bats. I had been inside unlit caverns, and had heard there the squeaking of the things, felt and heard the flapping of their wings—*but never in all my life before had I seen bats as large as men and women!*

Sick and dizzy from the blow on my head, and from disgust, I crept along the way they were going. If I touched one of them, I felt that I should die of horror.

Now, at last, the storm abated, and a heavy darkness made the whole world seem like the inside of a tomb.

Where the tents stood in a long row, the number of the monster bats seemed to diminish. It was as though—horrible thought!—they were creeping into the tents, with their slumbering occupants.

At last I came to a lighted tent, and paused, crouching so that the dim radiance which shone through the canvas did not touch me in the shadows. And there I waited, but not for long. There was a dark form silhouetted against the tent; a rustle and confusion, and the dark thing was again in silhouette—but with a difference in the quality of the shadow. The dark thing was *inside* the tent now, its bat wings extending across the entrance through which it had crept.

Fear held me spellbound. And as I looked, the shadow changed again, imperceptibly, so that I could not have told *how* it changed. But now it was not the shadow of a bat, but of a woman.

"The storm, the storm! I am lost, exhausted! I crept in here, to beg for refuge until the dawn!"

That low, thrilling, sibilant voice—too well I knew it!

Within the tent I heard a murmur of acquiescent voices. At last I began to understand.

I knew the nature of the woman I had carried over the river in my arms, the woman who would not even cross the canal until the water should have ceased utterly to flow. I remembered books I had read—*Dracula*—other books and stories. I knew they were true books and stories, now—I knew those horrors existed for me.

I had indeed kept my oath to the creature of darkness—I had brought her to her kind, under her guidance. I had let them loose in hordes upon the pleasure camps. The campers were doomed—and through them, others. . . .

I forgot my fear. I rushed from my hiding place up to the tent door, and there I screamed and called aloud.

"Don't take her in—don't let her stay—nor the others, that have crept into the other tents! Wake all the campers—they will sleep on to their destruction! Drive out the interlopers—drive them out quickly! *They are not human—no, and they are not bats!* Do you hear me?—Do you understand?"

I was fairly howling, in a voice that was strange to me.

"She is a vampire. They are all vampires. *Vampires!*"

Inside the tent I heard a new voice.

"What can be the matter with that poor man?" the voice said. It was a woman's, and gentle.

"Crazy—somebody out of his senses, dear," a man's voice answered. "Don't be frightened."

And then the voice I knew so well—so well: "I saw a falling rock strike a man on the head in the storm. He staggered away, but I suppose it crazed him."

I waited for no more. I ran away madly through the night and back across the bridge to the city.

Next day—today—I boarded the sunken canal-boat. It is the abode of death—no woman could have lived there—only such a one as *she*. The old man's corpse was there—he must have died long, long ago. The smell of death and decay on the boat was dreadful.

Again, I felt that I understood. Back in those awful houses, she had committed the crime when first she became the thing she is. And he—her father—less sin-steeped, and less accursed, attempted to destroy the evidence of her crime, and fled with her, but died without becoming like her. She had said that one of those two was always on watch—did he indeed divide her vigil on the boat? What more fitting—the dead standing watch with the undead! And no wonder that she would not let me board the craft of death, even to carry her away.

And still I feel the old compulsion. I have been spared her kiss—but for a little while. Yet I will not let the power of my oath draw me back, till I enter the caverns with her and creep forth in the form of a bat to prey upon mankind. Before that can happen, I too will die.

Today in the city I heard that a horde of strange insects or small animals infested the pleasure camps last night. Some said, with horror-bated breath, that they perhaps were rats. None of them was seen; but in the morning nearly every camper had a strange, deep wound in his throat.

I almost laughed aloud. They were so horrified at the idea of an army of rats, creeping into the tents and biting the sleeping occupants on their throats! If they had seen what I saw—if they knew that they are doomed to spread corruption—

So my own death will not be enough. Today I bought supplies for blasting. Tonight I will set my train of dynamite, from the hole I made in the cliff where the vampires creep in and out, along the row of tents, as far as the last one—then I shall light my fuse. It will be done before the dawn. Tomorrow, the city will mourn its dead and execrate my name.

And then, at last, in the slime beneath the unmoving waters of the canal, I shall find peace! But perhaps it will not be peace—for I shall seek it midway between the old boat with its cargo of death and the row of dismal houses where a little child was done to death when first *she* became the thing she is. This is my expiation.

ARTHUR J. BURKS (1898-1974) was one of the most prolific writers for the pulps, writing around a couple of million words a year throughout the 1930s. His earliest stories, dating from before he took on writing as a profession, are his best. These stories include "Bells of Oceana" from *Weird Tales* of December 1927.

BELLS OF OCEANA
by Arthur J. Burks

It was on a heavily laden troopship, westward heading. Hours before, the sun had gone down toward China, trailing ebon night behind her. For a full week, since dropping the California coast behind us, there had been nothing in all the wild waste of waters for us to see save ourselves. No ship's funnels broke the lowering horizon, no sign of land, for our skipper had chosen a passage lying somewhere in between the usual steamer lanes. The nearest land, save that which stretched in eternal darkness some three miles below us, was more than a thousand miles beyond the southern horizon. We were just a single ship, burdened with a precious freight of souls, upon an ocean that seemed endless. The first day out had been squally, and everyone had been sick, save those of us who had gone down to the sea in ships before. But with the dawning of the second morning the sea had calmed down, and our vessel rode through the blue, toward the horizon bowl which ever crept before us, in the golden wake of the setting sun. The voyage, if the old salts spoke truly, would be uneventful; but, with that strange premonitory feeling which comes to all of us at times, I did not believe them.

Something, from the very first, warned me that our voyage was ill-fated. I couldn't explain my feeling. It wasn't a feeling of dread, exactly, nor of fear. Just a strange feeling of unease, much like that which comes to people on their first voyage, when a ship is rolling slightly under their feet, and everything, until they get their sea-legs, seems strangely out of focus. That doesn't explain it, I know; but it is as near as I can put my feeling into words.

I knew, when the sun went down ahead of us, with the hundred and eightieth meridian less than twenty-four hours ahead, that we were on the eve of strange, momentous happenings. To add to my feeling of unease, and as though it had been all planned out by some invisible *something* or *somebody*, in the vague beginning, the officer who should have had the watch that night fell suddenly ill, and I was called upon to take his place. I knew, as I donned my belt, holster, and pistol, that I obeyed the will of some invisible prompter—a prompter without a name.

We had seven sentries out at various important places about the ship, and I made the routine inspections before turning in, less than an hour before midnight. When I entered my stateroom and turned on the light, that feeling of unease was more pronounced than it had been at any time previously. I had the feeling, though I had locked my door when I had last quitted my stateroom, that I had entered again immediately *after* someone had left it. Yet that was impossible. I had carried the key in my pocket all the time, and my cabin-boy was not provided with one. There was no way that anyone, or anything, could have entered my stateroom in my absence, save—

Still as though my every move had been ordered by some invisible prompter, my eyes darted to the port-hole beside my bed. It was quite too small for the passage of a human body. If anyone had gone out through the port-hole, that one had fallen, or plunged into the sea, for had the port-hole been ever so big, there was absolutely no way one could have left my stateroom by that way and still remained upon the ship—unless that one had gone out and were even now hanging by his hands along the ship's side. So strongly had the feeling of an alien presence intruded itself upon me that, in spite of knowing myself an utter fool for entertaining any doubt whatsoever, I strode to the port-hole and looked out. There was nothing, of course, save water, now black and forbidding, stretching away to the south, to a horizon that, since night had fallen, seemed to have crept quite close to us to watch our passing.

Still unsatisfied, in spite of arguing with myself, condemning myself for a fool, I deliberately closed the glass which masked the port, took my seat in a chair beside the bunk, facing the round glass—which resembled, to an imagination suddenly fevered, the eye of a huge one-eyed giant—of the port-hole, and began to undress. Mechanically I lifted first one foot and then the other, removing shoes and stockings.

But I kept my eyes upon the closed port-hole—and that feeling of an unseen presence in the room was stronger as the moments fled. My undressing completed, I stood erect to turn out the lights, and paused in the very act, a cry of terror smothered in my throat by a sheer act of will.

For, for the most fleeting of seconds, I had seen a dead-white face outside the glass which covered the port-hole! It was the face of a person who had drowned, I told myself wildly, and the dripping hair wore a coronet of fluttering seaweed. The eyes of this strange outsider stared straight into mine, devoid of expression, totally unwinking, and the lips, which seemed blue as though with icy cold long endured, smiled a thin and ironic smile. It took all the courage I possessed, which is little enough in the face of the unknown, to hurl myself across the bed, right hand extended toward the heavy screw which held the circular piece of glass in place. In the instant my hand would have touched the glass, the ship rode into the edge of the storm that was to fill the remainder of the night, and the stern of the steamer rose dizzily on the crest of a mighty wave, drag-ging all the vessel with it—and the face slid slowly out of sight below the port-hole, the bluish lips still smiling!

I admit that I was trembling, that my fingers were unsteady as I fumbled with the screw to unloose the glass. When the port-hole was open once more, and the cold breeze of this latitude came in to fan my fevered face, I thrust my head out of the port and gazed right and left, and up and down, along the curving side of the ship. But there was nothing—save straight ahead, on our port side. And even there there was nothing but black water, huge mountainous waves touched with whitecaps at their crests, like flying shrouds, or like lacy streamers created as a fringe for the mantle of night.

I watched several of the waves sweep under the vessel, which rose and fell sluggishly. The waves seemed to be traveling in no certain direction, but broke into a veritable welter of warring forces, roaring as they came together with the bellowing of maddened, deep-throated bulls. Valleys with darkness on their floors, mountain-tops touched with snow that shifted eerily in the breeze.

I was about to close the port when, many yards away from the ship, as though born of the womb of old ocean, I heard the bells!

Like the tiny bells which the bell-wether wears to signal the ewes and the lambs, was the tinkling of the bells—like those bells, yet not like them,

364

totally out of place in mid-ocean, and I felt a strange prickling of the scalp as I listened. Hurriedly, driven by a fear I could not have explained then, nor can I now explain, I closed the port-hole again. And whirled about with another scream, which this time came forth from my quivering lips in spite of all I could do to prevent.

Just inside my stateroom door stood my sergeant of the guard, and his lips were trembling more wildly than my own, his eyes protruded horribly, his face was chalk-white, and he was striving with all his power to speak! As I watched his manful struggle, I dreaded for him to speak—for I knew that what he had come to tell me would be something strange and terrible, something hitherto entirely outside my experience.

"Sir," he managed at last, when I stiffly nodded permission for him to speak, "I just made the rounds of the sentries!"

Here the poor fellow stopped, unable to go on, and his knees knocked together audibly.

"Yes, sergeant," I managed to mutter, "you went the usual rounds of the sentries, and then?"

"The sentry who should be on duty on the main deck, forward of the bridge, is missing!"

Of course I knew on the instant that there might be many reasons for the failure of the sergeant of the guard to find the sentry, many logical reasons. The sentry might have quitted his post (a violation of regulations, true) for a quiet cigarette in the lee of a lifeboat; he might have been walking his post in the direction taken by the sergeant, so that the latter had not overtaken him, even with a complete circling of the main deck; he might—oh, there were many logical explanations; but I guessed instinctively that none of these reasons fitted the case. For one thing, the sergeant of the guard was an old-timer, had spent many years of his life at sea—yet he was frightened half out of his wits, and I knew he held as many decorations for bravery as any other officer or man in the Marine Corps. There was something terrible, something—if you will—uncanny behind this disappearance of the sentry.

I muttered an oath, more to prod my own flagging courage than for any other reason, and started toward the door, motioning the sergeant to precede me. But he shook his head stubbornly and barred my way. I halted, for it was evident that he had not completed his report.

"You'll maybe think me daft," he said; "but I couldn't let you go out there, sir, without telling you everything. The corporal on watch at the head of the promenade gangway told me a strange story just before I made my rounds. He opened the door leading onto the starboard promenade, for a look at the weather outside, and just as he was about to close it again, the ship lifted on the crest of a huge wave—and out beyond the wave, many yards away from the ship, he heard something which he likened to the tinkling of little bells!"

"Good God!" I exclaimed.

"And," the sergeant continued, "all the time I was looking for the missing sentry, I had the idea there was someone behind me, following me every step of the way; yet when I whirled to look, the deck behind me was empty!"

"And you found no sign of the sentry?" I said stupidly.

The sergeant shook his head.

"Nothing," he said, "except—except—well, sir, you'll maybe think me daft, as I said before; but on the spot where the sentry had stood to wait for me on my last round, I found wet marks on the deck floor—the marks, as near as I could tell with my flashlight, of bare feet!"

Mechanically, as the sergeant spoke, I had been donning my clothes, leaving my shoes, however, unlaced. I felt an icy chill along my spine as the sergeant continued, and I dreaded, as I had never dreaded anything before, to ask him further about those wet footprints on the deck.

"The wet footprints," he went on, and he was talking wildly now, his words tripping over one another, so rapidly were they uttered, as though he wished to finish his report before I could interrupt again, "led away where the sentry should have been standing, straight to the starboard rail! Right at the rail I stooped to examine the prints more closely. They were the footprints of a human being, I was sure, and the marks of the toes were blurred, and very wide, as though whoever—or whatever—had made them had been carrying a burden in his arms!"

"Good God, sergeant!" I said again; "what are you driving at?"

"Just this, sir. There's something terribly wrong with this ship! *Something took that sentry bodily over the side!*"

I believe that putting a name, however meaningless, to what was in my own mind, caused a little of my courage to return, for I did not find it difficult now to bring myself to leave the stateroom. The sergeant almost trod on my heels as I hurried to the main deck, starboard side, where the wind wrapped icy fingers around me, chilling me to the bone.

As I hurried forward I looked over the side, into the welter of water—and stopped short!

Behind me the sergeant groaned—hollowly, like a man who has been mortally wounded. For out of the waters, away to starboard, came the sound of tinkling bells! I darted to the rail and leaned far outboard, striving to pierce the gloom. But there was nothing save the watery wastes, mountains and valleys—and two spots of greenish phosphorescence, far out, like serpent's eyes which watched the passing ship. But when I looked at them closely, straining my eyes, seeking the form below the eyes, the twin balls of eery flame vanished, a wall of water intruding itself between!

Well, we found the sentry, sprawled on his face, where the sergeant should have found him on his rounds. I turned the body over, and it was quite cold—with excellent reason! The corpse was dripping wet, entirely nude, and the lips and cheeks as coldly blue as though the corpse had been dragged for hours on a line in the wake of the ship!

No matter how secluded one's life may have been, no matter how carefully one may have been guarded during one's lifetime, there come into the lives of most of us certain inexplicable happenings which may never be forgotten. This matter of the dead sentry was one of these for me, and I shall go to my grave with the memory of his cold cheeks and bluish lips limned upon the retina of my very soul. So many strange circumstances—thank God that, at the moment, I could not look into the two hours or more of terror which even then stretched before me, else I should most surely have gone entirely mad!—were there connected with this matter that, taken altogether, it is little wonder that I have been unable to forget. The roaring of the wind which was lashing all the ocean into fury, a maelstrom in mid-ocean, ghostly whitecaps stretching away into darkness, into seeming infinity; the frightened sergeant behind me, his teeth chattering with fear; the dead sentry at my feet, his body blue with cold, entirely nude as I have said; the marks on the deck of huge bare feet, wet as though the feet had come up out of the sea; the eery sound of bells between our vessel and the lowering horizon—and that dead-white face which I had seen beyond the port-hole of my own cabin a half-hour before.

What was the explanation of it all? What was the cause of the bells, if bells there were? What had come up out of the sea to stride barefooted across the promenade deck of the slumbering troopship? Had my sentry seen whatever had come for him before he had been taken?

Add to all these circumstances the fact that all hell was loose in the watery wastes, that it was now after midnight, and you will understand a little of my feelings. Never before or since have I been as frightened as I was then. I don't regard myself as a coward, nor am I ordinarily superstitious;

but show me the man who is without fear in the presence of the unknown, the utterly uncanny, and I will show you a man who has no soul.

I whirled, bumping into the sergeant, who manfully muffled a scream at my unexpected movement, and started, almost blindly, toward the stern of the troopship. As I strode along, with the sergeant at my heels once more, strange images fled across my mind. I remembered the tale of *Die Lorelei*, the maiden who lured sailors to their death with her eery singing, and strained my eyes through the gloom, seeking shapes I feared to see. Then my mind went farther back, to the years before I could read, years in which, thirsty for knowledge, I studied pictures out of old histories to satisfy my longing for wisdom. One of these pictures came back to my mind as I hurried aft: a picture of a hideous monster of unbelievable proportions, who had come up from behind the ocean's horizon, blotting out the sunlight, long arms extended into the picture's foreground, the right hand holding aloft a medieval sailing vessel which had been lifted bodily from the ocean. A fantastic picture, I knew now, drawn to prove the existence of terrible monsters beyond the horizon to which, as yet, no caravel or galleon had dared travel. I wondered, as I strode aft, why this old picture should return to my mind at this time, and fear was at my throat again as I walked.

"I am coming, oh, my beloved!"

The words, high-pitched with ecstasy, came from straight ahead of me, and out of the heavy shadow cast by a huge funnel stepped one of my sentries. Just for a second, as he strode toward the starboard rail, I could see his face—and the face was transfigured, as though the man gazed into the very soul of the Perfect Sweetheart somewhere beyond the rail. Slowly, step by step, as though he would prolong the joy of anticipation, the sentry, who had hurled his rifle aside, approached the rail, still with his eyes fixed on the welter of waters overside, while I halted spellbound to watch what he would do. From out of the waters there came once more the tinkling of bells! And with the sound, as though the sound had been a signal, a huge shadow detached itself from the shadow whence the sentry had stepped but a moment ago, and loomed high above the luckless youth. At the same time the ship climbed high upon a monster wave, so that her starboard side went down, down, until white water came over the side—and when she straightened again, shuddering through all of her, the sentry had vanished! From well rearward of where the man had disappeared, from out of the smother of waters, there came a single long-drawn cry—and it was not a cry of terror, not a cry of pain, but a scream of ecstasy!

"He's gone, sergeant," I said stupidly, "but what took him? Not the wave: he had only to seize the rail to save himself."

"Did you see the shadow, Lieutenant?" the sergeant replied.

I did not answer. *He knew* I had seen it.

We strode on again, heading toward the stern—and all about us now, over the ship, on either side of her—but never on her—there tinkled the eery, unexplainable bells!

We stood at last in the very stern of the troopship, gazing into the ghostly wake far below our coign of vantage, and with certain care, I followed the wake rearward with my eyes. But one could not follow it far! That was the circumstance which impressed itself upon me almost at once. The wake died away, short off, within less than a dozen yards of the ship's stern—as though at the very moment of birth, it had been ignominiously smothered!

In a trice I understood the reason, and thought I understood many things besides. For, like a monster raft, stretching away rearward as far as I could see, and into the darkness beyond my vision to right and left, there followed us, close to, an undulating mass of odorless seaweed! Acres and acres of it there were, rising and falling sluggishly, but keeping pace with the troopship through the night and the storm! Came again that sound of bells, and my hair stiffened at the base of my skull when I saw, watching the seaweed, the result of the tinkling of the bells. The seaweed, when the bells sounded, seemed imbued suddenly with life that was utterly and completely rampant. Long tendrils of the stuff drew away to right and left below us, as though endowed with will of their own, and these tendrils, countless thousands of them, collided with other tendrils in the mass, and slithered over them so that all the mass of the seaweed writhed as though in torment, resembling countless hordes of serpents gathered together from all the evil places of the earth—and where the tendrils had drawn aside I could see black water in the rift as though the tendrils had drawn aside so that I *might* see. Some terrible fascination held me, my eyes fixed on that space of black water, for several moments after the tendrils of seaweed had drawn away to right and left—and up from the depths, into the opening, came two who filled all my being with abject terror—and something else.

One of the two was dead, I knew on the instant, for I could see his face, all white and drawn, yet with the blue lips smiling, of the ill-fated sentry who had gone over the side before my very eyes! And he had been brought up from the depths in the arms of—I hesitate to give the creature a name.

A woman? I scarcely know; yet this I do know: in the instant I looked into her eyes, I understood the ecstacy I had read in the face of the sentry whom she now held in her arms. Her breasts, nude and unashamed, were the breasts of a buxom woman, her lips as red as full-blown roses, her hair as black as the wings of a crow, a mantle of loveliness all about her wondrous body, whipping this way and that in the storm.

Her eyes swerved away from mine, and one arm, shapely and snowy, raised aloft from the water—and to my ears came again the sound of tinkling bells! Once more the seaweed writhed and twisted, pressed forward about the ship; but a single mass of it detached itself from the larger mass, pressed close to the—should I call her "woman"—and swerved away again; and the arms of the beautiful creature were empty. Instinctively I whirled about, knowing somehow that I must move my head before I met this creature's eyes again, and stared forward to the shadowy portion of the promenade whence the sentry had emerged before his plunge over the side. Up the starboard side of the ship crept a veritable wall of seaweed; up to the rail, pausing there for a moment, then to the deck, where it squirmed for a moment or two, taking a weird distorted shape that made me think of a man. From out of the heart of this monstrosity there dropped soggily a white, cold figure! The second sentry had returned, as the first had done!

I knew, as I searched through all my experience, seeking the key to this uncanny enigma, that we were heading westward outside the usually traveled sea-lanes; that ships seldom, if ever, came this way; that in seven days we had seen not one vessel, nor even the smoke of one upon the horizon. Why did not vessels come this way?

But I could not answer my many questions. I could only ask them, and hope within me that they be not answered, ever. Nauseated by the return of the dead sentry, nude as the first had been, I closed my eyes for a moment, and when I opened them again, there was no seaweed, no monstrous shape, upon the promenade; but even from where I stood I could see the wet footprints—and wondered whom next the creature of the deep would claim from aboard our ill-fated vessel.

I drew my pistol and returned once more toward the stern of the vessel. This creature of the depths, whatever it was, had taken life—twice. Whatever it was, it was mortal, and whatever is mortal a bullet will slay. But, in the very act of whirling, I stopped short—for between me and the stern of the vessel, smiling dreamily, water rippling over her nude and glorious body to splash upon the deck, stood the creature who had come up from the depths in the wake of the ship, bearing the dead man in her arms! My arm fell to my side, my weapon clattered to the deck, and as I moved forward once more, slowly, a step at a time as the sentry had done, the wondrous creature held out her dripping arms, and my eyes drank in all the glorious wonder of her—from head to—*but she had no feet!*

Where the feet should have been, and the legs, there were neither legs nor feet; but a scaly column, wet and dripping, like a serpent with a woman's body; I screamed in terror and unbelief; but it was too late, and her arms were about me, preventing all escape! But, with the touch of those arms, I did not wish to struggle. I knew what had happened to the two sentries; knew the same was the prospect for me; yet at the moment there seemed nothing in all the world more worth-while than to slip over the side, into the depths, with the arms of this wondrous creature about me.

"Lieutenant! Lieutenant! For the love of God what is happening to you?"

It was the voice of the sergeant of the guard, freighted with abysmal terror; but I did not care. The shapely, strangely warm arms of the sea-creature were about me, and the sound of the bells, unbelievably sweet now, was in my ears. For me the world had ceased to exist, save for knowledge that these two things were true. I was carried to the rail, and went over slowly, without commotion, as comfortably as though I had been riding on a couch of eiderdown—and came to myself to know myself lost indeed!

I was deep down, whirling over and over behind the whirling screws of the ship, holding my breath until my lungs were nigh to bursting, swimming with all my might, striving to reach the surface, and life-giving air, when I hadn't the slightest idea which way was upward. With all my power I fought toward the surface; but my progress was slow and drag-ging, for there was a weight about my knees, as though arms were clasped about them, striving to hold me down. A wordless voice was in my ears—begging, beseeching, and there was something in the voice which made my struggles seem foolish and unnecessary, so that I desired never to reach the air I needed. I closed my eyes, which I had opened instinctively upon striking the water, and two lips pressed firmly against my own—and those lips saved my life, and my reason; for they were the cold lips of a corpse, with neither love nor challenge in them. I flailed out once more, and my hand caught in the line which the steamer dragged over her stern to measure the knots she traveled. All about me as I was hurled forward, now under water, now with nostrils out for a brief breathing space, the mass of seaweed rose and fell on the heavy seas.

God knows how I ever got back aboard the troopship; but I awoke at mess-call in the morning, and sent immediately for the sergeant of the guard.

"What happened after I came back aboard last night, sergeant?" I asked abruptly.

The sergeant of the guard stared at me as though he thought me insane.

"I don't understand you," he managed finally.

"Have we finally passed through the area of seaweed?"

"Seaweed? Is the lieutenant making sport of me? We're two thousand miles from any land, save the ocean bottom, and there ain't any seaweed anywhere! I don't understand you!"

"Let it pass," I said. "When did you last visit the sentries last night?"

"Just before midnight, sir."

"And were all of them at their post of duty?"

"Yes sir."

"And what about the bells?"

Again the sergeant's puzzlement was so genuine that I knew he did not understand my meaning. How much of my experience had been real, how much fantasy? I tried another tack.

"Did you make a round of the sentries after midnight?"

The sergeant shook his head sheepishly—it is one of the rules of guard duty that one visit to all sentries must take place between midnight and morning.

"Then the guard hasn't been mustered this morning? Is everyone present? You don't know? Then go at once and find out!"

Ten minutes later the sergeant returned, chalk-white of face, to report that two of the guards were missing, and could not be found anywhere aboard. He told me their names—and instantly my mind went back to the night of uncanny happenings just past, and the two nude bodies brought back from the deep in the arms of—whom? Or what?

I never knew, and to this day the questions I have propounded have never been answered.

But this I know: there are strange things, and sounds, in the sea near the hundred and eightieth meridian, a thousand miles north of Honolulu—and this is the strangest incident in my night of terror: the clothing which I donned next morning was entirely dry; but my hair was stiff with salt water, and there was the tang of seaweed in my room when I awoke!

I looked, too, at the glass which covered the port-hole beside my bed—

Outside that glass were the smudged prints of thin lips, the blur above them which told of a face pressed against the glass from outside—as though somebody, or *something*, had tried to peer in, between nightfall and morning!

And the bells? I still can hear them, in memory, when sometimes I waken at sea after midnight, and the rolling and the plunging of the ship tell me that a storm is making.

JOHN MARTIN LEAHY (1886-1967) lived in the state of Washington. He published three novels in the 1920s: "Draconda" and "Drome" were serialized in *Weird Tales*, while his third, "Zandara" was published as "The Living Death" in *Science and Invention*. A small number of short stories also appeared in *Weird Tales*, including "In Amundsen's Tent," which was published in the January 1928 issue. At the time of publication, the famous Norwegian polar explorer Roald Amundson (1872-1928), whose team had been the first to reach the South Pole on 14 December 1911 (beating by one month Captain Robert Scott, who perished with his team on the return journey from the Pole), was still living, and his unsuccessful 1925 attempt to fly over the North Pole in an airplane was fresh in the public's imagination.

IN AMUNDSEN'S TENT
by John Martin Leahy

"Inside the tent, in a little bag, I left a letter, addressed to H. M. the King, giving information of what he (sic) had accomplished. . . . Besides this letter, I wrote a short epistle to Captain Scott, who, I assumed, would be the first to find the tent."

Captain Amundsen: The South Pole.

"We have just arrived at this tent, 2 miles from our camp, therefore about 1 1/2 miles from the pole. In the tent we find a record of five Norwegians having been here, as follows:

> Roald Amundsen
> Olav Olavson Bjaaland
> Hilmer Hanssen
> Sverre H. Hassel
> Oscar Wisting

16 Dec. 1911.

* * * * *

"Left a note to say I had visited the tent with companions."

Captain Scott: his last journal.

"Travelers," says Richard A. Proctor, "are sometimes said to tell marvelous stories; but it is a noteworthy fact that, in nine cases out of ten, the marvelous stories of travelers have been confirmed."

Certainly no traveler ever set down a more marvelous story than that of Robert Drumgold. This record I am at last giving to the world, with my humble apologies to the spirit of the hapless explorer for withholding it so long. But the truth is that Eastman, Dahlstrom and I thought it the work of a mind deranged; little wonder, forsooth, if his mind had given way, what with the fearful sufferings which he had gone through and the horror of that fate which was closing in upon him.

What was it, that *thing* (if thing it was) which came to him, the sole survivor of the party which had reached the Southern Pole, thrust itself into the tent and, issuing, left but the severed head of Drumgold there?

Our explanation at the time, and until recently, was that Drumgold had been set upon by his dogs and devoured. Why, though, the flesh had not been stripped from the head was to us an utter mystery. But that was only one of the many things that were utter mysteries.

But now we know—or feel certain—that this explanation was as far from the truth as that desolate, ice-mantled spot where he met his end is from the smiling, flower-spangled regions of the tropics.

Yes, we thought that the mind of poor Robert Drumgold had given way, that the horror in Amundsen's tent and that thing which came to Drumgold there in his own—we thought all was madness only. Hence our suppression of this part of the Drumgold manuscript. We feared that the publication of so extraordinary a record might cast a cloud of doubt upon the real achievements of the Sutherland expedition.

But of late our ideas and beliefs have undergone a change that is nothing less than a metamorphosis. This metamorphosis, it is scarcely necessary to say, was due to the startling discoveries made in the region of the Southern Pole by the late Captain Stanley Livingstone, as confirmed and extended by the ex-pedition conducted by Darwin Frontenac. Captain Livingstone, we now learn, kept his real discovery, what with the doubts and derision which met him on his return to the world, a secret from every living soul but two—Darwin Frontenac and Bond McQuestion. It is but now, on the return of Frontenac, that we learn how truly wonderful and amazing were those discoveries made by the ill-starred captain. And yet, despite the success of the Frontenac expedition, it must be admitted that the mystery down there in the Antarctic is enhanced rather than dissipated. Darwin Frontenac and his companions saw much; but we know that there are things and beings down there that they did not see. The Antarctic—or, rather, part of it—has thus suddenly become the most interesting and certainly the most fearful area on this globe of ours.

So another marvelous story told—or, rather, only partly told—by a traveler has been confirmed. And here are Eastman and I preparing to go once more to the Antarctic to confirm, as we hope, another story—one eery and fearful as any ever conceived by any romanticist.

And to think that it was ourselves, Eastman, Dahlstrom and I, who made the discovery! Yes, it was we who entered the tent, found there the head of Robert Drumgold and the pages whereon he had scrawled his story of mystery and horror. To think that we stood there, in the very spot where it had been, and thought the story but as the baseless fabric of some madman's vision!

How vividly it all rises before me again—the white expanse, glaring, blinding in the untempered light of the Antarctic sun; the dogs straining in the harness, the cases on the sleds, long and black like coffins; our sudden halt as Eastman fetched up in his tracks, pointed and said, "Hello! What's that?"

A half-mile or so off to the left, some object broke the blinding white of the plains.

"*Nunatak*, I suppose," was my answer.

"Looks to me like a cairn or a tent," Dahlstrom said.

"How on earth," I queried, "could a tent have got down here in 87° 30' south? We are far from the route of either Amundsen or Scott."

"H'm," said Eastman, shoving his amber-colored glasses up onto his forehead that he might get a better look, "I wonder. Jupiter Ammon, Nels," he added, glancing at Dahlstrom, "I believe that you are right."

"It certainly," Dahlstrom nodded, "looks like a cairn or a tent to me. I don't think it's a *nunatak.*'"

"Well," said I, "it would not be difficult to put it to the proof."

"And that, my hearties," exclaimed Eastman, "is just what we'll do! We'll soon see what it is—whether it is a cairn, a tent, or only a *nunatak*."

The next moment we were in motion, heading straight for that mysterious object there in the midst of the eternal desolation of snow and ice.

"Look there!" Eastman, who was leading the way, suddenly shouted. "See that? It *is* a tent!"

A few moments, and I saw that it was indeed so. But who had pitched it there? What were we to find within it?

I could never describe those thoughts and feelings which were ours as we approached that spot. The snow lay piled about the tent to a depth of four feet or more. Near by, a splintered ski protruded from the surface—and that was all.

And the stillness! The air, at the moment, was without the slightest movement. No sounds but those made by our movements, and those of the dogs, and our own breathing, broke that awful silence of death.

"Poor devils!" said Eastman at last. "One thing, they certainly pitched their tent well."

The tent was supported by a single pole, set in the middle. To this pole three guy-lines were fastened, one of them as taut as the day its stake had been driven into the surface. But this was not all: a half-dozen lines, or more, were attached to the sides of the tent. There it had stood for we knew not how long, bidding defiance to the fierce winds of that terrible region.

Dahlstrom and I each got a spade and began to remove the snow. The entrance we found unfastened but completely blocked by a couple of provision-cases (empty) and a piece of canvas. "How on earth," I exclaimed, "did those things get into that position?"

"The wind," said Dahlstrom. "And, if the entrance had not been blocked, there wouldn't have been any tent here now; the wind would have split and destroyed it long ago."

"H'm," mused Eastman. "The wind did it, Nels—blocked the place like that? I wonder."

The next moment we had cleared the entrance. I thrust my head through the opening. Strangely enough, very little snow had drifted in. The tent was dark green, a circumstance which rendered the light within somewhat weird and ghastly—or perhaps my imagination contributed not a little to that effect.

"What do you see, Bill?" asked Eastman. "What's inside?"

My answer was a cry, and the next instant I had sprung back from the entrance.

"What is it, Bill?" Eastman exclaimed. "Great heaven, what is it, man?"

377

"A head!" I told him.

"A head?"

"A human head!"

He and Dahlstrom stooped and peered in. "What is the meaning of this?" Eastman cried. "A severed human head!"

Dahlstrom dashed a mittened hand across his eyes.

"Are we dreaming?" he exclaimed.

" 'Tis no dream, Nels," returned our leader. "I wish to heaven it was. A head! A human head!"

"Is there nothing more?" I asked.

"Nothing. No body, not even stripped bone—only that severed head. Could the dogs—"

"Yes?" queried Dahlstrom.

"Could the dogs have done this?"

"Dogs!" Dahlstrom said. "This is not the work of dogs."

We entered and stood looking down upon that grisly remnant of mortality.

"It wasn't dogs," said Dahlstrom.

"Not dogs?" Eastman queried. "What other explanation is there—except cannibalism?"

Cannibalism! A shudder went through my heart. I may as well say at once, however, that our discovery of a good supply of pemmican and biscuit on the sled, at that moment completely hidden by the snow, was to show us that that fearful explanation was not the true one. The dogs! That was it, that was the explanation—even though what the victim himself had set down told us a very different story. Yes, the explorer had been set upon by his dogs and devoured. But there were things that militated against that theory. Why had the animals left that head—in the frozen eyes (they were blue eyes) and upon the frozen features of which was a look of horror that sends a shudder through my very soul even now? Why, the head did not have even the mark of a single fang, though it appeared to have been *chewed* from the trunk. Dahlstrom, however, was of the opinion that it had been *hacked* off.

And there, in the man's story, in the story of Robert Drumgold, we found another mystery—a mystery as insoluble (if it was true) as the presence here of his severed head. There the story was, scrawled in lead-pencil across the pages of his journal. But what were we to make of a record—the concluding pages of it, that is—so strange and so dreadful?

But enough of this, of what we thought and of what we wondered. The journal itself lies before me, and I now proceed to set down the story of Robert Drumgold in his own words. Not a word, not a comma shall be deleted, inserted or changed.

Let it begin with his entry for January the 3rd, at the end of which day the little party was only fifteen miles (geographical) from the Pole.

Here it is.

Jan. 3.—Lat. of our camp 89° 45' 10". Only fifteen miles more, and the Pole is ours—unless Amundsen or Scott has beaten us to it, or both. But it will be ours just the same, even though the glory of discovery is found to be another's. What, shall we find there?

All are in fine spirits. Even the dogs seem to know that this is the consummation of some great achievement. And a thing that is a mystery to us is the interest they have shown this day in the region before us. Did we halt, there they were gazing and gazing straight south and sometimes sniffing and sniffing. What does it mean?

Yes, in fine spirits all—dogs as well as we three men. Everything is auspicious. The weather for the last three days has been simply glorious. Not once, in this time, has the temperature been below minus 5. As I write this, the thermometer shows one degree above. The blue of the sky is like that of which painters dream, and, in that blue, tower cloud formations, violet-tinged in the shadows, that are beautiful beyond all description. If it were possible to forget the fact that nothing stands between ourselves and a horrible death save the meager supply of food on the sleds, one could think he was in some fairyland—a glorious fairyland of white and blue and violet.

A fairyland? Why has that thought so often occurred to me? Why have I so often likened this desolate, terrible region to fairyland? Terrible? Yes, to human beings it is terrible—frightful beyond all words. But, though so unutterably terrible to men, it may not be so in reality. After all, are all things, even of this earth of ours, to say nothing of the universe, made for man—this being (a god-like spirit in the body of a quasi-ape) who, set in the midst of wonders, leers and slavers in madness and hate and wallows in the muck of a thousand lusts? May there not be other beings—yes, even on this very earth of ours—more wonderful—yes, and more terrible too—than he?

Heaven knows, more than once, in this desolation of snow and ice, I have seemed to feel their presence in the air about us—nameless entities, disembodied, *watching* things.

Little wonder, forsooth, that I have again and again thought of these strange words of one of America's greatest scientists, Alexander Winchell:

"Nor is incorporated rational existence conditioned on warm blood, nor on any temperature which does not change the forms of matter of which the organism may be composed. There may be intelligences corporealized after some concept not involving the processes of ingestion, assimilation and reproduction. Such bodies would not require daily food and warmth. They might be lost in the abysses of the ocean, or laid up on a stormy cliff through the tempests of an arctic winter, or plunged in a volcano for a hundred years, and yet retain consciousness and thought."

All this Winchell tells us is conceivable, and he adds:

"Bodies are merely the local fitting of intelligence to particular modifications of universal matter and force."

And these entities, nameless things whose presence I seem to feel at times—are they benignant beings or things more fearful than even the madness of the human brain ever has fashioned?

But, then, I must stop this. If Sutherland or Travers were to read what I have set down here, they would think that I was losing my senses or would declare me already insane. And yet, as there is a heaven above us, it seems that I do actually be-lieve that this frightful place knows the presence of beings other than ourselves and our dogs—things which we cannot see but which are watching us.

Enough of this.

Only fifteen miles from the Pole. Now for a sleep and on to our goal in the morning. Morning! There is no morning here, but day unending. The sun now rides as high at midnight as it does at midday. Of course, there is a change in altitude, but it is so slight as to be imperceptible without an instrument.

But the Pole! Tomorrow the Pole! What will we find there? Only an unbroken expanse of white, or—

Jan. 4.—The mystery and horror of this day—oh, how could I ever set that down? Sometimes, so fearful were those hours through which we have just passed, I even find myself wondering if it wasn't all only a dream. A dream! I would to heaven that it had been but a dream! As for the end— I must keep such thoughts out of my head.

Got under way at an early hour. Weather more wondrous than ever. Sky an azure that would have sent a painter into ecstasies. Cloud-formations indescribably beautiful and grand. The going, however, was pretty difficult. The place a great plain stretching away with a monotonous uniformity of surface as far as the eye could reach. A plain never trod by human foot before? At length, when our dead reckoning showed that we were drawing near to the Pole, we had the answer to that. Then it was that the keen eyes of Travers detected some object rising above the blinding white of the snow.

On the instant Sutherland had thrust his amber glasses up onto his forehead and had his binoculars to his eyes.

"Cairn!" he exclaimed, and his voice sounded hollow and very strange. "A cairn or a—tent. Boys, they have beaten us to the Pole!"

He handed the glasses to Travers and leaned, as though a sudden weariness had settled upon him, against the provision-cases on his sled.

"Forestalled!" said he. "Forestalled!"

I felt very sorry for our brave leader in those, his moments of terrible disappointment, but for the life of me I did not know what to say. And so I said nothing.

At that moment a cloud concealed the sun, and the place where we stood was suddenly involved in a gloom that was deep and awful. So sudden and pronounced, indeed, was the change that we gazed about us with curious and wondering looks. Far off to the right and to the left, the plain blazed white and blinding. Soon, however, the last gleam of sunshine had vanished from off it. I raised my look up to the heavens. Here and there edges of cloud were touched as though with the light of wrathful golden fire. Even then, however, that light was fading. A few minutes, and the last angry gleam of the sun had vanished. The gloom seemed to deepen about us every moment. A curious haze was concealing the blue expanse of the sky overhead. There was not the slightest movement in the gloomy and weird atmosphere. The silence was heavy, awful, the silence of the abode of utter desolation and of death.

"What on earth are we in for now?" said Travers.

Sutherland moved from his sled and stood gazing about into the eery gloom.

"Queer change, this!" said he. "It would have delighted the heart of Doré."

"It means a blizzard, most likely," I observed. "Hadn't we better make camp before it strikes us? No telling what a blizzard may be like in this awful spot."

"Blizzard?" said Sutherland. "I don't think it means a blizzard, Bob. No telling, though. Mighty queer change, certainly. And how different the place looks now, in this strange gloom! It is surely weird and terrible—that is, it certainly looks weird and terrible."

He turned his look to Travers.

"Well, Bill," he asked, "what did you make of it?"

He waved a hand in the direction of that mysterious object the sight of which had so suddenly brought us to a halt. I say in the direction of the object, for the thing itself was no longer to be seen.

"I believe it is a tent," Travers told him.

"Well," said our leader, "we can soon find out what it is—cairn or tent, for one or the other it must certainly be."

The next instant the heavy, awful silence was broken by the sharp crack of his whip.

"Mush on, you poor brutes!" he cried. "On we go to see what is over there. Here we are at the South Pole. Let us see who has beaten us to it."

But the dogs didn't want to go on, which did not surprise me at all, because, for some time now, they had been showing signs of some strange, inexplicable uneasiness. What had got into the creatures, anyway? For a time we puzzled over it; then we *knew*, though the explanation was still an utter mystery to us. They were *afraid*. Afraid? An inadequate word, indeed. It was fear, stark, terrible, that had entered the poor brutes. But whence had come this inexplicable fear? That also we soon knew. The thing they feared, whatever it was, was in that very direction in which we were headed!

A cairn, a tent? What did this thing mean?

"What on earth is the matter with the critters?" exclaimed Travers. "Can it be that—"

"It's for us to find out what it means," said Sutherland.

Again we got in motion. The place was still involved in that strange, weird gloom. The silence was still that awful silence of desolation and of death.

Slowly but steadily we moved forward, urging on the reluctant, fearful animals with our whips.

At last Sutherland, who was leading, cried out that he saw it. He halted, peering forward into the gloom, and we urged our teams up alongside his.

"It must be a tent," he said.

And a tent we found it to be—a small one supported by a single bamboo and well guyed in all directions. Made of drab-colored gabardine. To the top of the tent-pole another had been lashed. From this, motionless in the still air, hung the remains of a small Norwegian flag and, underneath it, a pennant with the word "Fram" upon it. Amundsen's tent!

What should we find inside it? And what was the meaning of that—the strange way it bulged out on one side?

The entrance was securely laced. The tent, it was certain, had been here for a year, all through the long Antarctic night; and yet, to our astonishment, but little snow was piled up about it, and most of this was drift. The explanation of this must, I suppose, be that, before the air currents have reached the Pole, almost all the snow has been deposited from them.

For some minutes we just stood there, and many, and some of them dreadful enough, were the thoughts that came and went. Through the long Antarctic night! What strange things this tent could tell us had it been vouchsafed the power of words! But strange things it might tell us, nevertheless. For what was that inside, making the tent bulge out in so unaccountable a manner? I moved forward to feel of it there with my mittened hand, but, for some reason that I cannot explain, of a sudden I drew back. At that instant one of the dogs whined—the sound so strange and the terror of the animal so unmistakable that I shuddered and felt a chill pass through my heart. Others of the dogs began to whine in that mysterious manner, and all shrank back cowering from the tent.

"What does it mean?" said Travers, his voice sunk almost to a whisper. "Look at them. It is as though they are imploring us to—keep away."

"To keep away," echoed Sutherland, his look leaving the dogs and fixing itself once more on the tent.

"Their senses," said Travers, "are keener than ours. They already know what we can't know until we see it."

"See it!" Sutherland exclaimed. "I wonder. Boys, what are we going to see when we look into that tent? Poor fellows! They reached the Pole. But did they ever leave it? Are we going to find them in there dead?"

"Dead?" said Travers with a sudden start. "The dogs would never act that way if 'twas only a corpse inside. And, besides, if that theory was true, wouldn't the sleds be here to tell the story? Yet look around. The level uniformity of the place shows that no sled lies buried here;"

"That is true," said our leader. "What *can* it mean? What *could* make that tent bulge out like that? Well, here is the mystery before us, and all we have to do is unlace the entrance and look inside to solve it."

He stepped to the entrance, followed by Travers and me, and began to unlace it. At that instant an icy current of air struck the place and the pennant above our heads flapped with a dull and ominous sound. One of the dogs, too, thrust his muzzle skyward, and a deep and long-drawn howl arose. And while the mournful, savage sound yet filled the air, a strange thing happened.

Through a sudden rent in that gloomy curtain of cloud, the sun sent a golden, awful light down upon the spot where we stood. It was but a shaft of light, only three or four hundred feet wide, though miles in length, and there we stood in the very middle of it, the plain on each side involved in that weird gloom, now denser and more eery than ever in contrast to that sword of golden fire which thus so suddenly had been flung down across the snow.

"Queer place this!" said Travers. "Just like a beam lying across a stage in a theater."

Travers' smile was a most apposite one, more so than he perhaps ever dreamed himself. That place was a stage, our light the wrathful fire of the Antarctic sun, ourselves the actors in a scene stranger than any ever beheld in the mimic world.

For some moments, so strange was it all, we stood there looking about us in wonder and perhaps each one of us in not a little secret awe.

"Queer place, all right!" said Sutherland. "But—"

He laughed a hollow, sardonic laugh. Up above, the pennant flapped and flapped again, the sound of it hollow and ghostly. Again rose the long-drawn, mournful, fiercely sad howl of the wolf-dog.

"But,'" added our leader, "we don't want to be imagining things, you know."

"Of course not," said Travers.

"Of course not," I echoed.

A little space, and the entrance was open and Sutherland had thrust head and shoulders through it.

I don't know how long it was that he stood there like that. Perhaps it was only a few seconds, but to Travers and me it seemed rather long.

"What is it?" Travers exclaimed at last. "What do you see?" The answer was a scream—the horror of that sound I can never forget—and Sutherland came staggering back and, I be-lieve, would have fallen had we not sprung and caught him.

"What is it?" cried Travers. "In God's name, Sutherland, what did you see?"

Sutherland beat the side of his head with his hand, and his look was wild and horrible.

"What is it?" I exclaimed. "What did you see in there?"

"I can't tell you—I can't! Oh, oh, I wish that I had never seen it! Don't look! Boys, don't look into that tent—unless you are prepared to welcome madness, or worse."

"What gibberish is this?" Travers demanded, gazing at our leader in utter astonishment. "Come, come, man! Buck up. Get a grip on yourself. Let's have an end to this nonsense. Why should the sight of a dead man, or dead men, affect you in this mad fashion?"

"Dead men?" Sutherland laughed, the sound wild, maniacal.

"Dead men? If 'twas only that! Is this the South Pole? Is this the earth, or are we in a nightmare on some other planet?"

"For heaven's sake," cried Travers, "come out of it! What's got into you? Don't let your nerves go like this."

"A dead man?" queried our leader, peering into the face of Travers. "You think I saw a dead man? I wish it was only a dead man. Thank God, you two didn't look!"

On the instant Travers had turned.

"Well," said he, "I am going to look!"

But Sutherland cried out, screamed, sprang after him and tried to drag him back.

"It would mean horror and perhaps madness!" cried Suther-land. "Look at me. Do you want to be like me?"

"No!" Travers returned. "But I am going to see what is in that tent,"

He struggled to break free, but Sutherland clung to him in a frenzy of madness.

"Help me, Bob!" Sutherland cried.

"Hold him back, or we'll all go insane."

But I did not help him to hold Travers back, for, of course, it was my belief that Sutherland himself was insane. Nor did Sutherland hold Travers. With a sudden wrench, Travers was free. The next instant he had thrust head and shoulders through the entrance of the tent.

Sutherland groaned and watched him with eyes full of unutterable horror.

I moved toward the entrance, but Sutherland flung himself at me with such violence that I was sent over into the snow. I sprang to my feet full of anger and amazement.

"What the hell," I cried, "is the matter with you, anyway? Have you gone crazy?"

The answer was a groan, horrible beyond all words of man, but that sound did not come from Sutherland. I turned. Travers was staggering away from the entrance, a hand pressed over his face, sounds that I could never describe breaking from deep in his throat. Sutherland, as the man came staggering up to him, thrust forth an arm and touched Travers lightly on the shoulder. The effect was instantaneous and frightful. Travers sprang aside as though a serpent had struck at him, screamed and screamed yet again.

"There, there!" said Sutherland gently. "I told you not to do it. I tried to make you understand, but—but you thought that I was mad."

"It can't belong to this earth!" moaned Travers.

"No," said Sutherland. "That horror was never born on this planet of ours. And the inhabitants of earth, though they do not know it, can thank God Almighty for that."

"But it is *here!*" Travers exclaimed. "How did it come to this awful place? And where did it come from?"

"Well," consoled Sutherland, "it is dead—it must be dead."

"Dead? How do we know that it is dead? And don't forget this: it didn't come here alone!"

Sutherland started. At that moment the sunlight vanished, and everything was once more involved in gloom.

"What do you mean?" Sutherland asked. "Not alone? How do you know that it did not come alone?"

"Why, it is there *inside* the tent; but the entrance was laced from the *outside!*"

"Fool, fool that I am!" cried Sutherland a little fiercely. "Why didn't I think of that? Not alone! Of course it was not alone!"

He gazed about into the gloom, and I knew the nameless fear and horror that chilled him to the very heart, for they chilled me to my very own.

Of a sudden arose again that mournful, savage howl of the wolf-dog. We three men started as though it was the voice of some ghoul from hell's most dreadful corner.

"Shut up, you brute!" gritted Travers. "Shut up, or I'll brain you!"

Whether it was Travers' threat or not, I do not know; but that howl sank, ceased almost on the instant. Again the silence of desolation and of death lay upon the spot. But above the tent the pennant stirred and rustled, the sound of it, I thought, like the slithering of some repulsive serpent.

"What did you see in there?" I asked them.

"Bob—Bob," said Sutherland, "don't ask us that,"

"The thing itself," said I, turning, "can't be any worse than this mystery and nightmare of imagination."

But the two of them threw themselves before me and barred my way.

"No!" said Sutherland firmly. "You must not look into that tent, Bob. You must not see that—that—I don't know what to call it. Trust us; believe us, Bob! 'Tis for your sake that we say that you must not do it. We, Travers and I, can never be the same men again—the brains, the souls of us can never be what they were before we saw that!"

"Very well," I acquiesced. "I can't help saying, though, that the whole thing seems to me like the dream of a madman,"

"That," said Sutherland, "is a small matter indeed. Insane? Believe that it is the dream of a madman. Believe that we are insane. Believe that you are insane yourself. Believe anything you like. Only don't look!"

"Very well," I told them. "I won't look. I give in. You two have made a coward of me."

"A coward?" said Sutherland. "Don't talk nonsense, Bob. There are some things that a man should never know; there are some things that a man should never see; that horror there in Amundsen's tent is—both!"

"But you said that it is dead."

Travers groaned. Sutherland laughed a little wildly.

"Trust us," said the latter; "believe us, Bob. 'Tis for your sake, not for our own. For that is too late now. We have seen it, and you have not."

For some minutes we stood there by the tent, in that weird gloom, then turned to leave the cursed spot. I said that undoubtedly Amundsen had left some records inside, that possibly Scott had reached the Pole, and visited the tent, and that we ought to secure any such mementoes. Sutherland and Travers nodded, but each declared that he would not put his head through that entrance again for all the wealth of Ormus and of Ind—or words to that effect. We must, they said, get away from the awful place—get back to the world of men with our fearful message.

"You won't tell me what you saw," I said, "and yet you want to get back so that you can tell it to the world."

"We aren't going to tell the world what we saw," answered Sutherland. "In the first place, we couldn't, and, in the second place, if we could, not a living soul would believe us. But we can warn people, for that thing in there did not come alone. Where is the other one—or the others?"

"Dead, too, let us hope!" I exclaimed.

"Amen!" said Sutherland. "But maybe, as Bill says, it isn't dead. Probably—"

Sutherland paused, and a wild, indescribable look came into his eyes. "Maybe it—*can't die!*"

"Probably," said I nonchalantly, yet with secret disgust and with poignant sorrow.

What was the use? What good would it do to try to reason with a couple of madmen? Yes, we must get away from this spot, or they would have me insane, too. And the long road back? Could we ever make it now? And what *had* they seen? What unimaginable horror was there behind that thin wall of gabardine? Well, whatever it was, it was real. Of that I could not entertain the slightest doubt. Real? Real enough to wreck, virtually instantaneously, the strong brains of two strong men. But—were my poor companions really mad, after all?

"Or maybe," Sutherland was saying, "the other one, or the others, went back to Venus or Mars or Sirius or Algol, or hell itself, or wherever they came from, to get more of their kind. If that is so, heaven have pity on poor humanity! And, if it or they are still here on this earth, then sooner or later—it may be a dozen years, it may be a century—but sooner or later the world will know it, know it to its woe and to its horror. For they, if living, or if gone for others, will come again."

"I was thinking—" began Travers, his eyes fixed on the tent.

"Yes?" Sutherland queried.

"—that," Travers told him, "it might be a good plan to empty the rifle into that thing. Maybe it isn't dead; maybe it can't die—maybe it only *changes*. Probably it is just hibernating, so to speak."

"If so," I laughed, "it will probably hibernate till doomsday."

But neither one of my companions laughed.

"Or," said Travers, "it may be a demon, a ghost materialized. I can't say incarnated."

"A ghost materialized!" I exclaimed. "Well, may not every man or woman be just that? Heaven knows, many a one acts like a demon or a fiend incarnate."

"They may be," nodded Sutherland. "But that hypothesis doesn't help us any here."

"It may help things some," said Travers, starting toward his sled.

A moment or two, and he had got out the rifle.

"I thought," said he, "that nothing could ever take me back to that entrance. But the hope that I may—"

Sutherland groaned.

"It isn't earthly, Bill," he said hoarsely. "It's a nightmare. I think we had better go now."

Travers was going—straight toward the tent.

"Come back, Bill!" groaned Sutherland. "Come back! Let us go while we can."

But Travers did not come back. Slowly he moved forward, rifle thrust out before him, finger on the trigger. He reached the tent, hesitated a moment, then thrust the rifle-barrel through. As fast as he could work trigger and lever, he emptied the weapon into the tent—into that horror inside it.

He whirled and came back as though in fear the tent was about to spew forth behind him all the legions of foulest hell.

What was that? The blood seemed to freeze in my veins and heart as there arose from out the tent a sound—a sound low and throbbing—a sound that no man ever had heard on this earth—one that I hope no man will ever hear again.

A panic, a madness seized upon us, upon men and dogs alike, and away we fled from that cursed place.

The sound ceased. But again we heard it. It was more fearful, more unearthly, soul-maddening, hellish than before.

"Look!" cried Sutherland. "Oh, my God, *look at that!*"

The tent was barely visible now. A moment or two, and the curtain of gloom would conceal it. At first I could not imagine what had made Sutherland cry out like that. Then I saw it, in that very moment before the gloom hid it from view. The tent was moving! It swayed, jerked like some shapeless monster in the throes of death, like some nameless thing seen in the horror of nightmare or limned on the brain of utter madness itself.

And that is what happened there; that is what we saw. I have set it down at some length and to the best of my ability under the truly awful circumstances in which I am placed. In these hastily scrawled pages is recorded an experience that, I believe, is not surpassed by the wildest to be found in the pages of the most imaginative romanticist. Whether the record is destined ever to reach the world, ever to be scanned by the eye of another—only the future can answer that.

I will try to hope for the best. I cannot blink the fact, however, that things are pretty bad for us. It is not only this sinister, nameless mystery from which we are fleeing—though heaven knows that is horrible enough—but it is the *minds* of my companions. And, added to that, is the fear for my own. But there, I must get myself in hand. After all, as Sutherland said, I didn't see it. I must not give way. We must somehow get our story to the world, though we may have for our reward only the mockery of the world's unbelief, its scoffing—the world, against which is now moving, gathering, a menace more dreadful than any that ever moved in the fevered brain of any prophet of woe and blood and disaster.

We are a dozen miles or so from the Pole now. In that mad dash away from that tent of horror, we lost our bearings and for a time, I fear, went panicky. The strange, eery gloom denser than ever. Then came a fall of fine snow-crystals, which rendered things worse than ever. Just when about to give up in despair, chanced upon one of our beacons. This gave us our bearings, and we pressed on to this spot.

Travers has just thrust his head into the tent to tell us that he is sure he saw something moving off in the gloom. Something moving! This must be looked into.

(If Robert Drumgold could only have left as full a record of those days which followed as he had of that fearful 4th of January! No man can ever know what the three explorers went through in their struggle to escape that doom from which there was no escape—a doom the mystery and horror of which perhaps surpass in gruesomeness what the most dreadful Gothic imagination ever conceived in its utterest abandonment to delirium and madness.)

Jan. 5.—Travers *had* seen something, for we, the three of us, saw it again today. Was it that horror, that thing not of this earth, which they saw in Amundsen's tent? We don't know what it is. All we know is that it is something that moves. God have pity on us all—and on every man and woman and child on this earth of ours if this thing is what we fear!

6th.—Made 25 mi. today—20 yesterday. Did not see it today. *But heard it.* Seemed near—once, in fact, as though right over our heads. But that must have been imagination. Effect on dogs most terrible. Poor brutes! It is as horrible to them as it is to us. Sometimes I think even more. Why is it following us?

7th.—Two of dogs gone this morning. One or another of us on guard all "night". Nothing seen, not a sound heard, yet the animals have vanished. Did they desert us? We say that is what happened but each man of us knows that none of us believes it. Made 18 mi. Fear that Travers is going mad.

8th.—Travers gone! He took the watch last night at 12, relieving Sutherland. That was the last seen of Travers—the last that we shall ever see. No tracks—not a sign in the snow. Travers, poor Travers, gone! Who will be the next?

Jan. 9.—*Saw it again!* Why does it let us see it like this—sometimes? Is it that horror in Amundsen's tent? Sutherland declares that it is not—that it is something even more hellish. But then S. is mad now—mad—mad—mad. If I wasn't sane, I could think that it all was only imagination. *But I saw it!*

Jan. 11.—Think it is the 11th but not sure. I can no longer be sure of anything—save that I am alone and that it is watching me. Don't know how I know, for I cannot see it. But I do know—it is watching me. It is always watching. And sometime it will come and get me—as it got Travers and Sutherland and half of the dogs.

Yes, today must be the 11th. For it was yesterday—surely it was only yesterday—that it took Sutherland. I didn't see it take him, for a fog had come up, and Sutherland—he would go on in the fog—was so slow in following that the vapor hid him from view. At last when he didn't come, I went back. But S. was I gone—man, dogs, sled, everything was gone. Poor Sutherland! But then he was mad. Probably that was why it took him. Has it spared me because I am yet sane? S. had the rifle. Always he clung to that rifle—as though a bullet could save him from what we saw! My only weapon is an ax. But what good is an ax?

Jan. 13.—Maybe it is the 14th. I don't know. What does it matter? Saw it *three* times today. Each time it was closer. Dogs still whining about tent. There—that horrible hellish sound again. Dogs still now. That sound again. But I dare not look out. The ax.

Hours later. Can't write any more.

Silence. Voices—I seem to hear voices. But that sound again.

Coming nearer. At entrance now—now—

Cold Spring Press

An Imprint of Open Road Publishing
P.O. Box 284
Cold Spring Harbor, NY 11724
E-mail: jopenroad@aol.com

FICTION:

Book of the Three Dragons, by Kenneth Morris, $11.95
Lud-in-the-Mist, by Hope Mirrlees, $11.00
Thin Line Between: Book One of the Wandjina Quartet, by M.A.C. Petty, $11.00
The Sillymarillion, by D.R. Lloyd, $11.00
Seekers of Dreams: Masterpieces of Fantasy, selected by Douglas A. Anderson, $14.00
Adrift on the Haunted Seas: The Best Short Stories of William Hope Hodgson, $11.00
The Dark Chamber, by Leonard Cline, $6.99
H.P. Lovecraft's Favorite Weird Tales, $14.00
The Shadow at the Bottom of the World, by Thomas Ligotti, $13.00

NONFICTION:

The Science of Middle-earth, by Henry Gee, $14.00
More People's Guide to J.R.R. Tolkien, by TheOneRing.net, $14.00
The People's Guide to J.R.R. Tolkien, by TheOneRing.net, $16.95
The Tolkien Fan's Medieval Reader, by Turgon, $14.95
Tolkien in the Land of Heroes, by Anne C. Petty, $16.95
Dragons of Fantasy, by Anne C. Petty, $14.95
Myth & Middle-earth, by Leslie Ellen Jones, $14.95
The 100 Best Writers of Fantasy and Horror, by Douglas A. Anderson, $16.95

For US orders, include $5.00 for postage and handling for the first book ordered; for each additional book, add $1.00. Orders outside US, inquire first about shipping charges (money order payable in US dollars on US banks only for overseas shipments). We also offer bulk discounts. *Note:* Checks or money orders must be made out to **Open Road Publishing**.